THE BEST AMERICAN

NONREQUIRED

READING

2012

THE BEST AMERICAN

NONREQUIRED
READING™

2012

∎

EDITED BY
DAVE EGGERS

INTRODUCTION BY
RAY BRADBURY

MANAGING EDITORS
SCOTT COHEN
EM-J STAPLES

A MARINER ORIGINAL
HOUGHTON MIFFLIN HARCOURT
BOSTON ▪ NEW YORK
2012

www.hmhbooks.com

ISSN: 1539-316x
ISBN: 978-0-547-59596-2

Printed in the United States of America
DOC 10 9 8 7 6 5 4 3 2 1

CONTENTS

EDITOR'S NOTE

Hello, readers. Welcome to the *Best American Nonrequired Reading*. Given no one reads forewords written by editors, especially given this is the tenth foreword I've written, I will be brief.

How This Book Is Made

For ten years now, I've been teaching a class every Tuesday night, the class that puts this anthology together: the *Best American Nonrequired Reading*. Every year it's a new group of students, up to about twenty-two of them in a given year—students drawn from all over the Bay Area, from Oakland to San Rafael, from San Francisco's Excelsior to the Sunset and everywhere in between. Halfway across the country, a sister class, in the Ann Arbor/Ypsilanti area, is doing the same thing. For the students in California and Michigan, the class is voluntary and extracurricular and very simple: We read and discuss contemporary writing. We subscribe to a few hundred journals and magazines, and we read, desultorily, everything we can. And when we think something's worth sharing with the class, we all read it, and then we dig in and break it down and vote yes or no or maybe. The class discussions are electric, heated, funny, wide-ranging, and fluid.

We jump all over the place, and if something we read leads to a discussion about a larger issue, we go with it. The class crosses into politics, current events, history, philosophy, art history, literary theory, and a dozen other disciplines. We argue, we battle, we vote, and eventually, in order to get this book together, we compromise and we curate. It is a ringing testament to the fact that contrary to various uninformed pundits, young people read as much and as passionately as the generations before them, and that the future of the written—even printed—word is in good hands and good minds, if we trust and encourage those minds.

Ray Bradbury

It's very strange and humbling to be typing these words knowing they will appear very close to Ray Bradbury's introduction. Every year, the students who help put this anthology together vote on who they want to introduce the book, and every year it's a very interesting and revealing process. In the past, the students have chosen everyone from Matt Groening to Beck to Zadie Smith—people who inspire them and who might have something interesting to say about how and why and what they read—and thus it was wonderful, this year, when the students chose Ray Bradbury. We contacted Sam Weller, a young man who had worked with Ray the last handful of years, and Sam said he would see if Ray was up to it. Ray was ninety-one when we asked, so I warned the students that he might not be able to say yes, however much he might want to. But Sam came back and said that Ray would do it, he'd love to do it—but that he would likely be dictating it. Which Ray did, in May of 2012, a few weeks before he passed away. The message of his introduction is clear, and the message sent by his dictating the introduction so close to his passing is clear, too: that the man was a consummate, wall-to-wall, unmitigated book lover, committed to the end, no-nonsense, omnivorous, and unafraid. We thank him for giving us some time when his time was short, and we will miss him profoundly.

Brian Selznick and Ray

The cover artist is also someone chosen by the students, the multitalented author–illustrator–classic storyteller Brian Selznick. His name came up in our weekly discussions, and when the students realized that Brian was alive and well—this was more of a revelation than the fact that Ray Bradbury was alive; young people are born assuming all authors are dead—there was much hoopla thinking he might do the cover. We asked him, he said yes, and he produced the gorgeous cover that likely enticed you to pick up this volume.

I had never met Brian, but when I did—at the memorial service for yet another legendary author, Maurice Sendak—Brian told me a story about his own interactions with Ray Bradbury. Brian's *Invention of Hugo Cabret* had just been published, and one of the first notes of congratulation he received was from none other than Ray Bradbury. He told Brian how much he loved the book, and invited him to visit him in Los Angeles. When Brian did so, Ray was in a vast overstuffed chair, a recliner, and was wearing a medal around his neck. He'd just been given an important award in France, and liked to wear it around the house. For a middle-class kid from Waukegan, Illinois, a man who was so poor that he had to rent a typewriter, by the hour, to write *Farenheit 451*, he got a kick out of traveling to Paris to receive their equivalent of a knighthood. If anyone ever doubted one's ability to write oneself into existence, or doubted the power of words and stories as a means of self-empowerment and transformation, as a tool to leap over boundaries of class or time or even geography, Ray's life, culminating in his relishing his French honor while sitting on his recliner, is irrefutable proof.

Very Short Story
In earlier editions of this yearly anthology, I used to include very short stories I'd written. Then I stopped. But I've been writing short-shorts again, and I looked at a recent short-short I'd written, and thought of Ray.

Shoot
He has one memory of his grandmother, whom he met only once. They were in her house in Brattleboro, on a humid night devoid of stars. They were alone, he was ten, night had come. "You've never seen a shooting star?" she said, dropping her head theatrically. "Watch this." She walked outside, to the other side of the glass, where

she lit a match. "It's like this," she said, her voice muffled, the flame so small. She threw it to the ground. "Isn't that astounding?"

That's the end of the short-short, and the end of this Editor's Note. I hope you enjoy this collection.

DAVE EGGERS
San Francisco, 2012

INTRODUCTION

The Book and the Butterfly

WHEN I WAS SEVEN YEARS OLD, I started going to the library and I took out ten books a week. The librarian looked at me and asked, "What are you doing?"

I said, "What do you mean?"

And she said, "You can't possibly read all of those before they are due back."

I said, "Yes, I can."

And I came back the next week for ten more books.

In doing so, I told that librarian, politely, to get out of my way and let me happen. That's what books do. They are the building blocks, the DNA, if you will, of *you*.

Think of everything you have ever read, everything you have ever learned from holding a book in your hands and how that knowledge shaped you and made you who you are today.

Looking back now on all those years, to when I first discovered books at the library, I see that I was simply falling in love. Day, after day, after glorious day, I was falling in love with books.

The library in Waukegan, Illinois, the town where I grew up, was a temple to the imagination. It was built by Andrew Carnegie, the philanthropist, who built libraries all across this great land. I learned to read by studying the comic strips in the *Chicago Tribune*. But I fell in love with reading at that old Carnegie library. It was this library that served as the inspiration for the library in my 1962 novel, *Something Wicked This Way Comes.*

I will never forget the many magnificent autumn nights, running home with books in my hands and the October winds driving me home towards discovery. I found books on Egypt and dinosaurs, books about pirates, and books that took me to the stars.

I clearly remember checking out books on physiology, books that described what human beings were like, what their bodies were like, what the veins were like, what the feet were like, what the head was like, what the heart was like. So I learned about the physiology of humans from books when I was just a child. And I was curious about all the animals of the world, too. I couldn't believe that God had created so many species. Of course, in many ways, one of the most miraculous creatures of all is the butterfly. They fascinated me as a child. When I read about butterflies, I realized that they are a metaphor for the totality of the universe. How is any of this possible? How did any of this happen? From the formation of a galaxy to the wings of a monarch! No one truly knows the answers. It is all such a great mystery.

Think about the butterfly for a moment. A caterpillar crawls along, eating leaves, fastens itself to a tree, and then an impossible miracle occurs: all of a sudden it goes into a protective stage, and, after a time, that caterpillar emerges from its chrysalis, sprouts magnificent wings, and turns into a butterfly. Where is the impulse that tells the butterfly to do any of that? Where was the impulse that caused the stars to form?

The books I brought home from the library caused me to think about the origins of life and the universe. How did it start? Where does it end? I recall Midwestern summer nights, standing on my grandparents' hushed lawn, and looking up at the sky at the confetti field of stars. There were millions of suns out there, and millions of planets rotating around those suns. And I knew there was life out there, in the great vastness. We are just too far apart, separated by too great a distance to reach one another.

I pondered all of these things because of books. I asked big questions because of books. I dreamed because of books. I started to write because of books. I read everything from comic strips, to history books, to the fantastic tales of L. Frank Baum, Edgar Allan Poe, H. G.

Wells, and many others. None of this reading was required, mind you. I just did it. It was all impulsive. The *Best American Nonrequired Reading* reflects much of what I loved about reading when I first discovered its magical allure. Here you find cartoons next to great nonfiction magazine stories next to imaginative short fiction next to lists of curious arcana. Each page is a new discovery, a decorated Easter egg in the garden.

I am told the editorial process for this series is rooted in the involvement of high school students selecting the stories and assembling each year's edition. I published my own fan magazine, *Futuria Fantasia*, as a teenager in the late 1930s. I would have loved to work on this series. I imagine each young person who has poured his or her heart into this edition has been changed as a result.

The caterpillar sprouts wings.

And I know that, as with reading any book, you, dear reader, will change too.

Now go off and fly.

RAY BRADBURY

Ray Bradbury was one of the most celebrated writers of our time. Among his best-known works are Fahrenheit 451, The Martian Chronicles, The Illustrated Man, Dandelion Wine, *and* Something Wicked This Way Comes. *He wrote for theater and the cinema, including the screenplay for John Huston's classic film adaptation of* Moby Dick, *and was nominated for an Academy Award. In 2000, Mr. Bradbury was honored by the National Book Foundation with a medal for Distinguished Contribution to American Letters. He won an Emmy for his teleplay of* The Halloween Tree. *This introduction was written in the weeks just before he passed away, on June 6, 2012.*

BEST AMERICAN FRONT SECTION

EACH YEAR, the *BANR* committee compiles the Best American front section—this section here. It is an entirely haphazard stockpile of some pieces that don't fit anywhere else, and some that do but are here anyway. This year's front section is a bit longer and a bit more serious. Nonetheless it is still American, and like America, it is boundless and brave. We start with a sonnet from novelist, poet, and friend of the series Sherman Alexie.

Best American Sonnet with Vengeance

SHERMAN ALEXIE

FROM *Zone 3*

Sonnet, with Vengeance

1. I'm a poet who spends a lot of time in Hollywood. 2. I write screenplays for movies that will never get made. 3. Through the screenwriters' guild, I've earned a pension that will pay me nearly $3,000 a month when I retire from writing screenplays. 4. If my writing career goes to shit, I can certainly live well on my reservation for $3,000 a month. 5. Why does an Indian work in Hollywood? Who has done

Indians more harm than white filmmakers? 6. For instance: during the making of a western, the Italian director looked at a group of Indians, pointed at one paler Sioux, and said, "Get him out of there. He's not Indian enough." 7. For instance: *Dances With Wolves.* 8. I rarely write screenplays about Indians. I have written screenplays about superheroes, smoke jumpers, pediatric surgeons, all-girl football teams, and gay soldiers. 9. I often dream of writing a B-movie about an Indian vigilante. 10. No, not a vigilante. That would be too logical. Who needs more logical violence? Who needs yet another just war? 11. Though I haven't written a word of my B-movie screenplay, I have designed the movie poster: an Indian man, strong and impossibly handsome, glares at us, his audience. He's bare-chested and holds a sledgehammer in one hand and a pistol in the other. The name of the movie: *Johnny Fire.* The tagline: "He's just pissed." 12. No logic. It will be the simple story of an Indian man who wakes one morning and decides to destroy everything in his life. 13. "Rage, rage, against the dying of the light." 14. When I was seven, during a New Year's Eve party at my house, I watched two Indian men fist fight on our front lawn. Then one of the Indians pulled a pistol and shot the other Indian in the stomach. As my mother rushed me back inside the house, I heard the wounded man ask, "Why does it hurt so much?"

Best American Very Short Memoir

JUNOT DÍAZ

FROM *The New Yorker*

In June of 2011, The New Yorker *published a series of short essays in which five American writers reflected on moments from their childhood. Here, novelist Junot Díaz writes about his experience living in a predominantly Dominican neighborhood in New Jersey after emigrating from the Dominican Republic at a young age.*

The Money

All the Dominicans I knew in those days sent money home. My mother didn't have a regular job besides caring for us five kids, so she scrimped the loot together from whatever came her way. My father was always losing his forklift jobs, so it wasn't like she ever had a steady flow. But my grandparents were alone in Santo Domingo, and those remittances, beyond material support, were a way, I suspect, for Mami to negotiate the absence, the distance, caused by our Diaspora. She chipped dollars off the cash Papi gave her for our daily expenses, forced our already broke family to live even broker. That was how she built the nut—two, maybe three hundred dollars—that she sent home every six months or so.

We kids knew where the money was hidden, but we also knew that to touch it would have meant a violent punishment approaching death. I, who could take the change out of my mother's purse without thinking, couldn't have brought myself even to look at that forbidden stash.

So what happened? Exactly what you'd think. The summer I was twelve, my family went away on a "vacation"—one of my father's half-baked get-to-know-our-country-better-by-sleeping-in-the-van extravaganzas—and when we returned to Jersey, exhausted, battered, we found our front door unlocked. My parents' room, which was where the thieves had concentrated their search, looked as if it had been tornado-tossed. The thieves had kept it simple; they'd snatched a portable radio, some of my Dungeons & Dragons hardcovers, and of course, Mami's remittances.

It's not as if the robbery came as a huge surprise. In our neighborhood, cars and apartments were always getting jacked, and the kid stupid enough to leave a bike unattended for more than a tenth of a second was the kid who was never going to see that bike again. Everybody got hit; no matter who you were, eventually it would be your turn.

And that summer it was ours.

Still, we took the burglary pretty hard. When you're a recent immigrant, it's easy to feel targeted. Like it wasn't just a couple of hoodlums that had it in for you but the whole neighborhood—well, the whole block.

No one took the robbery as hard as my mom, though. She cursed the neighborhood, she cursed the country, she cursed my father, and of course she cursed us kids, swore that we had run our gums to our idiot friends and they had done it.

And this is where the tale should end, right? Wasn't as if there was going to be any *CSI*-style investigation or anything. Except that a couple of days later I was moaning about the robbery to these guys I was hanging with at that time and they were cursing sympathetically, and out of nowhere it struck me. You know when you get one of those moments of mental clarity? When the nictitating membrane obscuring the world suddenly lifts? That's what happened. I realized that these two dopes I called my friends had done it. They were shaking their heads, mouthing all the right words, but I could see the way they looked at each other, the Raskolnikov glances. I *knew*.

Now, it wasn't like I could publicly denounce these dolts or go to the police. That would have been about as useless as crying. Here's what I did: I asked the main dope to let me use his bathroom (we were in front of his apartment) and while I pretended to piss I unlatched the window. Then we all headed to the park as usual, but I pretended that I'd forgotten something back home. I ran to the dope's apartment, slid open the bathroom window, and in broad daylight wriggled my skinny ass in.

Where I got these ideas? I have not a clue. I guess I was reading way too much Encyclopedia Brown and the Three Investigators in those days. And if mine had been a normal neighborhood this is when the cops would have been called and my ass would have been caught *burglarizing*.

The dolt and his family had been in the U.S. all their lives and they had a ton of stuff, a TV in every room, but I didn't have to do much searching. I popped up the dolt's mattress and underneath I found my D&D books and most of my mother's money. He had thoughtfully kept it in the same envelope.

And that was how I solved the Case of the Stupid Morons. My one and only case.

The next day at the park, the dolt announced that someone had broken into his apartment and stolen all his savings. This place is full of thieves, he complained bitterly, and I was, like, No kidding.

It took me two days to return the money to my mother. The truth was I was seriously considering keeping it. But in the end the guilt got to me. I guess I was expecting my mother to run around with joy, to crown me her favorite son, to cook me my favorite meal. Nada. I'd wanted a party or least to see her happy, but there was nothing. Just two hundred and some dollars and fifteen hundred or so miles—that's all there was.

Best American Manifesto

FROM *The Occupied Wall Street Journal*

Occupy Wall Street began in September of 2011. The protest was initiated by the Canadian-based magazine Adbusters *to address growing income inequality, mounting student loan debt, and the influence of corporate power on politics. Speaking out for financial and bank reform, the curbing of greed and corruption, and global social justice, the following statement of purpose was accepted by OWS's New York City General Assembly on September 29, 2011.*

Declaration of the Occupation of New York City

As we gather together in solidarity to express a feeling of mass injustice, we must not lose sight of what brought us together. We write so that all people who feel wronged by the corporate forces of the world can know that we are your allies.

As one people, united, we acknowledge the reality: that the future of the human race requires the cooperation of its members; that our system must protect our rights, and upon corruption of that system, it is up to the individuals to protect their own rights, and those of their neighbors; that a democratic government derives its just power from the people, but corporations do not seek consent to extract wealth from the people and the Earth; and that no true democracy is attainable when the process is determined by economic power. We come to you at a time when corporations, which place profit over people, self-interest over justice, and oppression over equality, run our governments. We have peaceably assembled here, as is our right, to let these facts be known.

They have taken our houses through an illegal foreclosure process, despite not having the original mortgage.

- They have taken bailouts from taxpayers with impunity, and continue to give Executives exorbitant bonuses.
- They have perpetuated inequality and discrimination in the workplace based on age, the color of one's skin, sex, gender identity and sexual orientation.
- They have poisoned the food supply through negligence, and undermined the farming system through monopolization.
- They have profited off of the torture, confinement, and cruel treatment of countless animals, and actively hide these practices.
- They have continuously sought to strip employees of the right to negotiate for better pay and safer working conditions.
- They have held students hostage with tens of thousands of dollars of debt on education, which is itself a human right.
- They have consistently outsourced labor and used that outsourcing as leverage to cut workers' healthcare and pay.
- They have influenced the courts to achieve the same rights as people, with none of the culpability or responsibility.
- They have spent millions of dollars on legal teams that look for ways to get them out of contracts in regards to health insurance.
- They have sold our privacy as a commodity.
- They have used the military and police force to prevent freedom of the press.
- They have deliberately declined to recall faulty products endangering lives in pursuit of profit.

- They determine economic policy, despite the catastrophic failures their policies have produced and continue to produce.

- They have donated large sums of money to politicians, who are responsible for regulating them.

- They continue to block alternate forms of energy to keep us dependent on oil.

- They continue to block generic forms of medicine that could save people's lives or provide relief in order to protect investments that have already turned a substantial profit.

- They have purposely covered up oil spills, accidents, faulty bookkeeping, and inactive ingredients in pursuit of profit.

- They purposefully keep people misinformed and fearful through their control of the media.

- They have accepted private contracts to murder prisoners even when presented with serious doubts about their guilt.

- They have perpetuated colonialism at home and abroad.

- They have participated in the torture and murder of innocent civilians overseas.

- They continue to create weapons of mass destruction in order to receive government contracts.*

To the people of the world,

We, the New York City General Assembly occupying Wall Street in Liberty Square, urge you to assert your power.

Exercise your right to peaceably assemble; occupy public space; create a process to address the problems we face, and generate solutions accessible to everyone.

To all communities that take action and form groups in the spirit of direct democracy, we offer support, documentation, and all of the resources at our disposal.

Join us and make your voices heard!

These grievances are not all-inclusive.

Best American Minutes from the General Assembly of Occupy Wall Street

FROM www.nycga.net

Like New York City itself, the General Assembly of Occupy Wall Street represents an array of people. Gaining consensus was often rewarding, sometimes infuriating, and always challenging. Here are some of the most interesting and all-around best quotes from the meetings of OWS's General Assembly.

We will stay in Liberty Plaza indefinitely. We will rename Zuccotti Park to Liberty Plaza.

Greetings, ancestors of the future; there are no limits to this movement; origin of the world Responsibility.

Stay calm and totally peaceful and nonviolent no matter what! This whole event was featured on the front page of *The New York Times!* The mainstream media are opening their eyes to what's happening.

Anyone interested in rhythms and drumming meet at 5:00.

Hi everyone. You all look beautiful.

Consensus!!! It tastes so good!

We want to encourage reducing, reusing, recycling.

There is a new Working Group called WOW: Woman of Occupy Wall Street. We met a few times and are committed to working on issues that women think are most important. Meet at 9:30 at red sculpture we will determine where to go from there. Thank you.

Workshop tomorrow at noon: Theater of the Oppressed. Meet at Altar.

* * *

Speak Easy Caucus: Caucus for a broad spectrum of individuals from female-bodied people who identify as women to male-bodied people who do not identify 100% as men.

We the Occupiers of Wall Street wholly challenge the New York City Police Department's unconstitutional, racist, and inhumane Stop & Frisk policing practices.

Tomorrow, Thursday, September 29 at 6:30 there is a First Precinct Community Council for Anthony Bologna (Tony Balonie) at 16 Erickson Place New York, NY. He was the officer that maced us. Please make a presence.

I am a drag queen! I have a group of drag queens, nightlife entertainers, and political activists who want to join forces with OWS! They are coming with supplies. We will come with medical supplies, clothing, and food. We will also, if you would like, perform for you!

Can someone kindly remind the drum circles that it is 10:00 p.m. and time for quiet hours?

Monday, October 3rd: Zombie Flesh Mob all day! 8:00 a.m. onward!

Everyone come dressed as a corporate zombie! This means jacket and tie if possible, white face, fake blood, eating monopoly money, and doing a slow march so when people come to work on Monday in this neighborhood they see us reflecting the metaphor of their actions.

The Oakland occupation was evicted yesterday morning very violently by 500 riot police with rubber bullets and tear gas. Yesterday night they marched to reoccupy and were met with ten rounds of tear gas. The footage depicts what looks like a war zone. Of the injuries reported, there's an Iraq war veteran who is currently unconscious in critical condition, shot in the head with a rubber bullet. Another vet is still in the hospital with a head injury from a tear gas canister. Twelve people have injuries from the police that haven't gotten checked out because they were in jail. There have been more than 180 arrests. Twelve people are still in jail for $10,000 bail, being charged with remaining at a riot scene. Two other people have larger bails—one an

18-year-old arrested beside her mom, who is being held on $12,000 bail. A man beaten by the police is being charged with assault on an officer and is being held on $30,000 bail. Bonding out the fifteen people would amount to $16,200. The remaining funds will be used for medical bills, which will in no way amount to that much.

This money will also go for legal because tonight, at a 6:00 p.m. march, they will try to reoccupy. The NLG does not provide money for bail or medical expenses, therefore the responsibility is on the movement. Occupy Oakland has been the most economically and racially diverse occupation in the U.S. Thus it comes as no surprise that they were the first of this scale to be violently evicted. If we want to make any claim toward being a movement inclusive of everyone, it is crucial to show material solidarity with Oakland. The violent decimation and consequent violent attacks on Oakland will set a precedent for how occupations across the country will be dealt with. Both Atlanta and Denver were moved on last night. If we want people to resist this oppression, we need to support their resistance. Occupy Oakland has no material support and collected money dollar by dollar . . . It is in this spirit of mutual aid and solidarity that we ask for $20,000 for our fellow occupiers on the West Coast. It is only together that we can keep this thing going.

If we're going to say we're the 99% we have to stick with issues the 99% of this country agree with. He is an anarchist, bisexual environmentalist against the War on Drugs. This is not 99% of the United States. We are at an impasse where this can be symbolic or substantial. If we embrace all the causes the majority of us believe in, this will be a symbolic movement. If we focus on Wall Street and corporations, we have a chance of changing things and getting the 99% behind us.

What is the current drumming schedule and how was it negotiated (or not) with the community/neighbors?

Originally we were drumming here ten hours a day. We were requested to cut it down — to 4 hours.

I'm concerned there's not enough focus on specific objectives of this currently peaceful revolution.

Hi, my name's Aaron. This is Sophia. We represent the people. Yesterday, in Ocean Parkway, a number of cars were burned out, swastikas were scrawled, KKK signs were scrawled, and hatred was rampant. *The Daily News* is trying to pin this on us. Now I think we have to condemn these sorts of actions. This is bad. Anti-Semitism and racism are not okay. I think we need to, as a group, take a leadership role in our community with some of the other leaders and officially condemn this. We need to write a statement that we do not support these acts and we would like consensus on that. All in favor?

My name is Josh. I have a problem with the term "anti-Semitic." Anti-Semitic does not mean anti-Jewish. I am an Arab, but I am also a Semitic. Why are you playing into that term when so many Semitic people have a problem with also being tied into this? So maybe you can say "anti-Judaic."

The community board was under the impression drumming would be limited to two hours a day and that has not been the case.

I'm Rabbi Chim Gruver, and I'm going to start this with a sadly perverse joke, that sadly there was news today, that in terms of global warming, scientific government has come back that global warming is now worse than the worst forecasts. Then just a moment ago, I realized how lucky I was to have been poor so I didn't take as many taxis and took public transportation. And I realized the perversity, or rather the paradox of what's going on. Because it's, I think, the wealthiest people who are mostly destroying the world. So I don't know if wealth is the answer. The best thing to do may be somehow to impoverish everyone! That's the end of the joke.

Basically nonviolence is a tactic we can use to protect ourselves and those around us, while retaining and using power with our bodies. So what that looks like in this park for example, is doing a soft lockdown, which is using our bodies to block people, police, from entering, as long as possible. Just because I use the word nonviolence doesn't mean that this will be nonviolent. Police are violent, and nonviolence implies that we are willing to use our bodies and put our bodies in harm's way, with the safety in mind, of course, of those around us, to defend our space and to defend our cause.

Mylanta in water neutralizes the oils in pepper spray. Has anybody here been pepper sprayed before? It sucks. This works. For those of you who have been pepper sprayed, were you treated with LAAL (liquid anti-acid water)? It works . . . 50-50 water and mylanta. The active ingredient is magnesium hydroxide and aluminum hydroxide. 50-50 water and mylanta, non-flavored!

Not to get all conspiracy theory-ish . . . But when you take baked goods, maybe be careful. We just know that supposedly nice people want to give us treats.

I asked the drummers to stop, but they said it's a sacred dance and won't stop.

Best American Observations at a Modern Protest Movement

SAÏD SAYRAFIEZADEH

FROM *McSweeney's*

Notes from a Bystander

Zuccotti Park is located about a mile and a half from my house—three stops on the subway—but four weeks after Occupy Wall Street began, I had yet to even pass by. This was due in part to the fact that there was a very good chance I might run into my father there. I haven't seen him in six years, even though he still lives in Brooklyn—about ten stops away, on the subway.

The last time we'd been together was at my wedding reception. He'd missed the ceremony entirely. "Why do I care what the church and state have to say about love?" he'd told me over the phone. He showed up to the reception late, looking dapper in his suit and tie, and handed me a cheap key ring that he'd brought back from Iran as my wedding gift. (I'd gotten key rings from him before.) This was the first time I'd ever seen my mother and father together in the same room—he had abandoned us when I was nine months old. "You didn't seem to smile a whole lot that afternoon," my cousin has since mentioned a number of times. The photographs bear this out.

Shortly after the wedding, I published an essay about what it was like to have grown up without a father. In response, he stopped speaking to me. He is nearing eighty years old now, and we are running out of time for reconciliation. The last attempt I made to contact him was by way of a rather groveling and obsequious email; I pretended everything was fine between us and invited him over to play Scrabble and drink red wine, two things I know he loves. *Dear Popskaya,* I wrote, using my invented Russified term of endearment for him. His response was silence.

It was a humiliating silence, but also quite familiar, considering that except for the occasional phone call on my birthday, I barely had any contact with my father until I was eighteen years old. After that we had a few awkward but encouraging years where we made an effort to get to know one another, especially around the holidays; then a few irksome years where I tried unsuccessfully to get him to answer some questions about the past; then a decade or so where he was so busy with politics that he could only see me every six months. And then I wrote my essay.

The possibility, therefore, of suddenly encountering him on the sidewalk in the middle of Occupy Wall Street was one that filled me with apprehension.

Protests bore me. They also embarrass me. This is no doubt an unfortunate consequence of a childhood spent in the Socialist Workers

Party, that small left-wing organization with several hundred members (including my father) and a single objective: working-class revolution. Many of my earliest memories are of attending branch meetings and forums, conferences and conventions, and of my mother, each and every Saturday, attempting to sell the Party newspaper, *The Militant.* I would spend the morning playing on the sidewalk in various locations around the city while she announced that week's headline to a generally disinterested public. It was always miraculous to me when anyone actually stopped to listen. Even more miraculous when someone stopped to buy. (Twenty years later my mother would do the unthinkable, for a Party member, and drop out.)

It was the demonstrations, however, that were the most disagreeable. The disagreeableness would begin around five o'clock in the morning, when my mother would wake me so that we could catch yet another Greyhound bus to yet another city—usually Washington, DC—and make yet another demand on the American government: usually an end to war. The bus rides were always long and often overheated, and would cause me on occasion to succumb to motion sickness. I blamed myself when this happened, and I think my mother blamed me too.

As for the demonstrations themselves, I remember them always taking place in the dead of winter, though this can't possibly be true. The freezing cold was made worse by the endless waiting and milling that must attend any demonstration before it can commence. When the events did finally get under way, the pace was slow and the fervor unnerving: our power appeared to lie in how loud everyone, including my mother, could shout. She was a small, unassuming woman, and it was strange to see her behave with such aggression in public. I would follow beside her, sometimes shouting myself, as we made our way from point A to point B—a journey as long as the bus ride—and then, having arrived at the latest march's end, we would stand and listen to the speakers make our demands known one last time.

If there was ever any positive moment in the day, it was in the tender realization that we were not alone in our aspirations, my mother and I. We had been joined by like-minded others, sometimes thousands of others, sometimes tens of thousands, all of whom had made a great effort to come and be with us, and all of whom, we believed, would one day be members of the Socialist Workers Party. But no matter the size of the crowd, I was always plagued by a debilitating self-consciousness. I understood that there was something pathetic about our behavior. Helpless, even. We might appear large and vital all crammed into a city street, but the reality was that we were a minority with strange ideas. It made me feel like I was being gawked at by someone. (This was sometimes literally true, as when, at the smaller marches, the people staring from the sidewalk might outnumber us ten to one.) My self-consciousness was in equal proportion to my physical discomfort—or perhaps self-consciousness is by definition a form of physical discomfort.

But if my presence at protests embarrasses me, then my absence makes me feel guilty. This is also an unfortunate consequence of my childhood. Between these two realms there is neither compromise nor escape. As Occupy Wall Street stretched on, and as I followed it closely from the comfort of my couch, I tried to delude myself into thinking that my personal and private support was somehow a contribution to the cause. But absence, I know full well, contributes nothing to no one.

At times I would try to rouse myself into some sort of sacrifice. I considered donating a big bag of organic oranges I had bought, and which were going to go bad because my wife was out of town and I could not possibly eat them all myself. I considered spending an entire day down at Zuccotti Park, twenty-four hours, from one dawn to the next, waking up on the ground in my sleeping bag under the Manhattan skyline. Years from now I could regale my grandchildren with how I had been there then. Yet when a friend of mine called to say he was going to stop by Zuccotti Park one afternoon and wanted to know if I would like to join him, I responded by snorting derisively. It was an involuntary act, and thus an authentic one.

Then one evening, as I was coming out of my therapist's office in the West Village, I was confronted by a young man on the street.

"Can you tell me how to get to Wall Street?" he asked.

He couldn't have been more than twenty years old. He was wearing a light jacket, because it was fall now, and carrying a small bag. It took me a moment to understand that at eight o'clock at night there could be only one reason why he was interested in going to Wall Street.

His interest highlighted my disinterest. Feelings of guilt flooded through me, and also of sadness. He looked at me with an expression that seemed to say, *I know you know where I'm going, and you know I know you haven't been there.*

"Is it too far to walk?" he wanted to know. He seemed excited by the prospect of walking. He seemed up for anything. He was young. He had dark hair. He was skinny. He could have been me twenty years ago.

Yes, I told him, it was too far to walk. But maybe it was just too far for me? I pointed him in the general direction of the 2 train, mumbling something about "down there and around the corner." He thanked me. He was all smiles. He was clearly excited. He was clearly unfazed by being given such general directions. Perhaps, at the age of twenty, he had grown used to general directions. I imagined that he had arrived thirty minutes ago on a bus from Michigan, or Nebraska, although he didn't look like someone who had been riding across the country on a bus. Here he was now, in New York City, just like that. Him and his jacket and his little bag of belongings, heading down to change the world. My father would have been proud.

To get to Wall Street from my apartment, I have to take the J or the Z train. It was a Sunday, however, when I finally decided to go, and there appeared to be no train running at all. After just a few minutes of waiting on the platform I was overcome with that crushing lethargy I have always felt while en route to any political event. Five minutes more made me contemplate turning around and going home to watch football. It also made me regret not having chosen to ride my bicycle. I generally try to ride my bicycle everywhere in New York City, even in the rain and snow, but I'd felt a certain amount of anxiety about leaving it unattended down by the park—an admittedly faint-hearted concern. Moreover, I had scheduled a swimming lesson for later that afternoon, and the prospect of riding my bicycle downtown in order to then turn and ride eighty blocks uptown, to then swim for one hour, seemed like far too much exertion for someone who was lately over forty years old.

The subway trip was also turning out to be too much exertion, physical and mental. When the Z finally arrived I boarded it glumly, only to discover two stops later that it wasn't running all the way to Wall Street. I had to get off and wait ten more minutes to go one more stop. This was the kind of needling impediment that might have once made me suspect that unseen forces, unseen *governmental* forces, were at work; such is a common perspective among the paranoid, and I was happy to no longer count myself among them even as I watched the thought pass through my head.

When I was a boy I'd once made the mistake of asking my mother what the little black bars on the side of the milk carton indicated. I was referring to the UPC code.

"It's code," my mother had said.

"What's it code for?" I asked.

"I don't know," she said.

"Code for secrets?"

"Those are the kinds of questions," she told me, "that can get you into trouble. You might be working in a milk factory one day and you'll ask someone what the code's for and the next thing you know you'll be out of a job."

My new train eventually made it to the Fulton Street station, three stops away from where I'd started, forty minutes after I'd left home. Once I'd ascended to ground level, I could hear the faint sound of drumming in the distance.

It has been correctly pointed out by a number of people, mainly critics, that Occupy Wall Street did not technically occupy Wall Street but rather Zuccotti Park two blocks north. Like most everyone else, I had never heard of Zuccotti Park prior to its occupation, nor had I ever noticed it, though I'm sure I must have passed it many times. My accountant, not incidentally, has an office just a few blocks away, and he once rescued me, not incidentally, from a horrific audit about six months after Bear Stearns collapsed. ("They always go after the little man," a friend of mine said at the time, meaning that I was a little man.) But while the literal location of the protest may have been disappointing for those with an investment in the dramatic and historical, including myself, it certainly doesn't make much difference in the end precisely where such things take place. Occupy Wall Street's inaugural location, in fact, is a good illustration of the mercurial nature of the protest, its bendable nature, its ability to find something relatively benign—Zuccotti Park—and infuse it with far-reaching meaning. This is not something, sadly, that the Socialist Workers Party ever managed to do.

And while the veracity of the Occupy Wall Street message can be debated and argued and even mocked, it is apparently much more difficult to dismiss. There are quite a few hairs one could split if one thought about them long enough, but such objections ultimately wouldn't alter the essence of what has happened. For instance, it doesn't really matter that while most of those who have taken part in the protests certainly are not part of the top 1 percent, many are situated somewhere within the top 15, and would probably have more in common with the 1 percent than they would with the bulk of those below them. Nor does it matter that many protesters saw no contradiction, as one *New York Times* article described, between spending their afternoon denouncing capitalism and then going across the street to buy a cup of coffee at Starbucks. Nor does it matter that most of the protesters in Zuccotti Park were white, that lots of them were from out of town, that some of them were homeless freeloaders, that quite a few of them have no idea what they are talking about, and that probably all of them were hoping to get laid.

It was a beautiful fall day, this particular Sunday. The sky was clear, and the temperature was just right. It was one of the last beautiful days of the year, and this made me resent my decision to spend it at a protest, just as I would have felt resentment when I was a child. Now, though, I had only myself to blame. Walking toward the sound of the incessant drumming—yet another criticism of the occupation, the incessant drumming—I had the impulse again to turn around and go back home. But as I rounded the corner on Broadway, I was suddenly in view of a strange and magical world that made me instantly happy I had come all this way. It was the very thing I had dreamed about when I was a little boy, the very thing that had given me comfort when things were bleakest for my mother and me: *uprising*.

As my mother would patiently explain to me on many occasions, first would come economic collapse, then depression and repression, then the insurgence of the working class—to be followed, finally and lastly, by socialist revolution. Here, now, was the insurgency. To have wandered past Zuccotti Park without knowing anything, you might have thought that you were witnessing a youth hostel set outdoors, what with the sleeping bags and the backpacks and the unshaven faces—except that none of these hostelers appeared to have any intention of leaving for the day. This was the excursion they had come for.

The photos from the *Times* had led me to believe that I was going to encounter an enormous affair, but up close it was actually rather small. The smallness gave it even more power. Within this one city block, enough tumult had been created to be heard round the world. Imagine what would happen if it was *two* city blocks.

There might have been about five hundred protesters gathered just then. Maybe a thousand. Whatever the number was, it was minuscule in the scheme of protests, and many of the protesters were doing things other than protesting, like eating and lying on their sleeping bags. This is not to imply that things were calm and uneventful. I happened to arrive at the moment that one of those ubiquitous hop-on hop-off Gray Line sightseeing buses was idling at the red light. Fifty passengers were standing on the rooftop level, watching the proceedings down below.

"*We* are the ninety-nine percent!" a group of about twenty protesters chanted at them full voice. "*You* are the ninety-nine percent!"

Their message was inclusive, but their tone was upbraiding; the implication was that the sightseers should get off the bus right then and there and join the protest. To do otherwise would indicate that they were either too selfish or too brainless to grasp the basic mathematical premise, and preferred instead to ride around on a bus all day. I couldn't help but feel protective of the passengers. After all, I had been doing my own form of sightseeing for the last four weeks.

But the sightseers did not appear at all affronted. They smiled at the protesters, and took their pictures. I got the sense that most of them weren't American—maybe none of them were American. They might not have been clear about what was going on, or what was being said. They smiled in that way that people who don't know the language smile. I was once in Amsterdam admiring a parade that went marching through the Rembrandtplein; it was led by two police officers on horseback who were making their horses do an intricate sort of whimsical dance. The officers and their horses were skilled enough to be able to move to the rhythm of the beating drum. This must be a parade for some sort of circus, I thought. No, I later found out it was a demonstration against police brutality.

The bus pulled off; the protesters continued to shout after it. Then they shouted at the passersby. They stood like sentries, these protesters, facing out toward the street, some of them holding handmade signs. SHIT IS FUCKED UP, read one handmade sign, an example of how certain simple and straightforward phrases can, when held aloft, be made to feel profound.

People walked up and down the sidewalk, some to join, some to stare, some to distribute flyers on various topics, including one on how to start your own business. *I am presenting an Economic Development Strategy for the betterment of mankind to breathe new life into the economy,* it read in part. I took everything that was given to me, mainly to be nice, mainly to show everyone I sympathized, and because I knew what it felt like to hand things out on the street and be ignored. A man offered me a newspaper called *The Last Trumpet.* It cost fifty cents, but he gave it to me for free. It was eight pages long and printed in a variety of fonts and it looked like it had been made by a crazy person. TOMORROW'S NEWS TODAY, the front page read, but the photo was of a Russian tank from twenty years ago as it "thrust toward strategic Persian Gulf Oil Fields."

How awkward it would have been to see my father there. I suspect he'd look exactly the same as he did six years ago: big belly, bald head, round glasses, welcoming expression of great forbearance. At any moment he might have emerged from the crowd with a fresh stack of *The Militant,* which unfortunately doesn't look that much different from *The Last Trumpet.* He certainly wouldn't be giving it away for free, though. That remains his mission in life: to sell newspapers, to sign up members, to build the Party.

I've run into him before at demonstrations. About ten years ago, in Midtown, at a demonstration against the Israeli occupation; another time in Washington, DC, after the Iraq War had started, and where he seemed unable to recognize my voice on the cellphone even though he had told me to call him. "Pop, it's me," I shouted over the noise of the chanting crowd. "Who?" he kept asking. We never managed to find each other.

Every once in a while I'll think I see him somewhere in the city. There are lots of tall, older men with big bellies and bald heads wearing backpacks. But so far none of them have been him.

A few years ago I stopped in at Tekserve in Chelsea to get my laptop repaired. When the clerk checked to see if I was already in their records, he looked up after a moment and announced, "Here you are. Mahmoud Sayrafiezadeh," and swiveled the monitor around to show me that Mahmoud Sayrafiezadeh had moved to a new apartment near Prospect Park. It was like a ghost had suddenly appeared. Not long after that I sent him the groveling email inviting him over to play Scrabble and drink red wine.

"Let's keep moving," one of the police officers told me.

I didn't appreciate being spoken to like that, but I did as I was told. I walked down a short flight of steps that led into the park itself.

And just like that, I found myself enveloped by the industry of protest. The moment I entered the park, I had the feeling that I had become a participant. I wasn't comfortable with this feeling, but I respected it. It was yet another ingenious element of the occupation: anyone who is present is ipso facto occupying. The tourists, the reporters, the onlookers, the naysayers, the guys playing chess—all were part of the occupation. The only exception to this was the police.

I meandered. Zuccotti Park is a park only in the sense that it is outside and there are places to sit and trees that come out of the concrete. Other than that it is not really a park. It is more like a square or a plaza. It also falls under the oxymoronic category of a "privately owned public space," which indicates that it was constructed by a private developer for public use in exchange for tax breaks, and which meant that, perhaps because of limited foresight when writing their rules and regulations, the mayor and the park's current owner turned out to be somewhat helpless when it came to ridding the park of its occupiers.

The paths were lined with sleeping bags that had been clumped together. It was nearing noon, but some of them still contained bodies. Many of the young faces looked bleary and exhausted and unwashed. Occasionally there were older campers, too, including one woman knitting, who could have been my mother if my mother had gained weight and stayed in the Party and taken up knitting. Body odor wafted through the air. I passed a flowerbed filled with pink, red, and yellow flowers that had most likely been planted by the developers when times were good. There was a handmade sign nearby, written in purple marker on the bottom half of a pizza box, that read, PLEASE!! DO NOT STEP ON FLOWERS OR WALK THROUGH FLOWERBED. THANK YOU SO SO MUCH. The fact that the appeal had been honored gave the surroundings an air of civility.

On the north side of the park, which is to say facing Liberty Street, was a library with books overflowing from plastic bins. It had been named the People's Library, and there must have been at least a thousand titles on hand.

State and Society in the Taiwan Miracle, read one.

Cold Mountain, read another.

Beyond the library was a kitchen that was offering a breakfast buffet of bagels and cereal and peanut butter and lots of other things — all free. People helped themselves to generous portions. I thought of helping myself, too, so that I could be part of them, and so that I could have an authentic experience, but I wasn't hungry. I had a vision of reaching for a bagel and being admonished.

Further along was a poster board with an illustration of an eagle and a listing of the day's events.

7:30 A.M.	Breakfast
9:00 A.M.	Working Group Coordination Meeting
10:00 A.M.	Occupiers Meeting
12:00 P.M.	MARCH
1:30 P.M.	Lunch
1:30 to 5:30 P.M.	Working Group, Forums, Teach-Ins, Guest Speakers, etc.
5:30 P.M.	MARCH
7:00 P.M.	General Assembly

It was an impressive agenda. It made me feel old. All of the things in the park made me feel old. And jealous. Maybe I was the one who should have come up with the People's Library and the day's agenda.

Maybe I was the one who should have come up with Occupy Wall Street. It was what I had been groomed for all those years by the Socialist Workers Party. Now I was being shown the possibilities of the talent I had squandered.

And then I came to the end of the park. The drum circle marked the end. There was a full set of blue drums being pounded on by a young man who was very skilled and could yet make a career of it. Behind him stood a group of people using tom-toms and bongos and plastic buckets and whatever else they had been able to get their hands on. A thin, middle-aged man wove through the onlookers shaking maracas. People were dancing in the middle of the sidewalk, including a woman with balloons tied around her head. After a few minutes, I understood how the sound of drumming would make you angry if you had to listen to it in your apartment all day.

I had been at Occupy Wall Street all of fifteen minutes, and I was ready to leave. I had seen everything; 80 percent of it was sleeping bags. If something more was going to happen, I would have to wait for it to happen, and I didn't want to wait. Familiar boredom had set in. Plus my legs were hurting and my feet were sore. I'd walked one city block, but it felt like I'd walked a mile. It was the same physical sensation that I'd felt at every protest I'd ever attended in my life. Discomfort, I had learned years ago, was the essence of protest. If there was no pain, there could be no evidence of sacrifice.

But it wasn't even noon yet. I still had time before my swimming lesson, and to leave now would be some sort of admission of defeat. Or of cowardice. So for good measure I did a loop around the perimeter of the park. The sidewalk was crowded. The sidewalk counted as part of the protest. Police leaned on barricades, observing. Some of the protesters engaged with the police, chatting pleasantly. Don't engage with the police, the Socialist Workers Party would have told them; they are not your friends, and moreover they will crack your head open if Mayor Bloomberg tells them to do it. I probably wouldn't be seeing my father here, I realized. He probably wouldn't approve of any of this.

There were always things that he was able to see that no one else could see. Political things. He always had a more perceptive understanding than the average man. *The correct analysis*, he would call it. He wouldn't approve of the fact that the protesters were mainly white, mainly out-of-towners, mainly young people, mainly people speaking in vague terms without any real scientific understanding of political economy. These characteristics were an indication of something *reactionary*, he might say. These were the reasons why the movement had been so slow to spread to unions and black people and poor people. It was why it was leaderless, and a leaderless movement cannot make a revolution. He'd point out how the protesters were complaining about the collapse of the banking industry and the government bailout when what they really should be fixated on was capitalism in general. Capitalism in perpetuity. Even when capitalism was booming and times were good and the banks were lending, it was still capitalism, it was still exploitative, and economic crisis was still around the corner. Economic crisis to be followed by war and fascism. This was the logical progression. Capitalism could never be reformed; it could only be overthrown.

I passed a pay phone that had a sticker on it that read THIS PHONE IS TAPPED. I thought of my UPC code. A man in his sixties was standing beside the phone waving an enormous Chinese flag. He was wearing a leather aviator hat with flaps that came over his ears and scolding a group of protesters who looked confused. "This man defends the Cultural Revolution," the man with the aviator hat was shouting, "not I!" He was referring specifically to one of the protesters, as if they'd just finished carrying on a debate and he was now asking others in the area to make the final judgment. But the person who was being singled out appeared not to know exactly what was happening. "This man is a Stalinist," the man in the aviator hat went on, "not I!" He looked pleased with himself. He looked like he knew he'd won the debate.

About fifteen years ago I'd observed a man standing on a milk crate in the middle of SoHo and shouting through a megaphone about the mayoral election that was being held that day. He obviously thought he was helping to bring some enlightenment to the residents of New York, helping to alert them to the fact that they were being duped by the two major political parties; what he was really doing, though, was giving the impression that he was somewhat maniacal, clearly angry, possibly dangerous, a man who stands on a crowded sidewalk in the middle of the day shouting through a megaphone at strangers. He was reaching no one with his message; in fact, he was achieving the opposite result. He was repelling people. What made it so disturbing for me was that I knew this man. He was a member of the Socialist Workers Party, and I had known him since I was a little boy. I had always liked him. He was funny and hip, rare traits in a political organization that was not known for either. My mother had liked him, too. I had often imagined that perhaps they would become a couple one day, even though there was really no chance of that — my mother never dated anyone after my father left. One summer we played softball together at a Party picnic, this man and I, and he ended up pulling his hamstring sliding into home plate. Now here he was in SoHo, nearly thirty years later, standing on the street and screaming about the parties of capitalism.

Around I walked. To the north of the park was Brooks Brothers, to the south was Men's Wearhouse, to the west was Burger King, and on Broadway was the same group of protesters declaiming, "*We* are the ninety-nine percent! *You* are the ninety-nine percent!" A woman in a wedding dress stood nearby, on the sidewalk. A man in a black suit had his arm around her waist. They were posing for photographs. It wasn't clear if this was an actual bride and groom having their wedding pictures taken, or two people who were commenting on the inequality in society and marriage.

From somewhere within the crowd I heard someone shout, "Mic check!"

Then, from somewhere else, came the response: "Mic check!"

Throughout the park the words "Mic check" reverberated. It was the clever way the occupiers had gotten around the prohibition on the use of amplified sound.

"We are assembling for our march . . ." someone shouted.

"We are assembling for our march . . ." someone repeated.

"We are assembling for our march . . ."

"We are assembling for our march . . ."

" . . . on the corner of Broadway and Trinity . . ."

" . . . on the corner of Broadway and Trinity . . ."

Etc.

* * *

A low wall ran around the south side of the park, and I took a seat on it to rest my back and legs. Someone came by asking for money to aid his sister city's occupation. I didn't believe that was really what he was collecting for. Someone came by asking for a cigarette. A certain loneliness began to creep into me. Loneliness and isolation. Everyone, it seemed, had some purpose, even if that purpose was just to ask for something.

Sitting next to me on the wall were a young man and woman, possibly boyfriend and girlfriend, having a conversation, and I interrupted them to ask, disingenuously, if they could explain what a "Mic check" was. They explained what I already knew. They appeared happy to talk to me.

The young man told me his name was Mike; he was twenty-one years old. He was from North Dakota and he'd been at the protest for four days, sleeping outside every night, which accounted for his skin being close to gray. Nevertheless, he was spry and animated and articulate. He told me he wasn't going to college because he didn't want to end up in debt. Instead, he was making a living selling cars with his uncle. He seemed fine with this. Or at least resigned. But his story took a more optimistic turn when he told me how one night he'd come across news online about Occupy Wall Street. It had the timbre of a spiritual awakening. He was mesmerized by what was happening, and a few days later he told his uncle that he had made the decision to leave for New York City. He'd never been to New York City before. He'd never even ridden on a bus before. The first time he got on the city bus he tried to pay using his credit card. The three of us laughed at this.

The young woman was Tracy, and she'd been at the protests for two days. She too was nearing the color gray. She said she was originally from a small town outside of San Diego, and was now living in upstate New York because she was in the Air Force and was going to school for engineering. After graduating, however, she would have to satisfy her military-service requirements, including four years of active duty and four years in the reserves. It was a major commitment, and she admitted that she had not realized quite what she was getting herself into when she signed up. Now she regretted it. The good news, at least, was that she'd made it out of her small, conservative hometown where no one approved of the protests, not even her relatives who had lost their homes in the mortgage crisis.

I felt sympathetic toward them. I knew what it was like to be in your early twenties and not have a clue what the future held for you. I wanted to offer some advice, but I had none to offer. No one had ever offered me advice. All I could muster was the banal: "It's good you guys came." This was the moment when my father would have tried to sell them a copy of *The Militant*. He would have spoken to them patiently, forbearingly, as he opened the paper to show them such-and-such article that summed up everything that was happening in the world. From this interaction, he would later be able to draw conclusions about young people throughout the United States.

I said goodbye to Tracy and Mike and hobbled off with my sore feet.

The group that had been chanting "*We* are the ninety-nine percent!" had been replaced by a quiet, contemplative group calling itself the Center for Economic Progress. It was composed of about fifteen people sitting cross-legged in a circle on the sidewalk discussing macroeconomics. Standing behind them were about fifteen more people trying to get a word in edgewise. The leaders of the group appeared to be a young man and woman who did most of the talking and had the power to call on people when they raised their hands. They probably weren't yet thirty years old. The man had a calm, professorial air — he mentioned several times that he had taught a class in macroeconomics — while the woman looked world-weary and pompous. When anyone asked a question, whether it was about the debt or the credit rating or the Euro, she'd take a deep breath as if we should all be beyond these questions by now but she'd explain it one last time.

The man had more energy. He spoke engagingly about his proposals for a new economy. He made it sound like it was only a matter of time before they were put into practice. His tone was matter-of-fact. It was the tone of the Socialist Workers Party: the revolution is coming, of course it is coming. I had no idea what the man was talking about, but within minutes I could feel myself becoming convinced. Such is the power of conviction.

He was selective, however, about whose questions he answered, or whose statements he addressed, and this diminished his credibility in my eyes. When a man in the crowd launched into an impassioned speech about the Euro, he waited him out with a glazed stare before moving on to a subject with which he was clearly more comfortable.

I looped around the block again. Then I hobbled through the park. Everything was the same as it was before: the library, the buffet, the drum circle. No discernible progress had been made except for the passage of time. It was past noon, and I was going to have to leave soon for my swimming lesson. How strange it was to think that the protest had been going nonstop for four weeks. If I came back after my swimming lesson, it'd still be here. If I came back in two weeks, it'd still be here. There was something comforting in this. The endless protest, the endless striving, the next generation taking up the mantle from the exhausted generation preceding it. My mother and I had protested for almost twenty years, and what did we have to show for it? Not much. If anything had changed because of our efforts, it wasn't apparent. Too bad we had never thought to live in a park as a way to call attention to the problems of the world.

I listened to the drum circle for a while. The sound was louder and more insistent, and the crowd of dancers had grown. I watched them, the drummers and the dancers. It was nice, it was rhythmic. Sure, it might get annoying if you lived nearby, but people had come to this park to make a change. How could there be change without annoyance? I thought about dancing. It'd be fun. I could tell people I'd gone to Occupy Wall Street and danced.

In six weeks all of this would be gone, of course. The protesters chased out in the middle of the night by the police, the buffet dismantled, the sleeping bags cleared away, the books thrown into the garbage. My father could have predicted it all. In six weeks it would return to the Zuccotti Park it once was, the only difference being metal barricades and a sign unequivocally stating *Zuccotti Park is a privately owned space that is designed and intended for use and enjoyment by the general public for passive recreation . . .* , followed by a list of every conceivable rule and regulation that could make it impossible for Occupy Wall Street ever to happen again. That is when the commitment to change would be put to the test: when the cameras are gone and the reporters are gone and the glamour disappears and the tedium sets in—the crushing tedium. That is when you realize, in your solitary moments, how much of your life you will have to sacrifice to change the world.

But for now, the drums were going and the people were dancing and it was time for me to go swimming. I crossed the street by Men's Wearhouse and headed back to the subway. At the red light, a father and his son stood waiting to cross. The boy must have been about five years old. He was holding a small football because it was Sunday.

"What's that?" the boy exclaimed, pointing to Zuccotti Park. There was trepidation in his voice, and I could understand how if you were five years old the ragtag sight might be frightening.

"Oh, yes," the father said, as if he'd been waiting for his son to ask him. "Those people are upset because they don't have jobs. They want the world to be more fair." He spoke calmly, rationally, and he bent down to the boy with one hand on his shoulder. "But that's not something you have to worry about right now."

Then they crossed the street going one way, and I crossed the street going the other way.

Best American Reflection on Historic Protest Movements

ADAM HOCHSCHILD

FROM *The Occupied Wall Street Journal*

The Occupied Wall Street Journal *began as a media project of the Occupy Wall Street movement to deliver protest-centric news, essays, and opinion articles. This piece was published in the newspaper's fifth issue in November of 2011, two months into the movement.*

Common Threads

We're at a curious moment in this remarkable movement. Has there ever been one so widespread that has not yet made demands? Yet at the same time, Occupy Wall Street has accomplished something that takes other movements years. It has crystallized a sense of outrage—and made clear that this outrage is shared by tens of millions.

I think about other moments in my lifetime when it suddenly became thrillingly clear that millions of people felt the same way. One was in the late 1960s, when huge crowds poured into the streets, again and again, opposing America's war in Vietnam. It took years more to stop that war, and an appalling amount of bloodshed by the Vietnamese. But something changed after those demonstrations began. All of us who had vowed never to fight in Vietnam looked up and down the long lines of fellow marchers and knew we were not alone.

Another exhilarating moment came in East Germany in the fall of 1989. Wanting the freedom to travel, to read and speak as they chose, and to be rid of constant surveillance and threats by the secret police, thousands of people began massing one Monday evening in a public square in Leipzig. Quickly the Monday demonstrations spread to other cities, and the crowds grew to tens of thousands. Within two months it became hundreds of thousands, and the Berlin Wall came down.

Don't imagine, though, that real change will happen so quickly here. We are up against a system of deeply rooted, widening inequality that is a veritable Berlin Wall of corporate power. I think our progress, our pattern of defeats and advances, will be more like that of another movement.

Roll the clock back about 220 years. Up through the late 1700s, most people in Britain accepted slavery as unthinkingly as most Americans, until now, have accepted the rule of giant corporations. British ships dominated the Atlantic slave trade, and on occasion reaped hedge-fund-sized returns: a single voyage by the *Hawke* of Liverpool in 1780 made a 147% profit. Some half million slaves toiled 12-hour days on the lucrative sugar plantations of the British West Indies. The profits from their labor built many a mansion in London's most exclusive neighborhoods, and country estates whose grandeur rivals anything in the Hamptons today. Jamaican sugar mogul William Beckford could afford to hire Mozart to give his son piano lessons.

Yet this was an era when the French and American Revolutions put new ideas about human equality into the air. When a brilliantly organized antislavery movement began in London in 1787, it quickly found a following. As often happens, the grassroots outpaced headquarters, and, unorganized by anyone except a couple of pamphlets suggesting the idea, by 1792 at least 400,000 people in the British Isles were refusing to eat slave-grown sugar. It was the largest consumer boycott the world had yet seen—and one of those moments when people who cared deeply about something looked around and saw they were not alone.

Sugar planters and their lobbyists were as taken by surprise as Wall Street was when people began pouring into Liberty Square in September. They fulminated, they issued counter-pamphlets, they claimed that ending slavery would throw thousands of Britons out of work. And for a time they prevailed. But in the end the antislavery activists won. They discovered the strength of their numbers through the sugar boycott, through vast petition campaigns, and, in later years, in mass meetings. In 1807 they succeeded in abolishing the British slave trade. Stimulated by news of the ongoing movement, a series of ever-larger slave revolts broke out in the British West Indies, and in 1838 British Empire slavery came to an end—a full quarter century before that happened in the United States.

In combating entrenched power of a different sort—a system with obscene profits for the 1% and hardship and a downward slide for many of the rest—I think we're now at about 1792 in this process. We have a long way to go. But we know we're not alone.

Best American Reflection on a Modern Protest Movement

ROBERT HASS

FROM *The New York Times*

Known for its students' political engagement and activist culture, the University of California-Berkeley became the site of an unfortunate clash be-

tween Occupy protesters and police on November 9, 2011. Video footage of the day shows police using batons against students and faculty. Robert Hass is a professor of poetry at UC-Berkeley and former U.S. Poet Laureate who encountered police at the Occupy Cal protests. This was his response.

Beat Poets, Not Beat Poets

Life, I found myself thinking as a line of Alameda County deputy sheriffs in Darth Vader riot gear formed a cordon in front of me on a recent night on the campus of the University of California, Berkeley, is full of strange contingencies. The deputy sheriffs, all white men, except for one young woman, perhaps Filipino, who was trying to look severe but looked terrified, had black truncheons in their gloved hands that reporters later called batons and that were known, in the movies of my childhood, as billy clubs.

The first contingency that came to mind was the quick spread of the Occupy movement. The idea of occupying public space was so appealing that people in almost every large city in the country had begun to stake them out, including students at Berkeley, who, on that November night, occupied the public space in front of Sproul Hall, a gray granite Beaux-Arts edifice that houses the registrar's offices and, in the basement, the campus police department.

It is also the place where students almost 50 years ago touched off the Free Speech Movement, which transformed the life of American universities by guaranteeing students freedom of speech and self-governance. The steps are named for Mario Savio, the eloquent undergraduate student who was the symbolic face of the movement. There is even a Free Speech Movement Café on campus where some of Mr. Savio's words are prominently displayed: "There is a time . . . when the operation of the machine becomes so odious, makes you so sick at heart, that you can't take part. You can't even passively take part."

Earlier that day a colleague had written to say that the campus police had moved in to take down the Occupy tents and that students had been "beaten viciously." I didn't believe it. In broad daylight? And without provocation? So when we heard that the police had returned, my wife, Brenda Hillman, and I hurried to the campus. I wanted to see what was going to happen and how the police behaved, and how the students behaved. If there was trouble, we wanted to be there to do what we could to protect the students.

Once the cordon formed, the deputy sheriffs pointed their truncheons toward the crowd. It looked like the oldest of military maneuvers, a phalanx out of the Trojan War, but with billy clubs instead of spears. The students were wearing scarves for the first time that year, their cheeks rosy with the first bite of real cold after the long Californian Indian summer. The billy clubs were about the size of a boy's Little League baseball bat. My wife was speaking to the young deputies about the importance of nonviolence and explaining why they should be at home reading to their children, when one of the deputies reached out, shoved my wife in the chest, and knocked her down.

Another of the contingencies that came to my mind was a moment 30 years ago when Ronald Reagan's administration made it a priority to see to it that people like themselves, the talented, hardworking people who ran the country, got to keep the money they earned. Roosevelt's New Deal had to be undealt once and for all. A few years earlier, California voters had passed an amendment freezing the property taxes that finance public education and installing a rule that required a two-thirds majority in both houses of the legislature to raise tax revenues. My father-in-law said to me at the time, "It's going to take them 50 years to really see the damage they've done." But it took far fewer than 50 years.

My wife bounced nimbly to her feet. I tripped and almost fell over her trying to help her up, and at that moment the deputies in the cordon surged forward and, using their clubs as battering rams, began to hammer at the bodies of the line of students. It was stunning to see. They swung hard into their chests and bellies. Particularly shocking to me — it must be a generational reaction — was that they assaulted both the young men and the young women with the same indiscriminate force. If the students turned away, they pounded their ribs. If they turned further away to escape, they hit them on their spines.

None of the police officers invited us to disperse or gave any warning. We couldn't have dispersed if we'd wanted to because the crowd behind us was pushing forward to see what was going on. The descriptor for what I tried to do is "remonstrate." I screamed at the deputy who had knocked down my wife, "You just knocked down my wife, for Christ's sake!" A couple of students had pushed forward in the excitement and the deputies grabbed them, pulled them to the ground, and cudgeled them, raising the clubs above their heads and swinging. The line surged. I got whacked hard in the ribs twice and once across the forearm. Some of the deputies used their truncheons as bars and seemed to be trying to use minimum force to get people to move. And then, suddenly, they stopped, on some signal, and reformed their line. Apparently a group of deputies had beaten their way to the Occupy tents and taken them down. They stood, again immobile, clubs held across their chests, eyes carefully meeting no one's eyes, faces impassive. I imagined that their adrenaline was surging as much as mine.

My ribs didn't hurt very badly until the next day and then it hurt to laugh, so I skipped the gym for a couple mornings, and I was a little disappointed that the bruises weren't slightly more dramatic. It argued either for a kind of restraint or a kind of low cunning in the training of the police. They had hit me hard enough so that I was sore for days, but not hard enough to leave much of a mark. I wasn't so badly off. One of my colleagues, also a poet, Geoffrey O'Brien, had a broken rib. Another colleague, Celeste Langan, a Wordsworth scholar, got dragged across the grass by her hair when she presented herself for arrest.

I won't recite the statistics, but the entire university system in California is under great stress and the state legislature is paralyzed by a minority of legislators whose only idea is that they don't want to pay one more cent in taxes. Meanwhile, students at Berkeley are graduating with an average indebtedness of something like $16,000. It is no wonder that the real estate industry started inventing loans for people who couldn't pay them back.

"Whose university?" the students had chanted. Well, it is theirs, and it ought to be everyone else's in California. It also belongs to the future, and to the dead who paid taxes to build one of the greatest systems of public education in the world.

The next night the students put the tents back up. Students filled the plaza again with a festive atmosphere. And lots of signs. (The one from the English Department contingent read "Beat Poets, not beat poets.") A week later, at 3:30 a.m., the police officers returned in force, a hundred of them, and told the campers to leave or they would be arrested. All but two moved. The two who stayed were arrested, and the tents were removed. On Thursday afternoon when I returned toward sundown to the steps to see how the students had responded, the air was full of balloons, helium balloons to which tents had been attached, and attached to the tents was kite string. And they hovered over the plaza, large and awkward, almost lyrical, occupying the air.

Best American Letters in the Mail that Breathe New Life into the Epistolary Arts

FROM *The Rumpus*

TheRumpus.net is an online magazine that focuses on cultural commentary and personal essays. For those of us nostalgic for the lost art of the physical letter, The Rumpus *sends its subscribers a near-weekly letter from different authors, written on paper, and printed in actual ink. Here are four examples, each of them addressed to all subscribers.*

Stephen Elliott, 490 2nd St. #200, San Francisco, CA 94107

Hi,

I don't know if you know but I do this thing called The Daily Rumpus where I send an email out to a large group of people. They've been called "overly personal" and recently it's been difficult. Some things are harder to share than others.

My friend Matthew Zapruder was talking to me about exposing oneself in one's writing. The point was that sometimes you expose yourself at the expense of your writing. As if the exposure was the point. After all, it's not a requirement, unless it is. Unless the point you're making can only be made by opening yourself up so people can read the ink scrawled across your lungs.

A little more than a year ago I did an interview with a young woman in a hotel room. She had a boyfriend but decided against mentioning him. At some point I curled around her and put my head in her lap. She wrote an essay about it and published it in a literary journal online. The editor wrote to say they'd received an essay about me and was I OK with them publishing it. I couldn't say no, after all I've written about so many people in my life. Though I always change the details enough that no one from a literary journal would ever figure out who I was talking about. But she didn't want to change those details, and anyway it's a quibble. I hate people who say this is why it's OK for me to do this but not you, based on some small difference. If you write about other people you have to let go of that, though I've never met a writer who has.

I've been dizzy. That's why it's been hard to write. Of course long before I started getting dizzy I was having trouble writing. In 2005, for example, I didn't write anything particularly good despite sitting at a desk every day and trying for many hours. These things come and go. Part of writing is not writing.

I noticed the dizziness first in New York six month ago. It was much less pronounced then. It was just a twinkle, like minor heartburn, and I ignored it. But as it progressed I got worried and then saw a doctor and then, two weeks later, went back to the doctor again, because by then I was really profoundly dizzy almost every day. I was off balance enough that I was nervous crossing the street. Everything was shifting. Something about contrasts and shapes. Sometimes my vision would blur.

I don't know why it's easier to put this in a letter than an email, but it is. The medium is the message, as they say.

As I write this I'm imagining you're my ex-girlfriend. I miss you terribly. Last time I saw you I was struck by how thin you were, and how beautiful. There is something about your waist. I always loved how comfortable you were being desired. Until the end, of course. Other women seem to be offended if you tell them they're beautiful too often. They want to be loved for who they are, whatever that means. How are we not our bodies? I read a study that said the most predictable determinant of straight male desire is hip to waist ratio. Maybe it's your hip to waist ratio that makes you so interesting when we talk. I think over the things you say later and I can't even understand them. But the sound of your voice is kind of like a river, or a music. You have the sweetest, most calming voice.

I was talking about the dizziness. It gets worse and sometimes, when it's particularly bad, I can't stay focused on the person talking. There's a pressure in my left eye and when I look to the left the world seems to spin violently. That's when I realized I was really only dizzy on the left side.

My mother was dizzy one day and went to a doctor who said she had multiple sclerosis. Not long after that she was shaking so violently she couldn't get off the couch. Five years later, when I was thirteen, she died. Not long ago my sister was diagnosed with the same thing. So you see, dizzy runs in my family.

The doctor referred me this time to a neurologist. The neurologist asked if I was ever depressed and I said yes and explained I'd had some kind of breakdown two years earlier. Since then I'd been taking Wellbutrin and Adderall, though both in relatively small amounts. He looked in my ears and my eyes and turned my head one way and the other. He asked if I ever got headaches. He prescribed Lamictal. 25 milligrams in the morning and at night. He said I didn't need to take the Wellbutrin anymore. Lamictal is for bipolar disorder and I had all these strange side effects, like I threw out my back and then I became kind of inert. I was tired and nothing mattered so I just lay on the couch. I stopped taking the Lamictal and made an appointment with a psychopharmacologist who prescribed Cymbalta. The Cymbalta had similar effects. I could feel my life slipping from me.

When I think of my mother I don't remember much, the same few images, like stock photos. Late last year I read an advance copy of Cheryl Strayed's memoir *Wild*. She talks a lot about her relationship with her mother and how her mother's death impacted her life. The day my mother died I went with some friends to the canal and drank as much vodka and beer as I could then I went home and crawled into bed. Our house was quiet for a while. It wasn't like a home, it was like we were all homeless crawling into this empty place to sleep. After my mother died the walls would barely protect you from the wind. My father's girlfriend came around a lot. She had been coming around when my mother was still alive. They were having sex in the bedroom while Mom lay on the couch. My father said his girlfriend was my mother's best friend. And I guess now I'm getting into that territory Zapruder was warning me about. They had a daughter ten months after my mother died, but I was way out of the picture by then. It took all of about two weeks after my mother died before I ran away from that place.

Sometimes people, usually psychiatrists, ask if I was close with my mother. It's a softball but I never hit it. How would I know? I was thirteen when she died; I was eight when she got sick. How would I know if we were close? What do you talk about with your mother when you're ten? I was smoking by that time. By eleven I was wearing torn heavy metal t-shirts and huffing spray paint. By twelve I was taking acid and whatever else came my way, which wasn't much. I didn't have the kind of friends that gave away drugs. We were freebasing early but no one could afford cocaine. I remember my very first acid trip and I literally had this thought: This is what happiness feels like. I mean, I was twelve, my mother was dying, and I thought I was discovering happiness because I didn't care about anything, because my friend's girlfriend was wearing purple contacts, because I was comfortable in my own acne covered skin for a moment. Was I close with my mom?

When I read Cheryl's book I cried a lot in the beginning. Everything she wrote about her mother killed me. I even sent her a note asking why I was so much more upset about her mother dying than my own. She didn't answer that one. That's a tough one.

The neurologist thinks it's just migraines. Migraines without headaches are called silent migraines, or ocular migraines. A more specific diagnosis would be migraine associated vertigo. I've always been prone to migraines. At least once a month, if I'm not sleeping enough, I get laid out by a migraine. I get nauseous and a film of thick sweat layers my forehead. I cover my eyes to keep out light and my head pulses like someone is inside my skull tapping with an icepick. I can't drink alcohol anymore because alcohol triggers migraines. Flying triggers migraines unless I'm careful to sit by the window and stare out at the wing for part of the flight. Lack of sleep. And stress. Though I don't know if I buy the one about stress. There's something about that diagnosis I don't like. It feels like they're blaming the victim. Like, maybe if you lightened up you wouldn't get these paralyzing headaches. Or, it's an excuse to not participate. Be careful with me, I can't handle stress.

The girl that wrote the article about me. I was telling my friend about it and she said I sounded like a frat guy defending having sex with a drunk girl. I mean, all we did was cuddle. Do you have to explain cuddling with someone? This was not creepy, non-consensual cuddling. But she was upset because we didn't go further than that, we were not going to be part of each other's lives. I don't know how to love. Can we let go? Enjoy the moment for what it was? It was a nice moment that led to nothing. And when I told my ex-girlfriend about it she knew even before I got there. "You curled up in her lap, didn't you." The point was I took and I didn't give back. And a girl I'm currently dating, or whatever we're doing, read the article and wrote me a long note about it. She said I made people feel a certain way. I didn't respond and when she asked about the note she'd sent, worried she'd offended me, I just said that it sounded like she didn't like me very much.

So my migraines grew silent and frequent, leading to dizziness. It's weirdly progressive, each week the dizziness is stronger. Is the dizziness a metaphor for something else? Missed opportunities, paths not taken? What is a migraine, anyway?

I have a suspicion that I will learn to live with the dizziness and because of this the dizziness will pass. We learn to live with all sorts of things. Like, ten years ago, following a sinus infection, I got tinnitus. My ears were always ringing and I wasn't sure I could live with it. But it turned out I could live with it, and then I barely noticed anymore. Or sleeping in a youth shelter in a room with thirty other children. Or losing our mothers at an early age. Or, like the other day, I saw a girl I hadn't seen in years. She was wearing a blue dress and her legs were naked and I swear I fell head over heels in love. It passed quickly, but you won't convince me it wasn't love just because it didn't stick around.

I don't have many regrets, honestly. If anything I feel like I live a charmed life. Of course, I wish I had known my mother better, and not just because I would then have been more complete. I wish I knew her better because she was a nice person. She knew how to be; people felt comfortable around her. And, I'm going to say something horrible here, but my father is not a nice person. My mother had friends but they stopped visiting after my father chased them away. In better times I would sit on the couch with my mother and watch soap operas. I would make her coffee with lots of milk. My mother believed she was going to get better and leave but she didn't, she got worse and died. And you know, I mean, maybe I knew her better than I remember. I have a short memory. Sometimes it seems like every day I'm starting from scratch. After she died I spent a year sleeping on the streets. That's the short story. My father moved with his wife to the suburbs and started a new life. I think I might have been too preoccupied with survival and unable to process my feelings for my mother. But I did survive. I did. I slept on a rooftop and a broom closet and in boiler rooms during a Chicago winter and I made it out alive. The truth is I didn't cry thinking about my mother for years. After my homeless year I was made a ward of the state and placed in a state run mental hospital, then a tough group home, then a better one and things started to fall into place. I went to college.

Who are we, what are we made up of? I worry that I'll never find out. My childhood was filled with adventures. At night I'd slip from the window; my friends waiting in the yard. We'd run through Indian Boundary or Warren Park, chased by the police or tougher boys or each other. We'd play basketball in front of Boone School and drink beer at the canal where we dug furniture into the dirt. In the summer the dandelions would turn white and we'd light them on fire.

That girlfriend I was remembering, imagining I was talking to even as I was writing this letter to you, we loved each other like we were in the movies. We had the kind of passion you leave people for. We were never going to make a family. But, in the moments I remember most clearly, she looked at me the way a mother looks at a child.

xoxoxo

stephen

/ Elliott

Rick Moody
PO Box 750
Dover Plains, NY 12522

*

Dear People Whose Names I Don't Know Yet,

The identity theft problem has been getting to me, so I thought I'd write you about it. Maybe some of you have had some experience with this. I'm supposed to keep notes about everything, according to the Federal Trade Commission, as a way to document what's going on. Here is my summary so far:

*Notified of potential security compromise on bank account 10/31/2011
*Closed and reopened Citibank account in early November
*Closed and reopened Mastercard account in early November
*Paid a bunch of bounce fees that felt unjust to me
*Credit report requested, by hacker (denied), in November
*E-Trade account opened, or attempted, by hacker, in November
*$5000 debited against checking account in early November, restored by Citibank
*America Online account hacked in January
*Gmail account hacked repeatedly in Jan/Feb, account closed in February
*Amazon account hacked in early February, several purchases attempted, account closed
*American Express green card number hacked, early February
*Attempted purchases on AmEx card including, WalMart online, QVC online, totalling $8,000, all denied
*Amex account closed, reopened
*Fraudulent text messages from hacker, as shown above, between February 8-11 *[handwritten: below]*
*Address of hacker (or fraudulent address) obtained from Amazon, February 13
*Second gmail.com account hacked, and closed, mid-February
*Notified of PayPal account attempt, third week of February

So this is the story of my life in the last couple of months. Lots and lots of thinking about this, and worrying about whether I'm staying ahead of things or not. I called the police the other day, and I was told that until they actually manage to *take some money*, I can't file a report; or, rather, I could have filed a report in November when they got the $5000 out, but now I sort of can't bear to spend the hours searching through my records in order to get an affidavit from the Citibank people, that I might then file the police report. It's the time commitment that I really *am* irritated about here. I have a kid, I'm teaching a lot this semester, and a novel that I haven't worked on in weeks, and all I seem to do is chase around these guys, these Nigerian guys (according to Gmail—that's where their ISP is from), who want to highjack my credit cards.

I don't know if it's clear from the above, but eventually I got a text message from someone claiming to be Amex, but whose poor English-language skills made him/her seem dubious to me. I'll transcribe the entire text message conversation for you. This is all exactly as it appeared, by the way. I'm not exaggerating the brute English usage for comic effect. ("H" stands for hacker, and "R" stands for Rick.)

H: yes this is the Citi bank from CA
R: Have already tipped off the cops and Amex so you'd better move on.
H: What do you mean Hiram Moody
R: Tell me about your childhood dreams. Did you have a childhood dream? Did it involve bad grammar?
H: What do you mean i wanna ask you some Question about you Order
R: I just came from my Dante group. Did you ever read Dante? The thing I can't figure is why misappropriation of funds is punished in a circle right next to murderers. Well, maybe I can understand a little bit. By the way, I hope I'm not waking you up. In the lowest circle of Inferno a guy is stuck eating another guy's head for all eternity. What do you think? Is it a just punishment? An archbishop starved this guy's kids to death. But there's no spot in Inferno for people who mistreated other people's pets. What about you? Did you ever mistreat pets?
R: Hey, what gives? I thought we had a nice conversation going. Giving up already?
R: Hey James, or is it Phil, how come you never answer my texts anymore?
R: Phil, are you related to the famous lawyer of the same name? And how is the weather in Stockton today? Kinda cold back east!
H: Hello, who are you?
H: Who are you?
R: I am the guy who has been getting fradulent messages from your telephone number. Who are you?

At which point, the exchange ended (for now). For the sake of the story, let me say that I started calling him/her Phil, because somewhere in the middle of this barrage of text messages, I managed to get access to my blocked Amazon account (see timeline, above) whereupon I could bear witness to the new address that the hackers had installed there, which belonged to a guy named Philip James B---, in Stockton, CA. And Phil's phone number was the *very number* that had been texting me, alleging to be Amex and Citibank. How I got access to the Amazon account is kind of interesting, but I can't just go on and on about the byways of research here. You guys probably want the human dimension.

I thought to keep writing to Phil, of course, and what I thought I would do was write increasingly personal notes to him. For example, I wanted to write to Phil about my daughter, and to ask if Phil had any kids. I mean, there's a stereotype we all have about the hackers, that they are pimply Asian guys in their mid-twenties, who are using all the proceeds to buy X-box games or maybe to finance Internet start-ups. And I thought if I really used the only skill I have, the ability to render well the English tongue, and to create the perception of a sympathetic character, maybe I could, over a long period, cause Phil to regret what he was doing, or, if not, at least I could cause charges to accrue to his phone bill in the same way charges were accruing whenever I had to untie another knot of this whole identity theft problem.

But eventually I just got bored of Phil, and I felt sorry for him, a little bit. I did, however, go look at his house on Google Maps. Because I could. It like suburban sprawl, not much more, although his complex does have a pool in it. I notice that his dad lives a couple of towns over, and I think this is his *real* dad, not the famous crank lawyer who seems to have the very same name.

All of this makes me not want to bother to go online. In fact, I have become suddenly careless about the piling up of e-mail, and don't really want to bother to do it anymore. E-commerce seems even more unlikely. I think the Nigerians were basically reading everything I typed into a Gmail message, and that's how they came to possess my social security number, my home address, my phone number, *and* my mother's maiden name, all of my passwords, even the passwords that I changed, because whenever I changed a password they seemed to have it in their possession immediately. It just makes you want to buy nothing. Which is probably good for my dwindling finances anyhow.

In the absence of a vigorous online life I have been feeling, well, kind of free. When I go outside, I think of myself as only existing in this flesh and blood version. I am the arthritic shoulders and bad knee and thinning hair, and the calluses, and so on, the guy out on the street. I no longer feel that the words "Rick Moody" as they appear out in the world refer to me. I feel that that entity is specifically *not me.* This phrase "Rick Moody" refers to a possession of certain people in Nigeria (and some in the state of Washington, too, according to Google), who will use this possession in whatever way is useful to their very baroque, and very fluid manipulation of data. So who am I then? Just a body? Is there a sense of self that inevitably goes with having a body? Or can the consciousness of self just go the way of the digital self, into a shadowy state of communal ownership, in which the borders of self and the packaged commodity become increasingly difficult to tease apart.

Did I somehow bring this on myself? The commonplace wisdom is that if you ever used a porn site online you have somehow made yourself vulnerable to this sort of thing, the identity theft sort of thing, which implies—or here's he linkage in popular culture—that you *deserve* what you got, and you victimized yourself. If you support pornography, by using it, and if you are at peace with that particular kind of free expression, *you deserve what you get.* Well, I would like to be completely blameless in this regard, but I think it's more honest (and more routine) to say that though I am not a frequent user of such things these days, I did occasionally in the past, I have, and I did what I did because I was *lonely,* and that is what is really what you get from your avowed users of pornography, you get a class of people suffer from aggravated loneliness, and who are bent not on sexual conquest, or on the abasement of women (or whomever it is they desire), though that abasement may be an effect of the loneliness of pornography; what you get with porn are a lot of people who somehow can't break through in an intimate way with other human beings, and who are therefore constitutionally apart, and who, in the process of loneliness, make use of this rather joyless preserve of online porn, and who thereby make themselves *more* lonely, and more cut off from the bodies here in the world.

Maybe this activity, this pornographic consumption, involves some separation of self (body) from identity in the first place, so that the inevitable decoupling of self from credit card and identity is part and parcel of the process of unselfing, deselfing, that takes place as a result. It's a symbolic continuation of something that the user has elected to begin *himself.* This is not really my story, the syllogistic narrative I'm sketching out, but I can feel echoes of my story in this story, and when I'm wandering around these days, on my rounds, I can feel the shame of being stripped from my information, like I've been caught cheating, and I can also feel the liberation. It's not such a bad thing, really, and in this afterlife you use time in a different way, this afterlife in which you are not shackled to this Internet business, when you think of the Internet as something to be avoided. So this is like being dead. I feel dead in a way. And being dead is not so horrible. There's a condition that Freud described—can't remember the name of it right now—in which a patient is convinced that she is already dead, and no amount of evidence will convince her otherwise.

Identity theft has that aspect to it. I am dead, I am in exile, and yet it's just a bunch of numbers, a bunch of digits, a bunch of corporations arguing over whether I am able to spend this much money now, or this much money minus the five thousand that some Nigerian took out of my checking account in order to open a E-trade account. I am dead. And in my afterlife I am not so much looking, dear friends whose names I don't know yet, for suggestions about the legal procedure relevant to my identity theft, nor am I looking for ways to get back at the perps. Nope, what I am looking for here is the human moment.

Best wishes to you,

"*Rick Moody*"

Dear you,

I'm sorry. I must start out by recounting a dream. I agree with all the writers who say you should never write dreams, and all the friends who groan, inwardly or aloud, when you start telling them. In fact, it's one of the only rules of friendship or writing I believe in. And yet. Here we are:

In my dream, I am (or was—this is about a week ago now) a slim black woman in a tailored suit with an above-the-knee skirt, retro-chic. My hair is straightened and curled into a Jackie-O silhouette. I am, in other words, Michelle Obama's stunt double.

I have brought President Obama back to my place for a night of escape; he has driven so fast to get here that he has lost his security detail. They call him, as I stand awkwardly waiting in my bare-walled, furnished apartment. I have the vague feeling I'm on special assignment in DC: while I'm his junior, and nominally a stranger to him, we have some sense of rapport. Sometimes, in the dream, I _am_ him, feeling his frustration, his desire and failure to be present. His guards berate him for his selfishness, for jeopardizing not only his own safety but the nation's, in his pursuit of pleasure. It's not just pleasure he's after, though, it's escape:

②

he's sick of always being in the public eye. His nice is a night of anonymity. He argues with them, but then — there's a jump in time, and I don't know whether we have had sex during it, but if we did, I'm already past the glow — we're driving back, even faster than we drove out, lethal speed, while I pump my pumps into the passenger footwell and grip the dash.

I had just finished reading Monica Ali's Untold story, a novel imagining an afterlife for Princess Di: what if she only staged her death, and then rebuilt her face and her life? What would she be like, as a regular person in some small American town, no obligations, no paparazzi? I had also been reading a long article in The New Yorker about how Obama, for all his pre-election promises of breaking down partisan barriers, has proven to be, for one reason or another, the most polarizing president ever, about how the presidential office has changed him. Great article. So lucid that it made me forget, from time to time, how depressing it was.

I hadn't had an erotic dream about Obama since he took office. Do you remember that? Four years ago, we were all having them, as though he was climbing into our bedrooms at night, through windows left unbolted in

(3)

tremulous hope. And now, after four years of nitty-gritty, he's back, but it's like being married for a husband. It's different. I'm not even sure mine was an erotic dream. Though the car chase was exciting, I suppose.

The other day, I was sitting at my desk, but turned away from it. I am revising a novel, and it was stressing me, and I couldn't face my desk if I wasn't able to write. But I was thinking about the novel, though what exactly I was thinking I no longer recall, when my eye was caught by something on the floor under a side table: an eraser? Something cube-like on the floor. What? I was about to get up and investigate when suddenly the lens of my perception shifted and I saw it was a rectangular sticky-note (a Post-It), standing on its edge, like this:

It was, for all practical purposes, two-dimensional. My mind had supplied four additional sides, and volume. I'm very alert to possible distractions when I'm supposed to be writing. And yet it could have been, as with so many things, a channeling of suggestions.

yet another item from my recent reading: ④
Lawrence Weschler's new book of essays, Uncanny Valley
It includes one piece I couldn't smush a mention
of into my Rumpus review of the book, a piece on
the artists Trevor and Ryan Oakes, identical twins
who are single-handedly revolutionizing the
representation of perspective (except that they
work together, so double-handedly, I guess).
Among the Oakes twins' innovations is the use of
curved drawing surfaces to more accurately mimic
human perception.

I'm on my way to Chicago in a few weeks
and perhaps have been thinking of Trevor Oakes
drawing that cityscape using his method, and
particularly of Weschler watching him reproduce
Anish Kapoor's enormous, reflective Cloud Gate
sculpture, "... the Michigan Avenue skyline,
smeared in a vast, swooping reflection atop the
Bean's convex pate... beginning to show up in his
own concave rendering."

Thinking about perception changes the way we
perceive, even in small ways. I just wasn't
expecting the change right then. But perhaps that's
always the way.

I wasn't able to see the sticky-note as
anything but a piece of garbage once I realized
what it was. And we can never again see Obama
the way we did when we were infatuated. You
look at someone for that long, he starts to seem human

But then, you never know when the lens (5) might shift again.

Before I sign off, you need to know that I planned to send glitter or candy in this missive, but was refused by my intermediaries. Even back when all we had were letters, they were always better with enclosures. The point was to see how much you could stuff in an envelope without paying to send it as a package. But no. If Willie Wonka had lived, he would have invented scratch-and-sniff emoticons by now. That's why we still have a post office. Next time, I'll mail this myself.

Until then —

Padma

If you want to write back

Padma Viswanathan
213 N. Summit Ave.
Fayetteville, AR 72701
USA

Claire Bidwell Smith
2328 20ᵗʰ Street
Santa Monica, California 90405

Dear You,

Today I went for a long walk on a road that rims around the outskirts of the Palisades in Santa Monica. I was having a shit morning and for most of the beginning of the walk I thought I might cry. There's not much sense in going into the details of what was ailing me – it mostly had to do with simple writer's woes and wondering if I can sustain the not-knowingness of life. I know you understand.

Anyway, by the time I reached that part in the road that curves so magnificently around the Palisades, I was feeling better or clearer or something, and I stopped to watch a hummingbird perched on one of those weird California plants that droops down like a prehistoric phallus. This hummingbird was just sitting there, at the topmost point of the plant, with a view that would make even the wealthiest humble just a bit, and I suddenly decided that I'm being a coward.

See, the hummingbird made me think of my dad, who I've been thinking about a lot lately anyway. He always liked hummingbirds and kept a feeder outside of his condo in his later years. I'm not really one of those people who believes in signs from dead people, but if I were, then hummingbirds would definitely be a signal that my father was near. But all this hummingbird really did for me was somehow make me realize that I need more determination.

Sometimes I think that my generation is too good at self-reflection, and that we're just too neurotic. I'm not saying we're the first generation to be these things; I'm just saying that we do them well. This leads me back to my dad. He was from an entirely different generation. He was born in 1920 and grew up in a small town in Michigan. He was a teenager during the depression and I know for certain that he didn't have time to sit around pondering the existential angles of his accomplishments. How could he when he was spending his mornings delivering milk and his afternoons defeathering dead chickens, all to help with the family bills?

On the other hand, I spent my teenage years skipping Mr. Johnson's geometry class and smoking cigarettes on the backfield. I had *too* much time to think about my life. Then, back then, I never could have imagined that I would one day envy my elderly father and the world he hailed from. It never once occurred to me that my two biggest pursuits in life (writing and making out with boys) weren't very weighty.

My father and I both went to college. He went to Michigan State and began studying to be an engineer. I went to New York, to the New School, to pursue my dreams of becoming a writer. But whereas I lived in the East Village, did my homework in coffee shops and bartended at night, my father cut short his classes and double dates with best friend Bernie, to enlist in WWII the day Pearl Harbor was attacked. In these parallel stories, that were never actually parallel, I continue bartending and going to school and living with my alcoholic boyfriend while my father begins to train as a fighter pilot. Can you imagine that? He was twenty years old and he'd never even ridden in a plane, let alone imagined flying one, yet here he was training on some of the most sophisticated airplanes around.

Over the next four years in our adolescent timelines I graduate from college, work at a couple of magazines, move to Los Angeles, break up with the boyfriend and struggle to understand the purpose of my life. My father flies a couple dozen missions over Europe, drops bombs on strategic locales, crashes his airplane and eventually winds up in a POW camp in Germany. Oh and did I mention that he also gets married and has his first three kids somewhere in there too?

That's why standing there this morning, on the lip of the continent, staring at that hummingbird and thinking about my father, I felt like a coward. Like I just don't know how to just grit my teeth and commit to a thing. Like I don't know the first thing about how to be simply grateful that I'm alive. Maybe that's what's missing in our generation. Maybe we just feel too safe, too secure. We have too much stuff and no threat of any of it disappearing anytime soon.

When my father came home from the war he was a different person than when he left. He knew something about life, something big. He finished college and moved his little family to Pasadena. Years and years later when I was in college myself in New York I would fly out here to California often to visit him. My dad was in his early eighties by then and tethered to an oxygen tank. There wasn't much he was up for doing in those last years, so we went for a lot of drives.

Sometimes we'd snake around the San Bernadino Mountains, my father lazily spinning the wheel with one hand while he gesticulated with the other. Other times we'd drive out to Pasadena and cruise up and down the wide, tree-lined streets until we found the little Spanish-style number that he lived in with his first family all those years ago, after WWII. My dad would steer the car to the curb and gaze out across to the house, past all those years of history and living now shimmering between it and him and me.

"Well, kiddo," he'd say. "Life is a wondrous thing."

And me in all my New York-affected youth would smile at him and nod, not really having a clue what he meant.

I'm still not sure that I understand what he meant, not that I don't sometimes think life is wondrous – I do, I do – but more that I don't know that I'll ever really grasp what it must have felt like to be him, sitting in a grey-toned Acura with his impossibly young daughter, looking at a house he lived in whole lifetimes ago. What it must have felt like to see the whole long spread of his life in that way.

All I know is that something about this morning and the hummingbird and the ocean in the distance and me with all my empty worries standing there, made me think that even if bravery was a forced experience for my father, maybe it can be a learned one for me.

Yours,

Claire

p.s. Here's a photo of me and my dad when I was 24. We were trying to make mean faces.

Best American Palindrome

BARRY DUNCAN

FROM *The Believer*

The Believer is a general-interest magazine of the arts. In September of 2011, Barry Duncan, a former bookstore employee from Massachusetts, published a short story of 407 words that can be read backward and forward with the same result. The palindrome's full title is "The Greenward Palindrome: In which a conversation with two U.S. senators about climate change evolves quite naturally into a celebration of the Cambridge eco-boutique Greenward—its mission, its owners, its staff, its inventory, its patrons, its spirit—on the occasion of its third anniversary."

The Greenward Palindrome

Won't I note Ben? Oh, still a cold, raw NE. Ergo: two nos. Day as dismal, climate big. Get Sen. (R-OK), sir. One disputes data in "war"? Damn, I do. Oh, retro? Paper a sham, lacks a bite. Mine position won. Kyoto? Negate; J.I.'d abet. Saw one rot. (Sneer.) Gas to low temp. Oh, sad loser, eh? Sit. Ah. We sue re: caps, ocean?

Wows, is up: Mural a gem. It still, a ballet, how one in every 3 is awed. Art on!

At 1764 M. A., as I view Otsu, mill at some mags, I gab gab on. Sin. A catnip, a Reknitz on a pup. (Is it paw art?) Sleets? A Totes. "I was, I tote."

No. No, see? Seeps. We fed ample. He's so PC in a Gro diaper.

(A IPO to CEO? Greed, sir! A fast ego's evil. Slam in a tub! How?)

One do Rei me. Togs. All is soft, safe, no? Rattle. Moth. Asleep.

Store: no BPA. Can I spot SIGG? (Is not a bottle *beer*, then a refill?!) Listen, a LP tray. (A LP is naive.) Was gift—rats!—late, Mom? Gab. Keel. So ten, if smart, lug a bare hot pans: To-Go's tiffins (ha! sets!). A Taza tastes . . . ah! Sniff it. So, got snap? To HER, a bag (ul-tra-Ms.-fine-to-sleek bag). Mo' metal? Start. Figs? Awe. Via N.? Si. Play. Art.

Planet's ill. Life ran, eh? Tree. (Belt to baton, SIGG is tops in a cap.) Bone rots, peels. Ah, to melt tar, one fast fossil. (L.A.'s got 'em.) I erode now. Oh, but animals live, so get Safari's deer.

Go, ecotopia!

Repaid organic posse? Help! Made few. Speesees on one tot is a wise tot. A steel straw apt: I sip up an oz., tinker, a pint, a can. I, snob? AG bag is game. Most. All. I must owe, I. Visa. Am 46.71. Ta! No? Trade.

Was I 3 yr. even (i.e., now)? Oh, tell. A ball? It's time. Gala! Rumpus!

I, S.W., own a eco space. Reuse what is here sold. A shop. Me. Two lots. A green store. No, waste bad. I? Jet age no toy. Know. No, it is open. I met, I bask. Calm. Ah, S.A., rep a Porter 'hood in MA. Drawn? I? A tad. Set. Upside: no risk, or nest egg. I bet a mil clams, I'd say. Ad.

So now to Greenward: Local. Lit. Shone. Bet on it now.

* * *

ACRONYMS, REFERENCES, AND ABBREVIATIONS IN
THE GREENWARD PALINDROME

Ben • Ben Nelson, Democratic senator from Nebraska
NE • Nebraska
Sen. (R-OK), J.I. • James Inhofe, Republican senator from Oklahoma
Kyoto • the Kyoto Protocol, an international agreement to reduce greenhouse-gas emissions

Mural a gem • Greenward's brilliant and iconic in-store mural, created by artist Craig Bostick
1764 M. A. • 1764 Massachusetts Avenue, Greenward's address
PC • politically correct
IPO • Initial Public Offering
CEO • Chief Executive Officer
BPA • Bisphenol A, a potentially harmful chemical used in the making of plastic
LP • long-playing vinyl record album
L.A. • Los Angeles
oz. • ounce
S.W. • Scott Walker, owner of Greenward
S.A. • Simone Alpen, owner of Greenward
MA • Massachusetts

COMPANIES AND PRODUCTS MENTIONED
IN THE GREENWARD PALINDROME

Otsu • Little Otsu Publishing, stationery and greeting cards
A catnip, a Reknitz on a pup • catnip toys and Reknitz reclaimed-cotton dog sweater, both from West Paw Design
A Totes • Totes Umbrellas
in a Gro diaper • Gro Baby cloth diapers
One do Rei me • Toby + Rei, eco-friendly baby clothes and accessories
SIGG • SIGG of Switzerland water bottles
LP tray • LP snack tray by Vinylux
To-Go's tiffins • tiffin set by To-Go Ware
A Taza • Taza Chocolate, makers of organic, stone-ground chocolate
HER, a bag • HER Design, eco-friendly bags by Helen E. Riegle
Figs • jewelry by Figs & Ginger
Via N. • jewelry by Via Nativa
Safari's deer • Bucky Cardboard Deer Trophy by Cardboard Safari
Speesees on one tot • Speesees, organic gear for babies and tots
A steel straw • stainless steel straws from R.S.V.P. International
AG bag • bag made from upcycled materials by Alchemy Goods

Best American Tweets Responding to the Death of Osama bin Laden

FROM WWW.TWITTER.COM

Osama bin Laden was the leader of Al-Qaeda and mastermind of the 9/11 attacks. Nearly ten years after bin Laden had seared himself into American public consciousness, the nation responded to his death with reflection, euphoria, ignorance, comedy, and relief. These are some of the best tweets from the evening of May 1st, 2011, when Navy SEALS and CIA operatives invaded his compound in Abbottabad, Pakistan, and executed him.

@cibercrimen: "Osama bin Laden just ousted Hitler as the Mayor of Hell on @foursquare"

@whitegrlproblem: "Osama's been dead to me for a long time. #whitegirlproblems."

@gavin_mcinnes: "All it took was 40k dead and half a trillion $. In your FACE Osama!"

@citizenfox: "Obama is SO getting laid tonight."

@bretthickey: "2011: US allows gays into the army. Later in 2011: US army kills bin laden. WAY TO GO GAYS."

@shaycarl: "I bet Osama Bin Laden is pissed he came out of hiding to watch the royal wedding #ThanksEngland"

@Booth86: "Osama Bin Laden was responsible for 9/11, Tiger Wood's divorce, also me being grounded that whole weekend."

@miss_mykila: "I'm confused! Wat did Osama have to do with 9/11? Did he order those ppl to crash the plane?"

@PopeMaledictus: "The secret weapon Obama used to take on Osama? Anderson Cooper's biceps. #winning"

@onewhoharms: "A black ops mission to kill a terrorist in a Pakistani mansion? I'm pretty sure I played this level in Call of Duty . . ."

@marcinmrowca: "I bet Osama Bin Laden accidentally hit the 'Add your location' button during his last tweet."

Best American Lonely Guy

DAVID SHIELDS, JEFF RAGSDALE, MICHAEL LOGAN

FROM JEFF, THE LONELY GUY

In 2011, Jeff Ragsdale, an aspiring actor and comedian, was feeling adrift. He had recently gone through a painful breakup and he was living in a tiny room in a boarding house in Harlem. One day, he posted a flyer on a lamppost in New York City, telling passersby that he was lonely and encouraging them to call him. He listed his actual phone number, and expected a handful of phone calls. He received approximately a hundred calls and texts the first day. Soon thereafter, pictures of the flyer were posted on the Internet and Ragsdale turned into a sensation, receiving seven hundred calls and a thousand texts a day. He's spoken with people from all over and as far away as Spain, Switzerland, Saudi Arabia, Iraq, Taiwan, Australia.

In 2011, David Shields and Michael Logan edited a collection of the texts and the transcripts of phone calls Ragsdale received. Below is a sampling from the book titled Jeff, One Lonely Guy. *The italic text is Ragsdale's interstitial commentary.*

908-420-XXXX
I saw your ad and I just wanted to talk for a while.

219-688-XXXX
Hey is this Jeff? I just called you to see if it was for real, but I chickened out and couldn't talk.

949-572-XXXX
My son introduced me to Imgur.com. It's great to see your flyer. Jeff,

what you did took courage. I like it. It showed trust of humanity. You not lonely anymore?

912-656-XXXX
Hey. I'm in Georgia. Hey, do you know my sister, Barbara, by chance? . . . I guess it is a big city.

Sanitation Worker (917-359-XXXX)
Jeff, is it you who's been posting those flyers? We can fine you.

347-364-XXXX
Wass wrong with you? Y u got problems?

Betsy
I love this flyer. Is it weird that I love this? . . . It's also true I once went on a Craigslist date with a total stranger because it was his birthday and he had no one to celebrate with . . . So maybe it's not weird that I love this.

818-281-XXXX
Wait—who is this? . . . This doesn't sound like you . . . What flyer? . . . How old are you?

636-544-XXXX
You're semi-famous.

Kelly, 28, bartender, NYC
Loved the flyer. You never know who's calling ya. It's like a surreal movie.

Jason
U stole the show on imgur—200K hits in ten minutes.

Matt, Columbus (618-843-XXXX)
This's killer. You must get tons of ladies. Shout out for the ladies.

Flyer originally posted on a lamppost in New York City

Kathleen
Hi, is this Jeff, and was your sign posted in Union Square true? How are you doing now? I was really touched by your flyer. I understand all about tough breakups. I just wanted to tell you that you are deeply loved. If you still need to talk, I'd love to encourage you. Otherwise, have a very blessed day!

Erica, 26 (917-691-XXXX)
Did you ever wish on eyelashes?

847-770-XXXX
Oh, I expected this number to be fake.

Marsha (914-536-XXXX)
Question: is it smart to go for a degree, then pursue a career in acting? Or should I just go for it?

Ray
You are famous. I'm nobody. Who are you? Are you nobody, too? No, you're famous, asshole. I live in a box. Buy me a car.

Woman with thick, old-money British accent
Jeffrey, darling. It's Emma. We met the other evening. *(Have never met her.)* I saw your flyer. I'm perturbed that you're still advertising yourself this way. I don't think you quite need it. We hit it off rather smashingly. I'll ring you back, dear.

Melissa, geology major in Colorado, from Texas (281-620-XXXX)
Pow. Right in the head. Aunt Stacey's in prison for murder. She killed her ex with a gun. My grandmother beat my mother as soon as she started dating. Grandma was jealous, wanted her all to herself.

Tony
You look a little like Keanu Reeves ... Maybe you are Keanu Reeves — doing research for a film about a lonely guy who puts his number on the internet?

April (989-450-XXXX)
Hi Jeff—Brian Quinn sent me . . . I'm doing all right with the exception that I just broke a lamp . . . Are you going to be on Quinn's show?

Kori, Cincinnati
One lonely guy. One lonely country.

305-773-XXXX
It's like free therapy.

212-280-XXXX
I'm calling about the computer sale.

847-417-XXXX
I grew up in a bipolar family. I'm a forensic pysch student from Evanston. I work at a sex shop and a petting zoo. Such a pleasure to meet you!

306-280-XXXX
If you were a tree, what kind of tree would you be, Jeff?

Felicia, 15 (845-464-XXXX)
I wanted to tell you how happy I am after adopting a shelter cat last week. His name is Aleister, after Aleister Crowley.

Amy
I'm a case worker for CPS, taking care of children who have been abused. I go to their homes, or foster homes, and feed the kids and take them to school. It can be tough because the mothers often think I'm in the way, but I've been appointed by the state to make sure that the children get fed and get to school on time . . . I need to take some time off, though. I hate where my son and I live right now. I need to find a better place for both of us . . . There's a sex party happening on Saturday, if you're interested.

Anya, 13, North Carolina (252-955-XXXX)
I had counseling because my mom found out I was cutting myself. Please don't tell anyone ... Smiling makes you live longer ... I'm better than I was in the past so I'm really good ... In the beginning I got molested by my older stepbrother. I never told anybody for 4 to 5 years. He also rapidly hit my head against a wall and had 2 knives, 1 on me and 1 on my mom ... I will but he lives in New Hampshire so I don't think I'll ever see him again ... Will you be my friend? ... I am—it's just that I don't have a lot of friends. I'm not good at making friends or normal things that people do everyday ... Yeah without the bad you wouldn't appreciate the good ... Have you felt like no matter what you do it will never be right? ... Have you seen Paranormal Activity 1 & 2?

Theo (469-237-XXXX)
My parents argue about everything ... How do I ask people out? ... What if she says no? ... My mom just lost her job.

Nicole, college student, Oklahoma City
My godfather, who was very close to me, committed suicide last year. It came out of nowhere ... My mom works for Halliburton overseas. I see her once a year ... My dad's a dick. I don't talk to him ... My deity is the universe. If I died, I'd probably be content. On further introspection, I probably wouldn't ... He'd been fighting with his wife. She left with the kids for the weekend, came back, and he had shot himself in the bedroom.

Dana, 21, college student and babysitter
My mom died in Mexico during childbirth when I was eight. She tried to save money by going to a cheap doctor in Mexico City. The doctor didn't do a sonogram and took out the baby wrong. Mom lost too much blood and she and the baby died.

Caitlin
My sister has a degenerative brain disease. The doctors really don't know much about it or what to do.

Susie (469-335-XXXX)

I'm a security officer married to an abusive man. I've been very worried about my two-year-old because she started hitting her head on things and purposely running into walls. I googled it and found that when children can't verbalize things, they hit themselves. I'm very relieved.

In rages I can even understand WWII tyrants. It comes from a lack of love throughout my life, isolation, and pain. I can't believe how asinine people are when they ask, "How can someone like Hitler exist?" I can be riding the subway, wanting to blow up the entire world, then five minutes later I can look at a young child and start crying.

Kenny

Hi, Jeff. My boyfriend and I were sitting here looking through pictures online and we came across your number and I can't believe that this is for real. But if you're that lonely, here's two pix of good-hearted guys and a dog that would love to talk to you. I don't know why, but we would. Guess we're a little lonely, too. Call us. Bye.

321-402-XXXX

Did you ever try going out, Jeff? Clubs? Bars? The library? The park? The supermarket? Gas station? I'm out of places.

Vanessa, 22, Minnesota

My best friend was naked, hiding in the bathroom. He was still lying in bed when I walked in on them. I dated him for two years, thought I was going to marry him . . . I'm a psych major. I like rock climbing, snowmobiling, and skeet shooting . . . I didn't kill him because I was too devastated. A year later I met Jared. He's the love of my life.

Molly

I hate it when you say you'll try to see me :(

College girl, Silicon Valley

I went through a traumatic breakup. Now I want to work in finance.

707-843-XXXX
I go door to door talking about solar panels.

716-548-XXXX
I'm making gingerbread houses, so call back later.

Randi (616-821-XXXX)
Um lol hun I do so like talking to you but I recently lost my contacts and I'm not fully aware who I'm talking to.

Claire and Georgia
Why is it so hard to meet people in New York?

Erica
Look at the moon . . . I hope the universe is treating you well, Jeff.

224-622-XXXX
I wanna be your melody, going through your head when you think of me. I wanna be your favorite song, you can turn me up play me all night long. Lalalalalalalalala.

Musician (715-250-XXXX)
Jeff you are a badass.

Girl, college student, NYU
I ate one of those waffles you make in the griddle thingy. I like to eat the batter. But today it was a lil gritty and didn't have enough vanilla.

16-year-old high school boy
Illinois is boring. I'm moving to LA to be a movie star.

Man at General Atomics
We build the planes . . . If you're ever in California, Lonely Jeff, and want a plane ride, look us up.

Amy
Are you ready to go to a swingers' party?

217-954-XXXX
You're nerd famous, that's awesome.

617-921-XXXX
You should detox your soul.

Emily, 646-258-XXXX
Why text? Seems like the thing now, kind of stops real communication. I'd rather speak in person. Texting seems so artificial.

502-387-XXXX
Cool . . . This feels weird . . . I don't even know where to start.

Claude, 50, Brooklyn
Hey, Jeffrey. This situation actually presented itself to the writer Paul Auster, who was on a flight to Paris. He went to use the restroom. An exceptionally attractive French woman comes out of the restroom, smiling. Paul goes in and sees a humungous turd on the closed toilet lid. Would you get the airline stewardess and explain what happened, thinking there's a chance she might not believe you? The stewardess could think that you're a sicko and into toilet tricks. Or would you — I think the term today is "man up" — clean up this woman's mess?

352-406-XXXX
Aw cute! Water dogs are so fluffy! . . . What do I want out of life? Happiness. And to make others happy . . . Peace. The Beatles. Twizzlers . . . I'm having one of those nights where I'm feeling extremely sorry for myself . . . What do you want?

715-771-XXXX
What more can we do? . . . We can't just show up naked, can we? . . . There is little to be done beyond that.

910-336-XXXX
I just wanted to talk to somebody right now. Where'd you go?

* * *

Rob

This is Rob from Queens. I was the flamboyant dancer in snappy attire on *Jimmy Kimmel Live*. Shyness has degenerated my life. I can't communicate with people. I'm lonely because I'm in a shell. I'm not working now. I get money from New York state because I'm mentally different. I saw your flyer. I'll call you tomorrow, in the a.m., OK?

Three teens from Fresno

Jeff, we loved your poster, but you should've put a zombie on it, dude . . . We're watching a zombie video and hanging out.

Jason, Columbus (419-252-XXXX)

You had one of those rare moments of clarity that we get once or twice in our lives.

Maya

I tried to commit suicide, but my parents called in the middle of it. An ambulance and the cops came. I'd taken 100 pills. He wasn't even a boyfriend. My parents said I'd never have a man because I'm so ugly. I'm from the ugly tree. I love stray cats. I was abused as a child and now I've lost custody of my boy.

Anitchka, Russian, 24, college student (646-353-XXXX)

My father was murdered before I was born. I moved to the U.S. at age three, rebelled majorly as a teen. I had to go to a high school for addicts for a few years upstate . . . My mother's a hairdresser. My mom and her grandparents want to move back to Moscow because the American dream isn't what they thought it would be . . . I want to be a veterinarian.

Erica

Everyone just hurts me.

Brittany

My mother's second pregnancy ended at four months after she had a heart attack at age 21. The baby died inside her. After the baby died, Dad was angry all the time and he abused her. After she finally moved out, taking shelter with the father of a family friend, she received death threats from my dad. He was a military man and used to perfection.

Brittany

She went from being my mom to being my child. We were bowling at the alley on our military base. Mom took one step toward the foul line and cracked her femur all the way down the center like a giant, ugly fissure. Seven years and three failed surgeries later, she still can't walk. Sometimes I blame myself. Since her injury, my mother has had to be on many strong and varied medicines. I'm of the suspicion that they, along with the pain and the mental trauma of not being able to walk, are what changed her. It's like her past decided to catch up. Her dad used to beat her until she ran away from home. She went from loving me to depending on me. Simply put, my mom died, and in her place I was given the responsibility of taking care of a psychotic, hateful child.

Krystal

I have sex with men for cash. I'm a bad person . . . The others do it too . . . I will get in trouble if I call now. I can text . . . How am I not? I do horrible things . . . I got out . . . Mark said he had a lot to offer . . . If I can get out, would you take me? . . . After I graduate? . . . That's not until June. I don't want to do this for another year . . . I left my brother with the rents . . . He can't help me. Mark takes care of me now . . . He allows me to have a roof over my head and buys me clothes . . . If you can't because I'm 17, take me in then . . . I guess it would . . . I don't want to listen to men anymore but if I don't I get in trouble . . . I'd rather be living with you . . . I want to be normal . . . I don't want to be hurt . . . He takes advantage of me in front of others . . . I'm scared . . . I do feel horrible though . . . I feel gross and used. I feel like no man can ever love me . . . Mainly for what I have to do . . . One time I actually had an orgasm while making money. I felt so disgusting . . . I didn't do it to feel good. It just happened . . . I wasn't in control, the way he had me positioned and pinned . . . I don't know. There was something inside of me . . . I'm sorry . . . I don't want to get you into trouble . . . Still be friends? . . . I get a free breakfast and lunch at school so I do eat . . . We almost died, Jeff, but it was fun! . . . Black ice on highway, 2 wheel drive . . . We swerved into the other lane and drifted and did a Uturn. Other cars honked and had to slow . . . I do, but I wasn't driving. I don't have my license . . . I have no choice. I have to go to school . . . Hey talk to me . . . I'm bored . . . He's my boss . . . I am not a hooker . . . Okay I believe you . . . I know that's what it is, but I don't get to keep most of the $—it goes to Matt . . . What do you consider it? . . . I have to do it though . . . I don't have control of it. He pays for it . . . I want out. But I can't. I don't have anywhere else to go and I wouldn't be able to support myself . . . My stepmom won't deal with me . . . I want to be 18 so bad. What if I had a fake ID? Could I come live with you then? . . . I'll be in this situation for the rest of my life . . . Steal me . . . I want to leave . . . He could hurt me . . . Jeff? . . . Thank you . . . That's so cool! I would love to write. I have a book written but it's not published of course . . . I don't need help. Don't get me help . . . Just let it be . . . Forget it. Just be my friend. That's all I need . . . Just be my friend. That's it . . . . Please don't try to get anyone involved. I'm fine . . . Thanks. I will go away this weekend . . . It's so loud where you are . . . Where do you think I should go? . . . Hey talk to me.

Bethany, 24, White Plains, NY (845-282-XXXX)
I like a guy who is sweet but an asshole at the same time. He can't be overly sweet—that's just a pussy.

JD (914-215-XXXX)
Should I be aggressive or let her come to me?

Sorority sisters
Are you rich?

423-946-XXXX
Even fast food places aren't hiring.

407-535-XXXX
I'm the Minister of Depression.

Erica
My collar bones are really weird.

Brittany
Grr. My bra is being uncooperative.

Morgan (818-223-XXXX)
Thought of you in the shower.

Krystal
But I want to be with you. I would like you to become my best friend and then meet you and then date you and then be your girlfriend and then possibly marriage.

Serena
Ah, the simple joy of a menthol Camel.

Erica
I fell asleep on a lump of gigantic stuffed animals at Toys R Us.

REI
Jeff, hey, this is the REI team, and we just wanted to give you a call because we saw your flyer on a pole in front of our REI store on Lafayette Street. We just thought we'd invite you to come down here to REI and check out the store. It's for people who love the great outdoors, who are social, who love to talk, and apparently you love to talk and we don't want you to be lonely. "REI" stands for "recreational," "equipment," "incorporated."

973-283-XXXX
Thanks for telling me u think im intelligent. it's one of the most meaningful compliments you can give . . . ur helping a lot of ppl and probably earning urself lots and lots of good karma :)

Ashley
I love my old school Carl Sagan. Nothing better than a healthy dose of existential physics to make your mind spin before bed.

Goldman Sachs Trader (212-357-XXXX)
I'm not doing that well . . . I'm calling strangers who post flyers on
the internet from my trading desk . . . The economy's in a major
downturn and we have Occupy Wall Street keeping us prisoner. It's
combative. We're under siege down here.

718-910-XXXX
It's a big world out there though, Lonely Guy Jeff, and there are
friendships to be found on every street corner! . . . May I suggest a
book club? . . . Maybe take up an activity like bowling . . . What you
say?

Marcus, 58, Queens (917-215-XXXX)
I don't tend to know everything about the human condition, but you
are lonely, the flyer reads, is that correct? . . . Okay then. When it's
sunny, the farthest thing you can see is the sun. When it's dark, you
can see farther, much farther . . . Great works derive from genuine
despair . . . It allows one to see things inside other people and oneself clearer. I've helped a few people out in my life . . . I'm just lucky
I haven't been in a situation where I've had to kill people to survive.
Let's get together next week, I will pass on wisdom gained from others . . . Great ideas outlast us all.

Man, 65, Upper West Side
Write gratitude lists.

MK (646-755-XXXX)
You'll be ok . . . Bless you, Jeff . . . You've already accomplished great
things despite your losses and bumps in life . . . Turning in for 2nite.

Melinda, 54, therapist, breast cancer survivor, Corvallis, Oregon
You've hit on something in the collective. Reflection is the key to
learning. Anything is possible. My odds of survival were ice thin. I'm
alive, happy, and still learning.

616-957-XXXX
Actually it's more I'm motivated than super smart. I mean I failed

the last three years of school, then I came to this alternative school and now I'm getting all A's.

Paige (347-620-XXXX)
Who is this? . . . Omg I had you saved in my phone with my boy-friend's name!!!!!

Joaquin (305-799-XXXX)
I got a new shiatsu, Barney. We go to the dog park. When I tell Bar-ney that that woman's hot he really turns the charm on, wagging the tail. Barney's helping me meet beautiful women.

501-208-XXXX
Dude, I would totally be your wingman if I was there with you.

Taylor
I'm riding horses this weekend. I really miss the barn. I'm looking forward to volunteer work at the barn, even mucking stalls. It relaxes and frees me. Yoga with an odor.

Garrett
Everyone loves you. I looked you up on Google. You're a phenomenon!

Alison (646-258-XXX)
I once knew a photographer, Bruno Zehdnerha, who travelled to the Antarctic and photographed penguins. He created a penguin calen-dar. A blizzard took his life.

Sandi (630-209-XXXX)
I'd like to think you are the nice guy as advertised and not a serial killer.

715-410-XXXX
You seem intelligent. Mind if I ask what you do for a living?

832-622-9095
Hey Jeff. This is God.

Cassandra (501-736-XXXX)
Tomorrow's Tabby's birthday and I'm trying to finish her cake. She wanted a Scooby Doo themed cake. It kind of turned out like Chewbacca. I am not a lady of culinary talents. It's delicious, albeit not appetizing.

Jenna
My last name is Deadman.

646-460-XXXX
Do you even know my name?

Don, 39, Queens
You are a noble man, Lonely Jeff. Much stronger than I am. Which nearly begs the question why are you lonely? You deserve an award, Bold Boy.

NYC man, studying to be doctor (646-610-XXXX)
You got me thinking about my own issues.

Ella, 16 (636-544-XXXX)
Hi Jeff. Your flyer means more to me than just some guy that wants someone to talk to. To me it means that someone cares. Someone wants to know. I just wanted to let you know that your interest in my story and my poetry means so much to me. I've gone through a lot and when someone takes time to say they're interested, it means a lot. Thank you.

KEVIN BROCKMEIER

■

A Fable for the Living

FROM *Electric Literature*

ONCE THERE WAS A COUNTRY where no one addressed the dead except in writing. Whenever people felt the urge to speak to someone they had outlived, they would take a pen and set their thoughts down on paper: *You should have seen the sun coloring the puddles this morning,* or *Things were so much easier when you were alive, so much happier,* or *I wanted to tell you I got all A's on my report card, plus a C in algebra.* Then they would place the message atop the others they had written, in a basket or a folder, until the summer arrived and they could be delivered.

In this country it rained for most of the year. The landscape was lush with the kinds of trees and ivies that flourish in wet weather, their leaves the closest green to black. The creeks and pools swam with armies of tiny brown frogs. Usually, though, in the first or second week of June, the clouds would thin from the air little by little, in hundreds of parallel threads, as if someone were sweeping the sky clean with a broom, and the drought would set in. This did not happen every summer, but most. Between the glassy river to the west of the country and the fold of hills to the east, the grass withered and vanished, the puddles dried up, and the earth separated into countless oddly shaped plates. Deep rifts formed in the dirt. It was through these rifts that people slipped the letters they had written. The dead were buried underground, and tradition held that they were waiting there to collect each sheet of paper, from the most heartfelt expression of grief to the most trivial piece of gossip:

You won't believe it, but Ellie is finally leaving that boyfriend of hers.

What I want to know is whether you think I should take the teaching job.

The crazy thing is, when the phone rang last night, I was absolutely sure it was you.

Do you remember that time you dropped your earring in the pond and it surprised that fish?

I just don't know what I'm doing these days.

So it was that people surrendered the notes they had saved with a feeling of relief and accomplishment, letting them fall through the cracks one by one, then returned home, satisfied that they had been received.

This was the way it had always been, for who knows how long, with the dead turning their hands to the surface of the earth, and no orphans praying out loud to their parents, and no widows chitchatting with the ghosts of their husbands, and all the wish-it-weres and might-have-beens of the living oriented around a simple stack of paper and a cupful of pens. Then something very strange happened.

There was a woman, not quite old but not quite young, whose fiancé had died unexpectedly. It was barely a month into their engagement and the two of them were attending a chamber music concert when he began coughing into his sleeve and excused himself from his seat. Because they had quarreled earlier over the cost of the wedding, she did not worry about him when he failed to return. Instead, with exasperation, she thought, *What could possibly be keeping him?*—little realizing that what was keeping him was death.

When she went to the foyer to look for him, she found a ring of ushers clustered around his body as if he were a spill for which no one wanted to accept responsibility. She would never forget the sight of his tongue pressed to his teeth, struggling to form some word he had just missed his chance of saying.

More than a year had gone by since then, a terrible year of ill health, sleeplessness, and rainy days that layered themselves over her like blankets. Who was she? Who had she become? Her skin was paler than it used to be, her hair grayer. Recently she had noticed creases lingering around her eyes in the morning, and also across her forehead, as if she had spent the night squinting into a harsh light. These lines did not go away when she rubbed them, vanishing only gradually as the hours wore on. She could foresee a time when the mask of age that grief had placed over her face would simply be her face.

She missed her fiancé terribly. Sometimes it seemed to her that he was only a beautiful story she had told herself, so quickly had she fallen in love with him and so quickly had he left her. It was hard to believe that the man who refused to button his collar, whose kisses began so shyly and ended so fervidly, who never once looked at her as if she were foolish or tiresome or even ordinary, was the same man she had found splayed across the theater's staircase like an animal pinned to a board.

Frequently she had the feeling that he was standing just behind her, his breath tickling her ear like it used to when he came prowling over to seize her waist while she was cooking. All the same, she did not speak to him.

Instead, like everyone, she accumulated letters that would never be answered. *I don't understand how this can be my life,* she wrote, and *What am I going to do?* And occasionally, late at night, when she could not sleep, something longer such as *Do you know what it feels like? Shall I describe it for you? It feels like the two of us got on a boat together, and the deck tossed me into the water, and you went sailing away without me. Thrown overboard—that's how it feels. So I want you to tell me, because I really need to know, why did I spend my whole life waiting to fall in love with just the right person if you were just going to leave and it would all be for nothing?*

That first summer, immediately after he died, she had barely been able to pick up a pen, but by the time the earth split open a year later, she had amassed three heavy baskets of letters. One afternoon, she went to the parched field where the fair sat in the autumn and the soccer team practiced in the spring and dropped them into the deepest opening she could find. The ground swallowed them as neatly as a pay phone accepting coins, except for the last page, which continued to show through the dirt until gravity gave it a tug and it slipped out of sight. That was where her heart was, she thought, cradled underground with the roots and the bones. As she stood in the dust listening to the insects buzz, she dashed off one last note and let it go: *Are you even out there?*

The next morning, she received her answer.

Her house was built like all the others, with its roof projecting over the front door to keep it from opening directly into the rain, and it was her pleasure upon waking in the morning to step out onto the porch and take stock of the day. This particular morning arrived hot and bright, with the sky that oddly whitened blue it became when there was no moisture in the air. She was surprised to find a fissure interrupting her lawn. She kept the grass carefully trimmed and watered, and she was sure she would have seen the rift if it had been there the day before. The crack ran as straight as a line on a map. She traced it with her eyes, following it across her neighbor's yard and a few others before it vanished into the woods at the end of the block, and then back again until it dead-ended at her front steps.

But that was not the strange part. No, the strange part was the sheet of paper that was protruding from it. She picked it up and unfolded it.

Of course I am, it read.

The handwriting was familiar to her, with its walking-stick *r* and its *o*'s that didn't quite close at the top. But it took her a moment to figure out where she recognized it from.

She spent the next few hours twisting her engagement ring around and around her knuckle. A potato chip bag was dipping and spinning in the middle of the road, and she watched it ride the breeze until a boy rode by and flattened it beneath his bicycle. Finally, on a blank sheet of paper, she wrote, *If you are who I believe you are, tell me something only you would know about me.*

She was unaccountably nervous. She knelt on the porch, closing her eyes as she slipped the note into the fissure. Something deep within the ground seemed to wrest it from her fingers, like a fish plucking a cricket from a hook.

For the rest of the day, every time she went outside, she expected to see a flash of white paper waiting for her in the grass. But it was not until the next morning that she found one: *I love your gray coat with the circles like cloud-covered suns.*

She stared closely at the breach in her lawn. If she followed it on foot, she calculated, she would eventually reach the scorched field where she had gone to deposit her letters.

On a fresh sheet of paper, she replied, *Everyone we know has seen me in that coat. It doesn't prove a thing.*

Early that afternoon, an answer arrived: *I love how you laugh with your mouth wide open, and how you snort sometimes, and how embarrassed it makes you when you do.*

She wrote, *Well, yes, that's definitely me.*

I love the joke you told at Zach and Christina's wedding reception.

She wrote, *If this is a trick . . . this had better not be a trick. Is it?*

I love how easily you cry when you're happy.

So the correspondence went on, hour after hour and day after day, pushing across the distance of the soil. All his letters were love letters, delivered while she was sleeping or mopping the kitchen, weeding the garden or out buying milk. When she held them up to the sunlight, the faded marks of earlier messages emerged through the stationery: *Bailey had two kittens last week, and I named the first one Bowtie, and the second one Mike! I hope you're better now, I truly do, because I am, I tell you, I am. I think there's something terribly wrong with me.*

They came in a variety of hands and were often hard to decipher. She presumed he had salvaged the pages from under the ground, a few dozen among the many hundreds of thousands that had rained down over the generations of the dead.

I love the way you stand at the mirror in the morning picking the lip balm from your lips.

I love the inexplicable accent, from nowhere anyone has ever visited, you use when you're trying to sound French.

I love that first moment, at night, when you trace the curve of my ear with your fingernail.

Soon the situation no longer seemed strange to her. It was as if the two of them were kneeling on opposite sides of the bedroom door, sliding notes to each other along the floor. Then it was as if the door had vanished, vanished entirely, and they were simply sitting in the bedroom together. When she had crossed the threshold she could not say, only that she had. He was her fiancé—she did not doubt it—but what had brought him back to her?

The next day, a message came while she was sitting on her front steps. She glanced away for a moment, and there it was, nestled in the thick fringe of grass around the fissure, like a mushroom springing up after a thunderstorm. *I love you*, it read, and *I want you to join me. I want us to be together again, my jewel, my apple. Whatever the cost, I want it, I want it. And I don't want to wait until you die, because God knows how long that will be.*

It was his longest letter yet. She sensed that every word had demanded some mysterious payment from him, a fee that could only be understood by those who had already been laid to rest. What was he asking? That she end her life? That she suspend it? Or something else altogether, something she could hardly imagine?

For the next few days, he left no love notes in her yard, no entreaties, only a single question that appeared late one night on the back of a chewing gum wrapper: *Hello?*

He was giving her time to think. He was waiting for her below ground—she knew it, she knew it. Every day, the crack by her porch grew a little larger. At first, it was only a chink in the dirt, no wider than the slot where she dropped her mail at the post office, but gradually it stretched open until it was as big as an ice chest, and then a steamer trunk, and then a gulf into which she could easily have fit her entire body. She wondered what it would be like if she accepted his invitation. She began to dream that she was living beneath the field on the far side of the woods, moving through a long procession of rooms and hallways where the dead milled around like guests at a trade convention.

Throughout the day, at various angles, the sun pierced the hills and the pastures, sending bright silver needles through the ceiling of the earth, so that it was never completely dark, and at night, when the land was soaked in shadows, the people around her glowed with a strange heat. She watched them flare and shimmer through their skin, their bones going off like bombs, every limb a magnificent firework of carbon, phosphorus, and calcium. It seemed that the surface of the world had two sides: on one were the bereaved spouses, the outcast teenagers, the old men and women who had no one left to reminisce with, and on the other were the lovers and friends and parents they had outlived—all of them, whether above or below, aching for those who were gone; all of them, whether above or below, pressing their fingers to the soil. Her eyes flickered in her face and her teeth shone in her mouth, and when she woke, before the dream had lost its color, she felt that she was recalling some earlier existence, like a house she had lived in as a child, familiar down to its last curved faucet and last chipped floorboard.

The truth was that the thread connecting her to the world was as thin as could be. A sunrise here or there, the feel of suede against her skin, the aroma of strong coffee in the morning, and a few moments of forgetful well-being—that was it, that was all she had, and she knew that it could snap at any moment. She had always believed that one day someone would come along and love her and she would understand how to live. Maybe the idea was juvenile, but she had carried it with her all her life, like an ember smoldering in a pouch of green leaves. It was only the past awful year that had forced her to give it up. And now, here it was again, the hope that she had finally found him, the man who would wrench her into the world, the good and beautiful world, where people got married and had children and slowly grew old together.

One afternoon, as she was standing at the kitchen counter eating a turkey and diced olive sandwich, she realized that she had made up her mind. She swept the bread crumbs into her palm and brushed them gently, caressingly, into the sink, as if she were stroking a cat. Then she went outside and knelt at the edge of the crevice. Her neighbor was grilling a steak in his backyard. A forsythia bush rustled in the wind.

There she was, and then there she wasn't, and two large, pale ants were exploring the impression her knees had left in the grass.

It was the last the world would see of her, or at least the last the sun would, the last the sky. I am here to tell you what happened next.

Soon after the woman went to join her fiancé, as the final sweltering days of summer came to a close, an unusual event took place. Late one night, while everyone was sleeping, something shifted beneath the brown pastures and the dry creek beds, and a hundred thousand fissures spread across the landscape, leading to a hundred thousand front doors. Shortly after the sun rose, in one house after another, the lights went on, and people showered and got dressed, and then they stepped outside to go to work. Earlier that week, a mass of clouds had been seen at the horizon, which meant that it was almost time for the rains to begin again, but this particular day had dawned hard and clear. The heat rang out like a coin. The grass twitched and straightened in the morning air. And the lawns—they were split down the center, and from every rift projected a sheet of paper:

I love that perfect little cluster of freckles on your wrist.

I love the way your hair curls when you work up a sweat.

I love how good you were to me when I got sick.

I love watching you sit at your desk, the sun shining on you through the philodendron leaves.

I love your many doomed attempts to give up caffeine.

Once there was a country where it rained for most of the year, and everyone resided underground, and no one was quite sure who was dead and who was living.

But it did not matter, because they were happy. And they were ever. And they were after.

JUDY BUDNITZ

■

Tin Man

FROM *This American Life*

"WHAT KIND OF SON ARE YOU?" asks Aunt Fran.

Aunt Nina says, "Your own flesh and blood!"

"What your mother wouldn't do for you . . ." Aunt Fran goes on. "She'd do anything for you, anything in the world—"

"And now you won't give just a little back. For shame," says Aunt Nina. The heat is stifling, but she pulls her sweater closer.

We're sitting in the hospital waiting room, Aunt Fran and Aunt Nina and I. My mother suffered a heart attack this morning. We're waiting to see her.

The doctors told us her heart won't last much longer. Her old ticker is ticking its last. "We can't fix it," the doctors said. "She needs a new one, a transplant."

"Then give her one!" the aunts cried.

"It's not that easy," said the doctors. "We need a donor."

The doctors went away. The aunts looked at me.

"Arnie," Nina said, "what about your heart?"

"My heart?!" I shouted. "Are you crazy?"

That started them both off on what a bad son I was. It's impossible to argue with Nina, especially with Fran to back her up. They wept, at first, but now they sit grimly. A Styrofoam cup of coffee steams next to my foot but I can't reach for it. The aunts don't care, they are amazed that I bought it, amazed that I can even think of coffee at a time like this.

Aunt Fran wears a bally sweater and sensible shoes. Her lips are pressed tight. She taps her feet nervously. On my other side Nina licks her lips again and again.

"I saw it on *60 Minutes*," Aunt Fran announces. "They put the heart in a cooler, a regular Igloo cooler like we have at home, and they rush it in a helicopter to the hospital, and they put it in, connect up the pipes. It's just like plumbing."

"You must be your mother's tissue type, too. I'm sure you are," Aunt Nina puts in. "You're young, you're strong—you have a college education! Your heart is exactly what she needs."

"It looked like a fist—a blue fist," Aunt Fran goes on. "It wasn't heart-shaped at all, I wonder why . . ."

"You shouldn't have started smoking, though," Aunt Nina says, "it's bad for the heart. You should have thought of that when you started."

"But what about me?" I blurt out finally.

"That's what we're talking about, we're talking about your heart," Nina says.

"But what happens to me?" I say again.

"I can't believe he's thinking of himself at a time like this." Aunt Fran sniffs.

"*I* need my heart! You want me to die so my mother can live?"

"Of course we don't want that," says Aunt Fran. "Sylvie loves you so much, she'd want to die herself if you died."

"We can't both have my heart," I say.

"Of course not," says Nina. "You could get one of those monkey hearts, or that artificial heart they made such a fuss about on the news a while back."

"Why can't Mother get one of those? Or a transplant from someone else?"

"Do you want your mother to have a stranger's heart? Or a monkey's heart? Your poor mother. Do you remember how she never used to take you to the zoo because she couldn't stand to see the filthy monkeys? And you want her to have a monkey's heart? It would kill her!" Fran cries.

"She's so weak, she needs a heart that will agree with her," Aunt Nina adds. "Any heart but yours just wouldn't do. But you—you can handle anything. You're young, you're strong, you—"

"Have a college education," I finish for her.

Aunt Nina glares and says, "Your mother worked herself to the bone for you, so you could go to college. She nearly killed herself so you could go and study and make something of yourself. And now what do you do? Out of college four years already, and all you do is sit in front of a typewriter all day, call yourself a writer, smoke those cigarettes, never get a haircut—"

"And the first time your mother needs you, you turn your back on her!" Aunt Fran finishes. They both tighten their grips on my arms.

I don't remember ever wanting to go to college; it had seemed like my mother's idea all along. I went because I thought it would make her happy.

"I do things for Mother all the time—" I begin.

One of the doctors appears at the end of the hall. As he approaches, my aunts rise, pulling me with them. "Is she all right?" demands Fran when he is still twenty feet away.

"We've found a donor!" Nina announces.

The doctor greets us. He is a small man, completely bald. The eyes, behind thick glasses, are sad. He strokes his scalp as he talks, savoring the feel of it.

"She's all right. She's being monitored," he said. "We will look for a donor, but there's a long waiting list."

"We've got a donor. Sylvie's son. He's in the prime of health," Aunt Nina says.

"This is Arnie," Fran explains.

The doctor studies me carefully.

"Surely you don't do that sort of thing?" I say incredulously.

He gazes at me. "It's very rare, very rare indeed that a son will be so good as to donate his heart. In a few cases it has been done. But it's so rare to find such a son. A rare and beautiful thing." He takes off his glasses and polishes them on his sleeve. Without them his eyes are small, piggish.

He puts them back on and his eyes are sad and soulful once more. "You must love your mother very much," he says, gripping my shoulder with a firm hand.

"Oh, he does," Fran says. I shift my feet and knock over the cup of coffee. It spills on the floor. A sudden ugly brownness spreading over the empty white.

* * *

arse leads us to the intensive care unit where my mother is ly-
attached to machines and bags of fluid. The room has a window
through which the nurses watch our every move.

Aunt Fran rushes to one side of the bed, Aunt Nina the other. I
shuffle awkwardly at the foot of the bed. I touch my mother's feet.

"Sylvie! Are you all right?" the aunts cry. They are afraid to touch
her because of the tubes snaking into her arms, the needles held by
strips of tape.

My mother opens her eyes. There are purple circles around them.
She looks pale, but not so different from usual. Hardly on the verge
of death. She smiles dully at her sisters.

"Oh, Sylvie, you look wonderful! Just the same!" they say. Then
she raises her eyes to me.

"Oh, Arnie, you look terrible," she says. "That jacket—I told you
to throw it away. I'll find you another. There's no reason to go around
looking like a mess."

"Arnie has some good news," Nina says.

"Then why does he look like a thundercloud?" says my mother.
"Arnie, is something bothering you?"

Fran says, "Arnie wants to give you his heart."

"I never said that—" I cry.

There is a pause.

"Of course, Arnie, you shouldn't. You don't need to do that for me.
Really, you don't," my mother says. She looks terribly sad. The aunts'
faces have gone stony.

"You have your whole life ahead of you, after all," my mother says.
She looks down at her arms, at the branching veins that creep up
them like tendrils of a vine. "I never expected anything from you, you
know," she says. "Of course nothing like this."

I look down at her feet, two motionless humps under the blanket. "I'm considering it, Mother. Really, I am. I want to find out more
about it before I decide, that's all. It's not as simple as changing a car
battery or something." I force out a laugh.

No one else laughs, but the aunts' faces melt a little. My heart is
pounding. My mother closes her eyes. "You're a good boy, Arnie," she
says. "Your father would be proud."

*   *   *

A nurse comes in and tells us we should let my mother rest for a while. Aunt Fran and Aunt Nina head back to the waiting room. They sit down in the exact same seats and look up expectantly, waiting for me to sit between them.

"I think I'm going to take a little walk. I need to stretch my legs," I say.

I walk up and down halls of dull white where patients shuffle in slow motion, wheeling their IVs along beside them. I can feel in the floor the buzzing vibration of motors churning away somewhere in the heart of the building. I take the elevator and wander through more humming white halls until I find a pay phone.

I call up Mandy. She picks up on the first ring. "Hi," she says. "Where have you been?"

"My mother had a heart attack this morning," I say. "I'm at the hospital."

"Oh, I knew this would happen," Mandy says. "I burned my hand on the radiator this morning, and right away I thought, uh-oh, an omen, something bad's going to happen. How old's your mother?"

"Fifty-seven," I say.

"Oh, that's young for a heart attack. And she wasn't fat or anything. I feel like it's my fault, I should have warned you. Where did it happen?"

"At the bank, she was working," I tell her. "There was an ambulance, and her sisters are here, and I got here as soon as I could. Mandy, could I—"

"What?"

"I need to ask you something—" I shout into the phone.

"What—what?" Mandy's voice calls.

I tell her to come to the hospital and she says all right and hangs up. I don't need to tell her where to go; Mandy never gets lost. And she never has to wait in line. Strangers on the street talk to her. Jobs fall in her lap. She's nice-looking: freckles on her nose, good straight teeth. She keeps telling me that my signs indicate that my life will be on a big upswing soon, and I am just in a transition period right now. I hope she's right.

I finally reach the lobby and just as I do Mandy comes bursting in the doors, beaming at me. She doesn't smile; she beams. Not like sunlight.

Like lasers. "I knew I'd find you," she says. "How's your mother? Have you seen her?" Her breath in my face is like pine trees and toothpaste.

"Yeah, she's all right for now. Come on, let's go outside for a minute. I want to ask you something."

Outside, the afternoon is darkening to early evening. We wander in the parking lot among the cars, talking softly like we're afraid we'll wake them. It's cold. The wind sends trash and dry leaves scuttling along the ground. I keep looking back to see if anyone's following us.

"They say my mother's heart is bad. She needs a new one. They want me to donate my heart. What do you think of that?"

Mandy stops, her eyes and mouth open. Wind whips her frizzy hair around her face. She looks shocked. I breathe a sigh of relief: at last, someone who can see reason.

But then she says, "Oh, Arnie. How wonderful! Can they really do that? That's so wonderful—congratulations!"

"You mean you think I should do it?"

"Isn't technology incredible?" Mandy says. "These days doctors can do anything. Now you can share yourself, really give yourself to someone else in ways you never thought were possible before. Your mother must be thrilled."

"But it's crazy—"

She takes my hands in hers and looks up into my eyes. "Frankly, Arnie, I didn't think you had it in you. I'm really impressed. Really I am."

"Mandy, I thought you could be realistic about this. What about me? Do you want me dead? What am I supposed to do without a heart?"

"Oh, I'm sure they could fix you up. The important thing right now is to help your mother." She unzips my jacket and presses her hands against my chest. My heart twitches, flutters like a baby bird in her hands.

"What about *your* heart? If I give my mother my heart, would you give me yours?"

She draws away from me suddenly. "Now that's not fair," she says.

"You always said . . . you wanted . . ."

"You're just saying that. You're just thinking about yourself, what you need; you don't care about me. I think I'd better go—"

"But Mandy! Wait! What am I supposed to do?"

"Arnie, you know what the right thing to do is. You should get back to your mother now."

I watch her go. Brisk, determined steps, like a schoolteacher.

I find my way back to the waiting room. Someone has mopped up the coffee.

"Feel better?" Nina asks.

"Made a decision yet?" Fran says.

"Yes . . . no . . . I don't know," I say.

They are both quiet.

Then Aunt Nina says, "She carried you for nine months. More than nine months! You were late. Do you remember it?"

Fran turns to me. "Arnie, think about this: the heart's a little thing, really. Less than a pound. It's just a muscle. You've got muscles all over the place, can't you spare one?" She looks earnestly into my face. "Can't you spare a little bit of flesh?"

"Your mother's dying in there!" Nina blurts out. Then they are crying, both of them, drops sliding down the wrinkles in their faces.

Later we go visit my mother again. She looks worse, but perhaps it is the fluorescent lights. I stand again at the foot of her bed. I can see the veins and tendons on her neck. So delicate, so close to the surface, you could snip them with scissors.

"Arnie," she says softly, "you should go home and get some sleep. And shave, you look terrible. So tired. Go. I'll be here tomorrow, I'm not going anywhere."

Fran and Nina say they will stay a while longer, in case anything happens. I leave, but promise to come back soon.

I drive home in the dark. I go up to my apartment and turn on the lights. I take a shower and try to shave, but my body does not want to work properly. I stub my toes, jab my elbow, and poke a toothbrush in my eye.

I go into the kitchen and put a frying pan on the stove. I put in a dab of margarine and watch it slide around, leaving a sizzling trail. I think of eggs: scrambled? No—fried, sunny-side up, half-raw and runny. I get two eggs out of the refrigerator. I crack one into the pan. There's a blob of blood mixed in among the yellow.

I dump everything in the sink and run the garbage disposal, trying not to look at it too closely.

I want to call Mandy. Then I realize I don't want to call her at all.

Usually my mother calls in the evenings to tell me about TV programs and weather changes.

I turn off the lights and sit in the dark. I look at the ceiling, at the smoke detector. It has a blue light that pulses and flickers with a regular beat, like the blip on a cardiograph.

Early the next morning, at the hospital, I tell the doctor, "I want to do it. Give her my heart."

He gives me a long steady look, eyes huge behind the glasses. "I think you've made the right decision. I do," he says. His eyes drop to my chest. "We can get started right away."

"But what about a transplant for me?" I say. "Don't you need to arrange that first?"

"Oh, we'll take care of that when the time comes. I want to get your heart into your mother right away, before — before —"

"Before I change my mind," I say.

He hardly hears, he's already deep in his plans. His scalp is shiny with sweat.

"Is it a complicated kind of operation?" I ask.

"Not really," he says. "Making the decision is the hardest part. The incision is easy." He claps me on the back. "Have you told your mother yet? Well, go tell her, and then we'll get your chest shaved and get started."

This is what I've realized: all along I thought I'd publish a book. Lots of books. Get recognition, earn lots of money, support my mother in style in her old age. Give her gorgeous grandchildren. I thought that was the way to pay her back for everything I owe her.

But now it looks like I have to pay my debts with my heart instead. Under these circumstances, I don't have a choice. I'm almost glad; it seems easier this way. I'll just give her a piece of muscle and then I'll be free of her forever. One quick operation will be so much easier than struggling for the rest of my life to do for her all the things she thinks she's done for me.

It seems like a good bargain.

When I tell my mother the news, she cries a little, and smiles, and says: "Oh, I didn't expect it, oh, not for a minute, I wouldn't expect such a sacrifice from you, Arnie, I wouldn't dare to even mention such a thing. It's more than any mother could expect of her son. I'm so proud of you. I guess I did a good job raising you after all. You've turned into such a fine, good person. I worried that I may have made mistakes when I was bringing you up, but now I know I didn't."

On and on she goes.

And the aunts. They cry and clutch my arms. They say they doubted me but they never will again. What a good son, they keep saying. Looking at the aunts now, they seem smaller than they did before, shriveled.

I call Mandy, and she dashes over to the hospital. She kisses all over my face with her cherry-flavored Chap Stick, and she hugs me and presses her ear against my chest. She tells me she knew I'd do the right thing. I'm feeling pretty good now; I light up a cigarette. She takes it away from me and mashes it beneath her heel. That belongs to your mother now, she says.

They all give me flowers. I feel like a hero. I kiss my mother's cheek.

I hop on a stretcher. They wheel me out. They sedate me slightly, strip me, shave me.

And then they put the mask on and knock me out good; it's like I'm falling down a deep well and the circle of daylight above me grows smaller and smaller and smaller until it is a tiny white bird swooping and fluttering against a vast night sky.

How does it feel to have no heart? It feels light, hollow, rattly. Something huge is missing. It leaves an ache, like the ghost of a severed limb. I'm so light inside, but so heavy on the outside. Like gravity increased a hundredfold. Gravity holding me to the bed like the ropes and pegs of a thousand Lilliputians.

I lie at the bottom of a pool. Up above I see the light on the surface. It wavers, ripples, breaks, and comes together again. I can see the people moving about, far above in the light. I am down here in the dark, cradled in the algae. Curious fish nibble my eyelashes.

After a while I see a smooth pink face above me. The doctor? "Arnie," he says. "The operation went very well. Your mother is doing wonderfully. She loves the new heart." His words begin far away and drift closer, growing louder and louder until they plunk down next to me like pebbles.

"Arnie," he calls. The pool's surface shivers. His face balloons, shrinks to a dot, then unfolds itself. "Arnie, about you—we're having a little trouble. There's a shortage of spare hearts in this country right now. We're looking for some kind of replacement. But don't worry, you'll be fine."

Later I see Aunt Fran and Aunt Nina. They lean close. They're huge. Their faces bleed and run together like wet watercolors. "Your mother's doing so well!" they call. "She loves you, oh, she's so excited, she'll be in to see you soon!"

And later it's my mother gliding in, her face pink, her hair curled. "Arnie . . . Arnie . . . you good boy . . ." she calls and then they wheel her out.

They leave me alone for a long time. I lie in the deep. It sways me like a hammock. There is a deep, low humming all around, like whales moaning. My mother does not visit again. When do I get to go out and play?

Alone in the dark, no footsteps, no click of the light switch.

Then the doctor looms above me. "Your mother," he says, "is not doing well. The heart does not fit as well as we thought. It's a bit too small." He turns away and then leans over again. "As for you, we're working on it. There's nothing available at the moment. But don't worry."

And then Fran and Nina are back. "How could you?!" they scream, their voices shattering the surface into fragments. "Giving your mother a bad heart. How could you? What kind of son are you? She's dying, your mother's dying, all because of you." They weep together.

For a long time, no one comes. I know without anyone telling me that my mother is dead. It is my heart. When it ceases to beat I know. A high keening rises from the depths.

The doctor comes to tell me how sorry he is. "She was doing so well at first. But then it turned out the heart just wasn't enough. I tell you, though, she was thinking of you when she died. She asked for you." He sits quietly for a moment. "We haven't managed to find a heart for you. But you'll be fine. We've shot you up full of preservatives. You'll stay fresh for a while yet." He goes away.

Aunt Fran and Aunt Nina no longer visit.

Mandy? Gone.

I lie listening to the emptiness in my chest, like wind wailing through canyons.

These days the doctor comes in often to chat with me.

One day he tells me a story: "You know, when your mother died, we managed to save your heart. It was still healthy. We thought about giving it back to you. But there was a little girl here, about eight years old, and she needed a new heart too. Cute little blond girl. One time a basketball star came here to visit her and there were TV cameras and photographers and everything. She was in the papers a lot. Kids were always sending her cards. Anyway, we decided to give her your heart. She's only a kid, after all, she's got a whole life ahead of her — why should we deny her that? I'm sure your mother would have wanted it that way. She was such a caring, selfless woman. I'm sure deep down *you* want her to have it, too, don't you?"

Of course I do.

■

The Years of My Birth

FROM *The New Yorker*

THE NURSE HAD WRAPPED MY BROTHER in a blue flannel blanket and was just about to hand him to his mother when she whispered, "Oh, God, there's another one," and out I slid, half dead. I then proceeded to die in earnest, going from slightly pink to a dull gray-blue, at which point the nurse tried to scoop me into a bed warmed by lights. She was stopped by the doctor, who pointed out my head and legs. Stepping between me and the mother, the doctor addressed her.

"Mrs. Lasher, I have something important to say. Your other child has a congenital deformity and may die. Shall we use extraordinary means to salvage it?"

She looked at the doctor with utter incomprehension at first, then cried, "No!"

While the doctor's back was turned, the nurse cleared my mouth with her finger, shook me upside down, and swaddled me tightly in another blanket, pink. I took a blazing breath.

"Nurse," the doctor said.

"Too late," she answered.

I was left in the nursery with a bottle strapped to my face while the county tried to decide what to do with me. I was too young to be admitted to any state-run institution, and Mr. and Mrs. George Lasher refused to have me in their house, which was at the edge of a nearby town, where Mr. Lasher owned and ran a farm-implements dealership.

The night janitor at the hospital, a woman from the reservation named Betty Wishkob, asked the head maternity nurse for permission to hold me on her break. While cradling me, with her back to the observation window, Betty also nursed me—she was still nursing her youngest child at home. As she fed me, she molded and rounded my skull with her powerful hand. Nobody in the hospital knew that she was feeding me at night, or that she was doctoring me and had made up her mind to keep me. This was five decades ago. When Betty asked if she could take me home, there was relief and not a lot of paperwork involved, at least in the beginning. So I was saved, and grew up with the Wishkobs. I lived on the reservation and eventually was educated as my Chippewa siblings were—first at a school run by the Catholic mission and later at one run by the government.

Around the age of two, I was taken away for the first time and placed alone in a room. I remember the smell of disinfectant and what I would now call despair. Into this disinfected despair, there came a presence, someone or something, who grieved with me and held my hand. That presence would come to me again at other moments in my life. Its return is partly what this story is about.

The second time that an officious welfare officer decided to find a more suitable home for me, I was four. As Betty argued with her in the dust of our yard, the matted hackles on the dog's back rose. I stood beside Betty and held her skirt—green cotton. I pressed the fine weave between my fingers and hid my face in its scent of heated cloth. Then I was in the back seat of a car that sped soundlessly in some infinite direction. I slept. I woke alone in another white room. My bed was narrow, and the sheets were tucked tightly down, so that I had to struggle to get out. I sat on the edge of the bed for what seemed like a long time, waiting.

When you are little, you do not always know when you are screaming or crying—your feelings and the sound that comes out of you are all one thing. I remember that I opened my mouth, that is all, and that I did not shut it until I was back with Betty.

Every morning until I was about eleven, Betty and her husband, Albert, tried to round my head, and straighten me by stretching out my legs. They woke me before the other children and brought me into the kitchen. I drank a glass of thin, blue milk by the wood stove.

Then Betty sat in a kitchen chair and put me in her lap. She rubbed my head, then cupped her powerful fingers and pulled my skull into shape.

"You're gonna see things sometimes," she told me once. "Your soft spot stayed open longer than most babies. That's how spirits get in."

Albert sat across from us in another chair.

"Put your feet out, Tuffy," he said.

I put my feet in Albert's hands, and he pulled me one way while Betty pulled the other. Slowly, as I grew, my legs untwisted, though one was always a little shorter than the other. I was the youngest of their four children—it was Sheryl whom Betty had been nursing when she cared for me in the hospital. Their older son, Cedric, gave me the name Tuffy because he knew that once I went to school I would get a nickname anyway. He didn't want it to be one that mocked my rolling walk or my head. My head—so misshapen when I was born that the doctor had diagnosed a birth defect—was still a bit flat on one side, where I had been crushed in the womb by my twin. But it had been shaped enough by Betty's squeezing and kneading that by the time I was old enough to look in a mirror I thought I was pretty.

Neither Betty nor Albert ever told me I was wrong; it was Sheryl who gave me the news.

"Tuffy, you are so ugly you're cute," she said.

I looked in the mirror the next chance I got and realized that she was telling the truth.

The house we lived in had a smell that permeates it still—old wood, onions, fried coot, the salty outdoors scent of children. Betty was always trying to keep us clean, and Albert was always getting us dirty. He took us into the woods and showed us how to spot a rabbit run and set a snare. We yanked gophers from their holes with loops of string and picked pail after pail of berries. We rode a mean little bucking pony, fished perch from a nearby lake, dug potatoes every year to make money for school clothes. Betty's job at the hospital had not lasted. Albert sold firewood, corn, squash. We never went hungry. Not long ago, I read a memoir by a man named Peter Razor, who was abandoned like me, only he ended up in an institution. He wrote of the one time that he remembered being held, and said that it remained one of the strangest and happiest moments of his life. I don't remember being held as something special. Which tells me that I must have been held so often that the sensation became a part of me, inseparable from my memory of the world.

I know that I was loved, because it was a complicated matter for Betty and Albert to claim me from the welfare system, though I had aided their efforts with my endless scream. A full adoption involved hiring a lawyer, which they didn't have the money to do. I was afflicted with nightmares of being chased down and captured, and many nights I scrambled into the warm cleft of mattress between them, then held my breath and lay perfectly still until they had rolled over and gone back to sleep. When I knew that I was safe, I opened my eyes and looked into the darkness, which was never entirely black but alive with shifting green panels and tiny zigzags of fractured light. Then I'd feel myself sliding down into a safe, warm sleep, their slow and even breathing like a gentle rope, keeping me from slipping too far.

All of which is not to say that they were perfect. Albert drank from time to time and passed out on the floor. Betty's temper was explosive. She never hit, but she yelled and raved. She could say awful things. Once, Sheryl was twirling around in the house. There was a shelf set snugly in the corner of the living room, and on that shelf there was a cut-glass vase that was very precious to Betty. When we brought her wildflower bouquets, she'd put them in that vase. I'd seen her washing the vase with soap and polishing it with an old pillowcase. Sheryl's arm knocked the vase off the shelf, and it struck the floor with a bright sound and shattered into splinters.

Betty was working at the stove. She spun around, threw her hands out, and stared.

"Damn you, Sheryl," she said. "That was the only beautiful thing I ever had."

"Tuffy broke it!" Sheryl said, and bolted out the door.

I stood mute and too frozen to speak. Betty began to cry, harshly, wiping her face with her forearm. I moved to sweep up the pieces for her, but she said to leave them, in such a heartsick voice that I went to find Sheryl, who was hiding in her usual place on the far side of the henhouse. When I asked her why she'd blamed me, she gave me a glaring, hateful look and said, "Because you're white."

Children can be brutal when it comes to gaining the attention and favor of their parents. I didn't hold anything Sheryl did or said against her, and we became close later on. I am very glad for that, as I have never married, and I needed to confide in someone when, six months ago, I was contacted by my birth mother.

Until Betty and Albert died, I lived in an addition tacked onto the tiny house where all of us grew up. They died one right after the other, in the space of a few months, as the long-married sometimes do. By then, the other children had either moved off reservation or built new houses closer to town. I stayed on. Even now that Betty and Albert were gone and I had the whole house, I spent most of my time in my room. One difference was that I let the dog, a descendant of the one that had growled at the welfare lady, live inside with me. Betty had believed in outside dogs, but I petted and pampered this one. I'd had a fireplace installed, with a glass front and fans that threw the heat into a cozy circle in front of it, and there I'd sit every evening, with the dog at my feet, reading or crocheting while I listened to music.

Then one night the telephone rang.

I answered it with a simple hello. There was a pause. A woman asked if this was Linda Wishkob speaking.

"It is," I said, and then I experienced a skip of apprehension.

"This is Nancy Lasher." The voice was tight and nervous. "I am your mother."

I took a breath, let it out. I said nothing but simply set the phone back in the cradle. Later, that moment struck me as funny. It was a kind of replay of my birth. I'd done it over. But this time I had instinctively rejected my mother, left her in the cradle just as she'd left me.

I work in the reservation post office. I am a government employee. At any time, I could have found out my birth parents' address. I could have called them up or, had I been another sort of person, got drunk and stood in their yard and railed at them. But not only did I not care—I actively did not want to know where they lived. Why would I? Everything I did know about them was painful, and I have always tried to avoid pain—which is perhaps why I've never married or had children.

That night, after I'd hung up the phone, I made a cup of tea and busied myself with crossword puzzles. One stumped me. The clue was "double-goer," twelve spaces, and it took me the longest time and a dictionary to come up with the word "doppelganger."

I had always identified the visitations of my presence as one of the spirits Betty's doctoring had let into my head. The first time I was aware of it was when I was taken from Betty and put in a white room. After that, I occasionally had the sensation that there was someone walking beside me or sitting behind me, always just beyond my peripheral vision. One of the reasons I let the dog live inside was that it kept away this presence, which over the years had grown to seem anxious, needy, helpless in some way I could not define. I had never before thought of the presence in relation to my twin, who'd grown up not an hour's drive away from me, but that night the combination of the phone call out of the blue and the twelve-letter word in my puzzle set my thoughts flowing.

Betty had told me all she knew of the circumstances of my birth. She was never one to keep things from people for their own good. She always let you have the truth square. But as I'd never thought to ask her about my brother she hadn't talked about him. Nor had any of my siblings—mainly because I don't think they really cared. Perhaps they didn't even associate me with the Lashers. I searched my memory and could not pull out much, except that my twin had been a boy, born first. I had no idea what the Lashers had named him. Of course, we were fraternal twins and supposedly no more alike than any other brother and sister. So I was free, that night, to actually hate and resent him. I'd heard my birth mother's voice for the first time. He'd heard it all his life.

She had called herself, simply, my mother. Not my birth mother—that careful, distancing term—but my mother. It could have been plain arrogance, but then there had also been distress in her tone. My brain had taped the eight words she'd said. All that night and the next morning, too, they played on a loop. By the end of the second day, however, the intonation grew fainter, and I was relieved that on the third day it stopped.

On the fourth day, she called again.

She began by apologizing: "I am sorry to bother you." She went on to say that she had always wanted to meet me but had been afraid to find out where I was. She said that George, my father, was dead and she lived alone and that my twin brother was a postal worker in Bismarck. It was then that I couldn't help myself. I had to ask his name.

"Linden," she told me. "It's an old family name."

"Was mine an old family name as well?" I asked.

"No," she said, "but it matched your brother's name."

She told me that George had written my name down on the birth certificate, but that they had never seen me. She told me that he had died of a heart attack, and she had nearly moved down to Bismarck to be near Linden, but she couldn't sell her home. She said that she hadn't known I lived so close by or she would have called me long before. Her light, conversational chatter must have caused a dreamlike amnesia to come over me, because when she asked if we could meet, if she could take me out to dinner at Vert's Supper Club, the only place in the area that served full dinners with drinks, I said yes and agreed on a day.

When I finally hung up the phone, I stared for a long time at the little log fire in my fireplace. I'd laid the fire before the call and had been looking forward to popping some corn. Whenever I did, I threw kernels high in the air for the dog to catch. Now I was gripped by something new—a dreadful array of feelings. Which should I choose to succumb to first? I couldn't decide. The dog came and put his head in my lap, and we sat there until I realized that one of the reactions I could have was numbness. Relieved, feeling nothing, I let the dog out, let him in, and went to bed.

She was shorter than me. And so ordinary. I was sure that I must have seen her in the street, or at the grocery, or in the bank, perhaps. It would have been hard not to have crossed paths with her at some point around here. But I would not have suspected her of being my mother. I could detect nothing familiar or like myself about her.

We did not shake hands or hug. We sat across from each other in a leatherette booth.

"You aren't . . ."

"Retarded? Lame?"

She composed herself. "You got your coloring from your father," she said. "George had dark hair."

Nancy Lasher had red-rimmed blue eyes behind bifocals, a sharp nose, a tiny, lipless bow of a mouth. Her hair was typical for a woman of seventy-seven—tightly permanented, gray-white. At one time, she had been a handsome woman, I thought, with strong features. Now she wore stained dentures, big earrings made of cultured pearls, a pale-blue pants suit. Walking in, I'd noticed her square-toed lace-up therapy shoes. There wasn't anything about her that called to me. She was just any little old lady you wouldn't want to approach. People on the reservation didn't go near women who looked like her—I can't say why. A mutual instinct for avoidance, perhaps.

"Would you like to order?" she asked, touching the menu. "Have anything you like—it's all on me."

"No, thank you, we will split the check," I answered.

I'd thought about this in advance and concluded that, if she wanted to assuage her guilt in some way, taking me out to dinner was far too cheap. So we ordered and ate and drank our glasses of sour white wine. As we did so, she talked. She asked me about myself. She drew me out, as they might say in a novel. She made sounds of interest and surprise and sympathy. She said that she admired me. We got through the dinner of walleye and pilaf. Tears came into her eyes over a bowl of chocolate ice cream.

"I wish I'd known you were going to be so normal. I wish I hadn't ever given you up," she said.

I was alarmed at the effect that these words had on me, and quickly asked, "How's Linden?"

Her tears dried up and her face became sharp and direct.

"He's very sick," she said. "He's got kidney failure and is on dialysis. He's waiting for a kidney. I'd give him one of mine, but I'm a bad match and my kidney is old. George is dead. You are your brother's only hope."

I put my napkin to my lips and felt myself floating up off my chair. Someone floated with me, just barely with me, and I could feel his anxious breathing there. Now would be the time to call Sheryl, I thought. I should have called her before. She won't believe this. It seemed best to me, too, not to believe what I had just heard and felt. I had a twenty-dollar bill with me, and I put that money on the table and walked out the door. I got to my car, but before I could get in I had to run to the scarp of grass and weed that surrounded the parking lot. I was heaving and crying when I felt Nancy Lasher's hand stroking my back. It was the first time my birth mother had ever touched me, and although I quieted beneath her hand, I could detect a stupid triumph in her murmuring voice. She'd known where I lived all along, of course. I pushed her away, repelled by hatred, like an animal sprung from a trap.

Sheryl was all business.

"I'm calling Cedric." He lived in Bismarck. "Listen here, Tuffy. I'll get Cedric to go to the hospital and pull the plug on this Linden, and you can forget this crap."

That was Sheryl—who else could have made me laugh under the circumstances?

It was the morning after the dinner, and I was still in bed. I'd called in sick for the first time in years.

"You're not seriously even considering it," Sheryl said. Then, when I didn't answer, "Are you?"

"I don't know."

"Then I really am calling Cedric up. Those people ditched you. They turned their backs on you. They would have left you in the street to die. You're *my* sister. I don't want you to share your kidneys. Hey, what if I need one of your kidneys someday? Did you ever think of that? Save your damn kidney for me!

"I love you," she said, and I said it back.

"Tuffy, don't you do it," she warned, but her voice was suddenly small, vulnerable.

After she hung up, I called the numbers on the card my mother had given me and made appointments for the tests.

While I was down in Bismarck, I stayed with Cedric and his wife, whose name is Cheryl with a "C." She put out little towels for me that she had appliquéd with the shapes of cute animals. And tiny motel soaps she'd swiped. She made my bed. She tried to show me that she approved of what I was doing, although the others in my family did not. She is very Christian. But this was not a do-unto-others sort of thing for me. I've already said that I don't seek pain, and I would not have contemplated going through with it unless I found the alternative unbearable.

All my life, knowing without knowing it, I had waited for this to happen. My twin had been the one beside me, just out of sight. He did not know that he had been there, I was sure. When social services stole me from Betty and I was alone in the whiteness, he had held my hand, sat with me, and grieved. And now that I'd met his mother I understood something more. In a small town people knew everything; they knew what she had done by abandoning me. She'd have had to turn her fury with herself, her shame, on someone else—the child she'd chosen. She'd have blamed Linden. I had felt the contempt and the triumph in her touch. I was grateful now for the way things had turned out. Before we were born, my twin had had the compassion to crush me, to improve me by deforming me: I was the one who was spared.

"I'll tell you what," the doctor, an Iranian woman, who gave me the results of the tests and conducted the interview said. "You are a match, but I know your story. And I think it only fair that you know that Linden Lasher's kidney failure is his own fault. He has issues. He tried to commit suicide with a massive dose of acetaminophen, aspirin, and alcohol. That's why he is on dialysis. I think you should take that into account when making your decision."

Later that day, I sat with Linden, who said, "You don't have to do this. You don't have to be a Jesus."

"I know what you did," I said. "I'm not religious."

"Interesting," Linden said. He stared at me. "We sure don't look alike."

I realized that this was not a compliment, because he was nice-looking. He'd got the best of his mother's features. But there was something else, too—his eyes shifted around the room. He kept biting his lip, whistling, rolling his blanket between his fingers.

"Are you a mail carrier?" he asked.

"I work behind the counter, mostly."

"I've got a good route," he said, yawning. "A regular route—I could do it in my sleep. Every Christmas, my people leave me cards, money, cookies, that sort of thing. I know their habits so well. I could commit the perfect murder, you know?"

That took me aback. I did not answer.

Linden pursed his lips and scrutinized his hands.

Uncomfortable, I spoke.

"Did you ever think," I said, "that there was someone walking your route just beside you or just behind you? Someone there when you closed your eyes, gone when you opened them?"

"No," he said. "Are you crazy?"

"That was me," I said.

I picked up his hand, and he let it go limp. We sat there together, silent. After a while, he pulled his hand out of mine and massaged it as though my grip had hurt.

"Nothing against you," he said. "This was my mother's idea. I don't want your kidney. I have an aversion to ugly people. I don't want a piece of you inside me. I'd rather get on a list. Frankly, you're kind of a disgusting woman. I mean, I'm sorry, but you've probably heard this before."

"No," I said. "Nobody's ever told me that."

"You probably have a cat," he said. "Cats pretend to love whoever feeds them. I doubt you could get a husband, or whatever, unless you put a bag over your head. And even then it would have to come off at night."

"Are you saying this to drive me away?" My throat clamped down on my voice. I swallowed, drew a deep breath to stop the shakes that had started in my body. "You want to die. You don't want to be saved, right? I'm not saving you for any reason. You won't owe me anything."

"Owe you?"

He seemed genuinely surprised. His teeth were so straight that I was sure he'd had orthodontic work done when he was young. He started laughing now, showing all those beautiful teeth. He shook his head, wagged his finger at me, laughing so hard he seemed overcome. When I bent down awkwardly to pick up my purse, he was infected by such a bout of hilarity that he nearly choked. I tried to get away from him, to get to the door, but instead I backed up against the wall and was stuck there in that white, white room.

OLIVIA HAMILTON, ROBIN LEVI, AYELET WALDMAN

■

An Oral History of Olivia Hamilton

FROM *Inside This Place, Not of It: Narratives from Women's Prisons*

AGE 25, FORMERLY IMPRISONED

Olivia lives with her husband and three sons in an apartment that FEMA (Federal Emergency Management Agency) provided for her family because they evacuated New Orleans after Hurricane Katrina. We sit at a table in her breakfast nook as she shares her story: abandonment by her mother, teenage pregnancy, forced evacuation from her city, and imprisonment. Olivia gave birth to her youngest son while she was in prison serving a six-month sentence for embezzling money to pay her bills. During the birth, she was chained to an operating table and given a forced and medically unnecessary cesarean section. Olivia gave birth to another child in July 2011, but because of Olivia's c-section in prison, her local hospital was unwilling to allow her to try for a vaginal birth and she was forced to have another c-section. The son she birthed while imprisoned, now three years old, bounds around the apartment wearing only a diaper, occasionally interrupting our interview to squeeze his mother's leg. During the interview, Olivia describes her distrust of both the prison and the healthcare system, and describes her precarious journey toward reestablishing her life post-incarceration.

And Then the Hurricane Hit

My grandma tells a story about when I was a little girl, that one day I got a broom and started beating my doll with it, saying, "That's what my mom does." After that, my mom sent me to live with my grandma in Louisiana, St. Charles Parish. My relationship with my grandma was really good, but she was strict with me.

My brother and sisters stayed in Georgia with my mom. I talked with my mom some, not a lot. I had a lot of resentment, I guess, for her sending me to live with my grandma when I was so young. I think the problems began when I was around twelve. It was never my grades, it was just that I was in trouble with the juvenile detention people all the time for fighting and running away; I was trying everything to get my mom's attention. I think I realized I was doing it the day I got sent to juvenile hall. Usually I'd just go to the ADAPT Center[1] when I was in trouble, but the last time I ran away, when I was about twelve, I was sent to the St. James Parish Juvenile Detention Center in New Orleans for ten days. I was hurt and mad the day my mama came to see me in juvenile hall. But then I finally realized I shouldn't be doing all this, and when I went home to my grandmother's I just got myself back together.

I got pregnant at seventeen, and my boyfriend and I got an apartment together. I had my first son, Emmanuel, when I was a junior in high school, but I still graduated with a 3.8 GPA. I got help. For instance, there was this lady from Africa who'd opened a school for teen moms. She got government funding to open it, and she'd look after the students' babies, all the way till they were able to go to Head Start.[2] I didn't have to bring diapers, food, nothing. All I did was drop him off every day, and that was a blessing.

After I graduated high school in 2004 my then-boyfriend and I headed to Augusta, Georgia, in a raggedy car to live with my mom. But my mom let me down, and six months later I moved back to Louisiana to start all over again. I started Bryman College at the beginning of 2005 and I met my new boyfriend, who is now my husband. And then, that August, Hurricane Katrina hit. Before the storm reached us, I got in a car with my boyfriend and baby, and we started heading toward Georgia. We stayed with a friend of my brother's, which was a hectic situation every day. It was only a two-bedroom

---

1   A social work and child resources organization.
2   A federal program promoting school readiness for young children (ages three to five) in low-income families by offering educational, nutritional, health, and social services.

apartment, but at least it wasn't a shelter. During that time, I wrote a lot of bad checks because it was hard for me to get a job. I didn't have money for food, and you know, it was just a lot that we were dealing with. It was the only way really at the time that we could get anything.

Eventually I got a job at McDonald's. My brother was working, and my dad was coming up with some money to send us so we could maybe rent a trailer or something. But then three or four weeks after we got out here, I spoke with my mom, and eventually she let us stay with her.

I'd Made This Huge Mistake, and I Regretted It

By the end of 2007, I had two kids and was four months pregnant with another. I was living in Marietta, Georgia, and working two jobs, at Kmart and Pep Boys.

Well, one day I got an idea. I had a friend at Kmart who used to do fake refunds. She'd say a customer was coming in and she was refunding stuff that wasn't really being refunded. So I did it the first time and I didn't get caught, but of course I was scared. I said to my friend, "We didn't get caught. Let's not do it again." But we really needed the money. I was behind on a lot of bills, and I was trying to catch it up.

One night, my friend came through my line to check out little items like diapers and different things—some of the things I needed—and I didn't charge her for everything; diapers and stuff like that I would never ring up. We would do that a lot.

That night the Kmart loss prevention officer was outside smoking a cigarette, but I didn't see him at the time. When I got ready to close up, he called me and my friend to the back, and of course they'd caught it on tape. He asked us how long we'd been doing it, and I lied, "This is my first time." And then he basically told me, "Write what I tell you to write, and then I'll let you go home."

I think the total he had us taking was $1,200 worth of stuff, and I said, "I didn't take that much," because we'd only taken $300 worth. But he said, "But we have other stuff that's been taken," even though I told him I hadn't taken any of that.

Then he said, "Well, we're gonna press charges." I think he was trying to save his job at the time, 'cause they've got to catch people, and I don't think he'd been doing too good in that department. I got arrested and taken to jail that night, but I bonded out.

About two months later, I got a letter in the mail saying there was an arraignment. I honestly thought it was for Kmart, but when I got to court, I found out it was for Pep Boys—I'd been doing the same thing there. The judge was sending everybody to jail that day, and I was totally scared. So I got up there, and the Pep Boys loss prevention officer said he'd called his manager because he really felt bad for me. He said I was a good worker, and that he knew the situation I was in. He said, "Well, I asked my manager if there's a way that you can make payments, but he's not budging. He says it's too much." It came to something like $700. The judge put me on a bond on my own recognizance. She basically let me go home that day without my needing to post bail, and told me that I needed to turn myself in the following night. It was like her trusting me that I was going to come back. She said, "I think you made a very bad mistake. I want you to go home, pick your kids up from day care, and make sure they're stable. Tomorrow at nine o'clock, you need to turn yourself in."

In my mind, I was thinking, *Okay, well, I've never been in trouble before, so the only thing they can do is put me on probation.* And that's all I kept saying to myself. But when I finally got to court, I got a court-appointed lawyer, and he said, "Well, the judge is saying eighteen months." And I was like, "Huh? I've never been in trouble before! I can pay the money back!" At the time I had $1,500 on me, which I'd saved from my taxes. My lawyer talked to the prosecutor, who said, "No. She's got to serve time."

Then my lawyer told me, "Go home for the weekend and get yourself together with your kids." He said, "The only thing I can say is that I'll try and talk the prosecutor down. Any other judge, and I think you would've been okay. But I don't think she's gonna budge."

So I went home and finally I called my grandmother, my dad, and everybody, and let them know what was going on. Of course they were all shocked, because I had never said anything about it before. That weekend was real, real hard. I was scared, because I didn't want to leave my kids. I guess it just hurt me because I'd never been in trouble, and I was doing all I could to stay out of trouble. But I'd made this huge mistake and I regretted it. I think that was the most that I felt—regret. Leaving my kids—I didn't know how to handle that part.

And so that Monday came, February 18, 2008. I had to be in court at nine. I told my oldest son, "Mommy might have to go away for a while to help some people. But once I've helped them, I'll be home." My husband kept saying, "You're not going. You're not going." When I got to court, every part of me just knew what would happen.

So I got in front of the judge and I said to her, "I'm truly sorry. But you know, I have never been in trouble before this. I just graduated from college and I'm pregnant. This is not what I thought I would be doing right now." The judge had her head down the whole time; she looked real, real sad. And then she said, "The only thing I can say is that I have to send you to jail, because your codefendant has already gone. But I'm sorry. I think you're on the right track. I think you just made a mistake that you've got to serve the consequences for." I was sentenced to a year, and the judge said, "Hopefully, you'll do six months on good behavior, with nine years' probation." And I thought, *Okay, so you're going to send me to jail. And then I have to pay all this money back—one hundred a month until it's paid back—and then probation for nine years. Nine years.*

They Shackled My Stomach and My Feet

When the court bailiff took me from the court to a holding cell in Georgia, a guard put the cuffs around my belly and on my wrists, like a chain. When I sat down, the cuffs were real, real tight, so I was basically standing up the whole time. For a while, I was complaining about how tight it was, and other inmates were complaining too. Finally the guard came back and loosened the chain around my belly, and then I was able to sit down. The whole process was just long, and I was hungry and tired.

I think the thing that upset me the most was that they wouldn't give me water in a cup. I was not about to drink out of this faucet where you wash your hands; it was right over the toilet bowl. So I just stayed thirsty. By the time I did finally go through the holding cell, the guards gave me a sandwich to eat. Then they took us all on upstairs to the jail, and once I got upstairs, one of the female guards told me, "I won't be able to put you in a bottom bunk until you go see the doctor and he says you're pregnant." I was six months pregnant! I said, "No, for real?! You want me to climb this bunk bed?" She said, "Well, I can't give you a bottom bunk." I just said, "Ma'am, I can't climb this." And then she just walked out. Another inmate told me, "You can have my bed." So she put her stuff on the top bunk, and I took the bottom. And finally I went to sleep.

I was there about a month before I actually saw a doctor. I didn't have vitamins there, and I had no prenatal care. I didn't really complain if I was in pain or anything, because the infirmary was real nasty. There was poo on the walls. It was just nasty. Then one day, when I was seven months pregnant, the guards called me down. They shackled my stomach and my feet and took me to see an OB-GYN. I mean, you walk like this through the front door looking as if you've murdered someone, and I just thought it was really degrading. I know I made a mistake, but I don't think I deserved to be ashamed or embarrassed in this way. And even once I'd got in the back where the actual doctors' offices were, the shackles didn't come off. They took them off my feet, but nothing else; the shackles stayed on my stomach.

The doctor complained that I wasn't getting enough water, vitamins, or fresh fruits, and that it could affect my baby's brain. The county doesn't give you fruits, and it's not like I could buy them. So I just tried to drink as much water as I possibly could.

My kids came to visit me sometimes with my boyfriend. My boys were five and three then. The first time they came was really hard. They were beating on the glass, trying to come through it. I was so mad at myself for putting them through this.

It felt like my pregnancy was the only thing that was keeping me going. I was eight months pregnant when I finally left the county jail and went to prison.

Nobody Cares If You're Pregnant

When I was moved to prison in Pennsylvania, I couldn't take my books that had been sent to me in jail, or anything like that. I had one picture and I had my Bible, but all the rest I had to send home.

I was taken to prison with other inmates in a cramped, hot van. Some of them were also pregnant. When we got there and were getting off the van, the guards started yelling at us, "Nobody cares if you're pregnant! You shouldn't have got in trouble. You're a sad excuse for a mother. You don't care about your kids!" It was a mess. It was real hard. There was another girl there who was pregnant, and she'd been there before. She said to me, "Don't let them get to you, girl." But they had already gotten to me. I just felt like this wasn't the place I was supposed to be.

The guards wanted me to stand up straight, but I couldn't. I was totally drained because I hadn't slept since three that morning. I was eight months along at this point, and I was huge. Eventually, one of the male guards said, "Okay, go get her a wheelchair." The female guards were actually harder on me. So I got in a wheelchair, and they rolled me on inside. When I got inside, the guards made me strip, bend over, all that. Then they made me take a shower, and afterward they gave me a sandwich and a juice. You would think that they'd give you more food, being pregnant, but they don't. You just eat what everybody else eats.

It was a whole process. I had to learn how to talk to the guards, and that I had to address them with "Ma'am" or "Sir" and "Good morning." Or when they walked by, I had to stop. I had to ask permission to speak. Finally they gave me all my stuff in a bag to put on the bed.

I couldn't carry the bag like they wanted me to. There's a certain way you had to hold it, a certain way to walk, and I just kept dropping it. It was about ten pounds—it's your clothes, it's everything in there—and I wasn't even supposed to be lifting that. But the guards kept yelling, "You'd better not drop it again!" And I was like, "Uh, ma'am, this is heavy. I'm trying my best."

When I got in the dorm, the inmates were pretty cool and they helped me make my bed. I think, with most of the women in there being mothers, they could imagine how it felt to go through this while pregnant. Most of them were pretty understanding, and they didn't mind helping me out as much as they could.

My family was very supportive. My grandmother made sure that I had money in my account, my dad and uncles too. My mama did most of the writing as far as letters went, and she sent a lot of pictures and just different things to help me get through. I could call my grandma any time, but it was hard for me to call my boyfriend, because you couldn't call cell phones from prison, only landlines. Also, you couldn't get a visitation until about two months of being there. It didn't make any sense for me to even start that process, because my lawyer told me that, nine chances out of ten, I would be getting out in six months. By the time I got to the prison, I'd already been in county jail for two months. I had to wait another two months before I would be allowed visitation at the prison, so it would have been four months by then. And by the time they'd gone through processing everybody, it probably would have been time for me to go home.

I Said I Didn't Want to Be Induced, and the Captain Said, "These Are Orders"

My due date was May 24, 2008, just before Memorial Day weekend. A female doctor from the Atlanta Medical Center came to visit me on the 22nd. At that time, I wasn't showing any signs of labor. We did an ultrasound, and the baby hadn't moved one bit. I wasn't dilated at all, wasn't even close, and I wasn't having any pains. She said I should be fine through the weekend, and that everything was normal about my pregnancy.

Then, on the evening of the 23rd—this was a Friday evening—the guards called me, and they told me to pack my stuff. But I hadn't even had one contraction, so I asked a guard, "Where am I going?" And the guard said, "I don't know. They just called and said for you to pack your stuff." I thought, *Okay, maybe I'm going home!*

I got over to the infirmary, and the captain said, "Well, the doctor from the prison says he's going to send you in to be induced." When I asked why, she said, "Because your due date is May 24th, and this is a holiday weekend." I said, "But I'm not even in pain or anything! I don't want to be induced, I'm not even late. Nothing's wrong with me!" And she said, "Well, these are orders."

They put me in a room and shackled me. I was more upset than anything that the baby just wasn't ready, and I didn't want to be forced. They gave me Pitocin,[3] but it wasn't working. Later, in the middle of the night, the doctor came in to check on me. He came in and he started poking inside me with an instrument—I'm not sure exactly what it was, it looked like a little stick. He put it inside me and started poking the bag of water, where the amniotic fluid was, so he could bust it. It was a lot of pain, and I said, "You're hurting me." He stopped, but by then he had swollen up my insides, and the baby wouldn't move any more than six centimeters.

Then he said, "Well, if you don't move any more by tomorrow, we're going to have to do a c-section." I said, "So you come in here, and you poke me to death, and now I'm swollen! I have never had a c-section in my life. My oldest son was nine pounds—no cuts, no slits, no nothing. And you're going to make me have a c-section?"

The next day, the doctor came back and took me in to have the c-section done. A sergeant came in and said, "She needs to be shackled. She's no different from anybody else." I was hurting, and I was tired. I said to the sergeant, "Ma'am, there is no way I need these shackles. I'm not going anywhere; I'm in pain. You've got a guard in my room. And I don't know if you have kids, but this ain't something fun to have your hands shackled for." But she made them keep the shackles on me when I went in for the c-section.

The doctor gave me an epidural. I went through with the c-section, and finally, the baby came on out. It was a boy. The guard held him up to show him to me. Even then, they never took the shackles off me.

This c-section I was forced to have—I doubt that it's legal. I don't remember signing any paperwork, but I never looked into finding a lawyer. I was hoping there was something I could do, but I was told that I had no rights. The guard said to me, "You lost your rights the day you walked in here."

I named the baby Joshua. I wonder about him; does he remember all that we went through? The guards made me put the prison address on the birth certificate. That's something you have to deal with for the rest of your life.

---

3   Pitocin is an intravenous medication commonly used to induce labor.

I was fortunate, you know. One of the guards there gave me her cell phone because she didn't agree with a lot of what was going on. She said, "Call your boyfriend. Let him know you had the baby." She let me talk to him until the phone died. It was a blessing.

It Felt Like My Baby Was Dying

After I left the hospital, my boyfriend picked up the baby and took him home. I guess for me, walking out of that hospital, knowing I was leaving my son—it killed me inside. I felt like I was being punished for the one mistake that I'd made in my life. I just remember looking at my baby, and kissing him, and crying, and not wanting to go. The nurse who was holding him was really hurt too. She asked me, "Do you want to kiss him again?" And I kissed him one last time, and they took me out the door.[4]

It felt like my baby was dying, that I was abandoning him. I felt like I owed it to him to be there, and I wasn't. I felt like maybe he would hate me, or resent me, or when I got home, he wouldn't know who I was. It hurt. It just hurt.

I got back to the prison with staples in because of the c-section. But I couldn't go back to the dorm until the staples came out, and so, on top of me being hurt and stressed, they put me in this infirmary with nothing but four walls. I didn't have any of my personal property, and there was no TV, nothing.

I was supposed to stay there through the weekend. During that time, I had nobody to talk to, and all I could really do was cry. I didn't want

---

4   Most prisons separate parents and their newborn infants after 48 hours. As well as causing emotional distress, the separation of mothers and their children also threatens the health of infants by posing serious barriers to breastfeeding. The Fifth Circuit of Appeals ruled in the 1981 case *Dike v. School Board of Orange County, Florida,* that the right to nurse is protected by the Fourteenth Amendment. However, the same court determined in *Southerland v. Thigpen* that the state could overlook this guarantee in prison. Some states, like New York, have taken steps to recognize the universality of this right, guaranteeing women in prison the ability to breastfeed their children for a year after birth, though in other states the reality of prison life has rendered breastfeeding impossible.

In at least thirteen states, babies can be placed in prison nurseries, though access is often limited to women with short sentences for nonviolent offenses, and some parents prefer for their children to be raised outside prison walls.

to eat, I didn't want to do anything. And then one of the guards told me, "Well, if you don't eat, we're going to make you stay here longer." So I made myself eat because I didn't want to stay in there that long. All that was going to do was drive me more crazy than I already was.

By then I was mad at everything. I was mad at myself. I was mad at my mom. I was mad at everybody. I had only been back there but about five weeks from the hospital, and I got in a fight. It was with a girl who was looking for trouble, and she picked a fight with me one night. She hit me and hit me, and I fought her back. So of course, they took us to lockdown. That's the worst place to be. I mean, you can't look out the windows because they're all blacked out, and you can only bathe on certain days. I was down there for three weeks. My birthday was July 18th, and I was in lockdown for that. But my mom sent me a whole bunch of cards and pictures, and I would call my grandma, and she'd be like, "You still down there?" And I'd say, "Yes."

The day I got out of lockdown was the day I got the news that I was going home on August 14. I had two weeks left! I thought, *Thank God! Finally!* I stayed up the whole night before the 14th—I was so excited, and I just wanted to leave. I was just so ready to get out of there.

All Storms End

When I got out of prison, my boyfriend came to get me. At that time, his mom had the two younger kids and my grandmother had my oldest son. It took me a while to get the kids back. I missed them terribly, but things were bad. The gas in the house had been turned off, the phone was off, the cable was off. The truck I had was gone, and my credit was totally messed up. Everything was in a total wreck. I couldn't be bringing the kids back into that type of situation. I wanted to be able to have food stamps first, and I wanted to try to get the house together. It was nasty, it was dirty. I was just in a depressed situation, and I was upset with my boyfriend, who wasn't working at that time. I was mad because I'd left him with $1,500, and he got money every month from my dad and my grandmother, so I couldn't understand the house being in a total wreck when I got out of prison.

I was totally mad about my money, and why everything was gone. I also felt a lot of resentment toward society.

Eventually, I was able to get a job at the food court. I saved up, and I got a car. Once I got the car, I could get back and forth to work. And finally, when we were more financially stable, we got the kids back.

Once I got out, I got in the church. I always was in church, but I strayed for a while when I first moved out here to Georgia. But once I got out of prison, I joined a choir and I went to Bible study and Sunday school. And, you know, I got myself back together for me and God. For me and school. For me and work.

Eventually I got laid off from the food court because they didn't have enough work for me, and it's been totally hard for me to find a job since. Whenever I'm filling out a job application, I get scared when I get to that question where I have to put down that I have this conviction. I feel like I'll never have the opportunity to explain what happened. So it's like, do you lie, or do you tell the truth? And, you know, every time I get to that question, I stumble.

I think my medical treatment in prison was cruel, degrading, and shameful. Being shackled, being forced to have that c-section—it was the worst feeling, mentally and emotionally, that I have ever been through. And I feel like it would be so unfair for me to have been through all this and not say anything about it to somebody. I always felt like everything I went through was definitely for a reason, and that it made me a stronger person. So my goal now is to help prevent somebody else from making the same mistakes, with the stealing, the whole scenario. Right now I'm working with young women through my church. I want to work with these young women because when you get to a certain age, there are things you go through, there's pressure to do things that you may not want to do. I've also been without a mom, and I know how it feels to want that. There's a gap in your heart where you need it. A grandmother's love is awesome, but a mom's love is something totally different.

Through God, all things are possible. Even though I was mad at my boyfriend and my mom, God has built those relationships again. Now my mom and I share a beautiful relationship, and my boyfriend is now my husband. This shows that all storms end and the sun will shine again.

PHIL KLAY

■

Redeployment

FROM *Granta*

WE SHOT DOGS. Not by accident. We did it on purpose and we called it "Operation Scooby." I'm a dog person, so I thought about that a lot.

First time was instinct. I hear O'Leary go, "Jesus," and there's a skinny brown dog lapping up blood the same way he'd lap up water from a bowl. It wasn't American blood, but still, there's that dog, lapping it up. And that's the last straw, I guess, and then it's open season on dogs.

At the time you don't think about it. You're thinking about who's in that house, what's he armed with, how's he gonna kill you, your buddies. You're going block by block, fighting with rifles good to 550 meters and you're killing people at five in a concrete box.

The thinking comes later, when they give you the time. See, it's not a straight shot back, from war to the Jacksonville mall. When our deployment was up, they put us on TQ, this logistics base out in the desert, let us decompress a bit. I'm not sure what they meant by that. Decompress. We took it to mean jerk off a lot in the showers. Smoke a lot of cigarettes and play a lot of cards. And then they took us to Kuwait and put us on a commercial airliner to go home.

So there you are. You've been in a no-shit war zone and then you're sitting in a plush chair looking up at a little nozzle shooting air conditioning, thinking, what the fuck? You've got a rifle between your knees, and so does everyone else. Some Marines got M9 pistols, but they take away your bayonets because you aren't allowed to have knives on an airplane. Even though you've showered, you all look grimy and lean. Everybody's hollow-eyed and their cammies are beat to shit. And you sit there, and close your eyes, and think.

The problem is, your thoughts don't come out in any kind of straight order. You don't think, oh, I did A, then B, then C, then D. You try to think about home, then you're in the torture house. You see the body parts in the locker and the retarded guy in the cage. He squawked like a chicken. His head was shrunk down to a coconut. It takes you a while to remember Doc saying they'd shot mercury into his skull, and then it still doesn't make any sense.

You see the things you saw the times you nearly died. The broken television and the haji corpse. Eicholtz covered in blood. The lieutenant on the radio.

You see the little girl, the photographs Curtis found in a desk. First had a beautiful Iraqi kid, maybe seven or eight years old, in bare feet and a pretty white dress like it's First Communion. Next she's in a red dress, high heels, heavy makeup. Next photo, same dress but her face is smudged and she's holding a gun to her head.

I tried to think of other things, like my wife, Cheryl. She's got pale skin and fine dark hairs on her arms. She's ashamed of them but they're soft. Delicate.

But thinking of Cheryl made me feel guilty, and I'd think about Lance Corporal Hernandez, Corporal Smith, and Eicholtz. We were like brothers, Eicholtz and me. The two of us saved this Marine's life one time. A few weeks later Eicholtz is climbing over a wall. Insurgent pops out a window, shoots him in the back when he's halfway over.

So I'm thinking about that. And I'm seeing the retard, and the girl, and the wall Eicholtz died on. But here's the thing. I'm thinking a lot, and I mean, a lot, about those fucking dogs.

And I'm thinking about my dog. Vicar. About the shelter we'd got him from, where Cheryl said we had to get an older dog because nobody takes older dogs. How we could never teach him anything. How he'd throw up shit he shouldn't have eaten in the first place. How he'd slink away all guilty, tail down and head low and back legs crouched. How his fur started turning gray two years after we got him, and he had so many white hairs on his face it looked like a mustache.

So there it was. Vicar and Operation Scooby, all the way home.

Maybe, I don't know, you're prepared to kill people. You practice on man-shaped targets so you're ready. Of course, we got targets they call "dog targets." Target shape Delta. But they don't look like fucking dogs.

And it's not easy to kill people, either. Out of boot camp, Marines act like they're gonna play Rambo, but it's fucking serious, it's professional. Usually. We found this one insurgent doing the death rattle, foaming and shaking, fucked up, you know? He's hit with a 7.62 in the chest and pelvic girdle; he'll be gone in a second but the company XO walks up, pulls out his KA-BAR, and slits his throat. Says, "It's good to kill a man with a knife." All the Marines look at each other like, "What the fuck?" Didn't expect that from the XO. That's some PFC bullshit.

On the flight, I thought about that too.

It's so funny. You're sitting there with your rifle in your hands but no ammo in sight. And then you touch down in Ireland to refuel. And it's so foggy you can't see shit but, you know, this is Ireland, there's got to be beer. And the plane's captain, a fucking civilian, reads off some message about how general orders stay in effect until you reach the States, and you're still considered on duty. So no alcohol.

Well, our CO jumped up and said, "That makes about as much sense as a goddamn football bat. All right, Marines, you've got three hours. I hear they serve Guinness." Ooh-fucking-rah. Corporal Weissert ordered five beers at once and had them laid out in front of him. He didn't even drink for a while, just sat there looking at 'em, all happy. O'Leary said, "Look at you, smiling like a faggot in a dick tree," which is a DI expression Curtis loves. So Curtis laughs and says, "What a horrible fucking tree," and we all start cracking up, happy just knowing we can get fucked up, let our guard down.

We got crazy quick. Most of us had lost about twenty pounds and it'd been seven months since we'd had a drop of alcohol. MacManigan, Second Award PFC, was rolling around the bar with his nuts hanging out of his cammies telling Marines, "Stop looking at my balls, faggot." Lance Corporal Slaughter was there all of a half hour before he puked in the bathroom, with Corporal Craig, the sober Mormon, helping him out and Lance Corporal Greeley, the drunk Mormon, puking in the stall next to him. Even the Company Guns got wrecked.

It was good. We got back on the plane and passed the fuck out. Woke up in America.

Except, when we touched down in Cherry Point, there was nobody there. It was zero dark and cold and half of us were rocking the first hangover we'd had in months, which at that point was a kind of shitty that felt pretty fucking good. And we got off the plane and there's a big empty landing strip, maybe a half-dozen red patchers and a bunch of seven tons lined up. No families.

The Company Guns said that they were waiting for us at Lejeune. The sooner we get the gear loaded on the trucks, the sooner we see 'em.

Roger that. We set up working parties, tossed our rucks and seabags into the seven tons. Heavy work and it got the blood flowing in the cold. Sweat a little of the alcohol out too.

Then they pulled up a bunch of buses and we all got on, packed in, M16s sticking everywhere, muzzle awareness gone to shit but it didn't matter.

Cherry Point to Lejeune's an hour. First bit's through trees. You don't see much in the dark. Not much when you get on 24 either. Stores that haven't opened yet. Neon lights off at the gas stations and bars. Looking out, I sort of knew where I was but I didn't feel home. I figured I'd be home when I kissed my wife and pet my dog.

We went in through Lejeune's side gate, which is about ten minutes away from our battalion area. Fifteen, I told myself, way this fucker is driving. When we got to McHugh, everybody got a little excited. And then the driver turned on A Street. Battalion area's on A, and I saw the barracks and I thought, there it is. And then they stopped about four hundred meters short. Right in front of the armory. I could've jogged down to where the families were. I could see there was an area behind one of the barracks where they'd set up lights. And there were cars parked everywhere. I could hear the crowd down the way. The families were there. But we all got in line, thinking about them just down the way. Me thinking about Cheryl and Vicar. And we waited.

When I got to the window and handed in my rifle, though, it brought me up short. That was the first time I'd been separated from it in months. I didn't know where to rest my hands. First I put them in my pockets, then I took them out and crossed my arms, and then I just let them hang, useless, at my sides.

After all the rifles were turned in, First Sergeant had us get into a no-shit parade formation. We had a fucking guidon waving out front, and we marched down A Street. When we got to the edge of the first barracks, people started cheering. I couldn't see them until we turned the corner, and then there they were, a big wall of people holding signs under a bunch of outdoor lights, and the lights were bright and pointed straight at us so it was hard to look into the crowd and tell who was who. Off to the side there were picnic tables and a Marine in woodlands grilling hot dogs. And there was a bouncy castle. A fucking bouncy castle.

We kept marching. A couple more Marines in woodlands were holding the crowd back in a line, and we marched until we were straight alongside the crowd and then First Sergeant called us to a halt.

I saw some TV cameras. There were a lot of U.S. flags. The whole MacManigan clan was up front, right in the middle, holding a banner that read: OO-RAH PRIVATE FIRST CLASS BRADLEY MAC-MANI-GAN. WE ARE SO PROUD.

I scanned the crowd back and forth. I'd talked to Cheryl on the phone in Kuwait, not for very long, just "Hey, I'm good," and, "Yeah, within forty-eight hours, talk to the FRO, he'll tell you when to be there." And she said she'd be there, but it was strange, on the phone. I hadn't heard her voice in a while.

Then I saw Eicholtz's dad. He had a sign too. It said: WELCOME BACK HEROES OF BRAVO COMPANY. I looked right at him and remembered him from when we left and I thought, "That's Eicholtz's dad." And that's when they released us. And they released the crowd too.

I was standing still and the Marines around me, Curtis and O'Leary and MacManigan and Craig and Weissert, they were rushing out to the crowd. And the crowd was coming forward. Eicholtz's dad was coming forward.

He was shaking the hand of every Marine he passed. I don't think a lot of guys recognized him, and I knew I should say something but I didn't. I backed off. I looked around for my wife. And I saw my name on a sign: SGT. PRICE, it said. But the rest was blocked by the crowd and I couldn't see who was holding it. And then I was moving toward it, away from Eicholtz's dad, who was hugging Curtis, and I saw the rest of the sign. It said: SGT. PRICE, NOW THAT YOU'RE HOME YOU CAN DO SOME CHORES. HERE'S YOUR TO-DO LIST. 1) ME. 2) REPEAT NUMBER 1.

And there, holding the sign, was Cheryl.

She was wearing cammie shorts and a tank top, even though it was cold. She must have worn them for me. She was skinnier than I remembered. More makeup too. I was nervous and tired and she looked a bit different. But it was her.

All around us were families and big smiles and worn-out Marines. I walked up to her and she saw me and her face lit. No woman had smiled at me like that in a long time. I moved in and kissed her. I figured that was what I was supposed to do. But it'd been too long and we were both too nervous and it felt like just lip on lip pushed together, I don't know. She pulled back and looked at me and put her hands on my shoulders and started to cry. She reached up and rubbed her eyes and then she put her arms around me and pulled me into her.

Her body was soft and it fit into mine. All deployment I'd slept on the ground, or on canvas cots. I'd worn body armor and kept a rifle slung across my body. I hadn't felt anything like her in seven months. It was almost like I'd forgotten how she felt, or never really known it, and now here was this new feeling that made everything else black and white fading before color. Then she let me go and I took her by the hand and we got my gear and got out of there.

She asked me if I wanted to drive and hell yeah I did, so I got behind the wheel. A long time since I'd done that too. I put the car in reverse, pulled out, and started driving home. I was thinking I wanted to park somewhere dark and curl up with her in the back seat like high school. But I got the car out of the lot and down McHugh. And driving down McHugh it felt different from the bus. Like, this is Lejeune. This is the way I used to get to work. And it was so dark. And quiet.

Cheryl said, "How are you?" which meant, How was it? Are you crazy now?

I said, "Good. I'm fine."

And then it was quiet again and we turned down Holcomb. I was glad I was driving. It gave me something to focus on. Go down this street, turn the wheel, go down another. One step at a time. You can get through anything, one step at a time.

She said, "I'm so happy you're home."

Then she said, "I love you so much."

Then she said, "I'm proud of you."

I said, "I love you too."

When we got home she opened the door for me. I didn't even know where my house keys were. Vicar wasn't at the door to greet me. I stepped in and scanned around and there he was on the couch. When he saw me he got up slow.

His fur was grayer than before, and there were weird clumps of fat on his legs, these little tumors that Labs get but that Vicar's got a lot of now. He wagged his tail. He stepped down off the couch real careful, like he was hurting. And Cheryl said, "He remembers you."

"Why's he so skinny?" I said, and I bent down and scratched him behind the ears.

"The vet said we had to keep him on weight control. And he doesn't keep a lot of food down these days."

Cheryl was pulling on my arm. Pulling me away from Vicar. And I let her.

She said, "Isn't it good to be home?"

Her voice was shaky, like she wasn't sure of the answer. And I said, "Yeah, yeah it is." And she kissed me hard. I grabbed her in my arms and lifted her up and carried her to the bedroom. I put a big grin on my face, but it didn't help. She looked a bit scared of me, then. I guess all the wives were probably a little bit scared.

And that was my homecoming. It was fine, I guess. Getting back feels like your first breath after nearly drowning. Even if it hurts, it's good.

I can't complain. Cheryl handled it well. I saw Lance Corporal Curtis's wife back in Jacksonville. She spent all his combat pay before he got back, and she was five months pregnant, which, for a Marine coming back from a seven-month deployment, is not pregnant enough.

Corporal Weissert's wife wasn't there at all when we got back. He laughed, said she probably got the time wrong, and O'Leary gave him a ride to his house. They get there and it's empty. Not just of people, of everything: furniture, wall hangings, everything. Weissert looks at this shit and shakes his head, starts laughing. They went out, bought some whiskey, and got fucked up right there in his empty house.

Weissert drank himself to sleep and when he woke up, MacManigan was right next to him, sitting on the floor. And MacManigan, of all people, was the one who cleaned him up and got him into base on time for the classes they make you take, about don't kill yourself, don't beat your wife. And Weissert was like, "I can't beat my wife. I don't know where the fuck she is."

That weekend they gave us a 96, and I took on Weissert duty for Friday. He was in the middle of a three-day drunk, and hanging with him was a carnival freak show filled with whiskey and lap dances. Didn't get home until four, after I dropped him off at Slaughter's barracks room, and I woke Cheryl coming in. She didn't say a word. I figured she'd be mad and she looked it, but when I got in bed she rolled over to me and gave me a little hug, even though I was stinking of booze.

Slaughter passed Weissert to Addis, Addis passed him to Greeley, and so on. We had somebody with him the whole weekend until we were sure he was good.

When I wasn't with Weissert and the rest of the squad, I sat on the couch with Vicar, watching the baseball games Cheryl'd taped for me. Sometimes Cheryl and I talked about her seven months, about the wives left behind, about her family, her job, her boss. Sometimes she'd ask little questions. Sometimes I'd answer. And glad as I was to be in the States, and even though I hated the past seven months and the only thing that kept me going was the Marines I served with and the thought of coming home, I started feeling like I wanted to go back. Because fuck all this.

The next week at work was all half-days and bullshit. Medical appointments to deal with injuries guys had been hiding or sucking up. Dental appointments. Admin. And every evening, me and Vicar watching TV on the couch, waiting for Cheryl to get back from her shift at Texas Roadhouse.

Vicar'd sleep with his head in my lap, waking up whenever I'd reach down to feed him bits of salami. The vet told Cheryl that's bad, but he deserved something good. Half the time when I pet him I'd rub up against one of his tumors and that had to hurt. It looked like it hurt him to do everything, wag his tail, eat his chow. Walk. Sit. And when he'd vomit, which was every other day, he'd hack like he was choking, revving up for a good twenty seconds before anything came out. It was the noise that bothered me. I didn't mind cleaning the carpet.

And then Cheryl'd come home and look at us and shake her head and smile and say, "Well, you're a sorry bunch."

I wanted Vicar around, but I couldn't bear to look at him. I guess that's why I let Cheryl drag me out of the house that weekend. We took my combat pay and did a lot of shopping. Which is how America fights back against the terrorists.

So here's an experience. Your wife takes you shopping in Wilmington. Last time you walked down a city street, your Marine on point went down the side of the road, checking ahead and scanning the roofs across from him. The Marine behind him checks the windows on the top levels of the buildings, the Marine behind him gets the windows a little lower, and so on down until your guys have the street level covered, and the Marine in back has the rear. In a city there's a million places they can kill you from. It freaks you out at first. But you go through like you were trained and it works.

In Wilmington, you don't have a squad, you don't have a battle buddy, you don't even have a weapon. You startle ten times checking for it and it's not there. You're safe, so your alertness should be at white, but it's not.

Instead, you're stuck in an American Eagle Outfitters. Your wife gives you some clothes to try on and you walk into the tiny dressing room. You close the door, and you don't want to open it again.

Outside, there're people walking around by the windows like it's no big deal. People who have no idea where Fallujah is, where three members of your platoon died. People who've spent their whole lives at white.

They'll never get even close to orange. You can't, until the first time you're in a firefight, or the first time an IED goes off that you missed, and you realize that everybody's life, everybody's life, depends on you not fucking up. And you depend on them.

Some guys go straight to red. They stay like that for a while and then they crash, go down past white, down to whatever is lower than "I don't fucking care if I die." Most everybody else stays orange, all the time.

Here's what orange is. You don't see or hear like you used to. Your brain chemistry changes. You take in every piece of the environment, everything. I could spot a dime in the street twenty yards away. I had antennae out that stretched down the block. It's hard to even remember exactly what that felt like. I think you take in too much information to store so you just forget, free up brain space to take in everything about the next moment that might keep you alive. And then you forget that moment too, and focus on the next. And the next. And the next. For seven months.

So that's orange. And then you go shopping in Wilmington, unarmed, and you think you can get back down to white? It'll be a long fucking time before you get down to white.

By the end of it I was amped up. Cheryl didn't let me drive home. I would have gone a hundred miles per hour. And when we got back we saw Vicar had thrown up again, right by the door. I looked for him and he was there on the couch, trying to stand on shaky legs. And I said, "Goddamn it, Cheryl. It's fucking time."

She said, "You think I don't know?"

I looked at Vicar.

She said, "I'll take him to the vet tomorrow."

I said, "No."

She shook her head. She said, "I'll take care of it."

I said, "You mean you'll pay some asshole a hundred bucks to kill my dog."

She didn't say anything.

I said, "That's not how you do it. It's on me."

She was looking at me in this way I couldn't deal with. Soft. I looked out the window at nothing.

She said, "You want me to go with you?"

I said, "No. No."

"Okay," she said. "But it'd be better."

She walked over to Vicar, leaned down, and hugged him. Her hair fell over her face and I couldn't see if she was crying. Then she stood up, walked to the bedroom, and gently closed the door.

I sat down on the couch and scratched Vicar behind the ears and I came up with a plan. Not a good plan, but a plan. Sometimes that's enough.

There's a dirt road near where I live and a stream off the road where the light filters in around sunset. It's pretty. I used to go running there sometimes. I figured it'd be a good spot for it.

It's not a far drive. We got there right at sunset. I parked just off the road, got out, pulled my rifle out of the trunk, slung it over my shoulders, and moved to the passenger side. I opened the door and lifted Vicar up in my arms and carried him down to the stream. He was heavy and warm, and he licked my face as I carried him, slow lazy licks from a dog that's been happy all his life. When I put him down and stepped back he looked up at me. He wagged his tail. And I froze.

Only one other time I hesitated like that. Midway through Fallujah an insurgent snuck through our perimeter. When we raised the alarm he disappeared. We freaked, scanning everywhere, until Curtis looked down in this water cistern that'd been used as a cesspit, basically a big round container filled a quarter way with liquid shit.

The insurgent was floating in it, hiding beneath the liquid and only coming up for air. It was like a fish rising up to grab a fly sitting on the top of the water. His mouth would break the surface, open for a breath and then snap shut, and he'd submerge. I couldn't imagine it. Just smelling it was bad enough. About four or five Marines aimed straight down, fired into the shit. Except me.

Staring at Vicar it was the same thing. This feeling, like, something in me is going to break if I do this. And I thought of Cheryl bringing Vicar to the vet, of some stranger putting his hands on my dog, and I thought, I have to do this.

I didn't have a shotgun, I had an AR-15. Same, basically, as an M16, what I'd been trained on, and I'd been trained to do it right. Sight alignment, trigger control, breath control. Focus on the iron sights, not the target. The target should be blurry.

I focused on Vicar, then on the sights. Vicar disappeared into a gray blur. I switched off the safety.

There had to be three shots. It's not just pull the trigger and you're done. Got to do it right. Hammer pair to the body. A final well-aimed shot to the head.

The first two have to be fired quick, that's important. Your body is mostly water, so a bullet striking through is like a stone thrown in a pond. It creates ripples. Throw in a second stone soon after the first, and in between where they hit the water gets choppy. That happens in your body, especially when it's two 5.56 rounds traveling at supersonic speeds. Those ripples can tear organs apart.

If I were to shoot you on either side of your heart, one shot . . .

and then another, you'd have two punctured lungs, two sucking chest wounds. Now you're good and fucked. But you'll still be alive long enough to feel your lungs fill up with blood.

If I shoot you there with the shots coming fast, it's no problem. The ripples tear up your heart and lungs and you don't do the death rattle, you just die. There's shock, but no pain.

I pulled the trigger, felt the recoil, and focused on the sights, not on Vicar, three times. Two bullets tore through his chest, one through his skull, and the bullets came fast, too fast to feel. That's how it should be done, each shot coming quick after the last so you can't even try to recover, which is when it hurts.

I stayed there staring at the sights for a while. Vicar was a blur of gray and black. The light was dimming. I couldn't remember what I was going to do with the body.

NORA KRUG

■

Kamikaze

FROM *A Public Space*

KAMI KAZE

神 風

by Nora Krug

In December 1943, 20-year-old Ena Takehiko was drafted into the Japanese imperial navy.

In 1944, the political situation in Japan drastically worsened

Japan is in danger. who can protect us from this danger? Not the generals, but the young ones, the ones with the hearts of children.

and admiral Ohnishi proposed a "special attack unit" made up of kamikaze pilots

A young, very talented pilot named Seki was asked if he wanted to lead the first ever kamikaze attack and die a hero.

I accept your offer. Please assign me to the post.

Seki had recently gotten married.

You are already gods. And just like gods you don't have any desires. You will sleep for a long time.

He didn't want to commit suicide.

Right before his sortie, he handed one of the officers a lock of his hair

which was delivered to his mother right after his death.

From then on, young soldiers were asked if they would volunteer to be part of the "special attack units." Most of them were 17-26 years old.

Volunteers were asked to write down their names on a piece of paper. Everyone else was supposed to leave the sheet blank.

Almost all of the pilots volunteered. No one wanted to stay alive while seeing their friends die.

If a soldier refused, he was listed anyway.

Many weeks passed

until the day and time of the soldiers' sorties were scheduled.

An intense week of training would follow.

The night before the sortie was spent cele-brating, drinking sake, eating dried fish,

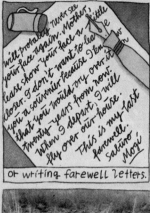

I will probably never see your face again. Mother, please show your face a little closer. I don't want to leave you a souvenir because I'm afraid that you would cry over it even twenty years from now. When I depart, I will fly over our house. This is my last farewell.
Saburo Mori

or writing farewell letters.

Village girls made dolls and waist-bands, stained with their own blood

and gave them to the pilots as gifts before takeoff.

Pilots had a ritual last cup of sake and bowed eastward, in the direction of the imperial palace.

The girls decorated the planes' cockpits with cherry branches.

Many of the planes were in very bad condition

and some of the soldiers crashed right after take-off. The cockpits became the soldiers' coffins.

The kamikaze plane units were escorted by two additional planes to ensure that the mission was carried out and also to protect pilots from attacks.

Only about 16 out of every 100 kamikaze planes were able to hit an enemy ship. Around 4000 kamikaze pilots gave their lives.

lost of them simply Vanished forever in the depth of the Ocean.

Sometimes the bodies of dead kamikaze pilots were recovered and buried at sea by American naval officers.

Pilots who returned due to bad weather or because they weren't able to locate the enemy planes, were pitied by their comrades and occasionally punished by their superiors.

Reportedly, one pilot returned to the base after nine failed attempts.

After an aborted mission, some pilots preferred crashing into the ocean on purpose, in order not to have to return to the base.

Toward the end of the war, pilots sometimes only received half a tank of petrol for their sortie. Sometimes the mechanics secretly filled the tank up to the brim.

By 1945, Japan's situation deteriorated. Pilots secretly picked up American radio signals, learning about Japan's large losses.

The war was already lost. Nonetheless, the Japanese military continued ordering young men to perform suicide attacks.

From that point, even regular soldiers were drafted into the "special attack unit."

Ena Takehiko was a student at the best university in Tokyo, when he was drafted into the navy.

In March 1945, Ena was assigned to a kamikaze unit.

Ena prepared for his mission and practiced how to descend on enemy ships at the air training base.

Ena's sortie as the commander of a three-man kamikaze unit was scheduled for April 28th, 1945.

Why didn't you drop the bomb? Do you mean to kill us all, or what?

Please forgive me!

Soon after, Ena's plane developed technical problems, and he and his comrades had to return to the base.

May 11th, 1945

After a final toast at the command post, I encounter my final hours. My doom looms, wretched and un—Just. I'm thinking of my family and silently bid my last farewell.

Ena's next sortie was scheduled for May 11th, 1945.

After days of waiting, the time had come for Ena and his two comrades to leave.

We have to drop the bomb! We have to hurry!

Hello?!?

Shortly after takeoff, Ena noticed a strange smell.

They dropped the bomb and landed.

The three soldiers arrived on Kutoshima, a Japanese island completely isolated from the world.

The islanders warmly welcomed the three navy soldiers.

There was no running water, nor electricity; there were no newspapers, nor transport ships.

Noone on the island knew about the status of the war, and Ena wasn't able to get in touch with the military base.

The islanders were going hungry, but they saved the most nutritious food for the newly arrived soldiers.

Shibata suffered bad burns during an emergency landing on Kuroshima. He was found only three days after the crash.

A group of young girls looked after Shibata's injuries. Even a horse was slaughtered, so that its fat could be used as an ointment for Shibata's wounds.

One of the girls, Shina, was particularly devoted to Shibata. She quietly endured his frequent angry outbursts when he cried out in pain and fever.

Ena frequently visited Shibata, and they became friends.

One day, Abe, the other stranded soldier, decided to return to the mainland together

With a boy from the island, despite the threat of enemy submarines. He promised Shibata he would fly over the island on his next kamikaze sortie and drop packages with medicine.

The small fishing boat weathered a storm, and after 31 hours finally arrived at Japan's mainland.

A few days later, a kamikaze plane circled kuroshima, and a package with medicine was dropped over the island.

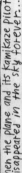

Then the plane and its kamikaze pilot disappeared in the sky forever...

Ena felt like a prisoner on death row. He used his time on the island as best as he could and instructed the islanders on what to do during an enemy attack.

Without any means of communication enemy planes could only be spotted by their sound. Sometimes American planes dropped spare bombs on the island.

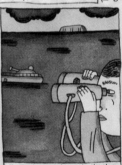

Every day, Ena went to the shore to look for ships. One day, he spotted a submarine near the shore.

Quick! Everyone get into the bunker!

Ena couldn't tell if the submarine was Japanese or American.

Shibata was still too weak to walk and Ena came to his aid.

I'm too heavy for you! Leave me behind! When the Americans are here I'll commit suicide!

No! I'm staying with you! Then we can die together right here!

Banzai

Banzai!

shortly after, the submarine raised a Japanese flag.

Finally we can die!

After their 82 days on the island, the soldiers were instructed to return to the mainland, and to accomplish their suicide mission.

On the night before the soldiers' departure, the islanders organized a farewell party with special foods.

But an unexpected American air raid put a sudden end to the gathering.

Back on the continent, Shibata was taken to hospital. Ena and his comrades were instructed to travel back to the base.

HIROSHIMA! HIROSHIMA! Please don't spend too much time outside.

On the way, the train stopped in Hiroshima, where Ena and his comrades changed into a different train, which was scheduled to leave from the center of town.

It was August 7th 1945

The three soldiers had to walk 13 miles, in order to get to the other train station. It was extremely hot.

What on earth is this?

It smelled of burnt flesh.

The things Ena saw then made him abandon all hope.

He saw a man who was alive, but whose intestines hung down from his belly.

He saw someone whose face was swollen to a degree that it was impossible to make out the person's eyes, nose and mouth.

Ena felt as though his soul was cleansed.

e swore to never again be involved in any form of war.

Why did you return alive?

On August 15th, the emperor broadcast his capitulation. Ena was no longer a soldier, but, as a surviving kamikaze pilot, despised by some.

Club soda makes you feel less hungry.

Ena went back to university in Tokyo. Only half of his former college friends had survived.

Ena and Shibata met frequently in Tokyo.

A few years after the war, Ena returned to Kuroshima. Shibata asked him to find Shina, the girl who had looked after him, and to ask her if she would marry Shibata.

I'm already married.

In 2004, Ena erected a Buddhist statue on Kuroshima, and he decided that he would commemorate his friends who had died as kamikaze pilots every year on the island.

na Takehiko is in his late 80s and lives as a retired soybean exporter in Japan.

ources: Wings of Defeat (Dir. Risa Morimoto), Kamikaze in Color (Dir. Ron Marans), Kamikaze Diaries (Auth. Emiko Ohnuki-Tierney), OKKOU NO MACHI: CHIRAN (AUTH. SANAE SATO). THANK YOU to: Ena Takehiko, Ai Tatebayashi, William Gordon (Wesley University).

ANTHONY MARRA

∎

The Palace of the People

FROM *Narrative Magazine*

You people with eyes are always so impatient.
——Daniel Alarcón

"IS THERE MORE, SERGEY FEDOROVICH?" my father demanded on
the day I received the notice of conscription from the Leningrad Military District headquarters. He stood in the doorway and held a half
gram of heroin in a slip of folded paper. I slouched to the floor of my
bedroom, my shoulder blades breaking paint peels from the wall.

"Is there more?" he asked again. His breaths were labored. Partially from shouting, partially from smoking three packs a day for
thirty years. I still hadn't answered the question. I certainly hoped
there was more, but I wasn't optimistic. He opened my dresser drawers and left my clothes piled on the floor. He upturned the mattress
and left the sheets dangling from the bedposts, left my club remix
tapes broken beneath his feet, left the spiderwebs hanging in the ceiling corners. When I was nine he had left to serve a prison term, and
four years later he returned.

"It there any more?" His voice was soft and beaten by my silence.
He sat in the rocking chair and pitched back and forth. His features
looked small and limp, as if drawn on a deflated balloon.

"More of what?" I said.

"More of this." He unfolded the paper.

"It's just brown sugar. For tea."

"Horseshit. You use a spoon to put sugar in tea. Not a hypodermic
needle."

I couldn't deny his logic, so I denied everything else. But he waved away my protestations.

"Do you have the virus?" he asked, a note of urgency in the question.

"No." I felt fairly confident in my answer. I'd shared needles with only three friends.

My father stood and lumbered to the door, his great belly leading the way. "Seryozha," he said without turning around. "Until the army takes you, you will spend your days working."

The next morning I followed my father to the top floor of the apartment building. A gash ran down the metal door of apartment 82. "Ridiculous," my father muttered as he knocked. "They make new doors from old tins to save metal, and now burglars need only a can opener to break in." I knew the next line was coming. Like a sigh, it punctuated all my father's lamentations on the state of modern Russia. "I miss Brezhnev."

Two doors opened, the outer made of recycled tins, the interior made of wood, and I saw the legless man. Midthirties, clean shaved, his hair as well oiled as a ball bearing. He smelled of cheap Ukrainian tobacco and vegetable shortening. He sat in a wheelchair. Two strips of leather stretching between the rubber wheels, shiny metal, all sorts of levers and adjustments. Likely the most advanced mode of transport owned by anyone in the building.

"This is my son, Sergey Fedorovich, but you may call him Seryozha," my father said, then gestured to the legless man. "And this is Kirill Ivanovich."

"Junior Sergeant Kirill Ivanovich," the legless man corrected. He didn't meet my outstretched hand. I felt slighted for a moment, then shrugged it off. A legless man must be wary of whom he trusts with his remaining appendages.

My father went into the kitchen to speak with Kirill, and I poked around the flat. The rooms were surprisingly well ordered, the furniture arranged at right angles. Nothing but dust and table legs touching the floor. A screen partitioned the lavatory into two chambers, one for the shower and sink, the other for the commode. Dirty dishes sat in the shower stall. Large glass jars of water stood along the baseboard, and clouds of rust hovered in the bottom inch of each. Did this legless man know something we didn't? Summer water shortages didn't usually begin for another month. I was thirsty and considered dipping my hand in for a sip, but it seemed unwise to drink anything found in the bathroom of a legless man.

A bookshelf stood in the living room. It was filled with yellowed Red Army field manuals and state-censored versions of nineteenth-century novels, the sort of kitsch sold to Western tourists outside the Winter Palace. I picked up a state-censored copy of *The Brothers Karamazov*. It was one hundred and thirty pages long and had blurbs from Lenin and Khrushchev. If I'd been born twenty years earlier, I'd have been assigned this slender copy of the book, and I'd have finished reading it. And if I'd finished reading it, I'd have passed my Unified State Examination in literature. But I was born in 1989 and was assigned the full, unexpurgated account of the devilish Karamazovs. I read only the first two hundred of the novel's nine hundred pages, and I did not pass my exam, and St. Petersburg State University did not want me. The army did.

A pistol sat on the coffee table, black metal polished to a warm luster. I picked it up, rubbed my thumb across the grip. I wondered if somewhere in Chechnya, a Muslim man my age was also holding a gun for the first time.

"Put it down."

Kirill wheeled through the doorway, my father behind him.

"Are you worried someone will steal the rest of your legs?" I asked, nodding to his stumps. Kirill didn't smile, and I put the gun on the table.

"You are now employed," my father said.

"By whom?"

"By Kirill Ivanovich."

"Junior Sergeant Kirill Ivanovich," the legless man corrected.

"Yes, you will be working for the junior sergeant."

"You must be joking," I said. My father never joked.

"Tomorrow morning," he said and appeared quite pleased. "You'll be the early bird."

I felt more like the worm. Some small part of me wished I had never tried heroin. The rest of me wanted to be high.

Deferments from military service were given to men in university or prison. Though some of my friends had the grades, none had the bribe money to gain admittance to university, so naturally we all planned on going to prison. We called it higher education. During our final spring in secondary school, we skipped class to drink beer in Tauride Gardens. Gaps in the gray snow revealed a field of dead grass. We stood in a small huddle and smoked cheap cigarettes that burned quick and harsh like dried leaves.

"No way I'm going to have some drill sergeant telling me what to do," Valeri said. He picked white grains from his scalp. I couldn't tell if they were lint or dandruff.

"Two hundred were beaten to death last year before they ever reached Chechnya. Dedovshchina, it's no joke."

"Forget dedovshchina. Two years with nothing but your palm to fuck, that's the worst."

"That's why I'm saying jail time is soft time. Anyone connected inside gets conjugal visits."

"Where's Big Pussy with those beers?" Our names were Aleksandr Kharlamov, Valeri Lebedev, Ivan Vladim, and Sergey Tretiak, but we called each other Tony Soprano, Silvio Dante, Big Pussy Bonpensiero, Christopher Moltisanti, and 2Pac. We watched bootlegged HBO and A&E crime shows, listened to rap, and smoked weed that was all seeds and stems. Our parents learned English from the Beatles, but we learned it from Biggie.

Another afternoon, in another park, the subject came up again.

"The trick is to go to higher education just until the war is over."

"And how do you do that?"

"Easy," I said. "You guess how long the war will last, how long you need to go to jail, then you find a crime that fits the punishment."

None of us had passed Russian civilization class, but we staked our futures on the progression of history. We took bets. The war in Chechnya would be finished in a year, two years, five. We found crimes with sentence lengths to fit each prediction. One year for assaulting an Ossetian, an Armenian, or a Jew. Two years for narcotics possession of over three grams. Five for assaulting an ethnic Russian. We wanted to become gangsters, but our fathers were all failures. They drove gypsy cabs, pumped gas, and mopped floors. They were relics from the past and didn't know how to make money by taking money. We needed higher education.

We all received conscription letters the same day, and we carried them with us to the park. The envelope was brown manila, the standard size and shape of all governmental correspondences. Even before I opened the letter, I knew it contained the conscription notice. It was the first letter I'd ever received, excluding those my father had written from prison.

Dear Sergey Fedorovich Tretiak, This letter is to inform you . . .

I compared the letters with those of my friends. But for our names, they were identical. We were all to report to the Military District of Leningrad Oblast on the last Friday of August. If we all died in Chechnya, I wondered, would our families receive form letters in brown manila identical but for our names?

"I'm going to knock off a liquor store," Aleksandr announced and killed a cigarette in three puffs. "Three years, I think that will cover it."

"Too long, Silvio," Ivan said. "The new president down there made a sex tape before getting tapped for the job. He's huge. I'm going with six months. I'll mug a tourist."

"Four years," Valeri stated as he picked at his scalp. The white grains in his hair were neither lint nor dandruff but lice. "I'm going to steal a car."

"You'll only get a year for that," Ivan objected.

"A year for a Lada or Volga, but a BMW or a Mercedes? That's four, easy."

They looked at me. "I haven't decided how many years," I said. "But don't worry. I'm in. I'm all in."

We pounded fists, then made our way to Ploshchad Lenina to pick up a six hundred-ruble envelope of heroin. The waters of the Neva sparkled, oil rainbows arcing over the swells. Tourists came to shore from pontoon boats, all oohs and ahhs, reaching for their cameras as if the pre-Revolution mansions lining the banks were flocks of rare birds. I didn't see the rush. Those pink and purple powder puffs weren't flying anywhere. We turned onto Arsenalnaya, then onto Komsomola. In the distance Kresty Prison looked like a palace. Great red brick walls, spires, and onion domes. In literature class we had once read an Anna Akhmatova poem about the prison. Our teacher told us about the poem's genesis. Akhmatova's son was detained for seventeen months, and with hundreds of other women she waited outside those great brick walls for word of the accusation, the verdict, the sentence. "Can you describe this?" a woman with blue lips whispered to Akhmatova, and she answered, "Yes, I can."

Now, outside the gates, a line of women waited, the wives and mothers of pretrial prisoners. We catcalled and whistled and asked if they wanted to party with us. Maybe seventy years ago we would have thought them tragic. But in this century we just thought they were alone and available. They didn't pay any attention to us, and we walked onward to Ploshchad Lenina.

"I'm not scared," I said, and Valeri, Ivan, and Aleksandr all agreed that they too were unafraid. I didn't know if they meant Kresty or Chechnya. Two blocks from Lenin's statue, I gathered crumbled bills from my friends and went to the third-floor flat of a communal housing complex to pick up the heroin.

The job was like nothing found in the classified sections of *Pravda* and *Novaya Gazeta*, the ads seeking multilingual men with business degrees, and attractive young women to work as dancers in Western Europe. No glamour, no status, no glitz to propel me past the face control at the Jakata or Decadence nightclubs. That first day I dragged my ass out of bed at four in the morning to help Kirill dress. The shirt and pants of his military uniform appeared to be cut from the same sheet of rough wool.

"How the hell do you normally get dressed?" I asked.

Kirill shrugged. "I can do it myself. It just takes longer."

"So what? You have an appointment with the sunrise?"

He smiled, his teeth the color of cooking oil. "With the city."

The pants were hemmed mid-thigh, and after I hoisted them up his knobby hips, Kirill pointed to a roll of duct tape on the divan. "You must tape the stumps."

"Fuck no."

"You must learn how."

"You're missing your legs, not your hands. Tape them yourself."

He just pointed to the duct tape, and I picked it up. I didn't want to fail my father. The stumps were taped within two minutes. Kirill greased his hair with vegetable shortening, combing it through a dozen times before he was satisfied with the part. The final touch was a squirt of knockoff Calvin Klein cologne, which smelled like flavored rum. I lifted Kirill into the wheelchair and pushed him into the hall.

"I'll go down by myself," he said when we reached the stairs. He used a sheet of plywood to sled down the steps and clasped onto the handrail, his hands protected in leather gloves. It took ten minutes to reach the ground floor.

"Wait," he said. The front door of the apartment building clunked closed behind us. "I want to catch my breath."

"You're in a wheelchair. All you can do is breathe."

Kirill shook his head and lit a cigarette. He looked disappointed. "You people with your legs," he said. "Always wanting to run."

I followed Kirill's example and lit a cigarette. The White Nights always ended in Gray Mornings. The clouds just sat in the sky, those big lazy bastards. Across the Neva River, smokestacks stood taller than any of the city's imperial obelisks. Across the street, a pack of feral dogs chased a homeless man through a vacant lot. Our school textbooks said as many as one thousand serfs died making St. Petersburg. Our teacher said the number was closer to one hundred thousand. The lead dog bit the vagrant on the ass. I didn't think this city was worth even the one thousand.

"I thought you wanted to get going," I said.

"Breakfast is the most important meal of the day," Kirill replied and looked at his cigarette. "It is important that we take the time to savor it."

The blue and white spires of Smolny Convent shrank behind us as I pushed Kirill along Shapalemaya Ulitsa. We took a left at Chernyshevskogo Prospekt. Casinos projected neon light across nineteenth-century palaces. Fires lifted through the grates of rusted cigarette cans. The darkened windows of sushi restaurants and Irish pubs, liquor stores opening before coffee shops, a Mercedes Benz with tinted windows and a driver frowning at his sidearm, Ladas so sooted over their license plates were unreadable. We waited for a break in traffic. St. Petersburg did not sleep in summertime.

"You must carry me over the gate," Kirill said when we reached the entrance of Chernyshevskaya Metro Station. I popped two tokens in the turnstile and lifted him by the armpits. He was heavy for half a body.

Newspaper vendors called the headlines as I broke down the wheelchair. *Sochi Prepares for 2014 Olympics. Kresty Prison to Be Turned into Hotel-Entertainment Complex. Two Dead and Twenty-Six Injured in Grozny Suicide Bombing.*

"On average, it takes three and a half minutes on the escalator to reach the platform," Kirill explained as we rode down the escalator. He sat, I stood. "Do you know why they built the metro so deep? So that the tunnels could be used as shelters for a nuclear attack."

"Do people hit by atomic bombs ever lose just their legs?" I asked.

"I don't know." Kirill looked at his stumps. "I've never been hit by one."

When we reached the platform, he put on his leather gloves. He crawled across the marble tiles on clenched fists.

"How do I look?" he asked.

"Short."

As a rush of hot air announced the approaching train, Kirill gave me instructions. The act was nothing new. One couldn't go more than three metro stops without seeing a crippled veteran from the Chechen Wars. They sang folk songs and played fiddles. They sat on wooden pallets and recited Pushkin. Some did acrobatics, contorting their lifeless limbs like pastry dough. Others merely drank and mumbled tales of Chechnya so harrowing we knew there could be no truth to them.

The train exhaled a stream of passengers. Kirill slipped through the shuffle of legs, and I followed. Young men offered their seats to women and the elderly, treating them with a level of propriety rarely seen above ground. The doors closed, the wheels hummed against the rails, and Kirill began. He didn't sing the national anthem, didn't pull a harmonica from his pocket or a horror story from his past. He just crawled through the parted crowd on clenched fists, his head raised to meet every glance. As instructed, I pushed the wheelchair behind him and watched the rubles fall into the basket.

"Give him a few rubles, Masha," a babushka in a kerchief whispered to her friend. "The poor man is sober."

"You are a hero," said a middle-aged man wearing pressed trousers. "It's better to lose your legs than your honor."

For the length of the train car, Kirill did not speak. He did not solicit charity or acknowledge the alms received from morning commuters. He just climbed over their feet.

One hundred and forty rubles made on the two-minute journey to Ploshchad Vosstaniya Station. I looked at the coins and wrinkled bills sitting in the basket. It was more than my father made in an hour.

"You don't want them to think you're making money," Kirill whispered as he pocketed the change. At Ploshchad Vosstaniya, we moved to the next car.

We rode the red and green lines until noon. Nine hundred rubles by eight o'clock. Seventeen hundred by eleven. I had never known my fellow citizens possessed such generosity. For lunch we surfaced at Baltiyskaya and bought sausages and kvass from a street vendor. Summer is the only bearable season in St. Petersburg. Long days and short skirts. But I didn't even bother whistling at the long, suntanned legs of passing women. Kirill made a poor wingman.

"Forty-one new stations are scheduled to be built in the next ten years," he told me between small bites of sausage. He chewed carefully and spoke only after swallowing, as if even eating was perilous for a crippled man. "Do you know what that means?"

"Only three will be built."

"It means more people will take the metro every day. More people, more money."

"You make too much as it is. Beggars shouldn't make more money than the people they beg from."

"We work harder." Kirill smiled at a flock of pedestrians running to catch the green crosswalk light. "I'm saving for a dacha outside Pavlovsk. Wheelchair accessible. I'll be able to wash the dishes in the sink."

The ambition alone impressed me. Only criminals, politicians, and businessmen could afford dachas. Men who could walk, who had never gone to Chechnya, whose sons would never go to Chechnya. And here was Kirill.

"What a racket."

"It's an art."

"Losing limbs?"

He shook his head. "Turning loss into gain, that is art."

Kirill's words hung within a moment that might have been profound had he not subsequently farted. I stared down the block, thinking of the lessons I had learned in history class. Crowds had stormed down this street toward the Winter Palace during the October Revolution. The city was renamed Petrograd, then Leningrad. The war, the siege, the nine hundred days of hunger. Bread was made from the plaster of a building that now housed Sbarro and KFC franchises. Perhaps this is what people mean when they call St. Petersburg an art museum.

When I returned home that night, my father lay supine on the orange divan. He ate sardines from the can and let the cat lick his fingers between bites.

"Come here," he said and examined my pupils by the flame of his cigarette lighter. "They're not constricted."

The cat wrapped its tail around my father's forearm and purred as it tongued the fish oil from his fingers. I've never trusted the little devil.

"What did you learn today?" he asked.

"The average length of an escalator ride."

"Anything else?"

"That Kirill makes more money than you." A dubbed Hollywood film played on the television, Clive Owen with a Vladivostok accent. The explosions made me flinch.

"And how much of that did you make?"

"None," I admitted.

"Then I still make more than you," he said and turned back to the TV.

"Kresty is going to be turned into a hotel," I mentioned, turning to gauge his reaction.

"Again? When?"

I shrugged. "The newspaper said as soon as they build a new prison outside the city."

My father smiled. "They've been saying that for years."

Sleep did not come easily that night. The midnight sun sat on the horizon, bars of light pressed against the shutters. I'd only begun using heroin a month earlier and never more than once or twice a week. Rubber cement, vodka, gas fumes, cough syrup, there were dozens of different ways to fall from reality. Chechnya or Kresty. I didn't know which scared me more. Kirill's woolen army uniform or my father's cotton prison uniform. In another two months, one would be my own.

*   *   *

Before cancer killed her, my mother worked as a cashier at the Billa supermarket. Fifteen minutes after she left the house, my father began his day. His mobile phone was larger than his left boot, and he took calls like a man in the trenches, following orders and always responding to his superiors with *sir*. He wore rubber gloves and painter's masks and cut heroin on the kitchen table. He let me watch, and even at the age of eight I knew this was something to be kept between us.

"This is bad for you," he said. "You must promise never to eat it."

I nodded. It was a promise I kept. He crumbled raw heroin into a spice grinder, blending it with powdered infant formula, quinine, and caffeine in a flour sifter. "What are you making?" I asked him as he used measuring spoons to scoop the powder into small folds of paper.

"A living," he replied.

He allowed me to make daytime deliveries in the summer, when I was out of school and my mother was at work. A few grams to nightclub managers and upscale prostitutes, those of his customers who made the most honest livings. Before I left he gave me a series of commandments.

"You must count the money before you give them the product."

"You must not look policemen in the eye."

"You must obey all laws except the one you are breaking."

"You must not stop to speak with anyone."

"You must pretend you are a man, and you will be treated like one."

I nodded and followed all of his instructions. I bought metro tokens rather than jumping the turnstile and waited for every crosswalk signal. I was too short to be seen through peepholes, and I had to knock repeatedly before anyone opened the door. The prostitutes gave the best tips and sometimes invited me in and offered me cake. This became a sore spot in my memory as I edged through adolescence. I had been invited into the hotel rooms of the most beautiful women in St. Petersburg and been tempted only by tea cakes.

Heroin on the kitchen table and snow on the windowsill; the tattoo of a wolf in mid-stride, running up his forearm; the surgery mask strapped over his mouth; gloved hands sifting through the powder, a delicate operation: this had been my father. He was a capitalist, a man built for the New Russia. He would never have put on a uniform and lost his legs in a distant war.

My mother knew but pretended she did not. As long as she and I benefited from but were not witness to my father's misconduct, all was well. We had the first color TV set over twenty inches in the apartment building. My mother was the only cashier at Billa who owned furs. But it came to an end when she discovered that I was my father's errand boy.

"Where were you?" she asked when I walked through the front door one warm August afternoon. She had come home from work early. "What were you doing?"

"Delivering a living," I said. She slapped me across the cheek, then embraced me as tears ran down my stinging flesh.

"I will not live with two criminals," she said.

The next day my father was arrested outside our apartment.

For the length of the summer, I avoided my friends. I did not return their phone calls and was careful to keep away from the parks and bars they frequented. I saw them only once, in mid-July, on the Gostiny Dvor metro platform, as Kirill described the forging of iron rails. Valeri saw me first. He was scratching his crotch, and I wondered if the lice had migrated southward.

"2Pac, where you been?" he asked. Ivan stood behind him, squinting at the cigarette in his hand as if hoping to light it by force of concentration.

I looked down at Kirill. "Just working."

"You hear about Aleksandr? He knocked off his liquor store two weeks back," Ivan said. "He got picked up down the block. Didn't even get a chance to spend the money."

"Is he in Kresty?" I asked.

Valeri nodded. "We visited him. He said it's not bad. No water shortages. Free electricity. Said he's making all sorts of connections. We're going to join him this weekend."

"On what charge?"

"We're going to steal a police car," Ivan said, forgetting about the cigarette. "You want in?"

I shook my head. "I'm going to wait a few more weeks. But I'll see you in there."

"You promise?" Ivan asked.

"Yeah, no doubt."

"It's your neck," Valeri said before walking off. "In prison, your head might stay attached to it."

Kirill didn't speak until Ivan and Valeri had disappeared into the white-tiled pedestrian tunnel toward the Nevsky Prospekt station. We watched vendors hawk individual Bic pens and hotel toiletries as we waited for the train.

"Are you going to go through with it?" Kirill asked. No disdain in his voice, nothing that even approached disapproval.

"I don't know," I said.

Kirill nodded. The breeze of an approaching train whipped through my hair, but Kirill's, slick with vegetable shortening, remained unmoved.

The weeks passed, days repeating without distinction. I hadn't touched heroin since the night my father found the half-gram in a fold of brown paper. Each morning I woke at four and helped Kirill dress. We breakfasted on Marlboro Mediums and worked the train cars till noon. We bought lunch from street vendors, and Kirill taught me the history of the metro system.

"It's the thirteenth busiest metro in the world," he said between small bites of sausage. It was a holy day, the Feast of Peter and Paul, and the city was woozy with warm weather and summer cocktails. "Yet Petersburg is just the world's forty-fifth biggest city. What does this tell you?"

I shrugged. It was like being back in school. "That we're too poor to afford cars."

Kirill continued as if he hadn't heard me. "It tells you that we have a metro system to be proud of. New York and London, do you think their metros have crystal chandeliers and marble floors and bronze statues?"

"Of course they do."

"They do not," he said adamantly. "They have graffiti and crumbling walls and floodlights. They do not have beauty. Have you heard of the Palace of the People?"

"I've seen commercials for the new season," I said. Finally Kirill was talking about something I cared about. "Ten newlyweds in one of those old palaces on the Fontanka Embankment. The first couple to cheat wins a trip to Paris, right?"

"I'm not talking about the TV show, I'm talking about the metro."
He breathed heavily. He'd completely forgotten about his sausage.
"The Palace of the People, that's what Lenin, Stalin, and Khrushchev
all called it. A palace not for czars and princes, but for you and me."

His face was red. I'd noticed that he was most comfortable below
ground. "Let's go back down," I suggested and wheeled him toward
the entrance of Pushkinskaya Station.

"You must not work on April twentieth," he advised as I lifted
him over the turnstile. "The skinhead gangs are the worst on
Hitler's birthday."

I nodded but still did not see how this advice applied to me.

On the platform we passed beggars with all manner of deformi-
ties. The civilians were worse than the vets. A three-meter-tall giant. A boy without bones pooled in a wooden crate. A woman whose
face was a seashell. They came out en masse on holy days to solicit
alms from the city's devout. Some held cardboard signs describing
the horrors of their ailments. Kirill climbed out of his wheelchair
and crawled past them, greeting each by name. I wondered if these
freaks and weirdos had social lives. If they made plans for the weekend and went on blind dates. If they gossiped and despised and loved
one another.

As we waited at the edge of the platform, I asked Kirill why he
never recounted how he'd lost his legs, why he was silent and defiant
to the point of ingratitude when seeking charity.

He thought for a moment before speaking. His words were almost lost in the clatter of the arriving train. "You can live off the pity
of others," he said. "But if you want a dacha, you must also make
them proud."

"How did it happen?" I asked. The question had been weighing
on me all summer, and I had only six days before my military service began.

"I don't like talking about it," he said. The rush of air from the
approaching train breezed down the track. It was all relief. As the
train pulled into the station, Kirill turned back to the assembled
beggars. I thought he would salute them, but he just smiled and
climbed aboard.

That evening a military uniform sat on the kitchen table. Blue-gray, the same rough wool as Kirill's. I unfolded the trousers, held them to my waist. The legs reached past my ankles and lay flat against the floor.

"I'll take them to the dry cleaner tomorrow," my father said from the doorway. The cat followed a few paces behind him. "You'll look smart once the legs are hemmed."

"I don't want to go," I said to the cat. It tilted its head, then snapped its tail as it strode from the room. The heartless animal, not a sliver of sympathy.

I met my father's eyes. "If we could, we'd all stay in the womb," he said. He walked over to me, put his hand on my shoulder. The half-smoked cigarette between his fingers made my eyes water. He dropped the cigarette into a soda can and wiped the tears from my cheeks with his thumbs.

"Look at you," he said and leaned down to kiss my forehead. "My Seryozha. You will make me proud."

The sky was cloudless the next morning. I ignored Kirill's history lessons as I pushed him to Chernyshevskaya. I didn't care if his grandfather had worked as a train conductor and later fought in the war under Zhukov, reaching Berlin and taking a shit in the Reichstag commode. In five days I was to report for duty in a pair of hemmed trousers.

For the first six hours I kept quiet. Kirill crawled across train cars, and I pushed the wheelchair behind him. Rubles fell into the basket, and he collected them at every stop.

"Let's have lunch," I said when we reached Ploshchad Lenina.

"It's only eleven-thirty."

"I want a cigarette."

Kirill sighed and scrambled into the wheelchair. I pushed him to the escalator, and he climbed out, sitting with his back to the stair. He counted the morning's earnings and appeared pleased with the sum.

"You must always keep your money in the front pockets of your pants," he said. "Most thieves will be too disgusted by your stumps to go anywhere near them."

"You keep saying 'you,'" I said softly. It was a quiet realization.

Frowning, he replied, "I'm talking to you. What else should I call you?"

"You keep giving instructions, like you're training me. 'You must do this, you must do that to be a good beggar.' "

"I was speaking in generalizations," he began, but I had already stopped listening. He was teaching me how to live without legs. I was his apprentice, and I was terrified.

I can't remember the faces of the bystanders. I don't know what was shouted by whom when I let the folded wheelchair fall down the escalator. I remember the headlines of the newspaper that day, pinned against kiosks of cigarette vendors: *Economic Turmoil in Western Europe Worsens, Sakhalin–Vladivostok Pipeline Begins Construction, Three Soldiers Killed on Chechen Border*. I remember punching him until my knuckles looked like broken raspberries, grabbing his greased hair at the part and slamming his face into the escalator step again and again.

Kirill went limp, and I reached into the front pockets of his pants, taking the bills and loose change and sprinting upstairs. Half a block away, I turned around and saw the escalator deposit Kirill at street level. Commuters stepped over his body. I spent the money on heroin, and I sat in a shooting gallery in an outer suburb, renting a needle for two rubles a blast.

Kresty Prison had originally been the imperial wine warehouse, storing enough alcohol to keep the nobility tanked through the long arctic winter. After the emancipation of the serfs, when the state assumed from landowners the responsibility of jailing newly liberated men and women, Kresty was converted into a penal facility. The renovation was performed by the prisoners themselves, my Russian civilization teacher said, and the prison was and remains the largest in Europe. After the Revolution, the prison mainly held political dissidents. After the Collapse, it mainly held drug offenders. Originally designed for 1,150 inmates, Kresty held 12,500 when my father was sent through the Komsomola Street gates.

I visited my father once in Kresty. Later I embellished the story for my friends. Made it sound like the prison scene in *Goodfellas*, my father the capo of the entire place. But there had been no scent of garlic or tomato sauce wafting down the corridors. Only ammonia, chlorine, and perspiration.

When I visited, the guards let me into the cell. The presence of a minor in the prison ward broke all manner of rules and regulations, but no one seemed to notice.

"It will scare him," one guard said in the waiting room. His nose looked like an overripe strawberry.

"It should," said another guard. "A few minutes in the cell now will save the little shit later on."

I followed the first guard down a long corridor to the cell blocks. His footsteps clicked over the linoleum as if he were wearing tap-dance shoes. Men with sheared heads and scrawny arms stared out from behind bars. My mother never visited my father. Maybe she would have if he'd been arrested in the purges, if his imprisonment and her hardship were worthy of an Akhmatova poem.

"Prisoner four-seven-six-three-two-eight-nine-seven-seven," the guard called out when we reached the second-to-last cell on the block. "You have a visitor."

The cell my father shared with nineteen other men was intended for solitary confinement. His head was shaved, his eyes swallowed by their sockets.

"You have any cigarettes?" he asked as he approached the bars. I shook my head. I was nine years old.

He was released four years later, serving only a third of his sentence. My mother had passed just before he was up for his first parole hearing. The state orphanages and foster homes were even more overcrowded than Kresty. The court took all this into consideration. After his release he became a civilian. He worked as a gypsy cab driver, and he stopped at every yellow light. Though I'd like to believe it was for my sake, it was for his own. He feared Kresty more than the disappointments of a lawful life. I don't know what happened to him in prison, what sucked the ambition and swagger from his heart. A few months after he was released, I got my ass beat by a couple of older kids. I came home with fat cheeks and a gashed forehead. The hollows of my eyes looked shined with black shoe polish. He opened the windowsill, brought in three icicles, and broke them with the back of a butcher knife. He slid them into a plastic shopping bag and pressed it against my face. Small splinters of glass were fixed in my forehead, and I screamed and cried as he pulled them out with bathroom tweezers. "You must be fearless," he said and gave me vodka before going back in with the tweezers. "A man who walks with fear only crawls. He deserves all the suffering of the world."

"I won't deserve it," I said, and even though my face was slick with mucus and tears, my father beamed at me with pride.

I lost two nights and all of Kirill's money. A headache and nausea, landlocked and seasick. The divan bolted to the floorboards. The diva lilting from the radio two floors below. The flutter of the high and the tremble of the comedown. Caught my reflection in a beer bottle, my pupils painted pinpricks. The room was lit by a shadeless lamp, the electricity stolen from the emergency outlet in the stairwell. A man appeared with crutches. His left arm and leg were swollen and useless, like the inflated appendages of a balloon animal. He pulled a bag of cocaine from his pocket, and he scattered it on a cooking sheet and mixed in the heroin with a phone card. He cooked it with a white plastic lighter, and the needle slurped it from the spoon, and I did not feel pain. Later he marked my veins with a Magic Marker, teaching me where the mainlines ran, saying he could tell I was new because my blood vessels sat close to the skin. I nodded, then nodded off. A woman came in the next morning and offered me a roll of toilet paper for fifty rubles. I told her I didn't need it, and she just said, "But you will someday. It is the only certainty besides death." It was the most profound statement I'd ever heard, and I bought twelve rolls and shot up again, the needle piercing through the blue star the man had drawn on my forearm. I couldn't make sense of my fingers. I had so many of them. Paint chips shook from the ceiling, and I waited for the whole thing to collapse. How many years would I get for beating a crippled veteran, for insulting the pride of our country? Twenty? Twenty-five? Others had received more time for lesser crimes. Show trials had not died with Stalin. I threw up six times. My muscles ached. I kept trying to quiet my head. It wouldn't shut the fuck up.

There was no crime greater than dishonoring a wounded war hero.

Twenty or twenty-five years in Kresty. I wondered if we would still be at war in Chechnya and if I would still have to serve.

When I returned home, I expected police cars. But just a couple of rusted bicycle frames locked to a lamppost and stripped of their hardware. Nothing had changed. The same dust sat on the same stairs, and I climbed to the eighth floor. Not to apologize, I just didn't want to face my father yet. Kirill's door was unlocked. He sat in the wheelchair, an ice pack pressed to his cheek, the pistol on the table beside him. The bruises on his face drew all attention from his stumps. He didn't reach for the phone, didn't call for help. Just reached for the gun and set it between his duct-taped thighs.

He looked at me with the expression I reserved for people like him.

"Go downstairs," he said, his voice possessing more control than it ever had before.

"Am I going to jail? Have you called the police?"

He looked offended by the question and answered simply, "I am a junior sergeant."

His face fell in and out of the shadows. He smiled, his remaining teeth standing like spare bowling pins. He was not afraid of me, and I hated him for it.

"Go downstairs, Seryozha. You're not going to prison."

But I took another step forward. Raised my hands. One step became a second and a third. One click released the safety, the second cocked the hammer. The gun sat between his stumps. My knee was a meter from the barrel when he realized what I was asking. He nodded, and I wanted to thank him, but the gunshot swallowed my breath. The floor fell from under me, and I screamed. I don't know how long I lay there before Kirill lifted me and I began to feel pain.

■

The Children

FROM *Granta*

WE LAID THEM DOWN GENTLY, in ditches and furrows and wicker baskets beneath the trees. We left them lying naked, atop blankets, on woven straw mats at the edges of the fields. We placed them in wooden apple boxes and nursed them every time we finished hoeing a row of beans. When they were older, and more rambunctious, we sometimes tied them to chairs. We strapped them onto our backs in the dead of winter in Redding and went out to prune the grapevines, but some mornings it was so cold that their ears froze and bled. In early summer, in Stockton, we left them in nearby gullies while we dug up onions and began picking the first plums. We gave them sticks to play with in our absence and called out to them from time to time to let them know we were still there. *Don't bother the dogs. Don't touch the bees. Don't wander away or Papa will get mad*. When they tired and began to cry out for us we kept on working because if we didn't we knew we would never pay off the debt on our lease. *Mama can't come*. After a while their voices grew fainter and their crying came to a stop. And at the end of the day when there was no more light in the sky, we woke them up from wherever it was they lay sleeping and brushed the dirt from their hair. *It's time to go home*.

Some of them were stubborn and willful and would not listen to a word we said. Others were more serene than the Buddha. *He came into the world smiling*. One loved her father more than anyone else. One hated bright colors. One would not go anywhere without his tin pail. One weaned herself at the age of thirteen months by pointing to a glass of milk on the counter and telling us, "I want." Several were wise beyond their years. *The fortune-teller told us he was born with the soul of an old man.* They ate at the table like grownups. They never cried. They never complained. They never left their chopsticks standing upright in their rice. They played by themselves all day long in the fields while we worked, without making a sound. They drew pictures in the dirt for hours. And whenever we tried to pick them up and carry them home they shook their heads and said, "I'm too heavy," or "Mama, rest." They worried about us when we were tired. They worried about us when we were sad. They knew, without our telling them, when our knees were bothering us or it was our time of the month. They slept with us, at night, like puppies, on wooden boards covered with hay, and for the first time since coming to America we did not mind having someone else beside us in the bed.

Always, we had favorites. Perhaps it was our firstborn, Ichiro, who made us feel so much less lonely than we had been before. *My husband has not spoken to me in more than two years.* Or our second son, Yoichi, who taught himself how to read English by the time he was four. *He's a genius.* Or Sunoko, who always tugged at our sleeve with such fierce urgency and then forgot what it was she wanted to say. "It will come to you later," we would tell her, even though it never did. Some of us preferred our daughters, who were gentle and good, and some of us, like our mothers before us, preferred our sons. *They're the better gain on the farm.* We fed them more than we did their sisters. We sided with them in arguments. We dressed them in nicer clothes. We scraped up our last pennies to take them to the doctor whenever they came down with fever, while our daughters we cared for at home. *I applied a mustard plaster to her chest and said a prayer to the god of wind and bad colds.* Because we knew that our daughters would leave us the moment they married, but our sons would provide for us in our old age.

Usually, our husbands had nothing to do with them. They never changed a single diaper. They never washed a dirty dish. They never touched a broom. In the evening, no matter how tired we were when we came in from the fields, they sat down and read the paper while we cooked dinner for the children and stayed up until late washing and mending piles of clothes. They never let us go to sleep before them. They never let us rise after the sun. *You'll set a bad example for the children.* They were silent, weathered men who tramped in and out of the house in their muddy overalls muttering to themselves about sucker growth, the price of green beans, how many crates of celery they thought we could pull from the fields. They rarely spoke to their children, or even seemed to remember their names. *Tell number three boy not to slouch when he walks.* And if things grew too noisy at the table, they clapped their hands and shouted out, "That's enough!" Their children, in turn, preferred not to speak to their fathers at all. Whenever one of them had something to say it always went through us. *Tell Papa I need a nickel. Tell Papa there's something wrong with one of the horses. Tell Papa he missed a spot shaving. Ask Papa how come he's so old.*

As soon as we could we put them to work in the fields. They picked strawberries with us in San Martin. They picked peas with us in Los Osos. They crawled behind us through the vineyards of Hughson and Del Rey as we cut down the raisin grapes and laid them out to dry on wooden trays in the sun. They hauled water. They cleared brush. They shovelled weeds. They chopped wood. They hoed in the blazing summer heat of the Imperial Valley before their bones were fully formed. Some of them were slow-moving and dreamy and planted entire rows of cauliflower sprouts upside down by mistake. Others could sort tomatoes faster than the fastest of the hired help. Many complained. They had stomachaches. Headaches. Their eyes were itching like crazy from the dust. Some of them pulled on their boots every morning without having to be told. One of them had a favorite pair of clippers, which he sharpened every evening in the barn after supper and would not let anyone else touch. One could not stop thinking about bugs. *They're everywhere.* One sat down one day in the middle of an onion patch and said she wished she'd never been born. And we wondered if we had done the right thing, bringing them into this world.

And yet they played for hours like calves in the fields. They made swords out of broken grape-stakes and dueled beneath the trees.

They made kites out of newspaper and balsa wood and tied knives to the strings and had dogfights on windy days in the sky. They made twist-up dolls out of wire and straw and did evil things to them with sharpened chopsticks in the woods. They played shadow catch shadow on moonlit nights in the orchards, just as we had back home in Japan. They played kick the can and mumblety-peg and *jan ken po*. They had contests to see who could nail together the most packing crates the night before we went to market and who could hang the longest from the walnut tree without letting go. They folded squares of paper into airplanes and birds and watched them fly away. They collected crows' nests and snakeskins, beetle shells, acorns, rusty iron stakes from down by the tracks. They learned the names of the planets. They read each other's palms. *Your lifeline is unusually short.* They told each other's fortunes. *One day you will take a long journey on a train.* They went out into the barn after supper with their kerosene lanterns and played mama and papa in the loft. *Now slap your belly and make a sound like you're dying.* And on hot summer nights, when it was ninety-eight degrees, they spread their blankets out beneath the peach trees and dreamed of picnics down by the river, a new eraser, a book, a ball, a china doll with blinking violet eyes, leaving home, one day, for the great world beyond.

Beyond the farm, they'd heard, there were strange pale children who grew up entirely indoors and knew nothing of the fields and streams. Some of these children, they'd heard, had never even seen a tree. *Their mothers won't let them go outside and play in the sun.* Beyond the farm, they'd heard, there were fancy white houses with gold-framed mirrors and crystal doorknobs and porcelain toilets that flushed with the yank of a chain. *And they don't even make a smell.* Beyond the farm, they'd heard, there were mattresses stuffed with hard metal springs that were somehow as soft as a cloud. (Goro's sister had gone away to work as a maid in the city, and when she came back she said that the beds there were so soft she had to sleep on the floor.) Beyond the farm, they'd heard, there were mothers who ate their breakfast every morning in bed and fathers who sat on cushioned chairs all day long in their offices shouting orders into a phone—and for this, they got paid. Beyond the farm, they'd heard, wherever you went you were always a stranger and if you got on the wrong bus by mistake you might never find your way home.

They caught tadpoles and dragonflies down by the creek and put them into glass jars. They watched us kill the chickens. They found the places in the hills where the deer had last slept and lay down in their round nests in the tall, flattened grass. They pulled the tails off lizards to see how long it would take them to grow back. *Nothing's happening.* They brought home baby sparrows that had fallen from the trees and fed them sweetened rice gruel with a toothpick but in the morning, when they woke, the sparrows were dead. "Nature doesn't care," we told them. They sat on the fence and watched the farmer in the next field over leading his cow up to meet with the bull. They saw a mother cat eating her own kittens. "It happens," we explained. They heard us being taken late at night by our husbands, who would not leave us alone even though we had long ago lost our looks. "It doesn't matter what you look like in the dark," we were told. They bathed with us every evening, out of doors, in giant wooden tubs heated over a fire, and sank down to their chins in the hot steaming water. They leaned back their heads. They closed their eyes. They reached out for our hands. They asked us questions. *How do you know when you're dead? What if there were no birds? What if you have red spots all over your body but nothing hurts? Is it true that the Chinese really eat pigs' feet?*

They had things to keep them safe. A red bottle cap. A glass marble. A postcard of two Russian beauties strolling along the Songhua River sent to them by an uncle who was stationed in Manchuria. They had lucky white feathers that they carried with them at all times in their pockets, and stones wrapped in soft cloth that they pulled out of drawers and held—just for a moment, until the bad feeling went away—in their hands. They had secret words that they whispered to themselves whenever they felt afraid. They had favorite trees that they climbed up into whenever they wanted to be alone. *Everyone please go away.* They had favorite sisters in whose arms they could instantly fall asleep. They had hated older brothers with whom they refused to be left alone in a room. *He'll kill me.* They had dogs from whom they were inseparable and to whom they could tell all the things they could not tell anyone else. *I broke Papa's pipe and buried it under a tree.* They had their own rules. *Never sleep with your pillow facing toward the north* (Hoshiko had gone to sleep with her pillow facing north and in the middle of the night she stopped breathing and died). They had their own rituals. *You must always throw salt where a hobo has been.* They had their own beliefs. *If you see a spider in the morning you will have good luck. If you lie down after eating you will turn into a cow. If you wear a basket on your head you will stop growing. A single flower means death.*

We told them stories about tongue-cut sparrows and grateful cranes and baby doves that always remembered to let their parents perch on the higher branch. We tried to teach them manners. *Never point with your chopsticks. Never suck on your chopsticks. Never take the last piece of food from a plate.* We praised them when they were kind to others but told them not to expect to be rewarded for their good deeds. We scolded them whenever they tried to talk back. We taught them never to accept a handout. We taught them never to brag. We taught them everything we knew. A fortune begins with a penny. It is better to suffer ill than to do ill. You must give back whatever you receive. Don't be loud like the Americans. Stay away from the Chinese. *They don't like us.* Watch out for the Koreans. *They hate us.* Be careful around the Filipinos. *They're worse than the Koreans.* Never marry an Okinawan. *They're not real Japanese.*

In the countryside, especially, we often lost them early. To diphtheria and the measles. Tonsillitis. Whooping cough. Mysterious infections that turned gangrenous overnight. One of them was bitten by a poisonous black spider in the outhouse and came down with fever. One was kicked in the stomach by our favorite gray mule. One disappeared while we were sorting the peaches in the packing shed and even though we looked under every rock and tree for her we never did find her and after that we were never the same. *I lost the will to live.* One tumbled out of the truck while we were driving the rhubarb to market and fell into a coma from which he never awoke. One was kidnapped by a pear-picker from a nearby orchard whose advances we had repeatedly rebuffed. *I should have just told him yes.* Another was badly burned when the moonshine still exploded out back behind the barn and lived for only a day. *The last thing she said to me was, "Mama, don't forget to look up at the sky."* Several drowned. One in the Calaveras River. One in the Nacimiento. One in an irrigation ditch. One in a laundry tub we knew we should not have left out overnight. And every year, in August, on the Feast of the Dead, we lit white paper lanterns on their gravestones and welcomed their spirits back to Earth for a day. And at the end of that day, when it was time for them to leave, we set the paper lanterns afloat on the river to guide them safely home. For they were Buddhas now, who resided in the Land of Bliss.

A few of us were unable to have them, and this was the worst fate of all. For without an heir to carry on the family name the spirits of our ancestors would cease to exist. *I feel like I came all the way to America for nothing.* Sometimes we tried going to the faith healer, who told us that our uterus was the wrong shape and there was nothing that could be done. "Your destiny is in the hands of the gods," she said to us, and then she showed us to the door. Or we consulted the acupuncturist, Dr. Ishida, who took one look at us and said, "Too much yang," and gave us herbs to nourish our yin and blood. And three months later we found ourselves miscarrying yet again. Sometimes we were sent by our husband back home to Japan, where the rumors would follow us for the rest of our lives. "Divorced," the neighbors would whisper. And, "I hear she's dry as a gourd." Sometimes we tried cutting off all our hair and offering it to the goddess of fertility if only she would make us conceive, but still, every month, we continued to bleed. And even though our husband had told us it made no difference to him whether he became a father or not—the only thing that mattered, he had said to us, was that we grew old side by side—we could not stop thinking of the children we'd never had. *Every night I can hear them playing in the fields outside my window.*

In J-Town they lived with us eight and nine to a room behind our barbershops and bathhouses and in tiny unpainted apartments that were so dark we had to leave the lights on all day long. They chopped carrots for us in our restaurants. They stacked apples for us at our fruit stands. They climbed up onto their bicycles and delivered bags of groceries to our customers' back doors. They separated the colors from the whites in our basement laundries and quickly learned to tell the difference between a red-wine stain and blood. They swept the floors of our boarding houses. They changed towels. They stripped sheets. They made up the beds. They opened doors on things that should never be seen. *I thought he was praying but he was dead.* They brought supper every evening to the elderly widow in 4A from Nagasaki, Mrs. Kawamura, who worked as a chambermaid at the Hotel Drexel and had no children of her own. *My husband was a gambler who left me with only forty-five cents.* They played *go* in the lobby with the bachelor, Mr. Morita, who started out as a presser at the Empress Hand Laundry thirty years ago and still worked there to this day. *It all went by so fast.* They trailed their fathers from one yard to the next as they made their gardening rounds and learned how to trim the hedges and mow the grass. They waited for us on wooden slatted benches in the park while we finished cleaning the houses across the street. *Don't talk to strangers,* we told them. *Study hard. Be patient. Whatever you do, don't end up like me.*

At school they sat in the back of the classroom in their homemade clothes with the Mexicans and spoke in timid, faltering voices. They never raised their hands. They never smiled. At recess they huddled together in a corner of the schoolyard and whispered among themselves in their secret, shameful language. In the cafeteria they were always last in line for lunch. Some of them — our firstborns — hardly knew any English and whenever they were called upon to speak, their knees began to shake. One of them, when asked her name by the teacher, replied, "Six," and the laughter rang in her ears for days. Another said his name was Pencil, and for the rest of his life that was what he was called. Many of them begged us not to be sent back, but within weeks, it seemed, they could name all the animals in English and read aloud every sign that they saw whenever we went shopping downtown — the street of the tall timber poles, they told us, was called State Street, and the street of the unfriendly barbers was Grove, and the bridge from which Mr. Itami had jumped after the stock market collapsed was the Last Chance Bridge—and wherever they went they were able to make their desires known. *One chocolate malt, please.*

One by one all the old words we had taught them began to disappear from their heads. They forgot the names of the flowers in Japanese. They forgot the names of the colors. They forgot the names of the fox god and the thunder god and the god of poverty, whom we could never escape. *No matter how long we live in this country they'll never let us buy land.* They forgot the name of the water goddess, Mizu Gami, who protected our rivers and streams and insisted that we keep our wells clean. They forgot the words for snow-light and bell cricket and fleeing in the night. They forgot what to say at the altar to our dead ancestors, who watched over us night and day. They forgot how to count. They forgot how to pray. They spent their days now living in the new language, whose twenty-six letters still eluded us even though we had been in America for years. *All I learned was the letter X so I could sign my name at the bank.* They pronounced their Ls and Rs with ease. And even when we sent them to the Buddhist temple on Saturdays to study Japanese they did not learn a thing. *The only reason my children go is to get out of working in the store.* But whenever we heard them talking out loud in their sleep the words that came out of their mouths came out—we were sure of it—in Japanese.

They gave themselves new names we had not chosen for them and could barely pronounce. One called herself Doris. One called herself Peggy. Many called themselves George. Saburo was called Chinky by all the others because he looked just like a Chinaman. Toshitachi was called Harlem because his skin was so dark. Etsuko was given the name Esther by her teacher, Mr. Slater, on her first day of school. "It's his mother's name," she explained. To which we replied, "So is yours." Sumire called herself Violet. Shizuko was Sugar. Makoto was just Mac. Shigeharu Takagi joined the Methodist Church at the age of nine and changed his name to Paul. Edison Kobayashi was born lazy but had a photographic memory and could tell you the name of every person he'd ever met. Grace Sugita didn't like ice cream. *Too cold.* Kitty Matsutaro expected nothing and got nothing in return. Six-foot-four Tiny Honda was the biggest Japanese we'd ever seen. Mop Yama-saki had long hair and liked to dress like a girl. Lefty Hayashi was the star pitcher at Emerson Junior High. Sam Nishimura had been sent to Tokyo to receive a proper Japanese education and had just returned to America after six and a half years. *They made him start all over again in the first grade.* Daisy Takada had perfect posture and liked to do things in sets of four. Mabel Ota's father had gone bankrupt three times. Lester Nakano's family bought all their clothes at the Goodwill. Tommy Takayama's mother was—everyone knew it—a whore. *She has six different children by five different men. And two of them are twins.*

Soon we could barely recognize them. They were taller than we were, and heavier. They were loud beyond belief. *I feel like a duck that's hatched goose's eggs.* They preferred their own company to ours and pretended not to understand a word that we said. Our daughters took big long steps, in the American manner, and moved with undignified haste. They wore their garments too loose. They swayed their hips like mares. They chattered away like coolies the moment they came home from school and said whatever popped into their minds. *Mr. Dempsey has a folded ear.* Our sons grew enormous. They insisted on eating bacon and eggs every morning for breakfast instead of bean-paste soup. They refused to use chopsticks. They drank gallons of milk. They poured ketchup all over their rice. They spoke perfect English just like on the radio and whenever they caught us bowing before the kitchen god in the kitchen and clapping our hands they rolled their eyes and said, "Mama, *please.*"

Mostly, they were ashamed of us. Our floppy straw hats and thread-bare clothes. Our heavy accents. *Every sing oh righ?* Our cracked, callused palms. Our deeply lined faces black from years of picking peaches and staking grape plants in the sun. They longed for real fathers with briefcases who went to work in a suit and tie and only mowed the grass on Sundays. They wanted different and better mothers who did not look so worn out. *Can't you put on a little lip-stick?* They dreaded rainy days in the country when we came to pick them up after school in our old battered pickups. They never invited friends over to our crowded homes in J-Town. *We live like beggars.*

They would not be seen with us at the temple on the Emperor's birthday. They would not celebrate the annual Freeing of the Insects with us at the end of summer in the park. They refused to join hands and dance with us in the streets on the Festival of the Autumnal Equinox. They laughed at us whenever we insisted that they bow to us first thing in the morning and with each passing day they seemed to slip further and further from our grasp.

Some of them developed unusually good vocabularies and became the best students in the class. They won prizes for best essay on California wildflowers. They received highest honors in science. They had more gold stars than anyone else on the teacher's chart. Others fell behind every year during harvest season and had to repeat the same grade twice. One got pregnant at fourteen and was sent away to live with her grandparents on a silkworm farm in remote western Japan. *Every week she writes to me asking when she can come home.* One took his own life. Several quit school. A few ran wild. They formed their own gangs. They made up their own rules. *No knives. No girls. No Chinese allowed.* They went around late at night looking for other people to fight. *Let's go beat up some Filipinos.* And when they were too lazy to leave the neighborhood they stayed at home and fought among themselves. *You goddamn Jap!* Others kept their heads down and tried not to be seen. They went to no parties (they were invited to no parties). They played no instruments. They never got valentines (they never sent valentines). They didn't like to dance (they didn't have the right shoes). They floated ghostlike through the halls, with their eyes turned away and their books clutched to their chests, as though lost in a dream. If someone called them a name behind their back they did not hear it. If someone called them a name to their face they just nodded and walked on. If they were given the oldest textbooks to use in math class they shrugged and took it in stride. *I never really liked algebra anyway.* If their pictures appeared at the end of the yearbook they pretended not to mind. "That's just the way it is," they said to themselves. And, "So what?" And, "Who cares?" Because they knew that no matter what they did they would never really fit in.

* * *

They learned which mothers would let them come over (Mrs. Henke, Mrs. Woodruff, Mrs. Alfred Chandler III) and which would not (all the other mothers). They learned which barbers would cut their hair (the Negro barbers) and which barbers to avoid (the grumpy barbers on the south side of Grove). They learned that there were certain things that would never be theirs: higher noses, fairer complexions, longer legs that might be noticed from afar. *Every morning I do my stretching exercises but it doesn't seem to help.* They learned when they could go swimming at the YMCA—*Colored days are on Mondays*—and when they could go to the picture show at the Pantages Theater downtown (never). They learned that they should always call the restaurant first. *Do you serve Japanese?* They learned not to go out alone during the daytime and what to do if they found themselves cornered in an alley after dark. *Just tell them you know judo.* And if that didn't work, they learned to fight back with their fists. *They respect you when you're strong.* They learned to find protectors. They learned to hide their anger. *No, of course. I don't mind. That's fine. Go ahead.* They learned never to show their fear. They learned that some people are born luckier than others and that things in this world do not always go as you plan.

Still, they dreamed. One swore she would one day marry a preacher so she wouldn't have to pick berries on Sundays. One wanted to save up enough money to buy his own farm. One wanted to become a tomato-grower like his father. One wanted to become anything but. One wanted to plant a vineyard. One wanted to start his own label. *I'd call it Fukuda Orchards.* One could not wait until the day she got off the ranch. One wanted to go to college even though no one she knew had ever left the town. *I know it's crazy, but . . .* One loved living out in the country and never wanted to leave. *It's better here. Nobody knows who we are.* One wanted something more but could not say exactly what it was. *This just isn't enough.* One wanted a Swing King drum set with hi-hat cymbals. One wanted a spotted pony. One wanted his own paper route. One wanted her own room, with a lock on the door. *Anyone who came in would have to knock first.* One wanted to become an artist and live in a garret in Paris. One wanted to go to refrigeration school. *You can do it through the mail.* One wanted to build bridges. One wanted to play the piano. One wanted to operate his own fruit stand alongside the highway instead of working for somebody else. One wanted to learn shorthand at the Merritt Secretarial Academy and get an inside job in an office. *Then I'd have it made.* One wanted to become the next Great Togo on the professional wrestling circuit. One wanted to become a state senator. One wanted to cut hair and open her own salon. One had polio and just wanted to breathe without her iron lung. One wanted to become a master seamstress. One wanted to become a teacher. One wanted to become a doctor. One wanted to become his sister. One wanted to become a gangster. One wanted to become a star. And even though we saw the darkness coming we said nothing and let them dream on.

∎

The Street of the House of the Sun

FROM *The Pinch*

MONTEZUMA, THE LAST OF THE AZTEC KINGS, left children who were lost and forgotten.

His enemy, Isabella, the Queen of Spain, left children, too. Her family faded like an oil painting left in the sun. In 1930, her distant grandnephew Don Organza Luis Rodrigo del Fonzo opened a Mexican restaurant in Tucson, Arizona.

In 1931, Montezuma's distant grandson Salvador Vigo opened another Mexican restaurant right across the street.

Bloodlines have a nose for such things.

The street between the restaurants was *El Camino del Casa del Sol*, the Street of the House of the Sun. Don Fonzo and Salvador Vigo observed one another across this street, and hated one another not like fire hates water, but the way only fire can hate fire.

Don Fonzo knew he came from royalty.

He sold Castilian wines, and burned candles in wrought iron chandeliers. His mustache was split, on one side, by a dueling scar.

Salvador Vigo was born poor, and had run away young to fight with Pancho Villa.

He had killed eleven men, that he knew of. At night, with dark and the devil close at hand, he was not proud of this.

The people who came to eat and drink on the Street of the House of the Sun were the gravediggers from the churchyard at Santo Domingo, the shopgirls from the pottery mall, and the rich men and women who owned these shops, owned the grave plots at Santo Domingo. When they felt like making noise and dancing and trouble, they attended Salvador's cantina. When they felt like eating to the music of phantom guitars, they filled the tables at Don Fonzo's.

Don Fonzo graced his patio with pots of Spanish roses. Salvador Vigo's patio was the street itself, a collage of broken glass and dark stains. Every night before the dinner hour, Don Fonzo swept his patio with a broom of dried mesquite. Every night after closing, Salvador Vigo stumbled across the street to urinate on Don Fonzo's roses.

In all the decades of their hatred, the two enemies fought only once, hand-to-hand.

Salvador Vigo decorated the front of his cantina with a painting of a fat, grinning whore. Don Fonzo strode into the street, drinking wine, insisting that Salvador Vigo erase this calamity.

"Unless," he said, "I am sorry, Don Vigo, this is a tribute to your honorable mother?"

They battered each other and cut each other until the police came and threatened to shoot them with rubber bullets, and then they went home.

Soon after Don Fonzo and Salvador Vigo both married, the Depression rolled west across the desert. Trucks filled with hungry men rumbled through Tucson. The shopgirls came to lunch less often. The gravediggers drank less at the bars. There were empty tables in both restaurants.

Each man thought to himself, "I'd better do more to turn a profit, or else join those scarecrows going west."

Salvador Vigo swept his back lot, and built a corral of saguaro ribs and twine. Anyone was welcome in that back lot after sundown, to place bets on Salvador Vigo's black rooster, El Negro, which, claimed Vigo, could kill any animal that challenged it.

The rooster killed other roosters. Then a tomcat. A wolfhound. A wolf.

He told no one how he coated El Negro's spurs with sea-snake venom from the Sea of Cortez. No one ever asked why he handled his bird with thick leather gloves.

Then one night El Negro spurred Salvador Vigo himself, drawing blood when his master was not looking. Salvador Vigo—they say—vanished into his kitchen, lay down on a table, and died. When he got to Heaven, he was so drunk and profane that they turned him away. When he got to Hell, he was so loud and so terrible that they cast him up until he awakened in his own bed, attended by his wife, as if Heaven and Hell were a good dream and a bad dream, no more.

His left eye was clouded and blue and forever blind. His left hand shook now. It would always shake.

Salvador Vigo stumbled to the wire cage in the cellar and wrung El Negro's neck.

Don Fonzo planted seeds smuggled from the Old World, and grew grapes and bottled wines. He sold the wine to men who came with trucks at night. He gave money and presents to treasury agents who left him in peace.

His wife bore a son. Don Fonzo taught the boy ancient signs and birthrights. He burned a sign into the boy's shoulder, and the boy knew better than to cry.

On the Christmas Eve Salvador Vigo's daughter was born, a dog which belonged to Carlos, his cook, was heard three times to bark the name of the Virgin.

"This child will be a holy and gentle child," whispered neighbors up and down the street. They brought gifts and prayers for the girl, then stopped in the kitchen to cross themselves before the dog.

One night, a sort of comet arced across the sky, burst on Don Fonzo's roof, and burned the restaurant down.

"Insurance," coughed Don Fonzo.

The restaurant reappeared before springtime, with a larger kitchen and a great stone oven.

Don Fonzo sent his enemy roses from the unblighted end of his garden.

Salvador Vigo marked his daughter's christening with the introduction of a wartime temptation: a monstrous and fantastic burrito, wrapped like a baby and called the *Stolen Child*.

The largest of the gravediggers swaggered in one Saturday night, and became the first to order this obscenity. But if the Stolen Child had indeed been a stolen child, he would barely have consumed the head before conceding defeat with ragged pork hanging from his teeth. This frightened no one. Every other day, it seemed, someone thought he could do better. No one ever did.

Don Fonzo's son Julian turned seven, turned ten.

Salvador Vigo's daughter Anna was rarely seen.

Nine more years passed, and when Julian Fonzo was nineteen, he met Anna Vigo for the first time. She had strayed from home after a rainstorm, and was patrolling a grassy strip near the pottery mall, picking up worms and carrying them to high ground.

Julian helped her. They barely spoke at all. Of course, they fell in love.

There were horror and tears two nights later, when they learned who their respective fathers were.

They glared at one another.

They rushed together. They fucked like delirious, moon-savage alley cats.

Their fathers stirred in their sleep.

Their mothers went to their windows and felt something looming toward them, something black and empty and shaped like a heart.

Impatient and hot-blooded, Julian Fonzo strode into Salvador Vigo's cantina, looked the old bandit in the eye, and ordered the Stolen Child.

Salvador Vigo brought the evil dish himself.

Julian's blood sang in his heart. Love widened his throat, but it didn't matter. Julian ate to the shoulders, then slumped in his chair, doubting his courage and his love.

Salvador Vigo knelt beside him and said terrible things. His voice was the voice of the man who had killed eleven men.

In the morning, Julian Fonzo was gone.

* * *

It was not necessary for Don Fonzo to engineer revenge.

Anna Vigo rode a bus to Sabino Canyon and jumped from the highest red cliff she could find. Her broken heart was a hollow thing, not a storm or a battle inside her. She did not wail or cry. She only felt an infinite weariness, and fell asleep while falling.

Men are silenced by the death of a child, quite often.

Salvador Vigo was not. He roared and laughed with the rowdiest drinkers. He gutted his kitchen, and rebuilt it by hand. He changed everything within his grasp, always moving, always shouting, as if he had grown immune to contentment.

Death and sadness were more direct with others.

Salvador Vigo's wife simply faded. She was like a song on the radio which is turned down until it cannot be heard. Salvador Vigo closed his doors for the day of the funeral, but could be heard inside, tearing down stucco to make room for a new oven.

Don Fonzo realized, one day, that he no longer loved anything. One month later he died in his sleep.

"Now what?" cried Salvador Vigo to the empty half of his bed.

There was peace then, for a while, although Don Fonzo's did not close. Who owned the place, no one could say. It was a mystery.

The Peace was a long peace. After a while there was a new cook and a new bartender.

The ghost of Anna Vigo was the patron saint of the Peace. She sat invisible on the hillside, overlooking the Street of the House of the Sun. The gravediggers made room for her when they lay themselves out for siesta between the stones.

When Julian Fonzo returned, he had become a young bull of a man. His eyes looked the way glass looks, reflecting the sun.

A new war began.

The new war was possible because these were new times. The gravediggers were fewer, because graves were dug with machines. The pottery mall had become part of a larger mall, and the shopgirls had changed into a new kind of shopgirl.

There were boys from the neighborhood on their way to Vietnam. Salvador Vigo snarled and said that if they were old enough to die they were old enough to drink, and swore he would put a bullet in the first cop who objected.

Julian Fonzo advertised something called Fondue, billed as *The Next New Thing!*

The roses on Don Fonzo's grave opened early, blood red.

Salvador Vigo installed a television over his bar.

It was an age of excitements which rose fast and faded fast. Fonzo's became a hookah bar for nine months, one time.

Then a famous man named Jimi Hendrix came to dinner at Fonzo's, and the Age of Celebrities dawned on the Street of the House of the Sun. Fonzo's overflowed, while Salvador Vigo and his cook watched television at their empty bar.

The next week, a famous man named Johnny Cash came to dinner at Salvador Vigo's, and this time Fonzo's emptied. No one noticed, or minded, that Johnny Cash wore sunglasses the whole time, didn't look much like himself, and could not be enticed to sing.

This was the form of the new war.

Like the old war, it seemed that it could never end, and could certainly never be won. Until it did end. Until Salvador Vigo won, until Salvador Vigo died.

Salvador Vigo planned nothing of great importance the day of his hundredth birthday. Only the week before, a famous woman had gone to dinner at Fonzo's, so Salvador Vigo sat watching television alone with his forty-second bartender. He called the bartender Carlos, although the bartender's name was Onofre. Salvador Vigo's memory shook sometimes, like the aim of an old soldier.

"I can't remember, Carlos," said Salvador Vigo. "Is the beer driver coming today?"

The front door opened, and two men stepped in, wearing dark suits and sunglasses.

This is how it happened that *El Presidente* came to Salvador's cantina.

The men looked around. They talked into radios.

El Presidente walked in. Tall, silver-haired, charming, with his Arkansas smile. A few sharply dressed men and women came with him, but no cameras, no crowds. Even *El Presidente* must have his quiet times with friends.

On the Street of the House of the Sun, the black cars with their dark windows did not go unnoticed. A few shopgirls even ventured inside, took tables, and whispered excitedly at the sight of *El Presidente* at the back table.

Then the men in the suits locked the doors and told Salvador Vigo that *El Presidente* had come to eat the Stolen Child.

Onofre's eyes flew wide. The shopgirls caught their breath and dug through their bags for disposable cameras.

On the hill at Santo Domingo, the hot afternoon breeze awakened the sleeping gravediggers. The ghost of Anna Vigo whispered in their dusty ears, and they knew in the graves and forests of their hearts that a wonderful thing was happening. Salvador Vigo himself stormed into his kitchen and baked tortillas. He sliced meat and conjured sauces. He, himself, delivered the Stolen Child, shook the hand of *El Presidente*, then retired to the bar and said, "Carlos, give me a cigarette."

Already cameras were on their way, and crowds, but the Street of the House of the Sun was far away from everything except for the things it was close to, and it would be quiet awhile, just yet.

Perhaps there are things which can only happen in some particular moment of perfection. Perhaps all impossibilities have flaws.

Horse races thundered, mute, on the television.

The Street of the House of the Sun seemed to vibrate. Salvador Vigo smoked. Roses grew. Ghosts waited and a hot breeze blew, and *El Presidente* ate the Stolen Child as if he were a fairy tale monster. Head to swaddled foot, and scraped the beans up, too, leaving the platter clean.

Salvador Vigo stood and bowed, and nearly fell. A camera flashed.

By the time *El Presidente* left, there were cameras. Instantly, he appeared on the television above the bar. And the television talked about Salvador Vigo's restaurant and the evil dish which had never been eaten before, which had been eaten by *El Presidente*.

Salvador Vigo's tables filled with strangers. He watched as they packed his bar and waited six-deep for tables.

The shopgirls turned the back table into a landmark. They carved their names. They left flowers. They ordered the Stolen Child, and sometimes managed to eat it. This was not a lean time, but a time of vast appetites and great changes in fortune. The Stolen Child ceased to be an impossibility in an age when impossibilities were simply unpopular.

Salvador Vigo could not have said when Julian Fonzo closed his doors and sold his father's restaurant. He only knew that one day he looked across the Street of the House of the Sun and Fonzo's had become a drugstore, and that night he snored a ragged snore and died.

It took only one gravedigger to bury Salvador Vigo, after the shopgirls and thirteen bartenders named Carlos had gone. One gravedigger with a Ditch Witch and a flask of tequila in his pocket. He was honorable enough to pour out a drop or two on the grave of Salvador Vigo, the last son of Montezuma.

Then he gunned his engine and pulled his levers, working with a sleepy ghost on his lap, the ghost of the dead man's daughter, singing songs about bullets and lizards.

Maybe Salvador Vigo rested and was still. Who could say? But there were footprints in the grass, on rainy mornings, from his grave to the grave of Don Fonzo, at least the last gravedigger said so, and from the morning after Salvador Vigo was buried, Don Fonzo's roses yellowed, and wilted into dust.

ERIC PUCHNER

■

Beautiful Monsters

FROM *Tin House*

THE BOY IS MAKING BREAKFAST for his sister—fried eggs and cheap frozen sausages, furred with ice—when he sees a man eating an apple from the tree outside the window. The boy drops his spatula. It is a gusty morning, sun-sharp and beautiful, and the man's shirt flags out to one side of him, rippling in the wind. The boy has never seen a grown man in real life, only in books, and the sight is both more and less frightening than he expected. The man picks another apple from high in the tree and devours it in several bites. He is bearded and tall as a shadow, but the weirdest things of all are his hands. They seem huge, grotesque, as clumsy as crabs. The veins on them bulge out, forking around his knuckles. The man plucks some more apples from the tree and sticks them in a knapsack at his feet, ducking his head so that the boy can see a saucer of scalp in the middle of his hair.

What do you think it wants? his sister whispers, joining him by the stove. She watches the hideous creature strip their tree of fruit; the boy might be out of work soon, and they need the apples themselves. The eggs have begun to scorch at the edges.

I don't know. He must have wandered away from the woods.

I thought they'd be less . . . ugly, his sister says.

The man's face is damp, streaked with ash, and it occurs to the boy that he's been crying. A twig dangles from his beard. The boy does not find the man ugly—he finds him, in fact, mesmerizing—but he does not mention this to his sister, who owns a comic book filled with pictures of handsome fathers, contraband drawings of twinkling, well-dressed men playing baseball with their daughters or throwing them high into the air. There is nothing well-dressed about this man, whose filthy pants—like his shirt—look like they've been sewn from deerskin. His bare feet are black with soot. Behind him the parched mountains seethe with smoke, charred by two-week-old wildfires. There have been rumors of encounters in the woods, of firefighters beset by giant, hairy-faced beasts stealing food or tents or sleeping bags, of girls being raped in their beds.

The man stops picking apples and stares right at the kitchen window, as if he smells the eggs. The boy's heart trips. The man wipes his mouth on his sleeve, then limps down the driveway and stoops inside the open door of the garage.

He's stealing something! the boy's sister says.

He barely fits, the boy says.

Trap him. We can padlock the door.

The boy goes and gets the .22 from the closet in the hall. He's never had cause to take it out before—their only intruders are skunks and possums, the occasional raccoon—but he knows exactly how to use it, a flash of certainty in his brain, just as he knows how to use the lawn mower and fix the plumbing and operate the worm-drive saw at work without thinking twice. He builds houses for other boys and girls to live in, it is what he's always done—he loves the smell of cut pine and sawdust in his nose, the *fzzzzdddt* of screws buzzing through Sheetrock into wood—and he can't imagine not doing it, any more than he can imagine leaving this gusty town ringed by mountains. He was born knowing these things, will always know them; they are as instinctive to him as breathing.

But he has no knowledge of men, only what he's learned from history books. And the illicit, sentimental fairy tales of his sister's comic.

He tells his sister to stay inside and then walks toward the garage, leading with the rifle. The wind swells the trees, and the few dead August leaves crunching under his feet smell like butterscotch. For some reason, perhaps because of the sadness in the man's face, he is not as scared as he would have imagined. The boy stops inside the shadow of the garage and sees the man hunched behind the lawn mower, bent down so his head doesn't scrape the rafters. One leg of the man's pants is rolled up to reveal a bloody gash on his calf.

He picks a fuel jug off the shelf and splashes some gasoline on the wound, grimacing. The boy clears his throat, loudly, but the man doesn't look up.

Get out of my garage, the boy says.

The man startles, banging his head on the rafters. He grabs a shovel leaning against the wall and holds it in front of him. The shovel, in his overgrown hands, looks as small as a baseball bat. The boy lifts the .22 up to his eye, so that it's leveled at the man's stomach. He tilts the barrel at the man's face.

What will you do?

Shoot you, the boy says.

The man smiles, dimpling his filthy cheeks. His teeth are as yellow as corn. I'd like to see you try.

I'd aim right for the apricot. The medulla. You'd die instantly.

You look like you're nine, the man mutters.

The boy doesn't respond to this. He suspects the man's disease has infected his brain. Slowly, the man puts down the shovel and ducks out of the garage, plucking cobwebs from his face. In the sunlight, the wound on his leg looks even worse, shreds of skin stuck to it like grass. He reeks of gasoline and smoke and something else, a foul body smell, like the inside of a ski boot.

I was sterilizing my leg.

Where do you live? the boy asks.

In the mountains. The man looks at his gun. Don't worry, I'm by myself. We split up so we'd be harder to kill.

Why?

Things are easier to hunt in a herd.

No, the boy says. Why did you leave?

The fire. Burned up everything we were storing for winter. The man squints at the house. Can I trouble you for a spot of water?

The boy lowers his gun, taking pity on this towering creature that seems to have stepped out of one of his dreams. In the dreams, the men are like beautiful monsters, stickered all over with leaves, roaming through town in the middle of the night. The boy leads the man inside the house, where his sister is still standing at the window. The man looks at her and nods. That someone should have hair growing out of his face appalls her even more than the smell. *There's a grown man in my house,* she says to herself, but she cannot reconcile the image this arouses in her brain with the stooped creature she sees limping into the kitchen. She's often imagined what it would be like to live with a father—a dashing giant, someone who'd buy her presents and whisk her chivalrously from danger, like the brave, mortal fathers she reads about—but this man is as far from these handsome creatures as can be.

And yet the sight of his sunburned hands, big enough to snap her neck, stirs something inside her, an unreachable itch.

They have no chairs large enough for him, so the boy puts two side by side. He goes to the sink and returns with a mug of water. The man drinks the water in a single gulp, then immediately asks for another.

How old are you? the girl says suspiciously.

The man picks the twig from his beard. Forty-six.

The girl snorts.

No, really. I'm aging by the second.

The girl blinks, amazed. She's lived for thirty years and can't imagine what it would be like for her body to mark the time. The man lays the twig on the table, ogling the cantaloupe sitting on the counter. The boy unsheathes a cleaver from the knife block and slices the melon in two, spooning out the pulp before chopping off a generous piece. He puts the orange smile of cantaloupe on a plate. The man devours it without a spoon, holding it like a harmonica.

Where do you work? the man asks suddenly, gazing out the window at the pickup in the driveway. The toolbox in the bed glitters in the sun.

Out by Old Harmony, the boy says. We're building some houses.

Anything to put your brilliant skills to use, eh?

Actually, we're almost finished, the boy says. The girl looks at him: increasingly, the boy and girl are worried about the future. The town has reached its population cap, and rumor is there are no plans to raise it again.

Don't worry, the man says, sighing. They'll just repurpose you. Presto chango.

How do *you* know? the girl asks.

I know about Perennials. You think I'm an ignorant ape? The man shakes his head. Jesus. The things I could teach you in my sleep.

The girl smirks at her brother. Like what?

The man opens his mouth as if to speak but then closes it again, staring at the pans hanging over the stove. They're arranged, like the tail bones of a dinosaur, from large to small. His face seems to droop. I bet you, um, can't make the sound of a loon.

What?

With your hands and mouth? A loon call?

The boy feels nothing in his brain: an exotic blankness. The feeling frightens him. The man perks up, seeming to recover his spirits. He cups his hands together as if warming them and blows into his thumbs, fluttering one hand like a wing. The noise is perfect and uncanny: the ghostly call of a loon.

The girl grabs the cleaver from the counter. How did you do that?

Ha! Experts of the universe! The man smiles, eyes bright with disdain. Come here and I'll teach you.

The girl refuses, still brandishing the knife, but the boy swallows his fear and approaches the table. The man shows him how to cup his hands together in a box and then tells him to blow into his knuckles. The boy tries, but no sound comes out. The man laughs. The boy blows until his cheeks hurt, until he's ready to give up, angry at the whole idea of bird calls and at loons for making them, which only makes the man laugh harder. He pinches the boy's thumbs together. The boy recoils, so rough and startling is the man's touch. Trembling, the boy presses his lips to his knuckles again and blows, producing a low, airy whistle that surprises him—his chest filling with something he can't explain, a shy, arrogant pleasure, like a blush.

The boy and girl let the man use their shower. While he's undressing, they creep outside and take turns at the bathroom window, their hands cupped to the glass, sneaking looks at his strange hairy body and giant shoulders tucked in like a vulture's and long, terrible penis, which shocks them when he turns. The girl is especially shocked by the scrotum. It's limp and bushy and speckled on one side with veiny bursts. She has read about the ancient way of making babies, has even tried to imagine what it would be like to grow a fetus in her belly, a tiny, bean-sized thing blooming into something curled and sac-bound and miraculous. She works as an assistant in a lab where frozen embryos are kept, and she wonders sometimes, staring at the incubators of black-eyed little beings, what it would be like to raise one of them and smoosh him to her breast, like a gorilla mother does. Sometimes she even feels a pang of loneliness when they're hatched, encoded with all the knowledge they'll ever need, sent off to the orphanage to be raised until they're old enough for treatments. But, of course, the same thing happened to her, and what does she have to feel lonely about?

Once in a while the girl will peek into her brother's room and see him getting dressed for work, see his little bobbing string of a penis, vestigial as his appendix, and her mouth will dry up. It lasts only for a second, this feeling, before her brain commands it to stop.

Now, staring at the man's hideous body, she feels her mouth dry up in the same way, aware of each silent bump of her heart.

The man spends the night. A fugitive, the boy calls him, closing the curtains so that no one can see in. The man's clothes are torn and stiff with blood, stinking of secret man-things, so the boy gives him his bathrobe to wear as a T-shirt and fashions a pair of shorts out of some sweatpants, slitting the elastic so that they fit his waist. The man changes into his new clothes, exposing the little beards under his arms. He seems happy with his ridiculous outfit and even does a funny bow that makes the boy laugh. He tries it on the girl as well, rolling his hand through the air in front of him, but she scowls and shuts the door to her room.

As the week stretches on, the girl grows more and more unhappy. There's the smell of him every morning, a sour blend of sweat and old-person breath and nightly blood seeping into the gauze that the boy uses to dress his wound. There's his ugly limp, the hockey stick he's taken to using as a cane and which you can hear clopping from every room of the house. There's the cosmic stench he leaves in the bathroom, so powerful it makes her eyes water. There are the paper airplanes littering the backyard, ones he's taught the boy to make, sleek and bird-nosed and complicated as origami. Normally, the boy and girl drink a beer together in the kitchen after work—sometimes he massages her feet while they listen to music—but all week when she gets home he's out back with the man, flying his stupid airplanes around the yard. He checks the man's face after every throw, which makes her feel like going outside with a flyswatter and batting the planes down. The yard is protected by a windbreak of pines, but the girl worries one of the neighbors might see somehow and call the police. If anyone finds out there's a man in their house, she could get fired from the lab. Perhaps they'll even put her in jail.

Sometimes the man yells at them. The outbursts are unpredictable. *Turn that awful noise down!* he'll yell if they're playing music while he's trying to watch the news. Once, when the girl answers her phone during dinner, the man grabs it from her hand and hurls it into the sink. Next time, he tells her, he'll smash it with a brick. The worst thing is that they have to do what he says to quiet him down.

If it comes to it, she will kill the man. She will grab the .22 and shoot him while he sleeps.

On Saturday, the girl comes back from the grocery store and the man is limping around the backyard with the boy on his shoulders. The lawn mower sits in a spiral of mown grass. The boy laughs, and she hisses at them that the neighbors will hear. The man plunks the boy down and then sweeps her up and heaves her onto his shoulders instead. The girl is taller than she's ever imagined, so tall that she can see into the windows of her upstairs room. The mulchy smell of grass fills her nose. She wraps her legs around the man's neck. A shiver goes through her, as if she's climbed out of a lake. The shiver doesn't end so much as wriggle its way inside of her, as elusive as a hair in her throat. The man trots around the yard and she can't help herself, she begins to laugh as the boy did, closing her legs more tightly around his neck, giggling in a way she's never giggled before—a weird, high-pitched sound, as if she can't control her own mouth—ducking under the lowest branches of the pin oak shading the back porch. The man starts to laugh, too. Then he sets her down and falls to all fours on the lawn and the boy climbs on top of him, spurring him with the heels of his feet, and the man tries in vain to buck him off, whinnying like a horse in the fresh-mown grass. The boy clutches the man's homemade shirt. The girl watches them ride around the yard for a minute, the man's face bright with joy, their long shadow bucking like a single creature, and then she comes up from behind and pushes the boy off, so hard it knocks the wind out of him.

The boy squints at the girl, whose face has turned red. She has never pushed him for any reason. The boy stares at her face, so small and smooth and freckled compared to the man's, and for the first time is filled with disgust.

The man hobbles to his feet, gritting his teeth. His leg is bleeding. The gauze is soaked, a dark splotch of blood leaking spidery trickles down his shin.

Look what you've done! the boy says before helping the man to the house.

That night, the girl startles from a dream, as if her spine has been plucked. The man is standing in the corner of her room, clutching the hockey stick. His face—hideous, weirdly agleam—floats in the moonlight coming through the window. Her heart begins to race. She wonders if he's come to rape her. The man wipes his eyes with the end of his robe, first one, then the other. Then he clops toward her and sits on the edge of the bed, so close she can smell the sourness of his breath. His eyes are still damp. I was just watching you sleep, he says. He begins to sing to her, the same sad song he croons in the shower, the one about traveling through this world of woe. *There's no sickness, toil, or danger, in that bright land to which I go.* While he sings, he strokes the girl's hair with the backs of his fingers, tucking some loose strands behind her ear. His knuckles, huge and scratchy, feel like acorns.

What's the bright land? the girl asks.

The man stops stroking her hair. Heaven, he says.

The girl has heard about these old beliefs; to think that you could live on after death is so quaint and gullible, it touches her strangely.

Did someone you know die?

The man doesn't answer her. She can smell the murk of his sweat. Trembling, the girl reaches out and touches his knee where the sweatpants end, feeling its wilderness of hair. She moves her fingers under the hem of his sweats. The man does not move, closing his eyes as she inches her fingers up his leg. His breathing coarsens. Outside, the wind picks up and rattles the window screen. Very suddenly, the man recoils, limping up from the bed.

You're just a girl, he whispers.

She stares at him. His face is turned, as if he can't bear to look at her. She does not know what she is.

He calls her Sleepyhead and hobbles out of the room. She wonders at this strange name for her, so clearly an insult. Her eyes burn. Outside her window the moon looks big and stupid, a sleeping head.

The next day, when the boy comes home from work, the house is humid with the smell of cooking. The man is bent over the stove, leaning to one side to avoid putting too much weight on his injured leg. It's been over a week now and the gash doesn't look any better; in fact, the smell has started to get worse, an almondy stink like something left out in the rain. Yesterday, when the boy changed the bandage, the skin underneath the pus was yellowish brown, the color of an old leaf. But the boy's not worried. He's begun to see the man as some kind of god. All day long he looks forward to driving home from work and finding this huge ducking presence in his house, smelling the day's sweat of his body through his robe. He feels a helpless urge to run to him. The man always seems slightly amazed to see him, unhappy, even, but in a grateful way, shaking his head as if he's spotted something he thought he'd lost, and though the boy can't articulate his feelings to himself, it's this amazement that he's been waiting for and that fills him with such restlessness at work. Ahoy there, the man says. It's not particularly funny, even kind of stupid, but the boy likes it. Ahoy, he says back. Sometimes the man clutches the boy's shoulder while he changes his bandage, squeezing so hard the boy can feel it like a live wire up his neck, and the boy looks forward to this, too, even though it hurts them both.

Now the man lifts the frying pan from the stove and serves the boy and girl dinner. The boy looks at his plate: a scrawny-looking thing with the fur skinned off, like a miniature greyhound fried to a crisp. A squirrel.

I caught them in the backyard, the man explains.

Disgusting! the girl says, making a face.

Would you rather go to your room, young lady? the man says.

She pushes her chair back.

No, please. I'm sorry. You don't have to eat. He looks at his plate and frowns. My mother was the real cook. She could have turned this into a fricassee.

What are they like? the boy asks.

What?

Mothers.

They're wonderful, the man says after a minute. Though sometimes you hate them. You hate them for years and years.

Why?

That's a good question. The man cuts off a piece of squirrel but doesn't eat it, instead staring at the window curtain, still bright with daylight at six o'clock. I remember when I was a kid, how hard it was to go to sleep in the summer. I used to tell my mom to turn off the day. That's what I'd say, *Turn off the day*, and she'd reach up and pretend to turn it off.

The man lifts his hand and yanks at the air, as if switching off a light.

The boy eats half his squirrel even though it tastes a little bit like turpentine. He wants to make the man happy. He knows that the man is sad, and that it has to do with something that happened in the woods. The man has told him about the town where he grew up, nestled in the mountains many miles away—the last colony of its kind—and how some boys and girls moved in eventually and forced everyone out of their homes. How they spent years traveling around, searching for a spot where there was enough wilderness to hide in so they wouldn't be discovered, where the food and water were plentiful, eventually settling in the parklands near the boy and girl's house. But the boy's favorite part is hearing about the disease itself: how exciting it was for the man to watch himself change, to grow tall and hairy and dark-headed, as strong as a beast. To feel ugly sometimes and hear his voice deepen into a stranger's. To fall in love with a woman's body and watch a baby come out of her stomach, still tied to her by a rope of flesh. The boy loves this part most of all, but when he asks about it, the man grows quiet and then says he understands why Perennials want to live forever. Did you have a baby like that? the boy asked him yesterday, and the man got up and limped into the backyard and stayed there for a while, picking up some stray airplanes and crumpling them into balls.

After dinner, they go into the living room to escape the lingering smell of squirrel. Sighing, the man walks to the picture window and opens up the curtains and looks out at the empty street. Bats flicker under the street lamps. He's told them that when he was young the streets were filled with children: they played until it was dark, building things or shooting each other with sticks or playing Butts Up and Capture the Flag and Ghost in the Graveyard, games that he's never explained.

It's a beautiful evening, he says, sighing again.

The girl does not look up from her pocket computer, her eyes burning as they did last night. She is not a child; if anything, it's the man's head that's sleepy, as dumb as the moon. Just listening to him talk about how nice it is outside, like he knows what's best for them, makes her clench her teeth.

What did you do when it rained? the boy asks.

Puppet shows, the man says, brightening.

Puppet shows?

The man frowns. Performances! For our mom and dad. My brother and I would write our own scripts and memorize them. The man glances at the girl on the floor, busy on her computer. He claps in her face, loudly, but she doesn't look up. Can you get me a marker and some different colored socks?

They won't fit you, the boy says.

We'll do a puppet show. The three of us.

The boy grins. What about?

Anything. Pretend you're kids like I was.

We'll do one for *you*, the boy says, sensing how much this would please the man.

He goes to get some socks from his room and then watches as the man draws eyes and a nose on each one. The girl watches, too, avoiding the man's face. If it will make the boy happy, she will do what he wants. They disappear into the boy's room to think up a script. After a while, they come out with the puppets on their hands and crouch behind the sofa, as the man's instructed them. The puppet show begins.

Hello, red puppet.

Hello, white puppet.

I can't even drive.

Me either.

Let's play Capture the Graveyard.

Okay.

In seventy years I'm going to die. First, though, I will grow old and weak and disease-ridden. This is called aging. It was thought to be incurable, in the Age of Senescence.

Will you lose your hair?

I am male, so there's a four-in-seven chance of baldness.

If you procreate with me, my breasts will become engorged with milk.

I'm sorry.

Don't apologize. The milk will feed my baby.

But how?

It will leak from my nipples.

I do not find you disgusting, red puppet. Many animals have milk-producing mammary glands. I just wish it wasn't so expensive to grow old and die.

Everyone will have to pay more taxes, because we'll be too feeble to work and pay for our useless medicines.

Jesus Christ, the man says, interrupting them. He limps over and yanks the socks from their hands. What's wrong with you?

Nothing, the girl says.

Can't you even do a fucking puppet show?

He limps into the boy's room and shuts the door. The boy does not know what he's done to make him angry. Bizarrely, he feels like he might cry. He sits on the couch for a long time, staring out the window at the empty street. Moths eddy under the street lamps like snow. The girl is jealous of his silence; she has never made the boy look like this, as if he might throw up from unhappiness. She walks to the window and shuts the curtains without speaking and shows him something on her computer: a news article, all about the tribe of Senescents. There have been twelve sightings in three days. Most have managed to elude capture, but one, a woman, was shot by a policeboy as she tried to climb through his neighbor's window. There's a close-up of her body, older even than the man's, her face gruesome with wrinkles. A detective holds her lips apart with two fingers to reveal the scant yellow teeth, as crooked as fence posts. The girl calls up another picture: a crowd of children, a search party, many of them holding rifles. They are standing in someone's yard, next to a garden looted of vegetables. The town is offering an official reward for any Senescent captured. Five thousand dollars, dead or alive. The girl widens her eyes, hoping the boy will widen his back, but he squints at her as if he doesn't know who she is.

At work, the boy has fallen behind on the house he's drywalling. The tapers have already begun on the walls downstairs. In the summer heat, the boy hangs the last panel of Sheetrock upstairs and then sits down to rest in the haze of gypsum dust. He has always liked this chalky smell, always felt that his work meant something: he was building homes for new Perennials to move into and begin their lives. But something has changed. The boy looks through the empty window square beside him and sees the evergreens that border the lot. Before long they'll turn white with snow and then drip themselves dry and then go back to being as green and silent and lonely-looking as they are now. It will happen, the boy thinks, in the blink of an eye.

There's a utility knife sitting by his boot, and he picks it up and imagines what it would be like to slit his throat.

Did you see the news this morning? his coworker, a taper who was perennialized so long ago he's stopped counting the years, asks at lunch.

The boy shakes his head, struggling to keep his eyes open. He has not been sleeping well on the couch.

They found another Senescent, at the hospital. He wanted shots.

But it's too late, the boy says. Their cells are corrupted.

Apparently the dumbfuck didn't know that. The police promised to treat him if he told them where the new camp is.

The boy's scalp tightens. What camp?

Where most of them ended up 'cause of the fire.

Did he tell them?

Conover Pass, the taper says, laughing. The info got online. I wouldn't be surprised if there's a mob on its way already.

The boy drives home after work, his eyes so heavy he can barely focus on the road. Conover Pass is not far from his house; he would have taken the man there, perhaps, if he'd known. It's been a month since the boy first saw him in the yard, devouring apples, so tall and mighty that he seemed invincible. Now the man can barely finish a piece of toast. The boy changes his bandages every night, without being asked, though secretly he's begun to dread it. The wound has stopped bleeding and is beginning to turn black and fungal. It smells horrible, like a dead possum. When the man needs a bath, the boy has to undress him, gripping his waist to help him into the tub. His arms are thinner than the boy's, angular as wings, and his penis floating in the bath looks shriveled and weedlike. The boy leaves the bathroom, embarrassed. It's amazing to think that this frail, bony creature ever filled him with awe.

Last night the man asked the boy to put his dead body under the ground. Don't let them take it away, he said.

Shhhh, the boy said, tucking a pillow under the man's head.

I don't want to end up in a museum or something.

You're not going to die, the boy said stupidly. He blushed, wondering why he felt compelled to lie. Perhaps this was what being a Senescent was like. You had to lie all the time, convincing yourself that you weren't going to disappear. He said it again, more vehemently, and saw a gleam of hope flicker in the man's eye.

Ahoy there, the man says now when he gets home.

Ahoy.

The smell is worse than usual. The man has soiled his sheets. The boy helps him from bed and lets him lean his weight on one shoulder and then walks him to the bathtub, where he cleans him off with a washcloth. The blackness has spread down to his foot; the leg looks like a rotting log. The boy has things to do—it's his turn to cook dinner, and there's a stack of bills that need to go out tomorrow—and now he has to do laundry on top of everything else. He grabs the man's wrists and tries to lift him out of the bathtub, but his arms are like dead things. The man won't flex them enough to be useful. The boy kneels and tries to get him out by his armpits, but the man slips from his hands and crashes back into the tub. He howls in pain, cursing the boy.

The boy leaves him in the tub and goes into the kitchen, where the girl is washing the dishes from breakfast. The bills on the table have not been touched.

He'll be dead in a week, the girl says.

The boy doesn't respond.

I did some math this morning. We've got about three months, after you're furloughed.

The boy looks at her. The man has become a burden to him as well—she can see this in his face. She can see, too, that he loves this pathetic creature that came into their life to die, though she knows just as certainly that he'll be relieved once it happens. He might not admit it, but he will be.

I'll take care of us, the girl says tenderly.

How?

She looks down at the counter. Go distract him.

The boy does not ask why. The man will die, but he and the girl will be together forever. He goes back into the bathroom; the man has tried to get out of the tub and has fallen onto the floor. He is whimpering. The boy slides an arm around his waist and helps him back to bed. A lightning bug has gotten through the window, strobing very slowly around the room, but the man doesn't seem to notice.

What do you think about when you're old? the boy asks.

The man laughs. Home, I guess.

Do you mean the woods?

Childhood, he says, as if it were a place.

So you miss it, the boy says after a minute.

When you're a child, you can't wait to get out. Sometimes it's hell.

Through the wall, the boy hears his sister on the phone: the careful, well-dressed voice she uses with strangers. He feels sick.

At least there's heaven, he says, trying to console the man.

The man looks at him oddly, then frowns. Where I can be like you?

A tiny feather, small as a snowflake, clings to the man's eyelash. The boy does something strange. He wets his finger in the glass on the bedside table and traces a T on the man's forehead. He has no idea what this means; it's half-remembered trivia. The man tries to smile. He reaches up and yanks the air.

The man closes his eyes; it takes the boy a moment to realize he's fallen asleep. The flares of the lightning bug are brighter now. Some water trickles from the man's forehead and drips down his withered face. The boy tries to remember what it was like to see it for the first time—chewing on an apple, covered in ash—but the image has already faded to a blur, distant as a dream.

He listens for sirens. The screech of tires. Except for the chirring of crickets, the evening is silent.

The boy feels suddenly trapped, frightened, as if he can't breathe. He walks into the living room, but it doesn't help. The hallway, too, oppresses him. It's like being imprisoned in his own skin. His heart beats inside his neck, strong and steady. Beats and beats and beats. Through the skylight in the hall, he can see the first stars beginning to glimmer out of the dusk. They will go out eventually, shrinking into nothing. When he lifts the .22 from the closet, his hands—so small and tame and birdlike—feel unbearably captive.

He does not think about what he's doing, or whether there's time or not to do it—only that he will give the man what he wants: bury his body in the ground, like a treasure.

He walks back into the bedroom with the gun. The man is sleeping quietly, his breathing dry and shallow. His robe sags open to reveal a pale triangle of chest, bony as a fossil. The boy tries to imagine what it would be like to be on earth for such a short time. Forty-six years. It would be like you never even lived. He can actually see the man's skin moving with his heart, fluttering up and down. The boy aims the gun at this mysterious, failing thing.

He touches the trigger, dampening it with sweat, and fears that he can't bring himself to squeeze it. He cannot kill this doomed and sickly creature. Helplessly, he imagines the policeboys carrying the man away, imagines the look on the man's face as he realizes what the boy has done. His eyes hard with blame. But no: the man wouldn't know he had anything to do with it. He won't get in trouble.

The boy and girl will go back to their old lives again. No one to grumble at them or cook them dinners they don't want or make him want to cry.

The boy's relief gives way to a ghastly feeling in his chest, as if he's done something terrible.

Voices echo from the street outside. The boy rushes to the window and pulls back the curtains. A mob of boys and girls is yelling in the dusk, parading from the direction of Conover Pass, holding poles with human heads on top of them. The skewered heads bob through the air like puppets. *Off to bed without your supper!* one of the boys says in a gruff voice, something he's read in a book, and the others copy him—*Off to bed! Off to bed!*—pretending to be grownups. The heads gawk at each other from their poles. They look startled to the boy, still surprised by their betrayal. One turns in the boy's direction, haloed by flies, and for a moment its eyes seem to get even bigger, as though it's seen a monster. Then it spins away to face the others. Freed from their bodies, nimble as children, the heads dance down the street.

MARK ROBERT RAPACZ

■

Bellwether

FROM *Water~Stone Review*

THE SHEEP HAD TROUBLE crossing the crick. It'd been flooded since early spring and the foot boards had washed downstream with the winter melt, so they had to ford it. My sister Louanne crossed to the other side first, and with her breeches soaked she made no sign that the icy chill bothered her.

"Paul, goddamn it! You stay over there and guide these sons a bitches. Count 'em going in. I'll count 'em going out."

I could barely hear her on account of the rushing water. It was muddy gray, iron gone liquid, like one long rail gliding to forge somewhere down south. The bank had softened so much that the sheep sank in to their knees. They squealed as I slapped them on their rumps to jump in. The crick was narrow at this point, so it didn't take them more than a few steps to reach Louanne, but the water rushed through in unexpected heaves, as if something sizable were getting in and out of this tub on some unseen far end. Every so often one of these heaves caught a sheep, tumbling it in the water. Either Louanne or I hopped in and righted it, usually by lifting the dripping critter up and out onto the bank where it scurried off like a spooked mutt.

We worked like this for the better part of an hour as the sheep collected in a clearing in the trees and munched on foliage that would more than likely give them the skitters.

"I'm gonna smack Horace good for that one, you varmint!" she yelled as one sheep nipped at her. She was pulling it out by the ears. "Ya told Pa that this weren't a good idea, didn't you?"

"Yeah, I told him and he told me how else they gonna eat."

The next, she yanked by the throat. "Not every good pasture is on the far side of the crick." Eventually impatient with our progress, she asked, "How many you at?"

"Twenty-seven."

"Good, good. That's what I got, too."

A few of the sheep were still off to my side, and I could hear them tugging at leaves and snipping off twiggy branches as they rustled about. One came and the next, then I hustled three more into the crick. They all looked the same: happy as mules until I booted them into the drink, and then it was all hell and dark loneliness as they floundered blindly into my sister's unforgiving arms.

"I could let them drown while freezing to death, or I can do it my way. Jesus never said saving would be painless."

I turned back, looking for our last one, the thirty-third, but it wasn't to be seen.

"Lou. What're you at?"

"I'm at thirty-two. Send the other over."

I looked back up the path, the one we'd trampled down through the light undergrowth to reach this narrow point in the crick. Then I scanned the foliage reaching off the banks and peered back into the deeper forest that hugged our makeshift trail. Not a black or white thing was seen.

"Count again!"

Louanne cursed me right after she cursed our pa—but before the sheep—which meant her most unpleasant thoughts lay on me. "Get off your ass, Paul. We only got thirty-two."

It wasn't her command that made me stand, it was the thought of our pa and the knowledge he'd have after we penned the sheep for the coming night. Someone would have to tell him before he went drunk.

Louanne had an answer before I could ask her anything. "There ain't a damn thing we can do about it. By the time we find it, it'll be drowned and bloated and on the other side of Buckthorn Township. Sheep ain't dumb enough to go running off."

She stood a moment longer, ruminating. True to her nature and true to her being the eldest, she said, "I'll take it this time."

* * *

It was getting on late morning, the sun already burning the cool out of the trees and the dew out of the grass, by the time I found Louanne. Pa was in his room off the kitchen, asleep and sobering. Outside, the sheep looked scared, likely taking their demeanor from their leader, Horace. I couldn't place him in the bunch since they all looked so wretched. Sheep don't have faces that tell they're worried. It's more a feeling they give off, something Louanne and I had a talk-through concerning.

She was in the barn. The only reason that matters is there was no work to do in the barn at this time. She wasn't crying any, but she was beating the hell out of a horse blanket with the handle of a spade. Dust and bits of hay flew off. Nearby, a pile of rugs and work blankets was draped off a bench, never looking so clean.

She stopped when she heard me come in.

"We oughta kill him while he's asleep," I said.

She beat the blanket a few times more and then chucked the handle toward the nearest corner. The spade didn't quite make it. It slapped down, startling us both. She waited a breath before she spoke. "That's the air that makes the crack. It's going faster than time." She was talking quiet, barely to me if at all, like she had a habit of doing when she was alone in the fields with the sheep.

"He's dead to the world already. We go in there with a pitchfork or an axe. We could have it done before lunch and have him buried by supper. Hell, we'll cook Horace for dinner. Use his bell as a servant's call."

Floating in a way I never seen her walk, she drifted to the open door and leaned against the thick oak jamb. Her tendency was to lope along, dragging her heels one moment and nearly skipping the next. There was no logic to her movements, but this time she moved like she did when she showed up in my dreams.

"He didn't hit me, Paul. He didn't do nothing of the sort."

"Then what's this all about?"

Looking back at the pile of beaten and bedraggled coverings, she said, "Cleaning up is all."

"Pa wasn't mad about the sheep?"

"Nah."

"He knows about the sheep, right?"

"Yeah, he does."

"Then where's our punishment? Where's the justice he always talks about?" I paced between the horse stalls, kicking up dust. "He was drunk, Louanne."

The sheep pen stretched out in front of the barn, the fence an extension of the northern wall. Their black heads snuck through the middle rungs one by one, sniffing what was going on.

"I just got tired of the beatings, Paul. We figured another way."

To ease the tension, I spoke more on his murder while those beady-eyed sheep tottered their heads back and forth like they understood human situations. Louanne did not delight in my gruesome plots to kill our father. She just stared off and said that'd be nice every so often. The sheep soon tired of our fantasies and snuffled and guffawed amongst themselves. Eventually, I also tired of my descriptions of exposing my pa's entrails to the world by hanging them from a weather vane. The silence broke the air fragile.

"I thought that one would get you going for sure," I finally said.

Louanne smiled and said, "Your ideas always do, Paul." She drifted toward the sheep pen and gently lifted the latch, but she did not yell and call them all good-for-nothing bastard coots, as was her way. They were guided out, not by slapping and hisses, but by her open palm. Horace timidly licked her hand to see if she tasted safe. After a moment of quiet expectedness, as they huddled at the edge of the fence, they all shuffled through the gate and moved silently down the road, following my sister.

A few weeks later, Pa helped me to tend the field and livestock while Louanne stayed back to prepare a meal. This usually meant he had no money, so the day would go on fairly well until sure enough there was a sheep that didn't look right. Something in the eye, he'd say. Something in how it couldn't keep up. According to his expertise, such an animal was only days from coming down with a deadly illness. Selling it off now would do us all some good.

"See that there. See the gimp in her step. That ain't right." He jogged a few paces to catch up to the sheep meandering away from us, up a shadowy crest, heading toward the fading light still blazing on its southwestern side. He caught one right before the crest, a sheep that looked as sure-footed as the rest. He then flipped her over in the usual way. He could always set them better than me or Louanne, smoother and quicker, a skill I attributed to the extra length in his arms.

She was down and splayed, bleating her warnings like a grinding wheel jammed with oil-gunked rust. It was unnatural if you'd never seen a sheep sheared, but Pa had his way and his way was in his bones.

"Come 'ere," he said. "You got a knife?"

I gave it to him. He had her head crooked under his armpit, as if he was about to sing her to sleep. Her foot was folded up and he was inspecting it, scraping off the mud and detritus with my blade. As I came close, he looked up in a way to place blame.

"What?" I said.

"These sheep are yours and Louanne's, ain't they?"

"They're all ours."

"Well, I entrusted them to you."

People always talk about the eyes in a person, whether they're there or they ain't, whether they can see through you or not at all. Well, our pa had all those eyes that people talk about and it was difficult to meet them full on.

"Sure. She ain't lame, though." I had grown four inches over the summer. Not quite filled out through the chest and back, but Pa wasn't much taller than me at that time. "Me and Louanne know what you want. You don't gotta go through your show anymore. We know you want money for booze. Just say it. We don't care no more."

Pa slid the knife between the toes to continue with his cleaning. From her heel to her toe, he scraped off swaths of her black foot, trimming it down to the invisible cause of its rottenness. Every so often she would squirm and scream louder than I heard a sheep scream before. A few sheep stopped at the top of the crest and looked back, but they couldn't see us. We might as well have been stumps and rocks to them.

"You got me pinned, huh, son? You got me pinned like I got her here?"

I moved close to inspect his handiwork and to show him I could back up the things I say. The moment I stood by him, Pa stopped abrupt, the sheep making a strange pig-like noise, and I found my own knife only inches from my nose.

"I'm well aware of who you think I am."

The blade was a breadth away, and a gash wouldn't have been anything new. Still, I did not move. We remained like this until it was clear the sheep could no longer handle our human peculiarities, so Pa returned the knife to its purpose with a quick slice between her toes.

A smell rose out of that sheep's foot. I did not pinch my nose, but I must've made a look.

"You smell that?" Pa asked.

"Yeah." It was the smell of cheese decaying in a bog.

"And that's the smell of a sheep that's right as rain?"

The noises increased in that poor beast and her twists, more violent. Pa squeezed tighter, putting her in an off-kilter sleeper hold meant only for a four-legger since the joints of a sheep don't move like that of a man. "You hold her hind legs now. She's not gonna appreciate this right off."

I gripped her tight as we laid her flat on her back. Pa stood over her and crouched, hovering above her chest as he got a better view of the lame foot. He pierced the blade in and a fluid oozed out, but she made no noise. All this field surgery my father did as the light begun to fail us and the herd traveled farther from us.

When it was done, the sheep leaped up like a playful dog. At first she was careful how she stepped, then went on regular-like.

"When's the last time you checked for rot?"

I couldn't answer him because I don't believe we ever had.

"That could infect the whole herd, you know." He still held the knife as if he were a doctor curing the world of all its disease.

"Louanne mentioned something about that—the foot rot—just the other day."

"Did she?"

"Sure, she did."

He slapped the hilt back in my hand as if he knew I was looking to stab something as well. My arm went dead, nearly paralyzed with shame as Pa went after the herd that was somewhere down in the gully by now or lazing on the other side of the hill. He loped the way Louanne used to, skipping toward the setting sun, pleased that he'd brought one sheep from florid decay. I could have rushed him and stabbed him in his back if it wasn't for him turning to tell me one last thing.

"When we get back, prepare a zinc bath for that ailing foot so we won't have to sell her in town. Make up for the one you lost."

He disappeared on the side of the hill before I decided to catch them. I could hear him whistling.

Louanne was getting bigger. She was filling out in her chest and belly and bottom, curving like a woman and becoming how I supposed our mama would've looked. One afternoon we were in the kitchen, Pa was snoozing, and it was drizzly outside. Wind picked up unexpected and chilled the air, turning a summer day into straight fall with a few quick breaths.

"You eatin' more?" I asked.

She was by the stove, mixing in flour to thicken up a lamb stew. "Excuse me?"

"You. You're fleshenin' up. You eating more?"

Her womanly tasks became slower for a while, contemplative. "I suppose so."

"Just wondering is all."

Her spoon clanked the edge of the pot softly, resonating like a bell as she scraped the bottom to keep the potatoes from sticking.

After a while Louanne asked me to go wake Pa for our meal.

His room smelled so much like Pa it would make you gag. Sour with man sweat unless the windows were open, which let in the boggy smells of the wetlands and deadened the sourness in the air. This neither worsened the room nor made it better, it just mingled two different fumes of decay—man and earth.

"Get up." I nudged his shoulder. He made no sound or movement. "You been drinkin'? Get up!" I dug my finger deeper between one of his shoulder blades.

His arm raised toward me and lazily swatted at me.

"I mean it. Louanne's got stew on."

The groggy son of a bitch rolled. "Oh, Paul," he said and continued with a few indecipherable mumblings. Finally wiping his face down a few times with his dry palms, the stubble making crackly noises as he did it, he said, "I had a dream."

"So what." He always had dreams.

"Would you like to hear it?"

I turned and walked out.

Everything was set at the table and we even had heifer milk because we ended up selling the gimped-up sheep anyway. After her zinc bath and a week of healing, she still had the signs, as Pa said, so it was better that she ruined someone else's herd than our own. Plus, we'd come away with a tidy profit.

The stew was in the big cast iron and the bread was all cut up and warm and slathered with lard. There were plenty of root vegetables softened in the stew, and the lamb was tender. The milk was fresh and made talking difficult. Despite the goodness that Louanne worked so hard to provide for us, she could not take a bite.

"Louanne," Pa said. "Eat some of this. You worked hard and it's marvelous. What a meal. I had a dream of this very meal not a moment ago and here it is." His face was creased with self-satisfaction, as if his genie dreams and not Louanne's hard work was the thing that made the dinner so.

"Paul's noticing I'm getting bigger," Louanne said.

Though he spoke to her, he turned his attention to me. "Really? Well, who wouldn't notice that you're becoming a woman. We should be happy. It's about time we had another woman around the home."

The silence in her became a whimper and then a sob and then my pa was yelling at her to shut it and save it for another time. "Not this. Not now!"

Louanne's sobs became bleating wails, and soon she left and went into Pa's room, the bread still on her plate.

I reached for Louanne's bowl after I finished mine, but as I touched her stoneware, my wrist was caught and twisted. Pain shot through the joint.

"Women are sensitive about their bodies," Pa said. "You should know this as a young man." He held my wrist a moment more, taking a few nibbles of bread with his free hand. Crumbs tumbled down his chin, some getting stabbed and caught in his two-day growth.

My eyes had trouble looking away from my hand. Something messy was happening with its fleshy color. "I know why she's bigger, Pa. I know it ain't no Christian magic that's bringing another child under this roof."

He flung off my hand as if he were tossing it away into the sand. His own chapped hands pawed at his watery eyes. I went in to check on my sister, who lay in the room full of foul smells, a room that had borne us into this world, and soon would do the same for my own flesh-and-blood sibling.

For months we got along fine. It was the winter months, and though we were miserable and cold, we spent much of it indoors and to-gether. Pa was withdrawing from the booze, changing himself for the better through deprivation and fits of illness. During the time of Louanne's magic growth, as he maintained outright, he determined that being a father and grandfather, melded as one, meant something more profound than being alone or drunk.

While Louanne nursed him, I did the sheep raising, the wood chopping, and the brunt of the chore hauling. The home ran its fire off my sweat and the sheep stayed healthy off my aches, and all the rest was done from Louanne's goodness. Most especially, making Pa whole again. She grew as the cold wind blew. Many nights while Pa was in his delirium, we warmed ourselves near the stove.

"This must've been how it was," Louanne said more than once. What she meant was what it must've been like with our mama and our pa before she passed and Pa became the man we knew.

"I should be drunk."

"No, Paul. No, you should not. You spend one second in that room with Pa, sick as he is, and your lips will fall off your face from fright."

The wood shifted in the stove.

"We always wanted to kill the man," I said. "We could right here now. You spend so much of your energy trying to save the bastard when you know he's just gonna take to drinking soon as the child can crawl and then what'll he do to it? Same as he done to you?"

"Not no more. Not this again, Paul." She shied away from me. "Things are different. I told you then and it's the same now. Now we just head on."

"Head on to what?"

Them heavy logs were being eaten ragged by the fire and I won-dered where their heaviness went after the fire ate it. All I could fig-ure was it went to nothingness, which was about the same place we were all going to in the end.

"It don't matter," I said.

"What don't?"

"That you and Pa don't know where we're heading and you don't know how it's all gonna be when the child comes."

"I know how it's gonna be."

Glow light came out of the knobs and switches and from the creases in the stove. It lit her up in beautiful ways. She carried herself like she always had, like the flesh was always in her. "It's gonna be like the fire in the stove. Everyone knows fire burns away all the unnecessaries around a thing and leaves only the Jesus dust it took to make it." She stared at me in the half-light. "Shush, Paul. Forget it. Right now Pa's in bed sweating out a past he don't ever want back and we're in here sweating for a home we finally find desirable. We're burnin' off what we never needed."

"What's that supposed to mean?"

"Jesus, Paul, I could draw it on a length of string and thread it through your eyes and you still wouldn't see it."

The logs burned down and the stove begun to cool before either one of us spoke again. Little noises reminded me that the world gone unseen can never rest. The heat whirled in the stove like a fiery twister, its metal dinging and tapping in agitation. The creature noises outside were drowned by the needle rain that spackled against our windowpanes. Words hung on our tongues.

This moment collapsed. Hackles exploded from the darkness of Pa's room. Quick rustles and the creak of his bed were followed by confused murmurings that sounded like a game bird felled and warbling through its blood.

"Maybelle," the voice said. "Water."

Louanne's body stiffened, which somehow—by the power she's always had—made clearer the sights in our little house. What once was dim now was bright. What once was concealed by the foggy smoke was dispersed. It was as if a quill-covered sun suddenly rose to the peak of our ceiling and shone down, burning away what Louanne would call the unnecessaries.

"He's had a terror," she said, staring toward the door. "He's just a sick man coming off a life of booze. He ain't ever been more than that."

She hucked up her dress, filled a basin with water, and disappeared into Pa's room. A few muffled things were done to him in the darkness.

Then a match was struck and a gas lamp lit. I only had a partial view of Louanne and Pa, framed as they were by the twilit doorway. She sat by him and felt his head, then wet the rag and dabbed him.

"It was that dream, Maybelle. That same damn dream," he said.

"Shush, shush, Pa . . . This here's Louanne."

Pa's voice had dropped somewhere below the vocal box, somewhere deep in the chest. It pained him to talk.

"Maybelle," he called her again. "Hold my hand."

Louanne did so.

"Like all them terrors before—Oh, Jesus!—I were reading the Book of Eternity!"

"Now there, Papa, just a terror—just a dream. You rest and warm yourself. Here." As Louanne lay down beside him, her head disappeared behind the door frame. Only her legs were visible. "'Tis nothin' but the dead playing tricks with the thoughts of the living."

Pa was quiet, still stuck between worlds.

"Pay them dead souls no mind," she bid him.

I did not move from my stool. Some unknowable force had reached us. This here was the death of our pa as true as the ice flecks that had begun to scratch like hobnails on our panes, truer still than the light that danced from dark corner to dark corner, looking for space to hide. No longer would Pa force my hand, making me the murderer I expected to become. The booze that drained from his veins, out his pores, like the wine out a ragged thin bladder, created in me a sense I had not known for some time. I was happy.

His voice went on, becoming clearer with each hack and wheeze. He was saying things to Louanne that she seemed to understand.

I crept nearer his door to hear the words of Pa, which filled him with greater intoxications than the booze leaching from his skin. After months of draining, you'd expect he'd be shriveled like a dried slug, but here he was, virile and energetic as ever after weeks of cold sweats and delirious rants.

". . . I dreamed of that book. Of scripture. A hundred times I must've had this dream. God Fearers alive!—My dream is true."

"But, Papa—" Louanne said, nuzzling into him.

He rolled to face her. "Dead or no, we brought this world new life, Maybelle. A glorious sight if there ever was one . . . All regrown from the earth here." He motioned around as if our decrepit and failing farm was the very place of the Beginning. "And the man and woman started again with child." He left it at that, supposing it sufficient for forgiveness, and perhaps for Louanne it was. But to me it only furthered the mystery of his fever dream and the treachery this family let grow like rotten gourds.

I walked out into the cold drizzle, my hatred for Pa receding some and settling on Louanne. There was nothing in her that had changed as far as I could see. She did not move. She did not say anything to my father. I had a feeling, a wave of movement descending on our household, as if the threads that tie this world together had suddenly tightened—or snapped—I cannot say, but I knew Louanne as its cause. As she lay next to my father with their unborn in her belly, she changed from one thing to the next as if her deeper spirit was a pile of tattered clothes. This child of theirs was to be raised without shame. All eyes would be averted from our farmstead for good because it was she who had chosen, who had rescinded the rightness we were born with.

Some of the sheep were standing at the fence. The sleet collected on their backs and glistened in the moonlight. Their black heads bobbed and they mewed in protest of the cold or the dark or both. I petted Horace, acting dog-like, nuzzling and licking, his teeth scraping at my palm as if I held a bit of carrot. Finding none, he nipped me. I walloped him with my open palm, sending the whole herd scurrying to the far corner of their pen. Disappointed in myself, I turned to go back in, but my home was no longer one I recognized, the candlelight flickering like beast eyes guttering in a hollow.

Well before daybreak I awoke still in the sheep's pen. I was alone but for Horace, who jumped up the moment I stirred, a noticeable gimp in his movements as he scuttled toward the rest of the stupid creatures that had left us some time in the night.

In early April, Louanne went to bed with labor pains. She spent a week in Pa's room, telling him what to do and how to do it. She screamed, he soothed, and I was in the pasture when it was born.

Pa didn't go out much to do the heavy work afterwards. He preferred to work in and around the home—puttering as I called it.

He'd fix wobbly stool legs and build little shelves. If you went around back he'd be there scrubbing the wash, coming in with cold, blue hands that he'd warm by kneading dough or rolling tallow into candles. His hair had lost its shine and dark color, and wrinkles crept across his face. His posture matched the position his chores put him in: hunched. Where once he did his duties mean-spirited and crudely, he now accomplished them lightly, carefully, as if each were part of one long task never to be fully done.

After an evening of chores, I found him straddling a bucket, his hat pushed back and his sleeves rolled up. He moved a paring knife dexterously across the curves of a potato, hardly looking at what he was doing. Peels dropped limply into the bucket or stuck to his forearms, hanging to him like leeches.

He looked up. "You been out long."

"Broken fence post down near the road." I moved toward Louanne's room.

"Don't," he said as he wiped down his arms, leaving slicks of white slime. "They're both finally sleeping." He stood up, not fully, but as high as he could and he worked the creaks out of his back. "How 'bout if I make Louanne some marrow broth? We need her spirits up for the baby."

"That'd be good," I said. "Probably should give her more than old bones and potatoes, though."

"Yeah, yeah." He sat back down on the stool and straddled the bucket. "Horace has been limping."

"Been gettin' worse," I said.

"Caught it just in time, then." He thought a moment longer and then resumed his work.

I left him to begin a miserable evening of slaughter, eviscerating the only sheep we'd ever given a name.

CHAZ REETZ-LAIOLO

■

The Love Act

FROM *Raritan*

1985

BY THE EARLY 1980s, my mother had taken her baccalaureate
and quit her nursing job in hopes of opening a natural food store
with two partners she might or might not have been dating (curly-
haired hippie men who, before the doors opened, blew the startup
money up their noses). These were optimistic times. We were riding a chunk of cash my father'd relented on, as sick as we were of
his sending one- and two-thousand-dollar disbursements every six
months. Money we'd erupt into the streets with, paying off back rent,
gas accounts, one-two-three bills slap in the palm out the window of
our Volvo. My brother and me upright and buoyant in the sunlit cab
of the car, headed for sporting goods stores, the finest clothes bou-
tique in town where we'd pick out a shirt, maybe a pair of pants if
Mom could finesse the owner. We'd spend it in a day. No pension-
ing. I recall touching the fine cloth of an imported shirt hanging in
my closet, the rest of my shirts flung to the far end of the rod. Hearing the neighborhood kids in the street, I pulled an old T-shirt over
my head, paused in the doorway for one last look at the shirt, near
shivering, and shut the light, three steps at a time down and off the
porch. This was Oregon, but Ashland, Oregon. Shakespearean Oregon where Mondale/Ferraro and Keep Tahoe Blue placards stood in
front yards.

My mother befriended a beautiful stylist named Jeanette who cut
our hair during those flush months. Popular music pulsed from ceil-
ing-mounted speakers across her sleek modernist salon. No blue cyl-

inders of comb water, no white-smocked barber, no *Playboy* magazines stacked on the television, as I'd encountered when lucky
enough to avoid my mother's bowl cut. Jeanette and the other wom-
en's feet seemed barely to grace the floors, their hair shaped like exotic birds. One of the stylists holding a plait of her customer's hair up
in the sunlight from the window: "I've never seen anything so shoul-
der-length. I mean, who did this to you? Your husband?"

Enjoying the invisibility of children in such places, I'd smuggle
cookies and finger sandwiches laid out on trays and gulp down Per-
rier. I'd watch the men in suits who'd sit with their eyes closed, flirt-
ing with their stylist. I'd study their gestures, unconsciously mimick-
ing them in my lap, then later, alone, I'd sit in my room crossing my
legs, brushing the air aside, laughing boldly with women I had not
nor ever would meet.

Some days, knowing my mother would be elsewhere, I'd stop in,
claiming I'd expected to find her. Jeanette would muss my hair or
seat me in front of the mirror and clean around my ears—a service
that terrified me the first time because I imagined I'd be expected to
pay. But I became accustomed to this luxury, arriving more and more
regularly. If Jeanette was with someone I'd hang around shooting off
phrases I'd heard pass among the clientele, watching her bottom,
faintly sickened and exhilarated by the panty lines under her skirt.
Then make out the door with a pocket full of cookies, the bell dinging
as I bolted onto the sunlit sidewalks.

Jeanette had me take two photographs of my mother, who was
beautiful, but, possibly because my brother and I were born when she
was still a child, had never become more than a beautiful girl. One
you'd expect to see in a small town. Long straight hair. No makeup. A
gap between her front teeth. In the first photograph she's in a salon
chair, tissue around her neck, her body concealed by a black smock
so her youthful face and her matte hair are disembodied. They appear
more like illustrations than authentic body parts. As though the illustration of her face will accompany the word *expectant* in the dictionary.

In the second photo, my mother is posed in the bleach sunlight
in front of the salon. There is a grandness to her stature, the picture having been snapped from the height of an eight-year-old. She
stands with her legs wide set, her head pitched back, arms raised in

some sort of Egyptian space-age dance, and her red hair is cropped in a tousle of short spikes. She's nearly unrecognizable, as in black-and-whites I'd seen of her as a teenager in South Dakota experimenting with lipstick. Jeanette's leg and arm remain blurred in the foreground. Either out of fondness for my mother's mane of hair, or through some gift of foresight, Jeanette had refused to participate in the cutting—at one point, while my mother's red hair stained the floor, Jeanette smoked a cigarette in the salon, something I'd never seen her do before.

In the background of the photo, beyond my mother in her silver leggings, our old Volvo can be discerned waiting under an oak. She never dared park it in front of the salon.

She and Jeanette began going out nights, dancing. My mother, who I believe had been (maybe still is) waiting for some stroke of life luck, must have felt as if everything was coming together. These jubilant nights—dancing in the arms of out-of-town businessmen—far as they were from the small rental we still slept in, would be life from here on out.

Of course the money was running out, my father refusing her phone calls. About the time I became aware the natural food store would never open—which could've been weeks in delay, I was a child—I overheard her on the telephone as I brought an empty cereal bowl into the kitchen. "Well, I can't very well sell my hair anymore, can I?" she said. "Jesus, Patti, why didn't someone tell me?"

After a brief dismayed period when I believe she simply couldn't come to terms with the hemorrhaging of money, our apartment stacked with wholesale boxes of bulk grain, almonds, pastas, the landlord cupping his hands to look through the windows where my mother sat alarmingly still on the sofa, she started interviewing for work. The positions in the newspaper were menial: clerks, personal attendants, retail. She'd been so close to owning something of her own. Now, interviewing with her hands folded in her lap, her hair grown out awkwardly.

I was selling magazine subscriptions door to door for a school contest. I'd stick to the wealthy neighborhoods, the high houses set into the hills, dragging my hand along the sides of Mercedes as I

came up the driveway. I was well versed. "Some are quite sophisticated," I'd shoot off. "From *House & Garden* to female matters." Always my prospects would raise their eyes from the list and smile,
shocked. Occasionally a woman would cover her mouth or touch my
arm. "And at one third the newsstand," I'd say.

I'd ready the coupon book they received with the purchase of a
subscription.

One afternoon my mother and I stood waiting in the lobby salon
of the only four-star hotel in town. She didn't say anything as the staff
bustled about without noticing us. Then, as if suddenly awakened,
she went to the counter and negotiated a walk-in that even then I
knew she'd pass a bad check for.

"There," she said, sitting, taking up a magazine, crossing her legs.
"That wasn't so bad, was it? Tea?"

She folded something in her hand and refolded it, running her
fingers along the edge, and in the gloss of it and the color at the edge
I recognized one of the coupons from the subscription gifts. When
she saw me looking she crossed her eyes and made a face, something
she did when we were joking. "It's not as nice a place, is it?"

A short, bony, strict-looking woman matadored the smock over
her. She stood behind my mother, touching her hair, conferring with
her in the mirror. I couldn't hear anything for the noise of hairdryers.
The two of them went back to the sinks, my mother's legs switching
from under the smock. She snuggled her head into the contoured
neck of the basin, leaving only her chin and the tip of her nose visible. The bony woman rapped on a dividing wall and a young Mexican girl came out chewing, wiping the corners of her mouth with
her thumb and forefinger. She didn't look old enough to have a job.
Maybe a few years older than me, a teenager. She patted her hands on
her thighs, then washed them quickly in the sink next to my mother.
When she came over and tested the water in the basin, my mother
sat up quickly and smiled at the girl, then I didn't see her face again
until I returned from the lobby.

I had to move; I went out and walked along the carpeted hall under
a huge tinkling chandelier. My head pitched back, turning so the thing
rotated galactically overhead. Only when a bellhop grazed me did I
become self-conscious again, believing both the counter men, in ties

and vests, were watching me. I nodded expertly to them and cruised as nonchalantly as I could past a young girl holding to her mother's leg among their suitcases. I jumped down a set of stairs, through a pair of double doors, and leaned finally over the railing to the empty flat surface of the indoor swimming pool. I felt for the bottom of the water with my eyes, the softened white bulge where the floor rose to the shallow end. I climbed to the middle rung of the rail, my knees pressed to the top, and leaned out into the soundless wobbling light.

"What're you waiting for?" A man's voice startled me. I'd not seen him, lying on a towel, bare-chested, as if he were sunbathing. "Somebody ought to swim in the thing, we're all paying for it," he said. "And god knows, the rooms are a disgrace."

"Ours doesn't even have cable," I said. I don't know why I lied, or what it meant to me for a hotel room not to have cable television, but when his laugh echoed in the hollow walls, I smiled.

"Where the hell are we?" he said. "Oregon?"

I looked at his tan legs crossed at the ankles and at the heaviness of his body, his hands behind his head. He stared off over the water at a woman in uniform passing back and forth in one of the dim rooms above us, vacuuming. I made a dismissive gesture, and sloughed off up the stairs.

Through the salon's glass doors my mother seemed both delicate and unnatural, seated too upright in the chair. She didn't look at the women grouped around her, though something in her profile made clear her anxiety. The bony woman a step back directed another two whose postures looked like those peering in on an animal. I came through the door; they all looked at me briefly. Except my mother. She remained still, her eyes looking in the mirror at the other customers who sat waiting, some turning to watch.

One of the stylists looked again, pushing the hair aside, her mouth turned down. "Just eczema, I think."

"Just?" the bony woman said.

"It's worse when I'm stressed," my mother said. I looked up, thinking in her voice that she'd turned to me. But she hadn't. They were still the three of them all looking at each other in the mirror. "I'm sorry, I should have mentioned it."

"No, no," the third woman said. "It's—"

"It would have been helpful," the bony woman said. "You're probably used to it but I'm not." She held her hands up slightly. "I'm definitely not. I think Maria will finish you." The two other stylists looked at her dubiously. "Maria will finish her," she repeated to them. She patted my mother on the shoulder in what seemed to me a very strange gesture.

My mother said something I couldn't hear, looking up at the woman as she turned away. She said whatever it was again, but the woman didn't respond. She watched her interrupt the girl who was shampooing another customer, and when the girl looked over towards my mother, she looked down, then quickly towards me, and smiled without parting her lips. She made a motion to wave, but the smock tented over her hand.

1993

"No, he wants to keep that surfer look," my guardian said from the swivel chair, his hairdresser, Sherry, tousling his hair as she looked over at me.

"What a heartbreaker," she cooed.

I got up and looked out the glass front door of the Mane Attraction, at the wintering parking lot, our lone car sooted from the salt roads. Then the two hairdressers' cars and, farther out, below the limp pennants a row of secondhand cars with snow on their hoods. Tractor-trailers wheezed through their gears on the roadway, dwindling into the smudged distance. In the few days since I'd arrived in Iowa it had snowed eighteen inches while I sat in the house watching HBO. When Tim, my guardian, got home from work we'd hustle out in the cold to dinner at a pool hall where he had league matches. I'd watch the silver-haired men shoot deliberately from ball to ball, cracking their necks between shots, bantering. Sometimes they'd have me rack for them, get a wild game between matches, or I'd shoot on the dollar tables with women who frequented the place. Women in outdated clothes whose breasts and perfume would smudge my cheek when they hugged me. We'd gone out to the mall for winter clothes one weekend and I'd watched the other teenagers milling around outside the theater, their hands tucked in the back pockets of their girls' jeans. And even in the arcade, I'd stood over the shoulders of a few kids my age as if waiting for the game they were on, in hopes of striking up a conversation.

"It's no beach out there, is it?" a second beautician said, snapping her gum. She was seated in her own chair, filing her nails. There were no other customers.

"I can't believe school's not canceled," I said.

"So Tim says you're from the West Coast," Sherry said.

"Oregon," I said. I looked at her and the other woman for response. "I was born in California."

The second beautician held her hand out to look at her nails. "Just say California, sweetie."

A week later I revisited the Mane Attraction, driving the unfamiliar roads in the old pickup I was allowed to use. I barreled through the slush, risking the tail end, savoring the loose exhilaration of it drifting along the edge of control, sliding to a halt at stop signs, or through them, finally stopping angled midway through the intersection.

I'd begun at the high school on the north side of town. The bell ringing through the halls, I'd duck into the chaotic bathroom, where boys pushed at each other, talking pussy, eyeing the new kid as I washed my hands, giving myself just enough time to check my collar for dandruff. Then in class with the teacher tapping away on the chalkboard I'd lean forward on my desk, glancing back quickly at whoever sat behind me.

Because I was early for my appointment I walked out in the bleak cold of the used cars, leaning to have a look in a few of the windows. The interiors looked stiff and dusty and unused. A salesman finally shuffled out with his hands in his pockets, and I waved him back toward the modular building.

"I'm just waiting for a haircut," I said.

He smiled and motioned over at the salon without moving his head, the way a person does when they're huddling the heat into themselves. "I hear you," he said. "I'd be over there every day if the wife wouldn't catch on."

I stomped my boots in the door of the Mane Attraction, waved briefly to Sherry, looked around the bare rectangular room, the heavy rear end of the other hairdresser. I was suddenly disappointed in the place. I'd allowed myself to explode the beauty parlor into something grander, had moved Sherry through it elegantly and, if not in bold ways, erotically. It was actually quite cold and undecorated, a thin carpet, and then linoleum under the chairs. Everything smelled of candy hair products. The building may have been an office once.

I watched Sherry in the mirror, dropping the hydraulic chair to her height, bringing the back of my hair up in her fingers. She was small, as I'd remembered, and her clothes were girlish, as if she were trying to keep up with a time that was not hers.

"Don't tell me you want to cut this all off?"—she smiled at me— "'cause I won't do it." She held up the spray bottle to warm me and shielded my eyes. "Imagine you're in Hawaii."

It was the first time, having closed my eyes, that I realized music was playing. Piano and saxophone rung out a lazy "White Christmas." She began picking through my curls, tugging my head, and I kept my eyes closed. "All this snow would melt," I said.

She made a sweet sound in her throat. "They're not gonna stand a chance around here," she said.

She drew my wet hair up between her fingers, scissored dark clumps down the slide of my apron. I glanced at them in my lap for signs of dandruff. Then at her hands working, her thin waist where her shirt was tucked in and then rose over her breasts that pressed against me intermittently. For some reason the photographs of her children along the edge of the mirror reinforced my adolescent idea of her as a sexual woman—not that she had a home life, kids storming the house in the afternoon, a husband she breakfasted with, but that she was someone who had had men between her legs and had the desire to be found attractive. With no other objects of affection I'd spent nights with her hovering idyllically over my new bed. Waking in the morning, dragging myself to the breakfast table, Tim had said more than once, *And the dead has risen.*

"Do you like cutting hair?" I asked her.

She nodded, her head tilted sideways, still cutting. Then she looked up at me, stopped working. "You know, I've never had anybody ask me that, but I do."

She combed my bangs down to measure across my forehead and I looked at myself and felt that I didn't look my best but I smiled to her anyway. "You know, I really like running my hands through people's hair," she said.

"Jesus, Sher," the other stylist said. "It's a kid, you're not interviewing for work here."

"I do though," she said. "I don't know why. Is that crazy?"

"I understand," I said, wanting to.

She laughed. She stepped back over me and messed up my hair in her hands, her fingers pressing my scalp. I closed my eyes over the other stylist's gum cracking, and imagined the jostle of my head as the movement of both of us bumping along in the cab of my truck, crossing a field, maybe in springtime, no, evening, a summer evening, why not, fireflies thrusting over the silvered grasslands where suddenly she is transported, naked and illuminated in my headlights.

1998

At twenty-two, never having been to Europe, never for that matter to New York, I had a thousand dollars in my duffel folded into a La Guardia/Heathrow itinerary. In the dome light of the Greyhound across Pennsylvania, I found myself taking my passport out, flipping the empty pages soon to be filled with foreign stamps, even pretending to hand it over for inspection to the seat back in front of me.

Twice the lights of the city hazed the hilltops in front of us. Then in the headlights, mile markers hovered brightly over the roadside: New York 110 miles; New York 63 miles. And already mighty and visible and trembling against the sun-fallen sky.

It was on the crest of this bubble that a friend—a Long Islander whose wedding I was to attend before flying out—convinced me that we should have our hair cut. *Don't come back looking stupid,* his fiancée said as we shouldered our coats at the door.

The women in the salon didn't stop laughing and barely regarded us in the doorway.

"What is so funny?" the younger stylist said. She'd dropped her comb and scissors to her side dramatically. "I'm not gonna apologize for knowing what I want. A baby by 30." She counted on her fingers. "And I want to be with my husband two years before the baby. So, that leaves a year to find a husband."

"Well, I hope the dog rolls over and sits for you," a second, heavy-set beautician said.

The girl snipped at her customer's hair for effect, her lips pursed so as not to laugh with the others. "I don't see the crime in a woman knowing what she wants?"

"Don't we all," the heavyset one said. She had her comb in her mouth, thumbing through the appointment pages. She gleamed up at us. "Aren't you two lucky I'm a hard worker."

I sat and switched through outdated hairstyle manuals. Men with tightly shorn beards, rosy lips, their hair perfectly wet. A few I held up for my friend to glimpse out of the corner of his eye, but the beautician straightened his head in the mirror.

I got up, had a waxed cup of cider from a thermos. Watched a small electric train shimmy its way around a built-in shelf below the ceiling. Its tinsel noise pushing through some snow-covered New England landscape. The whole place was Christmas lights and ornaments hung from the latticed walls. Several women came in from the cold and disappeared behind a bamboo curtain and tiki lamp. They'd come out fifteen minutes later, bright, their eyes raccooned, retucking their shirts, looking themselves over in the mirrors. They were obviously regulars, paid on account, made small talk with the stylists, had cider, their down coats folded over sunburned arms.

"No, seven days, *seven* nights," one said emphatically.

"You make it sound like two whole weeks."

"I hear those boats," said the young one, stooped, eyeing her color job. "I hear you wanna jump off by the end."

When the heavyset one cinched the smock on my neck I had to stretch my chin out to free my Adam's apple. I looked up to find her waiting for me in the mirror. "I trust you," I said. "Just shorter than it is now."

She spritzed my hair, shielding my face with her plump hand. She drew my hair up between her fingers, snapped at it, let it bend over in wet plates, drew up another row and went on. Her freckled chest pressed my shoulder. I raised my eyebrows to my friend but saw his shape go out the door.

When a telephone rang in the back, no one moved for it. The young stylist looked up from the aluminum foil of her color job after a few rings, and I understood someone was back there, working, or on break, and would answer.

In the time just after the phone stopped, my stylist said to the young stylist, "I'd think you'd be answering every call." She let out a sharp laugh, covered her mouth with her hand holding a spray bottle. "I'm sorry, I'll quit," she said. "I'm sure you'll get exactly what you want. We all will, won't we?" She spritzed water into the air for no reason, and it fell whitely around us.

A woman came out from behind the bamboo. "Brittany," she said.

The young stylist held up the brush and Tupperware as if to show she was busy.

"It's for you," the woman said.

"Well, I understand that, but can you bring it to me?"

My stylist raised her eyebrows at the back-and-forth.

"It's in the back," the woman said. Everyone was looking now, the customers in the mirrors, and the woman from the back shot a look at my stylist that made me uncomfortable.

The girl handed her the Tupperware and went out.

"I think it's about her grandmother," the woman said, coming near. Both of them looked to where the tiki lamps stood at an angle. "I was just giving her a hard time."

"The hospital doesn't just go around calling people."

I looked quickly out the door where in the dim evening light my friend jogged across the street to a convenience store.

"The dear thing still lives with her, doesn't she?"

"Her grandmother?" asked the color job.

The woman from the back nodded, but firmed up as if territorial with the information.

There was a noise from behind the bamboo. The woman from the back turned and stood rigid, Tupperware in hand, while the heavyset one started combing my hair over and over, without cutting. Everyone looked vaguely in front of themselves as the girl appeared from behind the bamboo. She retrieved the Tupperware and, without hesitation, examined her client's hair, finding where she'd left off. She sniffed once audibly, stirring the color. The woman from the back stood with nothing to do. Mine continued combing my hair, parting one side, then the other, glancing at the girl out of the corner of her eye. The train tooted coming out of the snow-covered tunnel. And my friend appeared in the glass door lit intermittently by the Christmas lights. He crossed his eyes and squished his cheek and nose, whitening them against the glass. I tried to motion to him without moving; all of the women watching him horrified, all but the girl concentrating on her work. He plugged his nose, pretended to swim with one arm, then the other, crossing the blue oval of glass, his silent slow movement, kicking a leg, rising as if through an aquarium, up and over the gray streets.

Finally the girl leaned her head back as though she had a bloody nose, smiled, and flicked her hair with the back of her gloved hand. But her chin trembled. She pinched her lips together so they disappeared. We were all watching now as she began to sob. "Oh," she said. "This is so silly."

My friend out on the sidewalk bowed grandly, his arm draped like an elephant's trunk. The heavyset stylist let out a sharp cry or laugh, I couldn't tell. None of us had any idea what to do.

2001

I had not spent much time in automobiles in Italy. As the interpreter swerved through traffic, connecting quarters of the city that, as a subway commuter, seemed to me like a system of ponds, I began to connect them one to another. He took the opportunity to tend to several errands with the car the agency had loaned him while I waited in the double-parked Fiat. Motorini zipped up and over the high cobbled surface of the piazzas, sending pigeons into the bright sky above the flower vendors and their newspapers.

I'd hoped when we set out that the interpreter would simply take me to a prearranged salon. Possibly that the agency would pay for it. But when he settled back into the seat after his last stop, sighed, then bumped us out into traffic, he said without looking at me from the side-view mirror, "And now, my friend, my pleasure. Where do we go?"

At the salon I sat rigid as the interpreter and stylist talked. The interpreter had gone for coffee while she washed my hair, then failed to return until midway through the cut. Flopping in the vacant chair next to me, he winked. "Looking very good," he said.

I regarded him out of the corner of my eye. "Well, I told her exactly what I wanted," I said.

He laughed and spoke to her and she laughed, but politely, for him. He got up and held his cigarette in front of her mouth unexpectedly. She hesitated, then leaned forward, smiled sheepishly through the smoke at him. He watched her exhale, his hand on my shoulder, eager to offer another drag, but she insisted he sit, glancing nervously around at the others in the shop.

The whole place was black, modern, great orchids stretched from the countertops like miniature giraffes. It was striking, the resemblances to Jeanette's salon. There was even a young boy in a school uniform who had several times been scolded by his mother when he lost a handle on an orange he was tossing from hand to hand.

A male employee escorted a customer past and heckled my stylist gently. I understood only *Americano* as she tried to continue working but couldn't help glancing at me in the mirror. I smiled with my lips together. The interpreter called something after the man, and the schoolboy looked up, surprised at the exchange. He stood and craned his neck, but was told to sit again although his mother and her stylist had stopped as well to watch. The interpreter spoke in a loud slow unaccented Italian, covering his heart for effect. He tried to egg the stylist on, but she only made brief eye contact with me in the mirror and went on with her work. She combed my hair down around the ears and flat against the back of my head, then focused on a point in the back, pushed it up with her comb, and studied it again. I edged up in the chair. There was a roar of laughter from the man in the back. The kid stood again, his mother having forgotten about him. Then in the quiet the girl said something to the interpreter. She motioned to the spot, and from under the smock I actually brought my hand back and felt my head.

"Marca de diavolo?" the interpreter said, rising from the chair. "Black hair? It does not look black to me," he said loudly, in English so no one understood him. He laughed anyway.

"It's a birthmark," I said, relieved. "My father had black hair."

One of the other stylists came over and stooped to look for herself. I shifted uncomfortably in the seat.

"She wants to know if you color it," the interpreter said.

The woman picked up several cut pieces of hair from my apron, squinted at them, then rolled them in her fingers until they fell separately into her palm.

"What's she doing?" I asked.

The interpreter shrugged me off, watching her. He said something and she smiled to herself, laughed finally, then clapped her hands clean as my stylist pulled the smock off unannounced and stood back waiting for me to stand.

"Eighty?" I said to the stylist at the counter. I looked at the interpreter, who shrugged.

The stylist said something to him that seemed annoyed.

He replied, gesturing apologetically toward the window where it was displayed: Primero — L 50,000.

One of the other stylists looked up at us from her cut. She said something and there was a quick agitated back-and-forth.

"Never mind," I said. I counted it out on the counter, then threw another twenty in, waving the money away.

The woman took only the eighty.

"Sir," the interpreter said. He put his hand on the extra money. "You don't need to."

"No, please," I said. I moved his hand from it.

"It is not custom."

The stylist said something that I spoke over.

"Of course she can. Please," I said to her. "It was a pleasure."

I squeezed the money into her complacent hand, held it there, nodded to her. She looked at the interpreter helplessly, and I pulled her hand closer, reached up her wrist with my other hand. I tried to get her to make eye contact with me, but she spoke to the interpreter.

"What did she say?"

He looked from my face to where I continued to hold her arm. "She's sorry if you're angry with the price."

She looked at me.

Over her shoulder several of the clients and stylists had stopped and sat watching. The boy's mother had come out nearly to the middle of the room.

"No," I said. "Forget it."

I took the wadded bill from her hand, held it up between my thumb and forefinger for the boy to see. Then gulped it into my mouth exaggeratedly, brushed my hands together like a stage magician, and opened my empty mouth to him.

2004

For nearly a year our unmarried house floated injuriously through the celestial whiteness of our daughter. I often lingered in her room after putting her down for the night, replacing her books on the bookshelf, preparing a morning diaper on the night-lit changing table. I'd look down over her dark eggshelled eyelids, her warm breath releasing, then stretch out on the floor dozing finally as the street lamp out the window broke apart into sleep. Anything to avoid the endless pursuit of arguments that awaited me downstairs.

Our own sleep was mainly cold, a draft of unfinished arguments as we tossed under the blankets, our shins bumping and retreating from each other. Or, I'd leave in one of the cars and park in an unfamiliar neighborhood. (I once looked up to see the iridescent street sign, *Oregon St.*—which seemed impossibly distant now—hovering in the night.) I'd cover myself in jackets and sleep until in the early dawn I'd have to run the engine for heat. Couples would emerge from their houses as if from Disney movies, kissing on the porch, and I'd think very melodramatically that it would be a long time before I had another woman. I'd stretch my face out in the rearview, looking for something I no longer saw in myself. It seemed clear to me my efforts to weather the cohabitation in order to be with my daughter would eventually be obscured by my leaving. I would be an absentee father, with a child growing up outside his home. I'd often start ill-fated conversations with women in grocery lines, or over the opened door of my car, asking for directions to a place I knew well, only to harass myself with the disappointment of the interaction for days.

It was on a morning like this, eating breakfast in the car, leaning forward so as not to spill on my shirt, that I watched a young woman hurry through the rain with her purse held over her head. She opened a salon and the lights came on in the gray street front. She stood in the oily window taking her shawl off, shaking it, squinting out at the cars raising walls of water towards the gutters. It was winter, northern California. Under the storm clouds the row of buildings seemed very low and dark, though it must only be the way I'm remembering it, like night. It must have been 9 a.m. But even that, for a salon, struck me as wasteful and somehow romantic. As if the place would remain vacant a few hours, the young woman alone mooning over the books or sweeping the place. Maybe she would dance by herself, twisting from mirror to mirror.

A man ducked in under her awning and peered out into the torrent like a wet cat. He propped his collar up. Then turned startled when she opened the salon door behind him. I hit the wipers to see them better. She motioned him in, but he refused, gesturing down the street. He was just getting out of the rain. She went back in and he raised his shoulders and ducked into the rainfall, splashing with each footfall.

I peeked my head in the door and then came into the loud music before she finally realized I was there. "Oh," she said, covering her heart.

"Sorry," I said. "Are you not open?"

"No, of course." She hurried to turn the music down. "I didn't hear you come in."

"Rock'n and roll'n in here," I said. I wiped the rain from my eyebrows, trying to smile as she looked me over. My disheveled appearance probably wasn't reassuring. I hung my jacket and rolled my sleeves to the elbow to cover the wrinkles. Then flattening the chest a bit, tucking the shirt bottom around my waist, I said, "May as well be sleeping at the office these days."

She gave me a pained look.

"Actually, do you have a bathroom?"

She motioned to a door beyond a set of mirrors and stood awkwardly as I passed her.

"Oh." I stopped. "Do you have any open appointments?"

She nodded. Her face was younger than I'd imagined.

"Good." I turned but stopped again. "How much?"

"Seventy-five dollars."

"Seventy-five dollars?" I tried to act casual, patting my front pockets. "Do you take cards?" I said, hoping they wouldn't, I could say I'd be right back with cash, and disappear.

"Of course."

Outside the bathroom window were a few sodden dumpsters in a courtyard they shared with a restaurant. No exit. Seventy-five dollars was a full day's work at both the jobs I'd taken (one doing yard work, and then at night, after putting our daughter down, crossing town to feed and bathe and carry to bed, in odd repetition of my rituals with my own little girl, a grown man stricken with cerebral palsy). There were better things—for my daughter, for the house—to spend the money on. But I was here, splashing water on my face in the bathroom. I'd sent out résumés for better work. Maybe through some act of grooming, or care—through some love act—the woman could hold my fears at bay, if only for an hour.

She massaged my head for several awkward minutes before I finally realized this was part of her service. I was able to relax, my neck loose in her hands, but was never able to forget where I was. I had never been in a salon alone before. Only her working, and me, watching her crane her neck to work the top of my head or scratching her own part using her third finger as she stood back and looked at my thinning hair. We were both quiet, the place cold; some of the rear chairs remained in near darkness. I listened to the scissors shear through a tall stand of my hair, falling around me, and puffed up the lap of the smock, pushing the hair to the floor. Her ankles there where she stood on the linoleum. Next to her another hydraulic chair. Cars passing in the rain. Twice someone stopped under the awning to get out of the rain before making a break for a car.

"I keep thinking they're gonna come in," she said. We both smiled towards the door where the back of a woman stood in the humid window. "I wish they would. I should probably switch all the lights on."

"I don't know," I said. "I kinda like being in here alone. It's nice. Makes it feel like we're at your house and you're just cutting my hair. This is a very fancy garage."

I hoped that she would laugh, but she only smiled.

"I don't think there's anything I like less than hair salons."

She raised her eyebrows at me and snorted. We both laughed in the mirror.

"I'm serious. Rather be at the dentist," I said. "I feel like everybody's watching me and that I have something wrong with my head.

Even now, with nobody else around, every time you stop I watch you in the mirror to see if there's something wrong."

She put her fingers on the top of my head like a claw and turned it a little. "Seems like a perfectly good head to me."

"I know, it's juvenile," I said. "I don't know, do you like cutting hair?"

She didn't look up and I thought she would let it die. With her head tilted, combing my hair through she said, "It's work. And you know, it's creative. In some ways. Or I keep it creative." She looked up at me as if to affirm something she was about to say. "I call the women that come in Milady. The boss doesn't like it, but it's all right. They like it. And to some of the men I jokingly say, 'Milord, how is the vestry today?'" She smiled to herself, working again. Her concentration returned. "It's steady work. People will always need haircuts I guess."

"Milady." I smiled.

"That sounds totally ridiculous, doesn't it? Milady," she said. Her hands fell to her side and she looked off towards the dim back end of the place. "I rolled my car last week—it's all I think about," she said. "I rolled my car and listen to me, all I can do is say into the back seat—to my dog—'Hang on, Buster, we're going over!'" She laughed outrageously, put her hand and comb to her mouth to try and stop herself, but couldn't. "His name is really Buster." She gagged. Her body twitching out some laugh against her will until finally, a deep breath, wiping a few tears from her cheek, she said, "Oh, do I like cutting hair."

At home, I hopped the fence and went around to the back door where I stopped briefly in the heavy drops from the eave and watched through the window as my daughter, in her long sleep shirt, came and went dragging an open umbrella. She scrunched her nose at me when I came in and we both looked at her mother, who was talking to her, and hadn't noticed I'd come in.

"—down and eat your breakfast."

I shot my daughter a look and squatted and she ran to me and took me around the neck. "Papa hair," she said.

"You went out and got a haircut?" her mother said. She snorted.

Tossed a spoon in the sink.

I looked up at her over our daughter's head. "It came with the room at the Hilton," I said.

She looked at the two of us, the girl like a chimpanzee on my chest now, and me dodging her hand with my head.

"You look militant."

"You trying to cut my hair too?" I said to my daughter. I growled at her and showed my teeth.

She shrieked, kicking up on my hip to reach my hair.

"You wanna cut it?"

She stopped and leaned back to look at me gravely in the face, then up at my hair, nodding, trying then to touch it in a more delicate way.

"You think you know how?" I said.

"Yes."

I stood her on the kitchen table, pushing her food away. Held my hands up in front of her. "Don't move, you're up very high." I inched away from her little body oddly levitating in front of me, like a doll on a countertop.

"Chaz, get her off the table. She's gonna hurt herself."

"No, she is not," I said, rummaging the drawer by the sink and finding, holding up for her mother, the scissors. "If anything, she's going to hurt me."

Our daughter stood perfectly still, hand extended for the scissors, teeth chattering with excitement.

"You are absolutely not going to do that in my house."

Without looking away from our daughter I said very clearly, "We're gonna learn two things today. One, how to cut Papa's hair. And two, how to use the vacuum."

She tested the scissors using both hands. Her eyes lit. And as I bowed my head I heard the metal shearing, felt the first tug at my scalp. I leaned into her, my eyes closed, holding to her porcelain legs until her small concentrated breaths lifted me, and I drifted, stolen of my weight as I'd once seen a horse rescued by crane from flood ground, its legs hanging free and weak and miles long.

■

South Beach

FROM *Annalemma*

AFTER EVE ATE THE APPLE, God created South Beach. He, Himself, was a bit stoned at the time.

He cut the water with a causeway: on one side He placed ships of garbage and cargo and gulls hovering in halos; on the other He set down mansions with yachts bobbing in ocean parking lots. He invented the rich and famous to fill the mansions and yachts—this was before Christ was born, in the bathroom of an after-hours club, with long hair He wore in solidarity for the meek.

Anyway.

"Night club city hall hotel houses!" God boomed. He crafted condos in the clouds and signs that burned onto the eyelids of the night sky—vacancy, heated pool, hourly rates—turning night into eternal day. The moon was made of neon lighting and advertised drink specials.

"Mango terra-cotta two-tone!" God bellowed. He built buzzing beach-front boutiques, vending machines to dispense designer drugs, glaring gift shops brimming with kitsch: ceramic alligators, plastic flamingos, cigars, suntan lotion, and rum. He poured people into the streets.

In the shadows of it all, He raised rundown walk-up tenements and implemented reverse rush hour for pornstar parents. He composed bass drones like baritone angels to sing their children to sleep. He provided them customers, waving soiled currency like flags of surrender.

And it was good.

When Christ turned sixteen, and realized His name came from a curse word spray-painted on a wall of the abandoned lifeguard tower in which He was conceived, He ran away from home.

God said, "Leave then! Utopian socialist! Bleeding heart hippie liberal leftnik! You're destined to die!"

God was feeling bellicose, so He invented evangelicals, fully equipped with mistresses from the South Pacific. He hired them to freeze Jesus in jewel-encrusted removable platinum pieces, to be sold on the Home Shopping Network to the mothers of aspiring rappers. But despite Christ's dismemberment and global distribution, God knew one day the boy would return.

Dear Father, the letter read, *You designed me to love unconditionally, knowing I'd grow up to resent you. You designed me to be everywhere, even after I left that hard-on you call home, so that I'd still be there in Spirit. But it doesn't matter, because you're incapable of love, you just make shit without a thought or a care. Even if you could love, you can't hug a ghost. You're sick, Dad. I pity you. But you already know that.* The letter was signed, *Your Begrudgingly Loving Son.*

God underwent a spiritual crisis. He took a second look at the Bible and diagnosed Himself bipolar. A self-prescribed binge of barbiturates brought Him to meet Barbarous in a rundown bar on the edge of the beach, where he plunged a broken beer bottle into the brute's back.

He left town for a while on a casino cruise until things cooled down.

For a while, God gave up on creation. He tried yoga and tai chi, yogurt and fruit, all fruitless. God was too restless. But eventually, God grew tired of sand and sun, of coke and orgies, and became indifferent, middle-aged, and alone.

He spent most hours in the den of a penthouse suite, making ghosts out of room service napkins, waiting for the boy. And then the headlines began to appear in all the papers that He read each morning before His swim:

Jesus Killed in the Mountains of Bolivia
Corpse of Christ Found in Congo
Holy Spirit Stabbed in Serbia
Holy Ghost Gutted in Gaza
Son of Man Suffers Sins of the World

God had to admit, the boy had balls. To die like that, again and again. To block the bowels of Hell instead of getting high in Heaven.

Knifed in Nicaragua
Burned Alive in Burma

And so on. The headlines continued, as God knew they would, for eternity.

With a semblance of parental pride, God installed a dimmer on the sky, turned down the neon, and pure daylight returned to the beach. He evicted the squatters from all the lifeguard towers, then razed the rickety structures. He reduced speakeasies and strip clubs to rubble, essentially erasing all history of His son's conception, and the unruly teenage years that followed. He used the scrap to make an artificial reef.

He hoped these gestures would register on His son's radar. That maybe the boy would pay the old man a visit.

He made preparations. He made adjustments. He made amends. And when Christ never showed, He made peace.

He made sure His final draft was suitable for humanity to inherit in His absence. And with that, God clapped the dust off His hands, unintentionally inventing the stars, and left for limbo.

Business went on without Him, despite a few hitches—shark bites, red tide, an investigative reporter who smuggled a black light into all the hotels.

Every now and then a tourist claimed the beach was haunted by a homeless man with sand lice dancing through the tangles of a bushy brown beard, shouting gibberish from atop the dunes.

∎

The Amazing Adventures
of Phoenix Jones

FROM *GQ*

I AM RUSHING THROUGH THE NIGHT to the emergency room to meet a real-life superhero called Phoenix Jones, who has fought one crime too many and is currently peeing a lot of blood. Phoenix has become famous these past months for his acts of anonymous heroism. He dresses in a superhero outfit of his invention and chases car thieves and breaks up bar fights and changes the tires of stranded strangers. I've flown to Seattle to join him on patrol. I only landed a few minutes ago, at midnight, and in the arrivals lounge I phoned his friend and adviser Peter Tangen, who told me the news.

"*Hospital?*" I said. "Is he okay?"

"I don't know," said Peter. He sounded worried. "The thing you have to remember about Phoenix," he added, "is that he's not impervious to pain."

"Okay," I said.

"I think you should get a taxi straight from the airport to the ER," he said.

So here I am, hurtling through the night, still with all my luggage. At 1:00 a.m. I arrive at the ER and am led into Phoenix's room. And there he is: lying in bed wearing a hospital smock, strapped to an IV, tubes going in and out of him. Still, he looks in good shape—muscular, black. Most disconcertingly, he's wearing an impeccably hand-crafted full-face black and gold rubber superhero mask.

Phoenix Jones, real-life superhero

"Good to see you!" he hollers enthusiastically through the mouth hole. He gives me the thumbs-up, which makes the IV needle tear his skin slightly.

"Ow," he says.

His two-year-old son and four-year-old stepson run fractiously around the room. "Daddy was out fighting bad guys in his Super Suit and now he has to wait here," he tells them. (I promise not to identify them, or his girlfriend, to protect his secret identity.)

He looks frustrated, hemmed in, fizzing with restless energy. "We break up two to three acts of violence a night," he says. "Two or three people are being hurt *right now* and I'm stuck here. It bothers me."

By "we" he means his ten-strong Seattle crew, the Rain City Superheroes. They were patrolling last night when they saw "this guy swinging at another guy outside a bar with a baseball bat. I ran across the street and he jabbed me in the stomach. Right under my armor."

Unfortunately the baseball bat landed exactly where he'd been punched a week earlier by another bar brawler holding a car key in his fist.

"A few hours ago I went to use the bathroom and I started peeing blood," he says. "A lot of it. So I came to the hospital."

I glance over at Phoenix's girlfriend. "There's no point worrying about it." She shrugs.

Finally, the doctor arrives with the test results. "The good news is there's no serious damage," he says. "You're bruised. It's very important that you rest. Go home and rest. By the way, why do you name a pediatrician as your doctor?"

"You're allowed to stay with your pediatrician until you're twenty-two," Phoenix explains.

We both look surprised: this huge, disguised man is barely out of childhood.

"Go home and rest," says the doctor, leaving the room.

"Let's hit the streets!" says Phoenix. "I'll get suited up!"

Phoenix didn't know this when he first donned the suit about a year ago, but he's one of around two hundred real-life superheroes currently patrolling America's streets, in Florida and New York City and Utah and Arizona and Oregon, and on and on, looking for wrongs to right. There's DC's Guardian in Washington, DC, who wears a full-body stars-and-stripes outfit and wanders the troubled areas behind the Capitol Building. According to Peter Tangen, the community's unofficial adviser, DC's Guardian has "extremely high clearance in the U.S. government. Nobody knows what he looks like. Nobody knows his name. Nobody knows his job. Nobody knows the color of his skin. I've seen him with his mask off. I've been to his house for dinner. But that's because of the level of trust he has in me."

And there are dozens more, like Salt Lake City's Citizen Prime, who wears steel armor and a yellow cape and is in real life "a vice-president of a Fortune 500 financial company," says Peter Tangen. Like the majority of real-life superheroes, Citizen Prime undertakes basically safe community work, helping the homeless, telling kids to stay off drugs, etc. All are regular men with jobs and families and responsibilities who somehow have enough energy at the end of the day to journey into America's more needy communities to do what they can. Phoenix is reputed to be by far the most daring of them all, leaping fearlessly into the kinds of life-threatening situations the other superheroes might well run shrieking from.

Every superhero has his origin story, and as we drive from the hospital to his apartment, Phoenix tells me his. His life, he says, hasn't been a breeze. He was raised in an orphanage in Texas and now spends his days teaching autistic kids how to read. One night last summer someone broke into his car. There was shattered glass on the floor. His stepson fell into it, badly gashing his knee.

"I got tired of people doing things that are morally questionable," he says. "Everyone's afraid. It just takes one person to say, 'I'm not afraid.' And I guess I'm that guy."

So he retrieved from the floor the mask the robber had used to break into his car, and he made his own mask from it. "They use the mask to conceal their identity," he says. "I use the mask to *become* an identity."

He called himself Phoenix Jones because the Phoenix rises from the ashes and Jones is America's most common surname. He was the common man rising from society's ashes.

* * *

2:30 a.m. Phoenix says he wouldn't normally invite a journalist to his Secret Identity apartment but they're moving on Monday as their safety was compromised: "You walk in and out in a mask enough times, people get to know where you live."

It is a very, very messy apartment. Comic books and toys and exercise videos are strewn everywhere. He disappears into the bedroom and emerges in his full bulletproof superhero attire.

"Let's bust some crime!" he hollers.

Downtown is deserted. We see neither his crew nor any crime.

"How are you feeling?" I ask him.

"I'm in a lot of pain," he says. "The cut's still bleeding. Internally and externally. A couple of my old injuries are flaring up. Like some broken ribs. I'm having a rough night."

I glance at him, concerned. "Maybe you're going too hard," I say. "Aren't you in danger of burning out?"

"Crime doesn't care how I feel," he says.

Just then a young man approaches us. He's sweating, looking distressed. "I've been in tears!" he yells.

He tells us his story. He's here on vacation, his parents live a two-hour bus ride away in central Washington, and he's only $9.40 short for the fare home. Can Phoenix please give him $9.40?

"I've been crying, dude," he says. "I've asked sixty or seventy people. Will you touch my heart, save my life, and give me nine dollars and forty cents?"

Phoenix turns to me. "You down for a car-ride adventure?" he says excitedly. "We're going to *drive the guy back to his parents!*"

The young man looks panicked. "Honestly, nine dollars and forty cents is fine," he says, backing away slightly.

"No, no!" says Phoenix. "We're going to *drive you home!* Where's your luggage?"

"Um, in storage at the train station . . ." he says.

"We'll meet you at the train station in ten minutes!" says Phoenix.

Thirty minutes later. The train station. The man hasn't showed up. Phoenix narrows his eyes. "I think he was trying to scam us," he says. "Hmm!"

"Can you be naive?" I ask him.

Phoenix Jones

There's a silence. "It happens to the best of us," he says.

Does this guilelessness make him delightfully naive or disturbingly naive? I wonder. He is, after all, planning to lead me into hazardous situations this weekend.

4:00 a.m. We finally locate his crew on a street corner near the train station. Tonight there's Pitch Black, Ghost, and Red Dragon. They're all costumed and masked and, although in good shape, shorter and stockier than Phoenix. He stands tall among them, and more eloquent, too. They're a little monosyllabic, as if they've decided to defer to their leader in all things.

They have a visitor—a superhero from Oregon named Knight Owl. He's been fighting crime since January 2008 and is in town for an impending comic-book convention. He's tall, masked, and muscular, in his mid-twenties, and dressed in a black-and-yellow costume.

They brief Phoenix on a group of crack addicts and dealers standing at a nearby bus stop. A plan is formed. They'll just walk slowly past them to show who's boss. No confrontation. Just a slow, intimidating walk past.

We spot the crack addicts right away. There're ten of them. They're huddled at the bus stop, looking old and wired, talking animatedly to each other about something. When they see us they stop talking and shoot us wary glances, wondering uneasily what the superheroes are covertly murmuring to each other.

This is what the superheroes are murmuring to each other:

KNIGHT OWL: "I've discovered a mask maker who does these really awesome owl masks. They're made out of old gas masks."

PHOENIX: "Like what Urban Avenger's got?"

KNIGHT OWL: "Sort of, but owl-themed. I'm going to ask her if she'll put my logo on it in brass."

PHOENIX: "That's awesome. By the way, I really like your black-and-yellow color scheme."

KNIGHT OWL: "Thank you. I think the yellow really pops."

PITCH BLACK: "I just want a straight-up black bandana. I can't find one for the life of me."

PHOENIX: "You should cut up a black T-shirt."

PITCH BLACK: "Hmm."

We're ten feet from the bus stop now. Close up these dealers and addicts look exhausted, burned out.

Leave them alone, I think. *Haven't they got enough to deal with? They'll be gone by the time the daytime people arrive. Why can't they have their hour at the bus stop? Plus, aren't we prodding a hornets' nest? Couldn't this be like the Taco Incident times a thousand?*

The Taco Incident. Ever since Phoenix burst onto the scene some weeks ago with a short item on CNN extolling his acts of derring-do, the wider superhero community has been rife with grumbling. Many of the two hundred real-life superheroes out there, evidently jealous of Phoenix's stunning rise, have been spreading rumors about him. The chief rumormongers have been New York City's Dark Guardian and Washington state's Mister Raven Blade. They say Phoenix is not as brave as he likes people to believe, and he's in it for personal gain, and his presence on the streets only serves to escalate matters. For this last criticism they cite the Taco Incident.

"Tell me about the Taco Incident," I ask Phoenix now.

He sighs. "It was a drunk driver. He was getting into his car so I tried to give him a taco and some water to sober him up. He didn't want it. I kept insisting. He kept saying no. Eventually he got kind of violent. He tried to shove me. So I pulled out my Taser and I fired some warning shots off. Then the police showed up . . ."

"I didn't realize he was a drunk driver," I said. "The other superheroes implied it was just a regular, random guy you were trying to force a taco onto. But still" — I indicate the nearby crack dealers — "the Taco Incident surely demonstrates how things can inadvertently spiral."

"They're in my house," he resolutely replies. "Any corner where people go — that's my corner. And I'm going to defend it."

We walk slowly through the drug dealers. Nothing happens. Everyone just stares at each other, muttering angrily. It is 5:00 a.m. Our first night's patrolling together ends. I'm glad, as I found the last part a little frightening. I am not a naturally confrontational person, and I still have all my luggage with me.

When I was growing up in the 1970s and devouring Batman comics, introverted geeks like me tended not to actually patrol the streets

Knight Owl

Pitch Black

looking for crimes to thwart. We were the lame ones, running shrieking from real-life danger, cheering Batman vicariously on from our homes. How did all that change? How did my nerd successors get to be so brave?

The Real-Life Superhero Movement actually began, their folklore goes, all the way back in 1985, in Winter Park, Florida, when a young man (whose real-life identity is still a closely guarded secret) built himself a silver suit, called himself Master Legend, and stepped out onto the streets. He was an influential, if erratic, inspiration to those who followed.

"Ninety percent of us think Master Legend is crazy," Phoenix Jones told me. "He's always drinking. He believes he was born wearing a purple veil and has died three times. But he does great deeds of heroism. He once saw someone try to rape a girl and he beat the guy so severely he ended up in a hospital for almost a month. He's an enigma."

The rise of the mega–comic conventions has surely helped fuel the movement. I remember a friend, the film director Edgar Wright, returning from his first San Diego Comic Con, saucer-eyed with tales of hitherto reclusive geeks wandering around in immaculate homemade costumes, their heads held high.

"It was like Geek Pride," he said.

But the community has really blossomed post 9/11 and especially during the recession of the past few years.

"It's in the zeitgeist of our nation to help strangers in need," says Phoenix's friend Peter Tangen. "Many RLSHs [real-life superheroes] were raised learning morality from comic books and have applied that to their everyday lives. It's our natural way of reacting to the challenges of the day."

There's no national convention or gathering, but Peter Tangen is doing all he can to make them a structured, self-respecting community, with a coherent online presence.

Peter's origin story is as remarkable as any of the RLSHs'. He is by day a Hollywood studio photographer. He's responsible for a great many of the instantly recognizable superhero movie posters—Tobey Maguire as Spider-Man, etc. But he's always felt like a cog in the machine.

"I'm one of those guys that toils in obscurity," he says. "Nobody knows my name because you don't get credit on a movie poster."

When he learned there were people doing in real life what the likes of Tobey Maguire only pretended to do on a film set, it unlocked something profound within him. So he approached them, offering to photograph them in heroic, un-ironic poses. His hope is to de-ridicule them—make them seem valiant, worthy of respect. The project has become Peter's calling in life.

It is testament to Phoenix that most people had no idea their world existed until he came along. The CNN report praising his bravery has now had six hundred thousand YouTube hits. Something about him, and not the others, has captured the imagination. I hope to work out what that thing is.

The next morning I have coffee at a downtown Seattle café with Knight Owl.

"Last night might have been dangerous," I tell him, sounding annoyed.

"We ruffled some feathers." He nods. "When we walked past that bus stop there were people mumbling under their breath. It could have got out of control. I don't think they would have gunned us down. But they may have taken potshots and run. Still, shots fired would have been a crime. It would have been attempted murder in my opinion."

"Well, I'm glad none of that actually happened," I say.

Knight Owl used to be a graphic designer. "There was no promotion potential. I simply existed. It was thankless. I wanted something more with my life." So he joined the movement.

There is, he says, a bit of a superhero trajectory. When they start out they make rookie mistakes. Then they hit their stride. Then they not infrequently start to believe they have actual superpowers. Then they burn out and quit.

The first rookie mistake is to adopt a superhero name that's already in use.

"It's a general faux pas," he says. "Anything with the words *Night, Shadow, Phantom,* those dark, vigilante-type-sounding names tend to get snapped up pretty fast."

"Have there been any other Knight Owls?" I ask.

"There was an Owl," he says. "The Owl. But he ended up changing his name to Scar Heart, as he'd had a heart transplant."

He says he chose his name before he knew there was a Nite Owl in the *Watchmen* comic, so when people online tell him, "You're a fucking fag and by the way, Knight Owl's taken, haven't you seen the *Watchmen*?" they don't know what they're talking about.

The second rookie mistake is to "get caught up in the paraphernalia. People should think more about the functionality."

"Capes clearly aren't functional," I say, "because they can get snagged on things. Is cape-wearing a rookie mistake?"

"If you're going to do some serious crime-fighting there'd better be a good reason for a cape." He nods. "And grappling hooks. No, no, no, no, no! What? You think you're going to scale a building? What are you going to do when you get up there? Swoop down? Parachute down? You're not going to have enough distance for the parachute to even open."

Grappling hooks was one of Phoenix Jones's rookie mistakes. He also had a net gun, but on one occasion it backfired and ensnared him and he fell on the floor and had to be cut loose by the police. So now he leaves it at home.

Then, at the other end of the trajectory, are the burnouts. I ask Knight Owl if he's worried about Phoenix. Maybe he could become a burnout.

"I think he should take his doctor's advice, rest up, get healthy, get strong," he replies. "The way he's going is a recipe for disaster."

I talk to Phoenix on the phone. He's frustrated that I never saw him engage in any proper crime-fighting. I promise to stick around with him and give it another chance. He says a trip to the dangerous Seattle suburb of Belltown at 4:00 a.m. on a Saturday night should do the trick. We make a date.

Meanwhile . . .

. . . San Diego. Wednesday night.

I've been wanting to see another superhero operation at work to compare Phoenix with, so I've flown here to meet Mr. Xtreme. He's

Ghost

been patrolling most nights for the past four years, the last eight months with his protégé, Urban Avenger.

They pick me up at 9:00 p.m. outside my hotel. Both are heavily costumed. Mr. Xtreme is a thickset man—a security guard by day—wearing a green and black cape, a bulletproof vest, a green helmet and visor upon which fake eyes have been eerily painted. His outfit is covered with stickers of a woman's face—Kitty Genovese. In March 1964, she was stabbed and seriously wounded in her doorway in Kew Gardens, Queens, New York. Her attacker ran away. During the next half-hour thirty-eight bystanders saw her lying there and did nothing. Then her attacker returned and killed her. She has become, understandably, a talisman for the RLSH movement.

You cannot see an inch of Urban Avenger's body. He's wearing a weird, customized gas mask, green-tinted sunglasses, a red full-length hoodie, and long black leather gloves. Underneath it all he looks quite small and skinny. He says he's in his late twenties, has children, and works "in the food-service industry." That's all he'll reveal to me about his secret identity.

He says he loves being covered from head to toe. "When I wear this I don't have to react to you in any way. Nobody knows what I'm thinking or feeling. It's great. I can be in my own little world in here."

"I know *exactly* what you mean," I say. "I was once at a Halloween party and I didn't take off my mask all night. It completely eliminated all social anxiety."

"Sometimes I wish I never had to take the mask off," says Urban Avenger.

We begin our patrol through the nice, clean, well-to-do downtown San Diego. We pass bars and clubs filled with polite-looking young drinkers. A few take pictures of them on their phones. Others yell, "It isn't Halloween anymore!" from car windows. Urban Avenger says he doesn't understand how Phoenix is forever chancing upon crimes being committed. He's so *lucky*.

"What are the odds?" He sighs. "I almost never see *anything*." He pauses. "Last October we got involved in breaking up some street fights."

"Five months ago?" I say.

"We haven't really seen anything since," he says. "It's been really quiet around here. Did you and Phoenix Jones patrol Belltown in Seattle?"

"I believe we're going to," I say.

"Google 'Gunshots in Belltown' and you'll come up with a hundred stories of gunshots being fired in, like, the last *year*," he says wistfully.

Some boys pass us. "Want some reefer? Ganja? Weed?" they quietly murmur.

"No, that's all right," says Urban Avenger, walking quickly on. The boys shrug and continue on their way.

"Good thing I got all that on video," Urban Avenger eventually calls after them, indicating a small camera attached to his shoulder.

"Crack? Heroin? PCP?" the boys call back.

"Did you really film it?" I ask.

"No," says Urban Avenger. We continue our patrol.

"I noticed that you didn't make citizen's arrests on the drug dealers," I say.

"We didn't have probable cause," explains Mr. Xtreme. "All they did is say something. If they'd shown us crack rocks or marijuana it might have been a different story."

"You could have said you wanted to buy some and then they'd have got the drugs out of their pockets and you could have arrested them," I say.

There's a short silence. "That's true," says Urban Avenger.

As we reach the end of the patrol we get talking about burnout.

"I can relate to burnout," says Mr. Xtreme. "All the times I thought about hanging it up. But what would I move on to?"

"The person under the mask really hasn't accomplished much," says Urban Avenger. "But as a superhero I can go out and do something. I can feel like a better person, kind of."

"If I wasn't trying to make a difference in the community, I'd just be sitting around drinking beer," says Mr. Xtreme. "Watching movies, going broke, just being negative."

* * *

The real-life superheroes like to portray their motives as wholly benevolent, but if they were being driven purely by philanthropy they'd have become police officers or firefighters or charity volunteers. Something else is evidently propelling them—a narcissism. It's an odd sort of narcissism, of course, when the narcissist disguises their face, but the lust for fame and glory is unmistakable.

Only one of them, however, is achieving it: Phoenix Jones.

Back in Seattle he said he knew why he, alone, has captured the public's imagination. It's his bravery amid a community of superheroes who talk the talk but in practice basically don't do much more than hand out food to the homeless.

"When you wake up one day and decide to put on spandex and give out sandwiches, something's a little off," he said. "I don't call them real-life superheroes. I call them real-life sandwich-handlers."

In fact there's only one other crew out there actively looking for dangerous scrapes, and that's the NYI—the New York Initiative. And so, in the days before returning to Seattle, I email to ask if I can join them. I receive a very non-comic-book response. Yes, I can, but only if I accord them " . . . professional respect by cooperating with our scheduling and more importantly our tactics in the field . . . A bullet-proof vest will be available for your use . . . The scheduling is not negotiable. —Zero, co-founder of the New York Initiative."

We meet for a strategy briefing outside a movie theater near Washington Square Park, Lower Manhattan, at 10:00 p.m. There are ten of them. They don't look much like superheroes. They look quite intimidating, in fact, like a street gang, or some kind of private security detachment dressed entirely in black, with only cursory flashes of color.

"I look at it like a homeland soldier who has stickers on his helmet," explains Zero, a tall, good-looking, blond man. "I'm an artist. I'm a fighter. I'm a radical. I'm in a state of unrest." He pauses. "I'm trying to promote a new term instead of *superhero*: X-Alt. It's short for Extreme Altruist. I think it's going to open a lot of doors for people who don't want to be directly linked to the superhero stigma."

"Is any of this because of Phoenix—" I begin.

"We're not going to comment on Phoenix Jones," snaps Zero, shooting me a look.

Before Phoenix came along Zero and his crew—headed by the

veteran superhero of nine years' standing Dark Guardian—were America's most famous RLSHs. But these days the media don't really want to know them.

They put a bulletproof vest on me and the night's maneuvers begin. The plan is to confront the pot dealers in Washington Square Park, those men who sell to the students at the adjacent New York University.

We enter the park at 11:00 p.m. It is all very quick and efficient. A dealer is standing alone, looking incredibly startled and upset to see ten frightening men rushing toward him.

"Are you the police?" he says, in a small voice.

The superheroes surround him, shining torches in his face, screaming, "This is a drug-free park! A drug-free park! People, not drugs!"

They look like a pack of dogs chasing a fox. The dealer practically chokes with fright.

"You don't know anything about me," he shouts, running away onto the Manhattan streets.

Even though the operation seemed to me to unfold with a textbook precision, an embarrassed-looking Zero asks to speak to me quietly.

"It was a disorganized clusterfuck," he says, evidently furious with himself, like a virtuoso opera singer who does a flawless performance and then beats himself up. "Please don't write about how disorganized we were. If the dealers read it they'll think they can take us . . ."

My night with the NYI leaves a bad taste in my mouth. These men just seemed menacing, with no fun to them. I don't want my superheroes to be bullies. I want goofy charm. When Phoenix Jones walks down the street passersby point and laugh and gasp. Whereas all the NYI seem to get are anxious sideways glances. I agree with Zero: there's nothing superheroish about them at all.

Seattle. Saturday night. Phoenix Jones is in a bad way. He's still sick from the stabbing and the baseball bat incidents and has now developed a fever of 102.5.

"I found out this morning I have tetanus," he tells me.

Red Dragon

"You have to sleep," I say.

"No sleeping for us," says Phoenix.

I'm starting to like Phoenix a lot. For all his naivety, there's something infectiously upbeat about him. He's forever cheerful and positive and energetic. I ask him if he's addicted to crime-fighting and he says, "Yeah, I guess you could put it in the addiction category. It's the highlight of my day. Addictions are normally detrimental to health. This is detrimental to my health."

He puts his positive spirit down to a stable home life: "Me and my girlfriend have been together since I was sixteen. I make my own money. To be a successful superhero, you've got to have your life in line."

This will be our final night patrolling together. Phoenix is still embarrassed about our essentially crime-free washout patrol of the other night and is hoping to show me something more dramatic. They're a small team tonight—Pitch Black and Ghost are his only companions.

We begin at 1:00 a.m. in Pioneer Square. The bars are closing and drunk kids are piling onto the streets, but there's still a frustrating absence of crime. Phoenix notices a girl sobbing in an alleyway.

"Are you okay?" he asks her, bounding over.

"We're good," her friend says, quite sharply.

But then, from somewhere up the street, we hear a shout: "*I'm going to fuck you, bitch.*"

"Let's go!" yells Phoenix. He, Ghost, Pitch Black, and I start to run frantically toward the mystery commotion.

"It's the YouTube guy!" a nearby teenager shouts delightedly. "Can I get a picture of you?"

Phoenix screeches to a halt.

"I'll be right with you guys!" he calls to us. He poses for the girl.

"Phoenix!" I sigh.

By the time Phoenix has had his picture taken, the potential criminal and victim are nowhere to be seen.

By 3:00 a.m. we are giving up hope. Phoenix is reduced to suggesting we rent a hotel room, phone some prostitutes, and ask them on their arrival if they need help escaping the web of prostitution.

"I think the problem with the plan," I say, "is if a prostitute turns up at a hotel room and sees three men in masks, she's not going to immediately think, *Superhero*. Plus, she may have to travel right across Seattle. It'll be an hour out of her night." They agree to abandon the idea.

Suddenly we notice a man across the street drop a small, clear bag onto the ground at the feet of another man.

"*Yahtsee!*" yells Phoenix. He rushes across the road. "What did you just drop?" he asks them.

"Pretzels," says the man, picking the bag up and showing it to us.

There's a silence.

"Good!" says Phoenix.

We adjourn to a nearby café. "Aargh!" says Phoenix, in frustration.

Our very last hope, at 4:00 a.m., is Belltown. When we turn the corner into the district, everything changes. By day this place is nice—with bars and restaurants and art galleries. It's just down the road from the famous Pike Place market. But now, at 4:00 a.m., the dealers staring at us look nothing like the exhausted old crack heads from the bus stop, nor the two-bit pot dealers from Washington Square Park. These are large gangs of wiry young men. They stand on every block. The police are nowhere to be seen. I take in the scene and instinctively take a small step backward.

"There's a possibility we could get into a fight," whispers Pitch Black. "If that happens, back off, okay?"

"*What are you doing?*" a man calls from across the street. He's part of a nine-strong gang.

"Patrolling," Phoenix calls back. "What are *you* doing?"

He, Pitch Black, and Ghost walk toward him. I reluctantly follow.

"You've got to respect people's block, man," he's saying. "You don't come down here with your ski masks on. What are you doing, getting yourselves entwined in people's lives? You guys are going to get hurt. You understand? You want to see our burners?"

I'm sure I remember from *The Wire* that a burner is a stolen cell phone. But that doesn't sound contextually right.

"I don't care," says Phoenix.

"You don't care?"

"Not really."

"Not really?"

"I've already been shot once," says Phoenix.

"I've been shot *three times!*" another member of the gang says, looking weirdly proud. "One motherfucker round here got shot in the nighttime. Innocent bystanders get shot here. Think about the bigger picture. You're putting your lives on the line. If you guys get killed, if you guys are in a casket, your mamas are going to be like, 'For *what?*'"

"Don't be a hero," another adds. "That superhero shit? This is real life! You're going to get hurt, fucking around." He pauses. "How you feed your family is not how we feed our family. For real. We're not out here just for the fun and just for the show-and-tell. This is *real life.*"

I am finding myself ostentatiously nodding at everything the crack dealers are saying, I suppose in the hope that if the shooting starts they'll remember my nods and make the effort to shoot around me.

"I appreciate the info," says Phoenix.

Suddenly a gang member takes a step forward and peers at Phoenix through his mask.

"You're a *brother?*" he says. "You're a BROTHER and you're out here looking like THIS? You've got to be out of your fucking mind, man."

And then, it all changes. "I feel threatened right now," he says. "You've got ski masks on. I don't know if you're trying to rob me. A guy got shot last Friday in Belltown by somebody with a mask on. Is that you?"

"You don't have to be here," says Phoenix. "You've got choices."

"I've been in the system since I was ten years old!" the man yells. "I haven't got no choices! When your kids get older this is going to be the same shit."

"I disagree," says Phoenix.

"It can't be better!" the man yells. "This is it!" A silence. Then, "When I see ski masks I'm thinking, *Are these guys going to rob me?*"

The nine men withdraw up the block to decide what to do next.

"Have a good night. Good meeting you," calls Phoenix.

They're watching us, murmuring to each other. Their problem is

Knight Owl, Phoenix Jones, and Red Dragon on patrol

that nobody wants to buy crack in front of three men dressed as superheroes. While Phoenix and his crew stand here, the dealers are losing all their business.

Phoenix points to two packets of cigarettes under the windshield wiper of a nearby car.

"Those are indications that you can buy here," he says. "So I'm going to take them off and annoy the crap out of them."

He scrunches the packets up and throws them onto the sidewalk.

At this, one of the gang steps forward. If you were watching from across the road it would seem as if he just wanders past us. But in fact he whispers something as he does: "You keep staying on our block we gonna have to show you what the burner do."

"Thank you, it's great meeting you," says Phoenix.

"What's a burner?" I whisper.

"A gun," Phoenix whispers back.

The man loops and rejoins the others.

The streets are deserted. It's just the dealers and us. But then, miraculously, a taxi passes. I flag it. The superheroes all have bulletproof vests. I have nothing. I have a cardigan. I want to see how the drama plays out but I don't want to be killed. "I'll give you twenty bucks to just *stay here*," I say to the driver.

He looks around, taking in the scene in an instant. "No," he says.

"Thirty?" I say.

And then, suddenly, the whole gang, all nine of them, some with their hands down their trousers, as if they're holding guns just under their waistlines, walk toward us. I can't see much of Phoenix's face under his mask but I can see by the way his hands are involuntarily shaking that he is terrified.

"My shift is over," calls the taxi driver. "I need to go home now."

"Forty!" I yell. "Just stay there!"

"*I don't care about the money!*" the driver yells. But he doesn't move.

The nine men get closer.

"Are we leaving or are we standing?" says Phoenix.

"We're standing," says Ghost.

"We're standing," says Pitch Black.

"You're willing to *die* for this shit?" one of the men is yelling.

"You're willing to *DIE* for this shit?" They reach us. "You guys are dumb motherfuckers," he says. "I don't even know what to say. You guys are *fucking stupid*." He stares at Phoenix. But then his voice softens. "If you guys are going to stand here and die for it I guess we're going to have to walk home. We should shoot your ass, but I guess we've got to go home."

And they do. They disperse. They go home.

"You *won!*" I tell Phoenix.

I can practically hear his heart pounding.

"They had the weapons, the numbers, but they backed down to the image of Phoenix Jones," he says.

"I'm going to bed," I say.

"We'll stand here for ten minutes and solidify the corner," he replies. "You don't want to stand with us?"

"No," I say. "I definitely don't."

I jump into the taxi. And when I arrive back at the hotel my legs buckle and I almost fall onto the floor.

5:00 a.m. Phoenix telephones. He's shrieking with laughter, babbling, hyperventilating, letting out all the adrenaline.

"That was *ridiculously intense!*" he's yelling. "In a few hours I've got to be a *day-care worker!*"

It is the next afternoon. There's a comic convention in town. I spot Knight Owl and one of Phoenix's friends, Skyman.

"Ooh, look, the Rocketeer!" says Skyman. "You *never* see Rocketeer costumes! That is *priceless!* I gotta get me a photo of that! Ooh! Lady Riddler! Nice!"

Skyman approaches a Batman.

"Is that a real bulletproof outfit?" he asks him.

"No," Batman replies, a little apologetically.

"This place," I tell Knight Owl, "is full of costumed people who would never confront drug dealers in the middle of the night. You and Phoenix and Skyman exist in some shadow world between fantasy and reality."

"Yeah, man," Knight Owl replies. "What we do is *hyper*reality!"

And then there are cheers and gasps and applause. Phoenix Jones has arrived. He is a superstar here. He sees me and we hug—two brave warriors who have been through a great adventure together.

"Thank you for making our city safe!" a woman in the crowd calls out to him.

"You're a very cool man!" someone else shouts.

I tell Phoenix it is time for me to leave.

"When you write this be sure to tell everyone that what we do is dangerous," he says.

"I think you're great," I say. "But I'm worried you're going to get yourself killed."

"Well, don't make it seem like I'd be dying for a choice," he replies. "I couldn't quit if I wanted. You know how many people in this city look up to me? I'm like the state's hero."

And I suddenly realize that I feel about Phoenix the same way everyone here does. I think he is an awesome superhero.

As I walk out I hear a father whisper to his young son, "That's a *real* superhero."

"Are you a *real superhero?*" the little boy asks Phoenix.

"I'm real as you can get," Phoenix replies.

Afterword

Six months pass and then, one day in mid-October 2011, Phoenix is everywhere. My first thought when I see, via my Google news search, that four hundred and thirty-three media outlets have in a matter of hours published articles about Phoenix, is that he must be dead.

It turns out that he isn't dead.

Self-proclaimed Seattle crime fighter "Phoenix Jones" was arrested early Sunday morning when he pepper sprayed a group of people leaving a club. Now, in the aftermath, his identity has been revealed. Phoenix Jones is actually Benjamin Fodor. He is 23 years old, lives in Seattle and is a Mixed Martial Artist. Seattle police detective Jeff Kappel said the group was leaving a club near 1st Avenue about 2:30 a.m. when Fodor, in costume, intervened.

"They were dancing and having a good time," Kappel said. "An unknown adult male suspect came up from behind and pepper sprayed the group."

— Seattle's Q13 Fox News Online, 10 October 2011

Hours later one of the partygoers—a woman named by the media only as Maria—gives an interview to a Seattle radio station, King/5:

> We were just walking down to our parking lot after having a good time in Seattle, when a little argument broke out between our group and another group, and all of a sudden we were attacked. I turn around and we're being attacked by these guys wearing Halloween costumes. He says, "I'm a superhero" and sprays everyone. Nothing gives him a right to do that. That's harassment and assault.

Oh, Phoenix, I think as I read these reports. I put my life on the line for you. What have you done?

I try to reach him but to no avail. He's in a jail cell somewhere in Seattle.

And then, a few hours later, a shakily filmed and chaotic thirteen-minute video appears on Vimeo. It turns out that one of Phoenix's group filmed the whole thing.

The video: it's late at night in some floodlit industrial part of Seattle. The superheroes are patrolling, as normal, when one of them suddenly yells: "Phoenix! Look down! Huge fight!"

"Go! Go! Go! Go! Go!" Phoenix yells, clearly thrilled, running instantly into the midst of the altercation. "Call nine-one-one!" he shouts to his friends. "Call nine-one-one!"

As soon as Phoenix enters the fray—and it's hard to tell how violent the fray had been because the moment Phoenix arrives everyone stops fighting and just stares, baffled, at him—a small woman begins to repeatedly hit him with her shoe.

"You piece of shit," she yells. (This is the woman later identified as Maria.)

Everything becomes chaotic. A car zooms in and deliberately hits a pedestrian. It is presumably a car driven by one of the party goers, and makes me suspect that the street fight Phoenix intervened in had not been a friendly little nothing thing, as the police and Maria had intimated, but something more serious.

"Where are the cops?" Phoenix yells. "We need the cops now. This is getting serious."

A young man races toward Phoenix and he responds by pepper-spraying him in the face.

"I got fucking pepper spray in my eye!" Maria yells at one point.

A terrified-looking bystander, a nerdy man in a sweater, calls the police and stammers into the phone: "A huge group of people are fighting and there's pepper spray and superheroes and I don't know."

"Protect yourselves!" Phoenix yells.

"Oh my God, oh my God," says the nerdy bystander, and as I watch this from the safety of my home I think, *There but for the grace of God go I.*

The video ends.

Phoenix is booked into jail on four counts of assault. He's released on bail the following afternoon. Two days later—a few hours before he is due to be arraigned in court—my Skype flickers into life.

"Phoenix!" I say, startled. "You're unmasked!"

"The police took my Super Suit," he says. He sounds sorrowful. "I was debating whether to show you my face or just these . . ." He waves his biceps in front of the Skype camera. "Hey!" he says, pretending to be the voice of his biceps. "Remember me?"

"I do remember you," I say.

Phoenix doesn't look like I'd imagined he would. All I'd had to go on was the muscular physique, so I assumed his face would be tougher, more stern or something. But, while handsome, he's also unexpectedly goofy-looking. He's wearing nerdy, quite effeminate spectacles, and has a strange haircut that looks like an upside-down bucket.

"That's an incredible haircut," I say.

"Yeah, it's like Kid 'n Play, the Black Elvis," he explains. "So. Anyway. The police stole my Super Suit. They said it was evidence of a crime. But if someone commits a so-called assault, you don't take their shirt and pants."

"It does seem punitive," I say. "What did you say to them when they took your suit?"

"I said, 'Really?' They said, 'Yeah, that way we can keep your big mouth shut.' It's been a rough road."

"How does it feel to be unmasked?" I ask.

"Extremely uncomfortable, to say the least," says Phoenix. "They're not going to charge me with a crime. They can't. So I'm going to be sitting there in court in a few hours, unmasked, not charged with anything. It's ridiculous."

"Unmasked and named," I say. "Will people knowing your name now be problematic for the superheroism?"

There's a short silence.

"Wait," Phoenix says. He looks startled. "People know my *name?*"

Oh my God, I think. *Nobody has told him.*

"Phoenix," I say with concern. "Yes. They do."

"Hehehehehe!" says Phoenix. "I knew that! I'm just kidding you!"

"Oh, Phoenix!" I say.

I thought I'd find him humbled, perhaps even broken, but he's as enthusiastic as ever. He's convinced there's no case against him. "The police said they were frolicking and dancing," he says. "My video comes out and there's no frolicking, no dancing. They're trying to make it seem like I was out of control. What kind of guy who's out of control stands there and lets a girl hit him in the face thirty-six times with a shoe?"

"She says she was pepper-sprayed," I say.

"My pepper spray has orange dye in it," Phoenix replies. "So no way was she pepper-sprayed by any spray belonging to Phoenix Jones. So she can take that claim and . . . throw it away."

"But still," I say. "In hindsight would you do anything differently?"

"Yeah," says Phoenix. "Next time I'm in a situation like that I'm going to use more of my superpowers. I'm going to freeze time so I can make every decision right." He pauses. "No. I didn't do anything wrong."

Phoenix seems in high spirits. He has a new girlfriend—a superhero named Purple Reign. She looks veiled and impressive and an excellent match. Phoenix says the assault charge is nothing about the incident and all about a pre-existing police agenda to shut him down.

"I dress up as a superhero and fight crime because I like to," he says. "They dress up as cops and don't fight crime because they like to."

But, he says, their agenda to disempower him by unmasking and naming him has failed: "You're not a superhero until you take the mask off. Think about it. Batman wasn't Batman until he was also Bruce Wayne. Phoenix Jones isn't Phoenix Jones until he's also the other man."

"Benjamin Fodor," I say. "Benjamin Fodor."

"You can't stay masked forever," he says. "I wanted to, sure. But now I can talk to kids in hospitals. I can check into any school in America. I can do a lot of stuff I couldn't do before. There are so many opportunities I never thought would open up. I can go in my Super Suit and meet the president of the United States if I want to. I can take my mask off and take photos with him."

"That might not be as easy as you think," one of Phoenix's friends murmurs in the background.

"They tried to take me out but they gave me a bigger voice," says Phoenix. "Everyone who thought I was crazy now sees I'm a man. I'm a man with a history of activism and no criminal record. I'm in great shape. Now everyone's going, 'Wait! He's a professional mixed martial arts trainer! Wait! He's CPR certified and trained! Wait! He's the main manager of an autistic home!' They turned me from a weird rubbered-out freak into an American Superhero. I think they thought they'd find someone who lives in his basement and doesn't have many friends and is sort of socially awkward, and instead they got a guy living . . ." Phoenix pauses. ". . . the American Dream."

Phoenix Jones. Unmasked but undimmed. As I write this the Seattle police are yet to decide whether to press charges.

GEORGE SAUNDERS

∎

Tenth of December

FROM *The New Yorker*

THE PALE BOY with unfortunate Prince Valiant bangs and cublike mannerisms hulked to the mudroom closet and requisitioned Dad's white coat. Then requisitioned the boots he'd spray-painted white. Painting the pellet gun white had been a no. That was a gift from Aunt Chloe. Every time she came over he had to haul it out so she could make a big stink about the woodgrain.

Today's assignation: walk to pond, ascertain beaver dam. Likely he would be detained. By that species that lived amongst the old rock wall. They were small but, upon emerging, assumed certain proportions. And gave chase. This was just their methodology. His aplomb threw them loops. He knew that. And reveled it. He would turn, level the pellet gun, intone: Are you aware of the usage of this human implement?

Blam!

They were Netherworlders. Or Nethers. They had a strange bond with him. Sometimes for whole days he would just nurse their wounds. Occasionally, for a joke, he would shoot one in the butt as it fled. Who henceforth would limp for the rest of its days. Which could be as long as an additional nine million years.

Safe inside the rock wall, the shot one would go, Guys, look at my butt.

As a group, all would look at Gzeemon's butt, exchanging sullen glances of: Gzeemon shall indeed be limping for the next nine million years, poor bloke.

Because yes: Nethers tended to talk like that guy in *Mary Poppins*.

Which naturally raised some mysteries as to their origin here on Earth.

Detaining him was problematic for the Nethers. He was wily. Plus could not fit through their rock-wall opening. When they tied him up and went inside to brew their special miniaturizing potion —

Wham!—he would snap their antiquated rope with a move from his self-invented martial arts system, Toi Foi, a.k.a. Deadly Forearms. And place at their doorway an implacable rock of suffocation, trapping them inside.

Later, imagining them in their death throes, taking pity on them, he would come back, move the rock.

Blimey, one of them might say from withal. Thanks, guv'nor. You are indeed a worthy adversary.

Sometimes there would be torture. They would make him lie on his back looking up at the racing clouds while they tortured him in ways he could actually take. They tended to leave his teeth alone. Which was lucky. He didn't even like to get a cleaning. They were dunderheads in that manner. They never messed with his peen and never messed with his fingernails. He'd just abide there, infuriating them with his snow angels. Sometimes, believing it their coup de grâce, not realizing he'd heard this since time in memorial from certain in-school cretins, they'd go, Wow, we didn't even know Robin could be a boy's name. And chortle their Nether laughs.

Today he had a feeling that the Nethers might kidnap Suzanne Bledsoe, the new girl in homeroom. She was from Montreal. He just loved the way she talked. So, apparently, did the Nethers, who planned to use her to repopulate their depleted numbers and bake various things they did not know how to bake.

All suited up now, NASA. Turning awkwardly to go out door.

Affirmative. We have your coordinates. Be careful out there, Robin.

Whoa, cold, dang.

Duck thermometer read ten. And that was without wind-chill. That made it fun. That made it real. A green Nissan was parked where Poole dead-ended into the soccer field. Hopefully the owner was not some perv he would have to outwit.

Or a Nether in the human guise.

Bright, bright blue and cold. Crunch went the snow as he crossed the soccer field. Why did cold such as this give a running guy a headache? Likely it was due to Prominent Windspeed Velocity.

The path into the woods was as wide as one human. It seemed the Nether had indeed kidnapped Suzanne Bledsoe. Damn him! And his ilk. Judging by the single set of tracks, the Nether appeared to be carrying her. Foul cad. He'd better not be touching Suzanne inappropriately while carrying her. If so, Suzanne would no doubt be resisting with untamable fury.

This was concerning, this was very concerning.

When he caught up to them, he would say, Look, Suzanne, I know you don't know my name, having misaddressed me as Roger that time you asked me to scoot over, but nevertheless I must confess I feel there is something to us. Do you feel the same?

Suzanne had the most amazing brown eyes. They were wet now, with fear and sudden reality.

Stop talking to her, mate, the Nether said.

I won't, he said. And Suzanne? Even if you don't feel there is something to us, rest assured I will still slay this fellow and return you home. Where do you live again? Over in El Cirro? By the water tower? Those are some nice houses back there.

Yes, Suzanne said. We also have a pool. You should come over next summer. It's cool if you swim with your shirt on. And also, yes to there being something to us. You are by far the most insightful boy in our class. Even when I take into consideration the boys I knew in Montreal, I am just like: no one can compare.

Well, that's nice to hear, he said. Thank you for saying that. I know I'm not the thinnest.

The thing about girls? Suzanne said. Is we are more content-driven.

Will you two stop already? the Nether said. Because now is the time for your death. Deaths.

Well, now is certainly the time for somebody's death, Robin said.

The twerpy thing was, you never really got to save anyone. Last summer there'd been a dying raccoon out here. He'd thought of lugging it home so Mom could call the vet. But up close it was too scary. Raccoons being actually bigger than they appear in cartoons. And this one looked like a potential biter. So he ran home to get it some water at least. Upon his return, he saw where the raccoon had done some apparent last-minute thrashing. That was sad. He didn't do well with sad. There had perchance been some pre-weeping, by him, in the woods.

That just means you have a big heart, Suzanne said.

Well, I don't know, he said modestly.

Here was the old truck tire. Where the high-school kids partied. Inside the tire, frosted with snow, were three beer cans and a wadded-up blanket.

You probably like to party, the Nether had cracked to Suzanne moments earlier as they passed this very spot.

No, I don't, Suzanne said. I like to play. And I like to hug.

Hoo boy, the Nether said. Sounds like Dullsville.

Somewhere there is a man who likes to play and hug, Suzanne said.

He came out of the woods now to the prettiest vista he knew. The pond was a pure frozen white. It struck him as somewhat Switzerlandish. Someday he would know for sure. When the Swiss threw him a parade or whatnot.

Here the Nether's tracks departed from the path, as if he had contemplatively taken a moment to gaze at the pond. Perhaps this Nether was not all bad. Perhaps he was having a debilitating conscience-attack vis-à-vis the valiantly struggling Suzanne atop his back. At least he seemed to somewhat love nature.

Then the tracks returned to the path, wound around the pond, and headed up Lexow Hill.

What was this strange object? A coat? On the bench? The bench the Nethers used for their human sacrifices?

No accumulated snow on coat. Inside of coat still slightly warm.

Ergo: the recently discarded coat of the Nether.

This was some strange juju. This was an intriguing conundrum, if he had ever encountered one. Which he had. Once, he'd found a bra on the handlebars of a bike. Once, he'd found an entire untouched steak dinner on a plate behind Fresno's. And hadn't eaten it. Though it had looked pretty good.

Something was afoot.

Then he beheld, halfway up Lexow Hill, a man.

Coatless, bald-headed man. Super skinny. In what looked like pajamas. Climbing plodfully, with tortoise patience, bare white arms sticking out of his p.j. shirt like two bare white branches sticking out of a p.j. shirt. Or grave.

What kind of person leaves his coat behind on a day like this? The mental kind, that was who. This guy looked sort of mental. Like an Auschwitz dude or sad confused grandpa.

Dad had once said, Trust your mind, Rob. If it smells like shit but has writing across it that says Happy Birthday and a candle stuck down in it, what is it?

Is there icing on it? he'd said.

Dad had done that thing of squinting his eyes when an answer was not quite there yet.

What was his mind telling him now?

Something was wrong here. A person needed a coat. Even if the person was a grownup. The pond was frozen. The duck thermometer said ten. If the person was mental, all the more reason to come to his aid, as had not Jesus said, Blessed are those who help those who cannot help themselves, but are too mental, doddering, or have a disability?

He snagged the coat off the bench.

It was a rescue. A real rescue, at last, sort of.

Ten minutes earlier, Don Eber had paused at the pond to catch his breath.

He was so tired. What a thing. Holy moly. When he used to walk Sasquatch out here they'd do six times around the pond, jog up the hill, tag the boulder on top, sprint back down.

Better get moving, said one of two guys who'd been in discussion in his head all morning.

That is, if you're still set on the boulder idea, the other said.

Which still strikes us as kind of fancy-pants.

Seemed like one guy was Dad and the other Kip Flemish.

Stupid cheaters. They'd switched spouses, abandoned the switched spouses, fled together to California. Had they been gay? Or just swingers? Gay swingers? The Dad and Kip in his head had acknowledged their sins and the three of them had struck a deal: he would forgive them for being possible gay swingers and leaving him to do Soap Box Derby alone, with just Mom, and they would consent to giving him some solid manly advice.

He wants it to be nice.

This was Dad now. It seemed Dad was somewhat on his side.

Nice? Kip said. *That is not the word I would use.*

A cardinal zinged across the day.

It was amazing. Amazing, really. He was young. He was fifty-three. Now he'd never deliver his major national speech on compassion. What about going down the Mississippi in a canoe? What about living in an A-frame near a shady creek with the two hippie girls he'd met in 1968 in that souvenir shop in the Ozarks, when Allen, his stepfather, wearing those crazy aviators, had bought him a bag of fossil rocks? One of the hippie girls had said that he, Eber, would be a fox when he grew up, and would he please be sure to call her at that time? Then the hippie girls had put their tawny heads together and giggled at his prospective foxiness. And that had never—

That had somehow never—

Sister Val had said, Why not shoot for being the next JFK? So he had run for class president. Allen had bought him a Styrofoam straw boater. They'd sat together, decorating the hatband with Magic Markers. WIN WITH EBER! On the back: GROOVY! Allen had helped him record a tape. Of a little speech. Allen had taken that tape somewhere and come back with thirty copies, "to pass around."

"Your message is good," Allen had said. "And you are incredibly well spoken. You can do this thing."

And he'd done it. He'd won. Allen had thrown him a victory party. A pizza party. All the kids had come.

Oh, Allen.

Kindest man ever. Had taken him swimming. Had taken him to découpage. Had combed out his hair so patiently that time he came home with lice. Never a harsh, etc., etc.

Not so once the suffering begat. Began. Goddamn it. More and more his words. Askew. More and more his words were not what he would hoped.

Hope.

Once the suffering began, Allen had raged. Said things no one should say. To Mom, to Eber, to the guy delivering water. Went from a shy man, always placing a reassuring hand on your back, to a diminished pale figure in a bed, shouting CUNT!

Except with some weird New England accent so it came out KANT!

The first time Allen had shouted KANT! there followed a funny moment during which he and Mom looked at each other to see which of them was being called KANT. But then Allen amended, for clarity: KANTS!

So it was clear he meant both of them. What a relief.

They'd cracked up.

Jeez, how long had he been standing here? Daylight was waiting. Wasting.

I honestly didn't know what to do. But he made it so simple.

Took it all on himself.

So what else is new?

Exactly.

This was Jodi and Tommy now.

Hi, kids.

Big day today.

I mean, sure, it would have been nice to have a chance to say a proper goodbye.

But at what cost?

Exactly. And see—he knew that.

He was a father. That's what a father does.

Eases the burdens of those he loves.

Saves the ones he loves from painful last images that might endure for a lifetime.

Soon Allen had become THAT. And no one was going to fault anybody for avoiding THAT. Sometimes he and Mom would huddle in the kitchen. Rather than risk incurring the wrath of THAT. Even THAT understood the deal. You'd trot in a glass of water, set it down, say, very politely, Anything else, Allen? And you'd see THAT thinking, All these years I was so good to you people and now I am merely THAT? Sometimes the gentle Allen would be inside there too, indicating, with his eyes, Look, go away, please go away, I am trying so hard not to call you KANT!

Rail-thin, ribs sticking out.

Catheter taped to dick.

Waft of shit smell.

You are not Allen and Allen is not you.

So Molly had said.

As for Dr. Spivey, he couldn't say. Wouldn't say. Was busy drawing a daisy on a Post-it. Then finally said, Well, honestly? As these things grow, they can tend to do weird things. But it doesn't necessarily have to be terrible. Had one guy? Just always craved him a Sprite.

And Eber had thought, Did you, dear doctor/savior/lifeline, just say *craved him a Sprite*?

That's how they got you. You thought, Maybe I'll just crave me a Sprite. Next thing you knew, you were THAT, shouting KANT!, shitting your bed, swatting at the people who were scrambling to clean you.

No, sir.

No sirree bob.

Wednesday he'd fallen out of the med-bed again. There on the floor in the dark it had come to him: I could spare them.

Spare us? Or spare you?

Get thee behind me.

Get thee behind me, sweetie.

A breeze sent down a sequence of linear snow puffs from somewhere above. Beautiful. Why were we made just so, to find so many things that happened every day pretty?

He took off his coat.

Good Christ.

Took off his hat and gloves, stuffed the hat and gloves in a sleeve of the coat, left the coat on the bench.

This way they'd know. They'd find the car, walk up the path, find the coat.

It was a miracle. That he'd got this far. Well, he'd always been strong. Once, he'd run a half-marathon with a broken foot. After his vasectomy he'd cleaned the garage, no problem.

He'd waited in the med-bed for Molly to go off to the pharmacy. That was the toughest part. Just calling out a normal goodbye.

His mind veered toward her now, and he jerked it back with a prayer: Let me pull this off. Lord, let me not fuck it up. Let me bring no dishonor. Leg me do it cling.

Let. Let me do it cling.

Clean.
Cleanly.

Estimated time of overtaking the Nether, handing him his coat? Approximately nine minutes. Six minutes to follow the path around the pond, an additional three minutes to fly up the hillside like a delivering wraith or mercy-angel, bearing the simple gift of a coat.

That is just an estimate, NASA. I pretty much made that up.

We know that, Robin. We know very well by now how irreverent you work.

Like that time you cut a fart on the moon.

Or the time you tricked Mel into saying, "Mr. President, what a delightful surprise it was to find an asteroid circling Uranus."

That estimate was particularly iffy. This Nether being surprisingly brisk. Robin himself was not the fastest wicket in the stick. He had a certain girth. Which Dad prognosticated would soon triumphantly congeal into linebackerish solidity. He hoped so. For now he just had the slight man-boobs.

Robin, hurry, Suzanne said. I feel so sorry for that poor old guy.

He's a fool, Robin said, because Suzanne was young, and did not yet understand that when a man was a fool he made hardships for other men, who were less foolish than he.

He doesn't have much time, Suzanne said, bordering on the hysterical.

There, there, he said, comforting her.

I'm just so frightened, she said.

And yet he is fortunate to have one such as I to hump his coat up that big-ass hill, which, due to its steepness, is not exactly my cup of tea, Robin said.

I guess that's the definition of "hero," Suzanne said.

I guess so, he said.

I don't mean to continue being insolent, she said. But he seems to be pulling away.

What would you suggest? he said.

With all due respect, she said, and because I know you consider us as equals but different, with me covering the brainy angle and special inventions and whatnot?

Yes, yes, go ahead, he said.

Well, just working through the math in terms of simple geometry—

He saw where she was going with this. And she was quite right. No wonder he loved her. He must cut across the pond, thereby decreasing the ambient angle, ergo trimming valuable seconds off his catch-up time.

Wait, Suzanne said. Is that dangerous?

It is not, he said. I have done it numerous times.

Please be careful, Suzanne implored.

Well, once, he said.

You have such aplomb, Suzanne demurred.

Actually never, he said softly, not wishing to alarm her.

Your bravery is irascible, Suzanne said.

He started across the pond.

It was actually pretty cool walking on water. In summer, canoes floated here. If Mom could see him, she'd have a conniption. Mom treated him like a piece of glass. Due to his alleged infant surgeries. She went on full alert if he so much as used a stapler.

But Mom was a good egg. A reliable counselor and steady hand of guidance. She had a munificent splay of long silver hair and a raspy voice, though she didn't smoke and was even a vegan. She'd never been a biker chick, although some of the in-school cretins claimed she resembled one.

He was actually quite fond of Mom.

He was now approximately three-quarters, or that would be sixty percent, across.

Between him and the shore lay a grayish patch. Here in summer a stream ran in. Looked a tad iffy. At the edge of the grayish patch he gave the ice a bonk with the butt of his gun. Solid as anything.

Here he went. Ice rolled a bit underfoot. Probably it was shallow here. Anyways he hoped so. Yikes.

How's it going? Suzanne said, trepidly.

Could be better, he said.

Maybe you should turn back, Suzanne said.

But wasn't this feeling of fear the exact feeling all heroes had to confront early in life? Wasn't overcoming this feeling of fear what truly distinguished the brave?

There could be no turning back.

Or could there? Maybe there could. Actually there should.

The ice gave way and the boy fell through.

Nausea had not been mentioned in *The Humbling Steppe*.

A blissful feeling overtook me as I drifted off to sleep at the base of the crevasse. No fear, no discomfort, only a vague sadness at the thought of all that remained undone. This is death? I thought. It is but nothing.

Author, whose name I cannot remember, I would like a word with you. A-hole.

The shivering was insane. Like a tremor. His head was shaking on his neck. He paused to puke a bit in the snow, white-yellow against the white-blue.

This was scary. This was scary now.

Every step was a victory. He had to remember that. With every step he was fleeing father and father. Farther from father. Stepfarther. What a victory he was wresting. From the jaws of the feet.

He felt a need at the back of his throat to say it right.

From the jaws of defeat. From the jaws of defeat.

Oh, Allen.

Even when you were THAT you were still Allen to me.

Please know that.

Falling, Dad said.

For some definite time he waited to see where he would land and how much it would hurt. Then there was a tree in his gut. He found himself wrapped fetally around some tree.

Fucksake.

Ouch, ouch. This was too much. He hadn't cried after the surgeries or during the chemo, but he felt like crying now. It wasn't fair. It happened to everyone supposedly but now it was happening specifically to him. He'd kept waiting for some special dispensation. But no. Something/someone bigger than him kept refusing. You were told the big something/someone loved you especially but in the end you saw it was otherwise. The big something/someone was neutral. Unconcerned. When it innocently moved, it crushed people.

Years ago at "The Illuminated Body" he and Molly had seen this brain slice. Marring the brain slice had been a nickel-sized brown spot. That brown spot was all it had taken to kill the guy. Guy must have had his hopes and dreams, closet full of pants, and so on, some treasured childhood memories: a mob of koi in the willow shade at Gage Park, say, Gram searching in her Wrigley's-smelling purse for a tissue—like that. If not for that brown spot, the guy might have been one of the people walking by on the way to lunch in the atrium. But no. He was defunct now, off rotting somewhere, no brain in his head.

Looking down at the brain slice Eber had felt a sense of superiority. Poor guy. It was pretty unlucky, what had happened to him.

He and Molly had fled to the atrium, had hot scones, watched a squirrel mess with a plastic cup.

Wrapped fetally around the tree Eber traced the scar on his head. Tried to sit. No dice. Tried to use the tree to sit up. His hand wouldn't close. Reaching around the tree with both hands, joining his hands at the wrists, he sat himself up, leaned back against the tree.

How was that?

Fine.

Good, actually.

Maybe this was it. Maybe this was as far as he got. He'd had it in mind to sit cross-legged against the boulder at the top of the hill, but really what difference did it make?

All he had to do now was stay put. Stay put by force-thinking the same thoughts he'd used to propel himself out of the med-bed and into the car and across the soccer field and through the woods: MollyTommyJodi huddling in the kitchen filled with pity/loathing, MollyTommyJodi recoiling at something cruel he'd said, Tommy hefting his thin torso up in his arms so that MollyJodi could get under there with a wash—

Then it would be done. He would have preempted all future debasement. All his fears about the coming months would be mute.

Moot.

This was it. Was it? Not yet. Soon, though. An hour? Forty minutes? Was he doing this? Really? He was. Was he? Would he be able to make it back to the car even if he changed his mind? He thought not. Here he was. He was here. This incredible opportunity to end things with dignity was right in his hands.

All he had to do was stay put.

I will fight no more forever.

Concentrate on the beauty of the pond, the beauty of the woods, the beauty you are returning to, the beauty that is everywhere as far as you can—

Oh, for shitsake.

Oh, for crying out loud.

Some kid was on the pond.

Chubby kid in white. With a gun. Carrying Eber's coat.

You little fart, put that coat down, get your ass home, mind your own—

Damn. Damn it.

Kid tapped the ice with the butt of his gun.

You wouldn't want some kid finding you. That could scar a kid. Although kids found freaky things all the time. Once he'd found a naked photo of Dad and Mrs. Flemish. That had been freaky. Of course, not as freaky as a grimacing cross-legged—

Kid was swimming.

Swimming was not allowed. That was clearly posted. *No Swimming.*

Kid was a bad swimmer. Real thrashfest down there. Kid was creating with his thrashing a rapidly expanding black pool. With each thrash the kid incrementally expanded the boundary of the black—

He was on his way down before he knew he'd started. *Kid in the pond, kid in the pond,* ran repetitively through his head as he minced. Progress was tree-to-tree. Standing there panting, you got to know a tree well. This one had three knots: eye, eye, nose. This started out as one tree and became two.

Suddenly he was not purely the dying guy who woke nights in the med-bed thinking, Make this not true make this not true, but again, partly, the guy who used to put bananas in the freezer, then crack them on the counter and pour chocolate over the broken chunks, the guy who'd once stood outside a classroom window in a rainstorm to see how Jodi was faring with that little red-headed shit who wouldn't give her a chance at the book table, the guy who used to hand-paint bird feeders in college and sell them on weekends in Boulder, wearing a jester hat and doing a little juggling routine he'd—

He started to fall again, caught himself, froze in a hunched-over position, hurtled forward, fell flat on his face, chucked his chin on a root.

You had to laugh.

You almost had to laugh.

He got up. Got doggedly up. His right hand presented as a bloody glove. Tough nuts, too bad. Once, in football, a tooth had come out. Later in the half, Eddie Blandik had found it. He'd taken it from Eddie, flung it away. That had also been him.

Here was the switchbank. It wasn't far now. Switchback.

What to do? When he got there? Get kid out of pond. Get kid moving. Force-walk kid through woods, across soccer field, to one of the houses on Poole. If nobody home, pile kid into Nissan, crank up heater, drive to—Our Lady of Sorrows? UrgentCare? Fastest route to UrgentCare?

Fifty yards to the trailhead.

Twenty yards to the trailhead.

Thank you, God, for my strength.

In the pond he was all animal-thought, no words, no self, blind panic. He resolved to really try. He grabbed for the edge. The edge broke away. Down he went. He hit mud and pushed up. He grabbed for the edge. The edge broke away. Down he went. It seemed like it should be easy, getting out. But he just couldn't do it. It was like at the carnival. It should be easy to knock three sawdust dogs off a ledge. And it was easy. It just wasn't easy with the amount of balls they gave you.

He wanted the shore. He knew that was the right place for him. But the pond kept saying no.

Then it said maybe.

The ice edge broke again, but, breaking it, he pulled himself infinitesimally toward shore, so that, when he went down, his feet found mud sooner. The bank was sloped. Suddenly there was hope. He went nuts. He went total spaz. Then he was out, water streaming off him, a piece of ice like a tiny pane of glass in the cuff of his coat.

Trapezoidal, he thought.

In his mind, the pond was not finite, circular, and behind him but infinite and all around.

He felt he'd better lie still or whatever had just tried to kill him would try again. What had tried to kill him was not just in the pond but out here, too, in every natural thing, and there was no him, no Suzanne, no Mom, no nothing, just the sound of some kid crying like a terrified baby.

Eber jog-hobbled out of the woods and found: no kid. Just black water. And a green coat. His coat. His former coat, out there on the ice. The water was calming already.

Oh, shit.

Your fault.

Kid was only out there because of—

Down on the beach near an overturned boat was some ignoramus. Lying face down. On the job. Lying down on the job. Must have been lying there even as that poor kid—

Wait, rewind.

It was the kid. Oh, thank Christ. Face down like a corpse in a Brady photo. Legs still in the pond. Like he'd lost steam crawling out. Kid was soaked through, the white coat gone gray with wet.

Eber dragged the kid out. It took four distinct pulls. He didn't have the strength to flip him over, but, turning the head, at least got the mouth out of the snow.

Kid was in trouble.

Soaking wet, ten degrees.

Doom.

Eber went down on one knee and told the kid in a grave fatherly way that he had to get up, had to get moving or he could lose his legs, he could die.

The kid looked at Eber, blinked, stayed where he was.

He grabbed the kid by the coat, rolled him over, roughly sat him up. The kid's shivers made his shivers look like nothing. Kid seemed to be holding a jackhammer. He had to get the kid warmed up. How to do it? Hug him, lie on top of him? That would be like Popsicle-on-Popsicle.

Eber remembered his coat, out on the ice, at the edge of the black water.

Ugh.

Find a branch. No branches anywhere. Where the heck was a good fallen branch when you—

All right, all right, he'd do it without a branch.

He walked fifty feet downshore, stepped onto the pond, walked a wide loop on the solid stuff, turned to shore, started toward the black water. His knees were shaking. Why? He was afraid he might fall in. Ha. Dope. Poser. The coat was fifteen feet away. His legs were in revolt. His legs were revolting.

Doctor, my legs are revolting.

You're telling me.

He tiny-stepped up. The coat was ten feet away. He went down on his knees, knee-walked slightly up. Went down on his belly. Stretched out an arm.

Slid forward on his belly.

Bit more.

Bit more.

Then had a tiny corner by two fingers. He hauled it in, slid himself back via something like a reverse breaststroke, got to his knees, stood, retreated a few steps, and was once again fifteen feet away and safe.

Then it was like the old days, getting Tommy or Jodi ready for bed when they were zonked. You said, "Arm," the kid lifted an arm. You said, "Other arm," the kid lifted the other arm. With the coat off, Eber could see that the boy's shirt was turning to ice. Eber peeled the shirt off. Poor little guy. A person was just some meat on a frame. Little guy wouldn't last long in this cold. Eber took off his pajama shirt, put it on the kid, slid the kid's arm into the arm of the coat. In the arm was Eber's hat and gloves. He put the hat and gloves on the kid, zipped the coat up.

The kid's pants were frozen solid. His boots were ice sculptures of boots.

You had to do things right. Eber sat on the boat, took off his boots and socks, peeled off his pajama pants, made the kid sit on the boat, knelt before the kid, got the kid's boots off. He loosened the pants up with little punches and soon had one leg partly out. He was stripping off a kid in ten-degree weather. Maybe this was exactly the wrong thing. Maybe he'd kill the kid. He didn't know. He just didn't know. Desperately, he gave the pants a few more punches. Then the kid was stepping out.

Eber put the pajama pants on him, then the socks, then the boots.

The kid was standing there in Eber's clothes, swaying, eyes closed.

We're going to walk now, okay? Eber said.

Nothing.

Eber gave the kid an encouraging pop in the shoulders. Like a football thing.

We're going to walk you home, he said. Do you live near here?

Nothing.

He gave a harder pop.

The kid gaped at him, baffled.

Pop.

Kid started walking.

Pop-pop.

Like fleeing.

Eber drove the kid out ahead of him. Like cowboy and cow. At first, fear of the popping seemed to be motivating the kid, but then good old panic kicked in and he started running. Soon Eber couldn't keep up.

Kid was at the bench. Kid was at the trailhead.

Good boy, get home.

Kid disappeared into the woods.

Eber came back to himself.

Oh, boy. Oh, wow.

He had never known cold. Had never known tired.

He was standing in the snow in his underwear near an overturned boat.

He hobbled to the boat and sat in the snow.

Robin ran.

Past the bench and the trailhead and into the woods on the old familiar path.

What the heck? What the heck had just happened? He'd fallen into the pond? His jeans had frozen solid? Had ceased being bluejeans. Were whitejeans. He looked down to see if his jeans were still whitejeans.

He had on pajama pants that, tucked into some tremendoid boots, looked like clown pants.

Had he been crying just now?

I think crying is healthy, Suzanne said. It means you're in touch with your feelings.

Ugh. That was done, that was stupid, talking in your head to some girl who in real life called you Roger.

Dang.

So tired.

Here was a stump.

He sat. It felt good to rest. He wasn't going to lose his legs. They didn't even hurt. He couldn't even feel them. He wasn't going to die. Dying was not something he had in mind at this early an age. To rest more efficiently, he lay down. The sky was blue. The pines swayed. Not all at the same rate. He raised one gloved hand and watched it tremor.

He might close his eyes for a bit. Sometimes in life one felt a feeling of wanting to quit. Then everyone would see. Everyone would see that teasing wasn't nice. Sometimes with all the teasing his days were subtenable. Sometimes he felt he couldn't take even one more lunchtime of meekly eating on that rolled-up wrestling mat in the cafeteria corner near the snapped parallel bars. He did not have to sit there. But preferred to. If he sat anywhere else, there was the chance of a comment or two. Upon which he would then have the rest of the day to reflect. Sometimes comments were made on the clutter of his home. Thanks to Bryce, who had once come over. Sometimes comments were made on his manner of speaking. Sometimes comments were made on the style faux pas of Mom. Who was, it must be said, a real eighties gal.

Mom.

He did not like it when they teased about Mom. Mom had no idea of his lowly school status. Mom seeing him more as the paragon or golden-boy type.

Once, he'd done a secret rendezvous of recording Mom's phone calls, just for the reconnaissance aspect. Mostly they were dull, mundane, not about him at all.

Except for this one with her friend Liz.

I never dreamed I could love someone so much, Mom had said. I just worry I might not be able to live up to him, you know? He's so *good*, so *grateful*. That kid deserves—that kid deserves it all. Better school, which we cannot afford, some trips, like abroad, but that is also, uh, out of our price range. I just don't want to *fail* him, you know? That's all I want from my life, you know? Liz? To feel, at the end, like I did right by that magnificent little dude.

At that point it seemed like Liz had maybe started vacuuming.

Magnificent little dude.

He should probably get going.

Magnificent Little Dude was like his Indian name.

He got to his feet and, gathering his massive amount of clothes up like some sort of encumbering royal train, started toward home.

Here was the truck tire, here the place where the trail briefly widened, here the place where the trees crossed overhead like reaching for one another. Weave-ceiling, Mom called it.

Here was the soccer field. Across the field, his house sat like a big sweet animal. It was amazing. He'd made it. He'd fallen into the pond and lived to tell the tale. He had somewhat cried, yes, but had then simply laughed off this moment of mortal weakness and made his way home, look of wry bemusement on his face, having, it must be acknowledged, benefited from the much appreciated assistance of a certain aged—

With a shock he remembered the old guy. What the heck? An image flashed of the old guy standing bereft and blue-skinned in his tighty-whities like a P.O.W. abandoned at the barbed wire due to no room on the truck. Or a sad traumatized stork bidding farewell to its young.

He'd bolted. He'd bolted on the old guy. Hadn't even given him a thought.

Blimey.

What a chickenshitish thing to do.

He had to go back. Right now. Help the old guy hobble out. But he was so tired. He wasn't sure he could do it. Probably the old guy was fine. Probably he had some sort of old-guy plan.

But he'd bolted. He couldn't live with that. His mind was telling him that the only way to undo the bolting was to go back now, save the day. His body was saying something else: It's too far, you're just a kid, get Mom, Mom will know what to do.

He stood paralyzed at the edge of the soccer field like a scarecrow in huge flowing clothes.

Eber sat slumped against the boat.

What a change in the weather. People were going around with

parasols and so forth in the open part of the park. There was a merry-go-round and a band and a gazebo. People were frying food on the backs of certain merry-go-round horses. And yet, on others, kids were riding. How did they know? Which horses were hot? For now there was still snow, but snow couldn't last long in this bomb.

Balm.

If you close your eyes, that's the end. You know that, right?

Hilarious.

Allen.

His exact voice. After all these years.

Where was he? The duck pond. So many times he'd come out here with the kids. He should go now. Goodbye, duck pond. Although hang on. He couldn't seem to stand. Plus you couldn't leave a couple of little kids behind. Not this close to water. They were four and six. For God's sake. What had he been thinking? Leaving those two little dears by the pond. They were good kids, they'd wait, but wouldn't they get bored? And swim? Without life jackets? No, no, no. It made him sick. He had to stay. Poor kids. Poor abandoned —

Wait, rewind.

His kids were excellent swimmers.

His kids had never come close to being abandoned.

His kids were grown.

Tom was thirty. Tall drink of water. Tried so hard to know things. But even when he thought he knew a thing (fighting kites, breeding rabbits), Tom would soon be shown for what he was: the dearest, most agreeable young fellow ever, who knew no more about fighting kites/breeding rabbits than the average person could pick up from ten minutes on the Internet. Not that Tom wasn't smart. Tom was smart. Tom was a damn quick study. O Tom, Tommy, Tommikins! The heart in that kid! He just worked and worked. For the love of his dad. Oh, kid, you had it, you have it, Tom, Tommy, even now I am thinking of you, you are very much on my mind.

And Jodi, Jodi was out there in Santa Fe. She'd said she'd take off work and fly home. As needed. But there was no need. He didn't like to impose. The kids had their own lives. Jodi-Jode. Little freckle-face. Pregnant now. Not married. Not even dating. Stupid Lars. What kind of man deserted a beautiful girl like that? A total dear. Just starting to make some progress in her job. You couldn't take that kind of time off when you'd only just started—

Reconstructing the kids in this way was having the effect of making them real to him again. Which—you didn't want to get that ball roiling. Jodi was having a baby. Rolling. He could have lasted long enough to see the baby. Hold the baby. It was sad, yes. That was a sacrifice he'd had to make. He'd explained it in the note. Hadn't he? No. Hadn't left a note. Couldn't. There'd been some reason he couldn't. Hadn't there? He was pretty sure there'd been some—

Insurance. It couldn't seem like he'd done it on purpose.

Little panic.

Little panic here.

He was offing himself. Offing himself, he'd involved a kid. Who was wandering the woods hypothermic. He was offing himself two weeks before Christmas. Molly's favorite holiday. Molly had a valve thing, a panic thing, this business might—

This was not—this was not him. This was not something he would have done. Not something he would ever do. Except he—he'd done it. He was doing it. It was in progress. If he didn't get moving, it would—it would be accomplished. It would be done.

This very day you will be with me in the kingdom of—

He had to fight.

But couldn't seem to keep his eyes open.

He tried to send some last thoughts to Molly. Sweetie, forgive me. Biggest fuckup ever. Forget this part. Forget I ended this thisly. You know me. You know I didn't mean this.

He was at his house. He wasn't at his house. He knew that. But could see every detail. Here was the empty med-bed, the studio portrait of HimMollyTommyJodi posed around that fake rodeo fence. Here was the little bedside table. His meds in the pillbox. The bell he rang to call Molly. What a thing. What a cruel thing. Suddenly he saw clearly how cruel it was. And selfish. Oh, God. Who was he? The front door swung open. Molly called his name. He'd hide in the sunroom. Jump out, surprise her. Somehow they'd remodeled. Their sunroom was now the sunroom of Mrs. Kendall, his childhood piano teacher. That would be fun for the kids, to take piano lessons in the same room where he'd—

Hello? said Mrs. Kendall.

What she meant was: Don't die yet. There are many of us who wish to judge you harshly in the sunroom.

Hello, hello! she shouted.

Coming around the pond was a silver-haired woman.

All he had to do was call out.

He called out.

To keep him alive she started piling on him various things from life, things smelling of a home—coats, sweaters, a rain of flowers, a hat, socks, sneakers—and with amazing strength had him on his feet and was maneuvering him into a maze of trees, a wonderland of trees, trees hung with ice. He was piled high with clothes. He was like the bed at a party on which they pile the coats. She had all the answers: where to step, when to rest. She was strong as a bull. He was on her hip now like a baby; she had both arms around his waist, lifting him over a root.

They walked for hours, seemed like. She sang. Cajoled. She hissed at him, reminding him, with pokes in the forehead (right in his forehead) that her freaking *kid* was at *home*, near-*frozen*, so they had to *book it*.

Good God, there was so much to do. If he made it. He'd make it. This gal wouldn't let him not make it. He'd have to try to get Molly to see—see why he'd done it. *I was scared, I was scared, Mol.* Maybe Molly would agree not to tell Tommy and Jodi. He didn't like the thought of them knowing he'd been scared. Didn't like the thought of them knowing what a fool he'd been. Oh, to hell with that! Tell everyone! He'd done it! He'd been driven to do it and he'd done it and that was it. That was him. That was part of who he was. No more lies, no more silence, it was going to be a new and different life, if only he—

They were crossing the soccer field.

Here was the Nissan.

His first thought was: Get in, drive it home.

Oh, no, you don't, she said with that smoky laugh and guided him into a house. A house on the park. He'd seen it a million times. And now was in it. It smelled of man-sweat and spaghetti sauce and old books. Like a library where sweaty men went to cook spaghetti. She sat him in front of a wood stove, brought him a brown blanket that smelled of medicine. Didn't talk but in directives: Drink this, let me take that, wrap up, what's your name, what's your number?

What a thing! To go from dying in your underwear in the snow to this! Warmth, colors, antlers on the walls, an old-time crank phone like you saw in silent movies. It was something. Every second was something. He hadn't died in his shorts by a pond in the snow. The kid wasn't dead. He'd killed no one. Ha! Somehow he'd got it all back. Everything was good now, everything was—

The woman reached down, touched his scar.

Oh, wow, ouch, she said. You didn't do that out there, did you?

At this he remembered that the brown spot was as much in his head as ever.

Oh, Lord, there was still all that to go through.

Did he still want it? Did he still want to live?

Yes, yes, oh, God, yes, please.

Because, okay, the thing was—he saw it now, was starting to see it—if some guy, at the end, fell apart, and said or did bad things, or had to be helped, helped to quite a considerable extent? So what? What of it? Why should he not do or say weird things or look strange or disgusting? Why should the shit not run down his legs? Why should those he loved not lift and bend and feed and wipe him, when he would gladly do the same for them? He'd been afraid to be lessened by the lifting and bending and feeding and wiping, and was still afraid of that, and yet, at the same time, now saw that there could still be many—many drops of goodness, is how it came to him—many drops of happy—of good fellowship—ahead, and those drops of fellowship were not—had never been—his to withheld.

Withhold.

The kid came out of the kitchen, lost in Eber's big coat, pajama pants pooling around his feet with the boots now off. He took Eber's bloody hand gently. Said he was sorry. Sorry for being such a dope in the woods. Sorry for running off. He'd just been out of it. Kind of scared and all.

Listen, Eber said hoarsely. You did amazing. You did perfect. I'm here. Who did that?

There. That was something you could do. The kid maybe felt better now? He'd given the kid that? That was a reason. To stay around. Wasn't it? Can't console anyone if not around? Can't do squat if gone?

When Allen was close to the end, Eber had done a presentation at school on the manatee. Got an A from Sister Eustace. Who could be quite tough. She was missing two fingers on her right hand from a lawn mower incident and sometimes used that hand to scare a kid silent.

He hadn't thought of this in years.

She'd put that hand on his shoulder not to scare him but as a form of praise. *That was just terrific. Everyone should take their work as seriously as Donald here. Donald, I hope you'll go home and share this with your parents.* He'd gone home and shared it with Mom. Who suggested he share it with Allen. Who, on that day, had been more Allen than THAT. And Allen—

Ha, wow, Allen. There was a man.

Tears sprang into his eyes as he sat by the wood stove.

Allen had—Allen had said it was great. Asked a few questions. About the manatee. What did they eat again? Did he think they could effectively communicate with one another? What a trial that must have been! In his condition. Forty minutes on the manatee? Including a poem Eber had composed? A sonnet? On the manatee?

He'd felt so happy to have Allen back.

I'll be like him, he thought. I'll try to be like him.

The voice in his head was shaky, hollow, unconvinced.

Then: sirens.

Somehow: Molly.

He heard her in the entryway. Mol, Molly, oh boy. When they were first married they used to fight. Say the most insane things. Afterward, sometimes there would be tears. Tears in bed? And then they would—Molly pressing her hot wet face against his hot wet face. They were sorry, they were saying with their bodies, they were accepting each other back, and that feeling, that feeling of being accepted back again and again, of someone's affection for you expanding to encompass whatever new flawed thing had just manifested in you, that was the deepest, dearest thing he'd ever—

She came in flustered and apologetic, a touch of anger in her face. He'd embarrassed her. He saw that. He'd embarrassed her by doing something that showed she hadn't sufficiently noticed him needing her. She'd been too busy nursing him to notice how scared he was. She was angry at him for pulling this stunt and ashamed of herself for feeling angry at him in his hour of need, and was trying to put the shame and anger behind her now so she could do what might be needed.

All of this was in her face. He knew her so well.

Also concern.

Overriding everything else in that lovely face was concern.

She came to him now, stumbling a bit on a swell in the floor of this stranger's house.

MONA SIMPSON

■

Transcription of a Eulogy

Mona Simpson is a novelist, professor, and sister of Steve Jobs. These words were delivered as a eulogy at a memorial service for her late brother at the Memorial Church of Stanford University on October 16, 2011.

I GREW UP AS AN ONLY CHILD, with a single mother. Because we were poor and because I knew my father had emigrated from Syria, I imagined he looked like Omar Sharif. I hoped he would be rich and kind and would come into our lives (and our not yet furnished apartment) and help us. Later, after I'd met my father, I tried to believe he'd changed his number and left no forwarding address because he was an idealistic revolutionary, plotting a new world for the Arab people.

Even as a feminist, my whole life I'd been waiting for a man to love, who could love me. For decades, I'd thought that man would be my father. When I was twenty-five, I met that man and he was my brother.

By then, I lived in New York, where I was trying to write my first novel. I had a job at a small magazine in an office the size of a closet, with three other aspiring writers. When one day a lawyer called me — me, the middle-class girl from California who hassled the boss to buy us health insurance — and said his client was rich and famous and was my long-lost brother, the young editors went wild. This was 1985 and we worked at a cutting-edge literary magazine, but I'd fallen into the plot of a Dickens novel and really, we all loved those best. The lawyer refused to tell me my brother's name and my colleagues started a betting pool. The leading candidate: John Travolta. I secretly hoped for a literary descendant of Henry James — someone more talented than I, someone brilliant without even trying.

When I met Steve, he was a guy my age in jeans, Arab- or Jewish-looking and handsomer than Omar Sharif.

We took a long walk—something, it happened, that we both liked to do. I don't remember much of what we said that first day, only that he felt like someone I'd pick to be a friend. He explained that he worked in computers.

I didn't know much about computers. I still worked on a manual Olivetti typewriter.

I told Steve I'd recently considered my first purchase of a computer: something called the Cromemco.

Steve told me it was a good thing I'd waited. He said he was making something that was going to be insanely beautiful.

I want to tell you a few things I learned from Steve, during three distinct periods, over the twenty-seven years I knew him. They're not periods of years, but of states of being. His full life. His illness. His dying.

Steve worked at what he loved. He worked really hard. Every day.

That's incredibly simple, but true.

He was the opposite of absent-minded.

He was never embarrassed about working hard, even if the results were failures. If someone as smart as Steve wasn't ashamed to admit trying, maybe I didn't have to be.

When he got kicked out of Apple, things were painful. He told me about a dinner at which five hundred Silicon Valley leaders met the then-sitting president. Steve hadn't been invited.

He was hurt but he still went to work at NeXT. Every single day.

Novelty was not Steve's highest value. Beauty was.

For an innovator, Steve was remarkably loyal. If he loved a shirt, he'd order ten or one hundred of them. In the Palo Alto house, there are probably enough black cotton turtlenecks for everyone in this church.

He didn't favor trends or gimmicks. He liked people his own age.

His philosophy of aesthetics reminds me of a quote that went something like this: "Fashion is what seems beautiful now but looks ugly later; art can be ugly at first but it becomes beautiful later."

Steve always aspired to make beautiful later.

He was willing to be misunderstood.

Uninvited to the ball, he drove the third or fourth iteration of his same black sports car to NeXT, where he and his team were quietly inventing the platform on which Tim Berners-Lee would write the program for the World Wide Web.

Steve was like a girl in the amount of time he spent talking about love. Love was his supreme virtue, his god of gods. He tracked and worried about the romantic lives of the people working with him.

Whenever he saw a man he thought a woman might find dashing, he called out, "Hey, are you single? Do you wanna come to dinner with my sister?"

I remember when he phoned the day he met Laurene. "There's this beautiful woman and she's really smart and she has this dog and I'm going to marry her."

When Reed was born, he began gushing and never stopped. He was a physical dad, with each of his children. He fretted over Lisa's boyfriends and Erin's travel and skirt lengths and Eve's safety around the horses she adored.

None of us who attended Reed's graduation party will ever forget the scene of Reed and Steve slow dancing.

His abiding love for Laurene sustained him. He believed that love happened all the time, everywhere. In that most important way, Steve was never ironic, never cynical, never pessimistic. I try to learn from that, still.

Steve had been successful at a young age, and he felt that had isolated him. Most of the choices he made from the time I knew him were designed to dissolve the walls around him. A middle-class boy from Los Altos, he fell in love with a middle-class girl from New Jersey. It was important to both of them to raise Lisa, Reed, Erin, and Eve as grounded, normal children. Their house didn't intimidate with art or polish; in fact, for many of the first years I knew Steve and Lo together, dinner was served on the grass, and sometimes consisted of just one vegetable. Lots of that one vegetable. But one. Broccoli. In season. Simply prepared. With just the right, recently snipped, herb.

Even as a young millionaire, Steve always picked me up at the airport. He'd be standing there in his jeans.

When a family member called him at work, his secretary Linetta answered, "Your dad's in a meeting. Would you like me to interrupt him?"

When Reed insisted on dressing up as a witch every Halloween, Steve, Laurene, Erin, and Eve all went wiccan.

They once embarked on a kitchen remodel; it took years. They cooked on a hotplate in the garage. The Pixar building, under construction during the same period, finished in half the time. And that was it for the Palo Alto house. The bathrooms stayed old. But—and this was a crucial distinction—it had been a great house to start with; Steve saw to that.

This is not to say that he didn't enjoy his success: he enjoyed his success a lot, just minus a few zeros. He told me how much he loved going to the Palo Alto bike store and gleefully realizing he could afford to buy the best bike there.

And he did.

Steve was humble. Steve liked to keep learning.

Once, he told me if he'd grown up differently, he might have become a mathematician. He spoke reverently about colleges and loved walking around the Stanford campus. In the last year of his life, he studied a book of paintings by Mark Rothko, an artist he hadn't known about before, thinking of what could inspire people on the walls of a future Apple campus.

Steve cultivated whimsy. What other CEO knows the history of English and Chinese tea roses and has a favorite David Austin rose?

He had surprises tucked in all his pockets. I'll venture that Laurene will discover treats—songs he loved, a poem he cut out and put in a drawer—even after twenty years of an exceptionally close marriage. I spoke to him every other day or so, but when I opened *The New York Times* and saw a feature on the company's patents, I was still surprised and delighted to see a sketch for a perfect staircase.

With his four children, with his wife, with all of us, Steve had a lot of fun.

He treasured happiness.

Then, Steve became ill and we watched his life compress into a smaller circle. Once, he'd loved walking through Paris. He'd discovered a small handmade soba shop in Kyoto. He downhill skied gracefully. He cross-country skied clumsily. No more.

Eventually, even ordinary pleasures, like a good peach, no longer appealed to him.

Yet, what amazed me, and what I learned from his illness, was how much was still left after so much had been taken away.

I remember my brother learning to walk again, with a chair. After his liver transplant, once a day he would get up on legs that seemed too thin to bear him, arms pitched to the chair back. He'd push that chair down the Memphis hospital corridor towards the nursing station and then he'd sit down on the chair, rest, turn around, and walk back again. He counted his steps and, each day, pressed a little farther.

Laurene got down on her knees and looked into his eyes.

"You can do this, Steve," she said. His eyes widened. His lips pressed into each other.

He tried. He always, always tried, and always with love at the core of that effort. He was an intensely emotional man.

I realized during that terrifying time that Steve was not enduring the pain for himself. He set destinations: his son Reed's graduation from high school, his daughter Erin's trip to Kyoto, the launching of a boat he was building on which he planned to take his family around the world and where he hoped he and Laurene would someday retire.

Even ill, his taste, his discrimination, and his judgment held. He went through sixty-seven nurses before finding kindred spirits and then he completely trusted the three who stayed with him to the end. Tracy. Arturo. Elham.

One time when Steve had contracted a tenacious pneumonia his doctor forbid everything—even ice. We were in a standard ICU unit. Steve, who generally disliked cutting in line or dropping his own name, confessed that this once, he'd like to be treated a little specially.

I told him: Steve, this is special treatment.

He leaned over to me, and said: "I want it to be a little more special."

Intubated, when he couldn't talk, he asked for a notepad. He sketched devices to hold an iPad in a hospital bed. He designed new fluid monitors and x-ray equipment. He redrew that not-quite-special-enough hospital unit. And every time his wife walked into the room, I watched his smile remake itself on his face.

For the really big, big things, you have to trust me, he wrote on his sketchpad. He looked up. You have to.

By that, he meant that we should disobey the doctors and give him a piece of ice.

None of us knows for certain how long we'll be here. On Steve's better days, even in the last year, he embarked upon projects and elicited promises from his friends at Apple to finish them. Some boat builders in the Netherlands have a gorgeous stainless steel hull ready to be covered with the finishing wood. His three daughters remain unmarried, his two youngest still girls, and he'd wanted to walk them down the aisle as he'd walked me the day of my wedding.

We all—in the end—die in medias res. In the middle of a story. Of many stories.

I suppose it's not quite accurate to call the death of someone who lived with cancer for years unexpected, but Steve's death was unexpected for us.

What I learned from my brother's death was that character is essential: What he was, was how he died.

Tuesday morning, he called me to ask me to hurry up to Palo Alto. His tone was affectionate, dear, loving, but like someone whose luggage was already strapped onto the vehicle, who was already on the beginning of his journey, even as he was sorry, truly deeply sorry, to be leaving us.

He started his farewell and I stopped him. I said, "Wait. I'm coming. I'm in a taxi to the airport. I'll be there."

"I'm telling you now because I'm afraid you won't make it on time, honey."

When I arrived, he and his Laurene were joking together like partners who'd lived and worked together every day of their lives. He looked into his children's eyes as if he couldn't unlock his gaze.

Until about two in the afternoon, his wife could rouse him, to talk to his friends from Apple.

Then, after a while, it was clear that he would no longer wake to us.

His breathing changed. It became severe, deliberate, purposeful. I could feel him counting his steps again, pushing farther than before.

This is what I learned: he was working at this, too. Death didn't happen to Steve, he achieved it.

He told me, when he was saying goodbye and telling me he was sorry, so sorry we wouldn't be able to be old together as we'd always planned, that he was going to a better place.

Dr. Fischer gave him a 50/50 chance of making it through the night.

He made it through the night. Laurene next to him on the bed sometimes jerked up when there was a longer pause between his breaths. She and I looked at each other, then he would heave a deep breath and begin again.

This had to be done. Even now, he had a stern, still handsome profile, the profile of an absolutist, a romantic. His breath indicated an arduous journey, some steep path, altitude.

He seemed to be climbing.

But with that will, that work ethic, that strength, there was also sweet Steve's capacity for wonderment, the artist's belief in the ideal, the still more beautiful later.

Steve's final words, hours earlier, were monosyllables, repeated three times.

Before embarking, he'd looked at his sister Patty, then for a long time at his children, then at his life's partner, Laurene, and then over their shoulders past them.

Steve's final words were:

OH WOW. OH WOW. OH WOW.

JOHN JEREMIAH SULLIVAN

■

Peyton's Place

FROM *GQ*

PRACTICALLY EVERY DAY, cars stop in front of our house, and people get out to take pictures of it, and of us—me and my wife and daughter—if we happen to be outside. Or they'll take one of Tony, who cuts the whole neighborhood's grass. Tony loves it. He poses for them, with his rake and lawn bags, grinning, one arm thrown wide as if to say, "All this, my friends." I've told him several times to start charging, but he won't even hear it. He does it, he says, because it makes him feel famous. Sometimes it's only one car. Other times it's eight or nine in a day. It depends what time of year it is, and what's happening on the Internet. Once there was an event of some kind in town, and we got more than twenty. I go for long stretches when I forget it's even happening. I really don't see them, since I don't leave the house that much, and they're always quiet, they never make trouble. But a month ago my new neighbor, Nicholas, who just moved in next door, came over to introduce himself. He's a tall thin guy in his fifties, glasses and a white beard. Very nice, very sociable. Before he left, he said, "Can I ask you something? Have you noticed that people are always taking pictures of your house?"

Yeah, I said—pressing PLAY on my spiel—it's silly, I know, but our house used to be on TV, not anymore, those people are fans . . . Isn't that funny?

"I mean, it is constant," he said.

I know! I said. Hope it doesn't bother you. Tell me if it ever gets annoying.

"No, no, I don't mind," he said. "They're always polite. They almost seem embarrassed."

Well, tell me if that changes, I said.

"Okay," he said. "I just can't believe how many there are."

Nicholas and I have had some version of that conversation three times, one for every week he's lived next door. Each time I've wanted to tell him it's going to end, except that I don't know if it will. It may increase.

My brother-in-law sells trailers in the Arizona desert—indeed he professes to "have the trailer game in a chokehold" in that part of the world. Not long ago he told me about the Stamp. He had a boss whose office was across from his in the trailer they worked out of. They sold trailers from a trailer. The boss had a huge, specially made rubber stamp on his desk that read APPROVED. Whenever things were getting tense in my brother-in-law's office, when the boss could hear that negotiations were becoming sticky, usually on the matter of the prospective buyer's gaining loan approval, he would saunter in with the Stamp. Saunter doesn't describe his walk, which my brother-in-law demonstrated. The boss was a little guy, and his legs sort of wheeled out from his body as he walked, like something you'd associate with a degenerative hip condition. He'd come wheeling up to the desk like that and *bam* bring down the Stamp on the application, APPROVED, and wheel away, leaving the buyers stunned and, as it dawned on them, delighted. "You understand," my brother-in-law said, "a lot of the people I was selling to were gypsies. As in, literal gypsies. They didn't have mailing addresses."

The story goes some way toward explaining how my wife and I got permission from a bank to buy a giant brick neo-colonial house—also how the world economy went into free fall, but that's for another time and a writer with nothing to do but an enormous amount of research. My wife was eight months pregnant, and we lived in a one-bedroom apartment, the converted ground floor of an antebellum house, on a noisy street downtown, with an eccentric upstairs neighbor, Keef, from Leland, who told me that I was a rich man—that's how he put it, "Y'er a rich man, ain't ye?"—who told us that he was going to shoot his daughter's boyfriend with an ultra-accurate sniper rifle he owned, for filling his daughter full of drugs, "shoot him below the knee," he said, "that way they cain't git ye with intent to kill." Keef had been a low-level white supremacist and still bore a few unfortunate tattoos but told us he'd lost his racism when, on a cruise in the Bahamas, he'd saved a drowning black boy's life, in the on-ship pool, and by this conversion experience "came to love some blacks." He later fell off a two-story painting ladder and broke all his bones. A fascinating man, but not the sort I wanted my daughter having unlimited exposure to in her formative years. Not my angel. We entered nesting panic. We wanted big and solid. We wanted Greatest Generation, but their parents, even greater. We found it. It had a sleeping porch, and a shiplike attic where I in my dotage would pull objects from a trunk and tell their histories to little ones. We asked for the money, and in some office, somebody's boss came forward with the Stamp.

Around the time it became clear that we'd gotten ahead of ourselves financially—and thinking back, that was a seismic twinge in advance of the market meltdown, a message from the bowels that people like the guy with four cell phones and a Jersey accent working out of a storage unit in Charlotte, who'd loaned us the money, probably shouldn't have been loaning hundreds of thousands of dollars to people like me, not that "magazine writer" isn't right there behind civil servant on the job-security pyramid—that was when we remembered something our buyer's agent, Andy, had said, something about a TV show that might want to use the house, and somebody might be calling us. We had written it down. A guy named Greg.

Often I think of Greg. What an amazing guy. Truly amazing, as in he brought us into a maze. We only ever saw him once. I've never seen him since. And this is a small town—you see people. It was like they flew him in for this meeting. He was a heavy guy in a tentlike Hawaiian shirt. Goatee, sunglasses. Did he tell me he played rugby or did he look exactly like someone I knew who played rugby? He sat across from us at our kitchen table, a thirteen-foot dark wood table that purportedly came in pieces from a Norwegian farmhouse, relic of nesting panic (long table, order). Greg sat across from us. He explained that they'd mostly be using only the front two rooms of the house. This was the place they mainly shot. The rest of our character's house had been re-created on a set, and the transitions would be made seamless in editing.

He laid out the deal they'd struck with the previous owners. We move you into a Hilton. Meals and per diem. We put everything back the way it was. We take Polaroids of your bookshelves to make sure we've put the books in order. That's how thorough we are. We even pay people to come in afterward and clean up. The house looks better than you left it. We'll pay you $—— for an exterior shoot, $—— for interiors.

The combined amount equaled our mortgage.

Yes, I think we can work something out.

"The front two rooms"—that phrase, in particular, we heard repeated: it has a poetic density to it, like "cellar door," so I remember. The front two rooms.

Maroon minivan, Greg gone.

A lot of movies and TV shows are shot here, in our adopted coastal hometown of Wilmington, North Carolina—Wilmywood. It started when the late Frank Capra Jr. came here to make *Firestarter* in the early eighties. He liked the place and stayed, and an industry evolved around him. Dennis Hopper bought property. Now half the kids who wait on you downtown are extras, or want to be actors. You'll be in Target and realize you're in line behind Val Kilmer. We have studios and a film school, and we're known in the business for our exceptionally wide variety of locations. You can be doing beachy beachy, and suddenly go leafy established suburb, go country hayride, then nighttime happening street, pretty much whatever.

For the last several years, the big ticket in town has been the teen melodrama *One Tree Hill*, which was on the WB and is now on the CW Network. Don't let the off brands fool you, though; a surprising number of people watch it, maybe even you, for all I know. It's one of the worst TV shows ever made, and I seriously do not mean that as an insult. It's bad in the way that Mexican TV is bad, superstylized bad. Good bad. Indeed, there are times when the particular campiness of its badness, although I can sense its presence, is in fact beyond me, beyond my frequency, like with that beep you play on the Internet that only kids can hear. Too many of my camp-receptor cells have died. Possibly *One Tree Hill* is a work of genius. Certainly it is about to go nine seasons, strongly suggesting that the mother of its creator, Mark Schwahn, did not give birth to any idiots, or if she did those people are Schwahn's siblings.

The *One Tree* character who supposedly lived in our house was Peyton, played by one of the stars, Hilarie Burton, a striking bone-thin blonde. Think coppery curls. I'd seen her on MTV right at the moment when I was first feeling too old to watch MTV. Superfriendly when we met her—superfriendly always. Hilarie has a golden reputation in Wilmington. She's one of the cast members who've made the place home, and she gets involved in local things. When we met, she gave us hugs, complimented the house, thanked us for letting them use it. She disarmed us—good manners had not been what we'd expected.

I don't know how our house became known as a place to shoot. It's not all that special. I think it's sort of immediately sturdy-looking—guys who come here to fix things invariably remark on "how much wood they used on this place"—in a way that's visually useful to a director who wants to say Big Brick House in as little time and with as few subtleties as possible. The studio has scouts who drive around looking for these things. And this is an interesting neighborhood. I learned from a local historian that it was created as a sort of colony by Christian Scientists in the 1920s. Lolita's house from *Lolita*—the Jeremy Irons version—is down the street (it's really pretty). One of the crew guys who came to paint our living room—a short, supermuscular dude with a biker's mustache and cap, who knew a lot of Wilmington film trivia—told me that our house was in *Blue Velvet*, which David Lynch made here. I looked it up. Sure enough. Just for a few seconds. During the car-chase scene, when Jeffrey thinks he's being trailed by psychotic Frank (in Dennis Hopper's immortal performance), but then is relieved to find it's only chuckle-head Mike, the moment when the hubcap comes off and goes rolling down the street like a toy hoop (an unintended effect that Lynch reportedly loved in editing, causing him to linger on that moment—if you watch it you can see that the beat is held unusually long, compared with what you'd normally do on a curb-scraping turn, namely cut it off to emphasize speed), that happens in front of our house. There were other shows. The dresser in the guest bedroom had been, we were told, Katie Holmes's on *Dawson's Creek*. They used us as a haunted house in one episode of that series.

Now Peyton lived here, and they needed to bring over her stuff. Greg had given us a choice: Either we can switch our furniture out with yours every time—load up your stuff and haul it away; haul in our stuff, use it, haul it away; reload your stuff—we're actually willing to do that before and after each shoot. Or we can just leave our stuff here. Treat it as your own. We'll take it away when the show is over. Let us decorate your new house for you. They may let you keep a few pieces.

Theoretically that made sense. In reality (a word I can hardly use without laughing), it meant that we lived on a TV set. Of course, they consulted us on everything, showing us furniture catalogues, guiding us toward choices that both suited our taste and looked like something Peyton would have in her home. It meant more tasteful floral patterns than I'd expected, but that was okay. Maybe there was a little Peyton in me.

She was complicated, deeper than the other teens on *One Tree*, which in teen-show terms meant that she often wore flannel shirts. The other teens would come to her for advice. She lived alone. Her biological parents were dead, her adoptive parents missing, or some combination. This created an explanation for how she'd come to possess her own large home while still in high school, and how it was that she often lay in bed with teenage boys in that home, talking and snuggling, unmolested by those awful ogrelike parents who beat on the door and scream, "I don't hear any studying in there!" Peyton Sawyer: Forced to grow up too fast. Harboring an inner innocence.

One thing we did not help choose: these dark charcoal drawings. In my memory they seem to appear overnight. There were a bunch of them, and they were the first thing you saw when you walked through the front door, and they looked as if they'd been executed during art therapy time at a prison. I said something to one of the crewmen at one point, something like, "Gosh, the whole front of the house is filled with some very intense and angry artwork."

"Yes," he said. "Those are not happy paintings."

Petyon was in a tortured-artist period that season.

"You can just put them in a closet when we're not shooting."

When it was quiet again, we sat on the new couch with the baby, taking it in. Wow—the rooms looked great. A little sterile, a little showroom. But we hadn't been able to afford to furnish this place ourselves anyway. What had our plan been, to pick up used stuff off the street that other people had put out for collection? I couldn't even remember. There hadn't been a plan.

I had a high school Latin teacher named Patty Papadopolous, an enormous person—she often needed a wheelchair to get about, for her girth and what it had done to her knees—also a brilliant teacher. She married young, but her husband was killed in Vietnam. Bottle-blond beehive hairdo. She schlepped between public schools, teaching the few Latin courses they could still fill, using a medical forklift thing that moved her in and out of her van. She was captivating on the ancient world. She told us how the Roman army at its most mercilessly efficient used to stop every afternoon, build a city, live in it that night, eat and fuck and play dice and argue strategy and sharpen weapons and go to the toilet in it, pack it up the next morning, and march.

That description sprang to mind when the show arrived for the season's first shoot. With the baby barely two weeks old, we'd felt that she was too small to be moving back and forth from house to Hilton. They did a series of scenes with us in the house, sequestered upstairs.

Boxy light trucks appeared in a row down the street, a line of white buffalo. It was very *E.T.*, the scene where they take him away. Cops were parked on the corners, directing traffic and shooing gawkers. In a nearby field they pitched the food tent, which soon buzzed with crew. The stars ate in a van. I looked out the window—miles of cable, banks of lights, Porta-Pottys. Walkie-talkies.

It was a day shoot, but a night scene. They had blacked most of the windows. Upstairs, where we were, it was afternoon. Downstairs it was about ten o'clock at night. From the sound I guessed there were twenty strangers in the house.

Silence. We listened.

Peyton's voice.

I can't remember the line. It was something like "That's not what I wanted." And then another character said something. Footsteps.

The director was having Hilarie do the line different ways.

"That's not what I wanted."

"That's NOT WHAT I WANTED."

"That's not what I WANTED."

You got a sense, even through the floorboards, of former-kid-star work ethic from Hilarie, giving 100 percent. And rolling. And rolling. No brattiness, every take usable.

We heard general chatter, and could tell they were breaking off the scene. As the baby nursed, we listened for the next one.

No next one. They were done, moving out. Gone by midnight, traffic barriers picked up. The city vanished. It had existed for about twenty seconds of footage.

When the following shoot came, an exterior this time, we had family in town. That was fun. It gratified us to see them get a little thrill from it all, the occasional celebrity sighting. It also meant that some memorable, life-changing moments from my first days of being a father—of holding my own child in the kitchen and seeing the generations together—happened while Peyton was on the back patio having equally intense times. One of her fathers, who'd been a merchant marine, had come to port, and was trying to get back into her world. I may be slightly off on that; I had to put it together from dialogue fragments.

You could see Hilarie's sweetness in the way she humored our families. The scene called for her to run through the backyard, up the steps to the back screen door, say, "*No*, Dad!" and slam the door behind her. Each time she executed a take, my mother and ninety-year-old Cuban grandmother-in-law, their faces squeezed together in the window of the porch door, would smile and furiously wave at her through the glass, as we begged them to sit. Hilarie waved back, just absorbing it into her process. "*No*, Dad." (Slam, smile, wave, turn.) "Dad, no!" (Slam, smile, wave, turn.)

Did she want some black beans? Abuela asked. She was so skinny!

"No, no, I'm fine. Thank you, though." (To my wife, behind the hand, "They're so sweet.")

She had a barbecue going out back. A grill, burgers. Picnic tables. All gone by dark. And at some point the next morning, a check flew in at the door, without a sound. As the ending voice-over of a *One Tree*

episode might have put it, things were a little crazy, but we were going to be all right.

One thing did happen during the set-decoration phase. It was small,
but the symbolism of it was so obvious, so articulate, I really should
have paid more attention. They wallpapered the stairwell, and put up
light sconces.

It was the first little toe-wander across the Greg Perimeter, that
line around the front two rooms. It was the first shy tentacle tap, the
first tendril nuzzle.

"But Greg distinctly said only the front two rooms."

Well, we only shoot in here. But everything you can see from this
room has to match her house, too. It's for continuity.

Needless to say we hadn't been around when Peyton had chosen
the wallpaper—or when one of her lost parents had chosen it. Not
that it was ugly or anything. Just somber. It didn't say newlywed or
newborn or anything newly. And it was our staircase. We had to walk
up and down it every day. We couldn't avoid it like we mostly came to
avoid the front two rooms, treating them as a parlor. Peyton's spirit
lived there.

The problem wasn't the wallpaper, though, it was this curious
thing the crew guys did with it once they got upstairs. They stopped
in the middle of a wall. The paper wrapped around at the top of the
stairs, so you'd see it if you were shooting up, and it did start down
the hall, but about a foot and a half before it reached the first doorway, the first natural obstacle, it just terminated. That wall was part
wallpaper, part paint, divided horizontally. It looked bad, and I'm a
person who could live happily in a cardboard box if I wouldn't miss
my loved ones.

The next morning, when we pointed out the anomaly, they corrected it instantly. Inconvenience was hardly an issue. The crew were
hyperprofessional (film crews almost always are—the constant time
intensity of the work creates an autoflushing mechanism, instantly
getting rid of the lazy and sloppy). It was rather the oddity of their
having done something so glaring, when with everything else, they'd
been so meticulous (because it turned out they really did take pictures of your bookshelves). The wallpaper ended precisely where the

camera's peripheral vision did. What the camera couldn't see wasn't totally real.

If our daughter later in her life finds that she possesses any of those contextless, purely visual, prememory memories, like some people have from their first two years, hers will be of a suite at the Riverside Hilton, in downtown Wilmington, North Carolina. It rises beigely beside the Cape Fear River. My Lord, did we spend some time there. They knew us by sight at the check-in counter. We developed a game with pillows. Not a game, but a child stunt that could be endlessly repeated. We stacked up every pillow in the suite, maybe a dozen, in the center of the king bed, and laid my daughter on top of the highest one like the princess and the pea, and let it crash down onto the bed like a falling tower. She laughed until she gave herself hiccups. She was a toddler by then, of course. You wouldn't toss an infant about like that, although with an infant, they're so easy to balance, you could have done even more pillows, you could have done fifteen or twenty. My Cuban grandmother-in-law was given her own room, and she would watch the baby at night, while we hit the restaurants by the river with our meal vouchers. Mornings I woke around sunrise, before the baby even, and read by the window during that quiet hour. Best was when they gave us a room on the city side. You could watch the dawn invade the streets one by one, and see the old eighteenth-century layout of the town illuminated.

Those junkets gave me a ghostly feeling. It's strange to stay in a hotel in your own city. We had moved here, we'd found property here, and now they were paying us not to stay there, like people who lived elsewhere. People in the lobby would say, "Where are you visiting from?"

It became unsettling, though, when we started to watch the show. The hours of Hilton boredom brought on epic jags of cable flipping (oh, sad and too-hard colorful rubber buttons of hotel cable remotes). In the dark we'd look for the house to come on. We competed like in charades to say "There it is!" first. (Not as a formal competition but spontaneously.)

We formed memories of our house that weren't memories; we'd experienced them solely through television. We hadn't been there for them, yet they'd occurred while we lived there. It felt something like what I imagine amnesiacs feel when they are shown pictures from their unremembered lives. You thought, How could I not remember this, how can I not have known that this happened? Coming back home after a big shoot, and finding everything just as you'd left it, despite your certain knowledge that dramatic and often violent things had occurred there while you were gone, it kept bringing to mind a Steven Wright joke, from one of his comedy specials in the eighties. "Thieves broke into my house," he said. "They took all my things and replaced them with exact replicas."

Once we'd boarded the Hilton gravy train, the Greg Perimeter vanished like a knocked-out laser security grid at a museum. Breached by the wallpaper, it had suffered other small incursions during the early shoots—lights in the upstairs windows, for instance, to boost the artificial sunlight during a night shoot/day scene, a truly disorienting scene, the last we stayed home for, when they made it afternoon in the front yard. Now they were actually setting scenes in other rooms. Peyton and Lucas (Chad Michael Murray's character, the Chachi to Peyton's Joanie) baked cookies in the kitchen. They got into a food fight and started slinging dough at each other. All over our kitchen, dough balls hitting the wall. Splat, in the cracks, on the cupboards, sailing out into the hallway. Surely this was grounds for a lucrative contract readjustment. I checked the terms—Arrgh! I'd signed over the whole property! "Equal to the amount of the mortgage," said the guy on my shoulder.

And besides, when we got home, everything was spotless. Couldn't find a fleck of dough anywhere. Couldn't find a chocolate chip (wish I had—it might be worth something on eBay). The only way the scene had affected us, in a strict material sense, was that we got our kitchen professionally cleaned for free. We'd faced harder challenges.

That's when Psycho Derek appeared.

Much later, when we were no longer on friendly terms with *One Tree*, I caught myself wondering if Psycho Derek had not perhaps been created purely as an instrument for abusing our house, to make sure we never forgot the name Peyton Sawyer. Who was he? Who was Psycho Derek?

In another country, in another world, "Ian Banks" is a young blond Scottish writer. He has a pretty wife, and one night they're out driving. He's drunk and messing with the wheel. Crash, she dies. In his guilt and grief, he goes on the Internet and starts looking for girls who look like his wife. Guess what, his wife looked just like Peyton. He does some research. He learns that Peyton has a biological brother, separated at birth, name: Derek. Lightbulb—he'll impersonate the brother. From behind that mask he worms his way into her world. But Peyton figures out he's a violent obsessive. She cuts him off. That's when he starts to attack. Our house.

He tied up Peyton and her best friend, Brooke, in the basement, as a prelude to raping them (*One Tree* was getting dark, that's where its campiness lost me, with the darkness—I don't see how you get to be teeny-dumb and do psychotic teen rape fantasies, but as I say, the irony of the genre has evolved, found new crevices). In one episode Psycho Derek was pushed down our staircase, violently grabbing at the antique banister to save himself as he fell. In another he got thrown through our bedroom window onto a safety bag on the front lawn. Our house had become the stunt house (they don't care, they're at the Hilton, they need the money!).

The crew couldn't clean up after this stuff as easily. Everything was not the same when we got home. The yard was full of shattered safety glass. The handrail on the stairs was a few centimeters more rickety, thanks to Psycho Derek's heavy grasping (when we watched it on TV we realized that the stunt guy had actually fallen backward onto the rail, with all his weight). Not to mention that in our minds the basement was now permanently a onetime BDSM sex dungeon, and not a mutual-consent swinger dungeon, either. Psycho Derek had created some seriously bad visual associations in the house, ones our daughter might not enjoy discovering come her own teen years—the basement bondage pre-rape had taken place on Peyton's prom night. (Prom was hard on our house: Peyton's friend, Brooke, mad at Peyton for something, had egged it on the day of the prom; deranged Brooke fans later re-created this incident in "reality," hitting our house with eggs in the very same spots; at least we assumed that's who did it. Could have been vandals.)

I can't blame Derek for everything. And I should take this opportunity to thank the real Derek, Peyton's true half brother, who turned out to be black, and showed up just in time, wearing a varsity jacket, to save her from Psycho Derek, and our home from any more trauma. No, Psycho Derek had been neutralized by the time we ended the contract.

What did happen? I don't know how to explain it, except to say that it was a sort of caveman thing. Instincts that had lain dormant in my genome for generations awoke. Who were these strangers in my rock shelter? Why were they walking in and out without knocking or saying goodbye, why did they keep referring to it as "Peyton's House"? This is my house. The more the story line expanded through the rooms, the worse the feeling became. And of course the crew guys, who'd now been coming to the house for several years—who knew it in some ways better than we did—couldn't help making themselves more comfortable in it over time, sneaking in for more bathroom breaks. On one shoot, I remember, I'd been confused about where they needed to set up, and as a result neglected to clean the bedroom. Later a crew guy—the same one who'd told me about *Blue Velvet*—said, "I'm not used to picking up other people's underwear." I felt like saying, Then don't go into their bedrooms at nine o'clock in the morning! Except he was paying to be in my bedroom.

Isn't there another profession where people pay to be in your bedroom?

One day, we were at the Hilton, and I realized I'd forgotten something. I drove back to the house in the middle of a shoot. On my way out, having found what I needed, I ran into one of the crew. He had dinner plates in his hands. I knew those plates—they were plates we'd been given when we got married.

He got nervous, obviously aware that he'd crossed some line. He told me that the stars, in their dining van, had asked for real plates. These were the first he'd seen. In that awkward moment on the brick path there, something came into my head that my across-the-street neighbor, Arnie, kept saying to me, rather passive-aggressively I thought, when I would pass him on the sidewalk. Inevitably remarking on the *One Tree Hill* stuff, he'd say, "The way my wife and I feel is, we don't have much, but it's ours."

By then I was fairly certain that all the neighbors hated us. I'm sure that when we moved in, they were praying we wouldn't resume the previous owners' contract with the show, that the nightmare would end. These shoots couldn't help disrupting the whole psychogeography of the block. To have to be waved through by cops into your own neighborhood, how obnoxious! The lights, the noise (the crew were always scrupulously hushed outside, but when you have that many people, there's a hive hum). I felt how much I'd hate it, if I were one of them. And why our house, anyway? There was just some bad anthropological juju going on in our little barrio. And that's not good. You don't want that. When Armageddon comes and the village is reset to a primitive state, your clan will be shunned and denied resources.

When a disagreement about money came up—we thought we were owed for an extra day—my subconscious seized on it as an excuse (though I didn't really need one, they were unpleasant about the money, which seemed weird, given we'd never been complainers). Finally one day we told them they couldn't film there anymore. It was all too big a pain in the ass. I had a suspicion they were thinking about the attic. I've never had that confirmed, but the attic is neat-looking, and it would have been the next logical step. Psycho Derek isn't dead, he's in the attic, boring peepholes. Our daughter was getting older, old enough to start wondering why we regularly moved out of the house and then right back in again, and who was living there in the meantime? If my brain couldn't handle the metaphysical implications of it all, what chance did she have? A producer called and offered us a lot more money at one point—so Peyton could say goodbye—but it had become a principle thing by then, and it felt good to say no, to reclaim the cave. And so, for primarily petty and neurotic reasons, I made a decision that negatively impacted our financial future. It's called being a good father.

I remember when they came to get Peyton's furniture. Because she'd moved in at the same time as us, her things and ours had mingled at the edges. My wife was at work, and with some pieces, I didn't know whose they were. The guy who was in charge that day held up a vase that had been on the table. "I honestly don't know if that's ours or hers," I said. I suspected it was hers, but had always liked it. "You know what," the guy said, "let's just say it's yours."

They sent painters in, which I thought was classy. Many of the walls had been scuffed by equipment and gaffer's tape and whatnot. My wife gave them a bunch of bold colors, colors we'd never tended to before. The place looks totally different. It's ours again, or rather for the first time. We burned a sage stick. Both literally and metaphorically.

Our only worry was that maybe we'd caused trouble for Hilarie somehow, affected the plotline in some way that made Peyton less essential to the cast, but when we ran into her some weeks later and voiced this concern, she was characteristically ultramature about it, and said, "You know, I think you really helped her grow up." Her being Peyton. The producers had decided to zip forward the story line four years—just skip college, go straight from right after high-school graduation to right after college graduation, with the characters all back home, in order to avoid the dorm-room doldrums that have brought down other teen shows, like *Felicity*. Now Peyton lived downtown. She managed bands. "She doesn't live in her parents' house anymore," Hilarie said. "She has her own apartment. I think it's about time."

A year passed. We were at the airport in London—my wife had a conference there. Standing in the ticket line, we started talking about the show—probably we'd seen an old episode in one of the hotels we'd stayed at in Scotland—and we were having a what-an-experience type of conversation. At one point, the woman in front of us turned around. Business suit, dark bun. She leaned forward, and in an unplaceable European accent said, "You have a lovely home." Not in a creepy way. She said it about as nicely as you could say something like that. "Are you a fan of the show?" my wife asked. "Oh, yes," the woman said. "I always watch it." She knew exactly what Petyon's house looked like. She described it for us. The white railing, the hallway.

By then we'd grown inured to fans coming by, frequently knocking on the door. They acted more passionate in the early days, or at least more brazen. They wanted pictures of themselves, of them with you, of you and the house, them and the house, one at a time. They were 90 percent female, teens and early twenties, but lots of their moms came with them. One of the few males, a tall skinny stonery guy, gave me half of a dollar bill, and asked me to hide it inside something on the set. I put it inside a little African-looking wooden bowl that we and Peyton kept by the front door. The bowl had a lid. He thanked us profusely and said that now he could sit at home with his girlfriend, who loved Peyton, and they'd know the other half of the dollar bill was in her house. When they came for Peyton's stuff, it was still in there; I checked.

Nobody was ever scary or rude. One time we did get these Belgian girls. They were perhaps unwholesomely fixated on the show. Six of them showed up, with a Lebanese taxi-van driver who'd brought them straight from the airport, four minutes away. He'd evidently picked them up outside baggage claim and, hearing their talk of *One Tree Hill*, offered to give them a tour of locations. Now here they were. The driver stood behind them the whole time, as if presenting them to us for consideration. We gave them a couple of souvenirs from the show, a script from an old episode that had been lying around, something else I don't remember. At these modest acts of kindness they broke down into tears, which caused my wife to go and get more things to give them, which made them cry harder. I can see them standing in the hallway, these beautiful girls, crying and laughing. They gave us a jar of excellent honey from their country, and an Eiffel Tower key chain that my daughter loved and we still use. Bless you, girls, wherever you are. Watching *One Tree*, probably.

The farthest away that anyone ever came from—another mother-daughter team—was Thailand. "Peyton House?" Mostly Ohio, Florida, places like that.

Just this week, we had two from South Carolina knock at the door. My daughter and I met them on the porch. If I had to guess, I'd say they were about to embark on their senior year of high school. You could tell they were good friends, because they never said a word to each other. They stared at us, and past us into the house.

"Can I help you?" I said.

The smaller girl, a brunet with a haircut somewhat matronly for one so young, said, "Okay . . . Did you know that your house used to be on a show?"

"Yes," I said. "In fact, we were living here when they did that filming."

Their eyes widened. "May we come in?" I glanced down at my daughter. She looked excited—big girls!

"Why not?"

The brunet's question had given me a small, surprising tilt of nostalgia. Did we know that we used to be on a show? Did we know that? The time-lapse sands of pop-cultural oblivion, which will not be stayed, had overtaken us in just a few short years. We were trivia. These girls had come, before college separated them, to see something they remembered from when they were even younger, watching it together. Peyton isn't on the show anymore. Hilarie and Chad Michael Murray both failed to return for the most recent season. Contract disputes, they said. Chad, in a wild merging of life and art, ended up marrying a girl from the local high school here, right down the street, New Hanover High. The girl was still a high school student when they met. Chad had to wait for her to become legal, before they could marry. We heard him once in the front yard on his cell phone, on a night we were slow to get out of the house before a shoot, giving her advice about the SATs.

Hilarie's still in Wilmington, doing her own production company, Southern Gothic. Last year we saw her in a serious movie, *Provinces of Night*, based on a William Gay book. Val Kilmer was in it. Hilarie played an "oft-unconscious junkie," and she was good. She can act. She'll be fine.

The girls wanted to see the basement—they remembered the prom episode well—but I said no. I took pictures to make it up to them.

After they left, I was walking back down the hallway with my daughter, who's almost five. She's turned into a lovely child. Little brown helmet of smooth hair. She reminds me of the tiny Martian from Looney Tunes—"Illudium Pu-36 Explosive Space Modulator." Purely in terms of silhouette. She marches around in a very deliberate way.

"Daddy," she said, "why did those girls want to see our house?"

"Remember how I told you this house used to be on a TV show?"

"Yes," she said.

"Those girls love the show, so they wanted to see where it was made." She stopped.

"Is our house still on TV?" she asked.

"Well," I said, "there are reruns, so, I guess it's still on sometimes."

She got a concerned look on her face. Standing with her feet apart, she threw her arms out, looking from room to room.

"Are we on a show right now?!" she demanded.

I said I didn't think so.

ADRIAN TOMINE

■

A Brief History of the Art Form Known as "Hortisculpture"

FROM *Optic Nerve*

Hortisculpture

I'M TELLING YOU, JOE... THESE THINGS ARE GONNA FLY OUT THE DOOR!

I JUST DON'T KNOW IF THEY'RE RIGHT FOR US, HAROLD. WE SELL PLAIN POTS... REGULAR OL' TERRA COTTA AND THE LIKE.

APPLES AND ORANGES, JOE! THIS IS A VITAL NEW ART FORM!

WELL, THEY'RE AWFUL BIG, AND I JUST DON'T KNOW IF WE CAN SPARE THAT KIND OF REAL ESTATE RIGHT NOW.

HERE'S WHAT YOU DO, JOE: YOU PUT ONE ON DISPLAY, AND WHEN THAT ONE SELLS, YOU CALL ME.

GOSH... I DON'T KNOW, HAROLD. I DON'T THINK I'D FEEL COMFORTABLE ASKING A CUSTOMER TO HIRE YOU TO MAINTAIN THE THING, UH... AD INFINITUM.

PERFECTLY UNDER-STANDABLE! I KNOW IT TAKES PEOPLE AWHILE TO GET USED TO SOMETHING NEW, WHICH IS WHY--

UH, LOOK, HAROLD...

I'VE GOTTA GET BACK TO WORK, BUT HAVE YOU PROTECTED THIS IDEA? YOU KNOW... COPYRIGHT OR WHATEVER?

JOE, THAT'S NEITHER HERE NOR THERE, BUT--

OOH... I'D LOOK INTO THAT IF I WAS YOU, HAROLD.

YOU DON'T WANT SOME SHYSTER RIPPING YOU OFF RIGHT OUT OF THE GATE, DO YOU?

WELL...

LOOK... YOU GET ALL THE LEGALITIES SQUARED AWAY, AND THEN WE'LL TALK. OKAY, HAROLD?

...AND THAT'S WHY JOE CHOI IS A SUCCESSFUL BUSINESSMAN AND I'M NOT! HOW COULD I BE SO STUPID?!

"HORTISCULPTURE"

OKAY... TRY TO LOOK ON THE BRIGHT SIDE.

I'LL PROBABLY SLEEP BETTER OUT HERE, ACTUALLY. PROPPING MY FEET UP LIKE THIS IS GOOD FOR THE OL' PLANTAR FASCIITIS.

AND SOMETIMES A LITTLE "COOLING OFF" PERIOD IS ALL THAT--

HEY!

THIS IS NOTHING THAT AN ALL-NIGHT JUNK FOOD BENDER CAN'T DISTRACT ME FROM!

"HORTISCULPTURE"

I WAS BORN AT THE WRONG TIME. I GUESS I DIDN'T REALIZE HOW DUMBED-DOWN OUR CULTURE HAS BECOME.

NO ONE CARES ABOUT ART ANY-MORE. NO, THAT'S PUTTING IT TOO MILDLY. PEOPLE ARE **HOSTILE** TOWARDS ART NOW, JUST LIKE ANYTHING ELSE THEY DON'T UNDERSTAND.

EVERYONE'S BEEN BEATEN INTO SUBMISSION BY THE ADVERTISING INDUSTRY... TELEVISION... FAST-FOOD CHAINS... HOLLYWOOD... OUR STANDARDS HAVE BEEN SYSTEMATICALLY--

HEY! YOU GOT ANY MORE OF THESE CHOCOLATE "HOME RUN" PIES?

YOU SPEAK ENGLISH?!

JOSE ANTONIO VARGAS

■

Outlaw

FROM *The New York Times Magazine*

ONE AUGUST MORNING NEARLY TWO DECADES AGO, my mother woke me and put me in a cab. She handed me a jacket. *"Baka malamig doon"* were among the few words she said. ("It might be cold there.") When I arrived at the Philippines' Ninoy Aquino International Airport with her, my aunt, and a family friend, I was introduced to a man I'd never seen. They told me he was my uncle. He held my hand as I boarded an airplane for the first time. It was 1993, and I was twelve.

My mother wanted to give me a better life, so she sent me thousands of miles away to live with her parents in America — my grandfather (*Lolo* in Tagalog) and grandmother (*Lola*). After I arrived in Mountain View, California, in the San Francisco Bay Area, I entered sixth grade and quickly grew to love my new home, family, and culture. I discovered a passion for language, though it was hard to learn the difference between formal English and American slang. One of my early memories is of a freckled kid in middle school asking me, "What's up?" I replied, "The sky," and he and a couple of other kids laughed. I won the eighth-grade spelling bee by memorizing words I couldn't properly pronounce. (The winning word was "indefatigable.")

One day when I was sixteen, I rode my bike to the nearby DMV office to get my driver's permit. Some of my friends already had their licenses, so I figured it was time. But when I handed the clerk my green card as proof of U.S. residency, she flipped it around, examining it. "This is fake," she whispered. "Don't come back here again."

Confused and scared, I pedaled home and confronted Lolo. I remember him sitting in the garage, cutting coupons. I dropped my bike and ran over to him, showing him the green card. *"Peke ba ito?"* I asked in Tagalog. ("Is this fake?") My grandparents were naturalized American citizens—he worked as a security guard, she as a food server—and they had begun supporting my mother and me financially when I was three, after my father's wandering eye and inability to properly provide for us led to my parents' separation. Lolo was a proud man, and I saw the shame on his face as he told me he purchased the card, along with other fake documents, for me. "Don't show it to other people," he warned.

I decided then that I could never give anyone reason to doubt I was an American. I convinced myself that if I worked enough, if I achieved enough, I would be rewarded with citizenship. I felt I could earn it.

I've tried. Over the past fourteen years, I've graduated from high school and college and built a career as a journalist, interviewing some of the most famous people in the country. On the surface, I've created a good life. I've lived the American dream.

But I am still an undocumented immigrant. And that means living a different kind of reality. It means going about my day in fear of being found out. It means rarely trusting people, even those closest to me, with who I really am. It means keeping my family photos in a shoebox rather than displaying them on shelves in my home, so friends don't ask about them. It means reluctantly, even painfully, doing things I know are wrong and unlawful. And it has meant relying on a sort of twenty-first century underground railroad of supporters, people who took an interest in my future and took risks for me.

Last year I read about four students who walked from Miami to Washington to lobby for the Dream Act, a nearly decade-old immigration bill that would provide a path to legal permanent residency for young people who have been educated in this country. At the risk of deportation—the Obama administration has deported almost 800,000 people in the last two years—they are speaking out. Their courage has inspired me.

There are believed to be 11 million undocumented immigrants in the United States. We're not always who you think we are. Some pick your strawberries or care for your children. Some are in high school or college. And some, it turns out, write news articles you might read. I grew up here. This is my home. Yet even though I think of myself as an American and consider America my country, my country doesn't think of me as one of its own.

My first challenge was the language. Though I learned English in the Philippines, I wanted to lose my accent. During high school, I spent hours at a time watching television (especially *Frasier, Home Improvement,* and reruns of *The Golden Girls*) and movies (from *Goodfellas* to *Anne of Green Gables*), pausing the VHS to try to copy how various characters enunciated their words. At the local library, I read magazines, books, and newspapers—anything to learn how to write better. Kathy Dewar, my high school English teacher, introduced me to journalism. From the moment I wrote my first article for the student paper, I convinced myself that having my name in print—writing in English, interviewing Americans—validated my presence here.

The debates over "illegal aliens" intensified my anxieties. In 1994, only a year after my flight from the Philippines, Governor Pete Wilson was re-elected in part because of his support for Proposition 187, which prohibited undocumented immigrants from attending public school and accessing other services. (A federal court later found the law unconstitutional.) After my encounter at the DMV in 1997, I grew more aware of anti-immigrant sentiments and stereotypes: *they don't want to assimilate, they are a drain on society.* They're not talking about me, I would tell myself. I have something to contribute.

To do that, I had to work—and for that, I needed a Social Security number. Fortunately, my grandfather had already managed to get one for me. Lolo had always taken care of everyone in the family. He and my grandmother emigrated legally in 1984 from Zambales, a province in the Philippines of rice fields and bamboo houses, following Lolo's sister, who married a Filipino-American serving in the American military. She petitioned for her brother and his wife to join her. When they got here, Lolo petitioned for his two children—my mother and her younger brother—to follow them. But instead of mentioning that my mother was a married woman, he listed her as single. Legal residents can't petition for their married children. Besides, Lolo didn't care for my father. He didn't want him coming here too.

But soon Lolo grew nervous that the immigration authorities reviewing the petition would discover my mother was married, thus derailing not only her chances of coming here but those of my uncle as well. So he withdrew her petition. After my uncle came to America legally in 1991, Lolo tried to get my mother here through a tourist visa, but she wasn't able to obtain one. That's when she decided to send me. My mother told me later that she figured she would follow me soon. She never did.

The "uncle" who brought me here turned out to be a coyote, not a relative, my grandfather later explained. Lolo scraped together enough money—I eventually learned it was $4,500, a huge sum for him—to pay him to smuggle me here under a fake name and fake passport. (I never saw the passport again after the flight and have always assumed that the coyote kept it.) After I arrived in America, Lolo obtained a new fake Filipino passport, in my real name this time, adorned with a fake student visa, in addition to the fraudulent green card.

Using the fake passport, we went to the local Social Security Administration office and applied for a Social Security number and card. It was, I remember, a quick visit. When the card came in the mail, it had my full, real name, but it also clearly stated: "Valid for work only with INS authorization."

When I began looking for work, a short time after the DMV incident, my grandfather and I took the Social Security card to Kinko's, where he covered the "INS authorization" text with a sliver of white tape. We then made photocopies of the card. At a glance, at least, the copies would look like copies of a regular, unrestricted Social Security card.

Lolo always imagined I would work the kind of low-paying jobs that undocumented people often take. (Once I married an American, he said, I would get my real papers, and everything would be fine.) But even menial jobs require documents, so he and I hoped the doctored card would work for now. The more documents I had, he said, the better.

While in high school, I worked part time at Subway, then at the front desk of the local YMCA, then at a tennis club, until I landed an unpaid internship at *The Mountain View Voice*, my hometown newspaper. First I brought coffee and helped around the office; eventually I began covering city-hall meetings and other assignments for pay.

For more than a decade of getting part-time and full-time jobs, employers have rarely asked to check my original Social Security card. When they did, I showed the photocopied version, which they accepted. Over time, I also began checking the citizenship box on my federal I-9 employment eligibility forms. (Claiming full citizenship was actually easier than declaring permanent resident "green card" status, which would have required me to provide an alien registration number.)

This deceit never got easier. The more I did it, the more I felt like an impostor, the more guilt I carried—and the more I worried that I would get caught. But I kept doing it. I needed to live and survive on my own, and I decided this was the way.

Mountain View High School became my second home. I was elected to represent my school at school board meetings, which gave me the chance to meet and befriend Rich Fischer, the superintendent for our school district. I joined the speech and debate team, acted in school plays, and eventually became co-editor of *The Oracle*, the student newspaper. That drew the attention of my principal, Pat Hyland. "You're at school just as much as I am," she told me. Pat and Rich would soon become mentors, and over time, almost surrogate parents for me.

After a choir rehearsal during my junior year, Jill Denny, the choir director, told me she was considering a Japan trip for our singing group. I told her I couldn't afford it, but she said we'd figure out a way. I hesitated, and then decided to tell her the truth. "It's not really the money," I remember saying. "I don't have the right passport." When she assured me we'd get the proper documents, I finally told her. "I can't get the right passport," I said. "I'm not supposed to be here."

She understood. So the choir toured Hawaii instead, with me in tow. (Mrs. Denny and I spoke a couple of months ago, and she told me she hadn't wanted to leave any student behind.)

Later that school year, my history class watched a documentary on Harvey Milk, the openly gay San Francisco city official who was assassinated. This was 1999, just six months after Matthew Shepard's body was found tied to a fence in Wyoming. During the discussion, I raised my hand and said something like: "I'm sorry Harvey Milk got killed for being gay . . . I've been meaning to say this . . . I'm gay."

I hadn't planned on coming out that morning, though I had

known that I was gay for several years. With that announcement, I became the only openly gay student at school, and it caused turmoil with my grandparents. Lolo kicked me out of the house for a few weeks. Though we eventually reconciled, I had disappointed him on two fronts. First, as a Catholic, he considered homosexuality a sin and was embarrassed about having *"ang apo na bakla"* ("a grandson who is gay"). Even worse, I was making matters more difficult for myself, he said. I needed to marry an American woman in order to gain a green card.

Tough as it was, coming out about being gay seemed less daunting than coming out about my legal status. I kept my other secret mostly hidden.

While my classmates awaited their college acceptance letters, I hoped to get a full-time job at *The Mountain View Voice* after graduation. It's not that I didn't want to go to college, but I couldn't apply for state and federal financial aid. Without that, my family couldn't afford to send me.

But when I finally told Pat and Rich about my immigration "problem"—as we called it from then on—they helped me look for a solution. At first, they even wondered if one of them could adopt me and fix the situation that way, but a lawyer Rich consulted told him it wouldn't change my legal status because I was too old. Eventually they connected me to a new scholarship fund for high-potential students who were usually the first in their families to attend college. Most important, the fund was not concerned with immigration status. I was among the first recipients, with the scholarship covering tuition, lodging, books, and other expenses for my studies at San Francisco State University.

As a college freshman, I found a job working part time at *The San Francisco Chronicle,* where I sorted mail and wrote some freelance articles. My ambition was to get a reporting job, so I embarked on a series of internships. First I landed at *The Philadelphia Daily News,* in the summer of 2001, where I covered a drive-by shooting and the wedding of the 76ers star Allen Iverson. Using those articles I applied to *The Seattle Times* and got an internship for the following summer.

But then my lack of proper documents became a problem again.

The Times's recruiter, Pat Foote, asked all incoming interns to bring certain paperwork on their first day: a birth certificate, or a passport, or a driver's license plus an original Social Security card. I panicked, thinking my documents wouldn't pass muster. So before starting the job, I called Pat and told her about my legal status. After consulting with management, she called me back with the answer I feared: I couldn't do the internship.

This was devastating. What good was college if I couldn't then pursue the career I wanted? I decided then that if I was to succeed in a profession that is all about truth-telling, I couldn't tell the truth about myself.

After this episode, Jim Strand, the venture capitalist who sponsored my scholarship, offered to pay for an immigration lawyer. Rich and I went to meet her in San Francisco's financial district.

I was hopeful. This was in early 2002, shortly after Senators Orrin Hatch, the Utah Republican, and Dick Durbin, the Illinois Democrat, introduced the Dream Act—Development, Relief and Education for Alien Minors. It seemed like the legislative version of what I'd told myself: If I work hard and contribute, things will work out.

But the meeting left me crushed. My only solution, the lawyer said, was to go back to the Philippines and accept a ten year ban before I could apply to return legally.

If Rich was discouraged, he hid it well. "Put this problem on a shelf," he told me. "Compartmentalize it. Keep going."

And I did. For the summer of 2003, I applied for internships across the country. Several newspapers, including *The Wall Street Journal, The Boston Globe,* and *The Chicago Tribune,* expressed interest. But when *The Washington Post* offered me a spot, I knew where I would go. And this time, I had no intention of acknowledging my "problem."

The Post internship posed a tricky obstacle: It required a driver's license. (After my close call at the California DMV, I'd never gotten one.) So I spent an afternoon at the Mountain View Public Library, studying various states' requirements. Oregon was among the most welcoming—and it was just a few hours' drive north.

Again, my support network came through. A friend's father lived in Portland, and he allowed me to use his address as proof of residency. Pat, Rich, and Rich's longtime assistant, Mary Moore, sent letters to me at that address. Rich taught me how to do three-point turns in a parking lot, and a friend accompanied me to Portland.

The license meant everything to me—it would let me drive, fly, and work. But my grandparents worried about the Portland trip and the Washington internship. While Lola offered daily prayers so that I would not get caught, Lolo told me that I was dreaming too big, risking too much.

I was determined to pursue my ambitions. I was twenty-two, I told them, responsible for my own actions. But this was different from Lolo's driving a confused teenager to Kinko's. I knew what I was doing now, and I knew it wasn't right. But what was I supposed to do?

I was paying state and federal taxes, but I was using an invalid Social Security card and writing false information on my employment forms. But that seemed better than depending on my grandparents or on Pat, Rich, and Jim—or returning to a country I barely remembered. I convinced myself all would be okay if I lived up to the qualities of a "citizen": hard work, self-reliance, love of my country.

At the DMV in Portland, I arrived with my photocopied Social Security card, my college ID, a pay stub from *The San Francisco Chronicle*, and my proof of state residence—the letters to the Portland address that my support network had sent. It worked. My license, issued in 2003, was set to expire eight years later, on my thirtieth birthday, on February 3, 2011. I had eight years to succeed professionally, and to hope that some sort of immigration reform would pass in the meantime and allow me to stay.

It seemed like all the time in the world.

My summer in Washington was exhilarating. I was intimidated to be in a major newsroom but was assigned a mentor—Peter Perl, a veteran magazine writer—to help me navigate it. A few weeks into the internship, he printed out one of my articles, about a guy who recovered a long-lost wallet, circled the first two paragraphs, and left it on my desk. "Great eye for details—awesome!" he wrote. Though I didn't know it then, Peter would become one more member of my network.

At the end of the summer, I returned to *The San Francisco Chronicle*. My plan was to finish school—I was now a senior—while I worked for *The Chronicle* as a reporter for the city desk. But when *The Post* beckoned again, offering me a full-time, two-year paid internship that I could start when I graduated in June 2004, it was too tempting to pass up. I moved back to Washington.

About four months into my job as a reporter for *The Post*, I began feeling increasingly paranoid, as if I had "illegal immigrant" tattooed on my forehead—and in Washington, of all places, where the debates over immigration seemed never-ending. I was so eager to prove myself that I feared I was annoying some colleagues and editors—and worried that any one of these professional journalists could discover my secret. The anxiety was nearly paralyzing. I decided I had to tell one of the higher-ups about my situation. I turned to Peter.

By this time, Peter, who still works at *The Post*, had become part of management as the paper's director of newsroom training and professional development. One afternoon in late October, we walked a couple of blocks to Lafayette Square, across from the White House. Over some twenty minutes, sitting on a bench, I told him everything: the Social Security card, the driver's license, Pat and Rich, my family.

Peter was shocked. "I understand you one hundred times better now," he said. He told me that I had done the right thing by telling him, and that it was now our shared problem. He said he didn't want to do anything about it just yet. I had just been hired, he said, and I needed to prove myself. "When you've done enough," he said, "we'll tell Don and Len together." (Don Graham is the chairman of the Washington Post Company; Leonard Downie Jr. was then the paper's executive editor.) A month later, I spent my first Thanksgiving in Washington with Peter and his family.

In the five years that followed, I did my best to "do enough." I was promoted to staff writer, reported on video-game culture, wrote a series on Washington's HIV/AIDS epidemic, and covered the role of technology and social media in the 2008 presidential race. I visited the White House, where I interviewed senior aides and covered a state dinner—and gave the Secret Service the Social Security number I obtained with false documents.

I did my best to steer clear of reporting on immigration policy but couldn't always avoid it. On two occasions, I wrote about Hillary Clinton's position on driver's licenses for undocumented immigrants. I also wrote an article about Senator Mel Martinez of Florida, then the chairman of the Republican National Committee, who was defending his party's stance toward Latinos after only one Republican presidential candidate—John McCain, the co-author of a failed immigration bill—agreed to participate in a debate sponsored by Univision, the Spanish-language network.

It was an odd sort of dance: I was trying to stand out in a highly competitive newsroom, yet I was terrified that if I stood out too much, I'd invite unwanted scrutiny. I tried to compartmentalize my fears, distract myself by reporting on the lives of other people, but there was no escaping the central conflict in my life. Maintaining a deception for so long distorts your sense of self. You start wondering who you've become, and why.

In April 2008, I was part of a *Post* team that won a Pulitzer Prize for the paper's coverage of the Virginia Tech shootings a year earlier. Lolo died a year earlier, so it was Lola who called me the day of the announcement. The first thing she said was, *"Anong mangyayari kung malaman ng mga tao?"*

What will happen if people find out?

I couldn't say anything. After we got off the phone, I rushed to the bathroom on the fourth floor of the newsroom, sat down on the toilet, and cried.

In the summer of 2009, without ever having had that follow-up talk with top *Post* management, I left the paper and moved to New York to join *The Huffington Post*. I met Arianna Huffington at a Washington Press Club Foundation dinner I was covering for *The Post* two years earlier, and she later recruited me to join her news site. I wanted to learn more about Web publishing, and I thought the new job would provide a useful education.

Still, I was apprehensive about the move: many companies were already using E-Verify, a program set up by the Department of Homeland Security that checks if prospective employees are eligible to work, and I didn't know if my new employer was among them. But I'd been able to get jobs in other newsrooms, I figured, so I filled out the paperwork as usual and succeeded in landing on the payroll.

While I worked at *The Huffington Post*, other opportunities emerged. My HIV/AIDS series became a documentary film called *The Other City*, which opened at the Tribeca Film Festival last year and was broadcast on Showtime. I began writing for magazines and landed a dream assignment: profiling Facebook's Mark Zuckerberg for *The New Yorker*.

The more I achieved, the more scared and depressed I became. I was proud of my work, but there was always a cloud hanging over it, over me. My old eight-year deadline—the expiration of my Oregon driver's license—was approaching.

After slightly less than a year, I decided to leave *The Huffington Post*. In part, this was because I wanted to promote the documentary and write a book about online culture—or so I told my friends. But the real reason was, after so many years of trying to be a part of the system, of focusing all my energy on my professional life, I learned that no amount of professional success would solve my problem or ease the sense of loss and displacement I felt. I lied to a friend about why I couldn't take a weekend trip to Mexico. Another time I concocted an excuse for why I couldn't go on an all-expenses-paid trip to Switzerland. I have been unwilling, for years, to be in a long-term relationship because I never wanted anyone to get too close and ask too many questions. All the while, Lola's question was stuck in my head: What will happen if people find out?

Early this year, just two weeks before my thirtieth birthday, I won a small reprieve: I obtained a driver's license in the state of Washington. The license is valid until 2016. This offered me five more years of acceptable identification—but also five more years of fear, of lying to people I respect and institutions that trusted me, of running away from who I am.

I'm done running. I'm exhausted. I don't want that life anymore.

So I've decided to come forward, own up to what I've done, and tell my story to the best of my recollection. I've reached out to former bosses and employers and apologized for misleading them—a mix of humiliation and liberation coming with each disclosure. All the people mentioned in this article gave me permission to use their names. I've also talked to family and friends about my situation and am working with legal counsel to review my options. I don't know what the consequences will be of telling my story.

I do know that I am grateful to my grandparents, my Lolo and Lola, for giving me the chance for a better life. I'm also grateful to my other family—the support network I found here in America—for encouraging me to pursue my dreams.

It's been almost eighteen years since I've seen my mother. Early on, I was mad at her for putting me in this position, and then mad at myself for being angry and ungrateful. By the time I got to college, we rarely spoke by phone. It became too painful; after a while it was easier to just send money to help support her and my two half-siblings. My sister, almost two years old when I left, is almost twenty now. I've never met my fourteen-year-old brother. I would love to see them.

Not long ago, I called my mother. I wanted to fill the gaps in my memory about that August morning so many years ago. We had never discussed it. Part of me wanted to shove the memory aside, but to write this article and face the facts of my life, I needed more details. Did I cry? Did she? Did we kiss goodbye?

My mother told me I was excited about meeting a stewardess, about getting on a plane. She also reminded me of the one piece of advice she gave me for blending in: If anyone asked why I was coming to America, I should say I was going to Disneyland.

JESS WALTER

■

Don't Eat Cat

FROM *Byliner*

1.

AT NIGHT I DEADBOLT DOORS and hard-bar windows, and it's not bad living in the city. I stay home a lot. Turn off outdoor lights, bring in garbage cans: simple, commonsense stuff. Obviously, I don't have pets. I leave my car unlocked so they won't break the windows looking for food and trinkets. Play music all night to drown out the yowling. But nights aren't bad. Daytime is when I get fed up with zombies.

I know. I shouldn't call them that.

I'm not one of those reactionaries who believe they should be locked up, or sterilized, or confined to Z towns. I think there are perfectly good jobs for people with hypo-endocrinal-thyro-encephalitis: day labor, night janitors. But hiring zombies for food service? I just think that's wrong.

That day, I'd had another doctor's appointment and had gotten the unhappy results from a battery of invasive tests. I was already late for a sim-skype in Jakarta when I popped into the Starbucks Financial near my office. I got to the front of the line and who should greet me behind the counter but some guy in his early twenties with all the symptoms: translucent skin, rotting teeth, skim-milk eyes — the whole deal. Full zombie. (I know: we shouldn't call them that.)

His voice was ice in a blender. "I help you."

"Grande. Soy. Cran. Latte," I said as clearly and patiently as possible.

He said back to me in that curdled grunt: "Gramma sing con verde?"

I stared at him. "Grande . . . Soy . . . Cran . . . Latte."

"Gramma say come hurry?" His dull eyes blinked, and he must've heard the impatience in my voice—"No!"—because he started humming the way they do when they get agitated. "Gran-maw!" he yelled, and the manager, standing at the drive-through banking/coffee window behind him, gave me a look like, *Dude* . . . and I looked back at the manager: *you're blaming me for this?* The other people in the Starbucks Financial all took a step back.

Look, I understand the economics. I work in multinational food/finance. I know there has been some difficulty in staffing service jobs in the States since the borders were closed. More than that, I get the *humanity* of hiring them. Hey, my ex-girlfriend started shooting Replexen *after* researchers made the connection between hypo-ETE and the popular club drug. Marci actually *chose* that life. So yes, I know how their brains work; I know abstraction and contextual language give them problems; I know they're prone to agitation; but I also know that as long as they're not drunk or riled up, zombies can be as peaceful as anyone. And yes, I know we're not supposed to call them zombies.

But come on. *Gramma sing con verde?* What does that even mean?

That day, the Starbucks Financial manager came over and put a hand on the zombie's shoulder. "You're doing fine, Brando," the manager said. He was in his fifties, in a headset, tie, and short sleeves, one of those sorry men who try to overcome a lack of education and breeding by working up from food service into retail finance. The manager smiled at me and then pointed to "latte" on Brando's touchscreen sim, and they debited the sixty bucks from my iVice while I walked over to the other line. And over at the drink counter, who should be making my actual coffee but another zombie, a girl who couldn't have been more than eighteen, standing there dead-gaze-steaming my soy milk.

Two zombies. At morning rush hour in a Starbucks Financial. In the multinat/finance district of downtown Seattle. Really?

The manager was watching the girl zombie steam my milk when Brando screwed up the next order, too, turning a simple double cappuccino into "Dapple *cat* beano," a hungry hitch on that word *cat*, and you could feel the other businesspeople in the Starbucks Financial

cial tense, and even the short-sleeved manager knew this could be trouble, no doubt thinking back to their training (apparently they put four or five of them in a room with an actual cat and repeatedly stress *"Don't eat cat,"* which has to be tough when every fiber of the zombie's being is telling him *Eat cat*), and in the meantime, poor Brando was humming, just about full tilt. At that point, of course, the manager should have called the Starbucks Financial security guards to come over from the banking side or called whatever priva-police firm had that contract, but instead he put a hand up to the dozen or so of us in the store and walked calmly over to the kid and said, "Brando, why don't you go into the break room and relax for a few minutes." But Brando's red-veined eyes were darting around the room and he started making those deeper guttural noises, and look, I was not without sympathy for the manager, or for Brando, or for the twitchy zombie girl running the steamer, who looked over at her fish-skinned counterpart, both of them now thinking *ca-a-a-at*, salivating as if someone had yelled "chocolate" in a kindergarten, the girl zombie humming too now, the soy milk for my latte climbing to two hundred degrees — "Miss," I said — and still my soy was hissing and burbling, half to China Syndrome, the boiling riling every-one up, the manager calmly saying, "Brando, Brando, Brando," and I suppose I was still freaked by the bad news from my doctor's appointment, because I admit it, I raised my voice: "Miss, you're *burning* it," and when she didn't even acknowledge me, just kept humming and watching Brando, I clapped my hands and yelled, "Stop it!" And that's when the manager shot me a look that said *You're not helping!* And hell, I knew I wasn't helping, but who doesn't get frustrated, I mean, I wouldn't want that manager's life, and I certainly wouldn't want to be some twenty-one-year-old with full-on hypo-ETE, but we all have our crosses to bear, right? I just wanted a stupid cup of coffee. And I'd have stormed out right then, but my iVice had already been debited, and I suppose there was something else, too, something personal — I'm willing to acknowledge that — I mean, how would *you* feel if your girlfriend got so depressed that she actually *chose* to start taking Replexen, knowing it could make her a slow-witted, oversexed night crawler, how would you feel if the woman you loved actually *chose* zombie life over the apparently unbearable pain of a normal life with you? So *fuck me, sue me, yes yes yes*, I was short-tempered! You bet your ass I was short-tempered, and I yelled at that poor pale girl, "Hey, zombie! You're scalding my fucking latte!"

I know.

We're not supposed to call them zombies.

What was I supposed to say? "Excuse me, *unfortunate sufferer of hypo-endocrinal-thyro-encephalitis,* please stop burning my latte"?

I suppose it was inevitable what happened next. As it unfolded, I felt awful. I still feel awful—but in my defense, I was the only customer who didn't turn and run right then, as Brando flashed his teeth and pit-bulled the manager, leaped right into the poor guy's chest, both of them tumbling to the ground. In fact, I actually tried to distract him, clapping my hands and yelling as he worked over the poor, screaming manager. And to be fair, Brando didn't get far. *He bit, but he didn't chew* is I guess how you'd say it. He really wasn't trying to eat the manager; he was just scared and agitated. Probably not a distinction the manager was making at that time, with Brando yowling, biting, and scratching, sinewy veins popping beneath translucent skin, the manager lying on his back, covering his face, weeping, *"Oh God,"* as Brando snarled and struck and the girl zombie yowled in sympathy, still standing there, steaming my soy milk, which was like magma now, gurgling over the side of the pitcher. And if I give myself credit for anything, it's that I thought quickly on my feet, grabbing the scalding pitcher out of her hand and throwing the boiling milk on Brando, who reared his head like a bridled horse, snarled, and spun on me. I turned and ran for the door, Brando now bounding over the counter and toward me like a hungry wolf, knocking over displays of coffee cups and food-finance brochures as he ran straight into the arms of two Starbucks Financial security guys who quickly Tasered him to the ground and, eventually, into submission.

I stood on the sidewalk with the gathered crowd as the security guys loaded the hog-tied, muzzled Brando into the back of a Halliburton priva-police car, the poor kid still making that awful yowling noise, which shivered up my neck.

"What happened?" a young man asked.

"Zombie attack," a woman said.

I muttered, "You're not supposed to call them that."

It was the first documented attack in months, and the sim-tweets went crazy, as they always do when the subject is hypo-ETE. The tweet was up for hours, twice as long as any election news; only the Florida evacuation tweet was up longer that week. Most of the noise came from Apocalyptics ranting about Revelations, law-and-order types calling for another crackdown on Replexen, and, on the other side, hypo-ETE activists calling for mercy, for understanding, and for more government funding for programs aimed at those kids *born into* Replexen addiction, family support groups accusing the "irate customer" of being an agitator (thankfully, I wasn't named). Starbucks Financial stock dropped a couple of points after that (I managed to short the whole coffee/finance sector for my Indonesian clients), and the company announced it would "revisit its hypo-ETE retraining program." But honestly, it just seemed like the whole thing would fade. The manager would get a good payout, I'd get a free latte, the zombies would get retrained ("Brando. Do not eat cat"), and the world would go on. Or so I thought.

2.

Everyone has an opinion about when it all went to hell: this war, that epidemic, the ten-billion-people threshold, the twelve-, this environmental disaster, the repeated economic collapses, suicide pacts, anti-procreation laws, nuclear accidents, terrorist dirty bombs, polar thaws, rolling famines, *blah blah blah*. It's getting to where you can't watch the sim-tweets without someone saying *this* is the end of the world, or *that*—genetic piracy, food factory contaminations, the Wasatch uprising, Saudi death squads, the Arizona border war. Animal extinctions. Ozone tumors. And, of course, the so-called zombie drug.

But here's what I've come to believe. That maybe it's no different now than it ever was. Maybe it's *always* the end of the world. Maybe you're alive for a while and then you realize you're going to die, and that's such an insane thing to comprehend, you look around for answers and the only answer is that the world *must die with* you.

Sure, the world seems crazy *now*. But wouldn't it seem just as crazy if you were alive when they sacrificed peasants, when people were born into slavery, when they killed firstborn sons, crucified priests, fed people to lions, burned them at the stake, when they intentionally gave people smallpox or syphilis, when they gassed them, tortured them, dropped atomic bombs on them, when entire races tried to wipe other races off the planet?

Yes, we've ruined the planet and melted the ice caps and depleted the ozone, and we're always finding new ways to kill one another. Yeah, we're getting cancer at an alarming rate, and suicides are at an all-time high, and sure, we've got people so depressed they take a drug that could turn them into pasty-skinned animals who go around all night dancing and having sex and eating stray cats and small dogs and squirrels and mice and very, *very rarely*—the statistics say you're more likely to be killed by lightning—a person.

But *this* is the Apocalypse? Fuck you! It's always the Apocalypse. The world hasn't gone to shit. The world *is* shit.

All I'd asked was that it be better managed.

But four days after the Starbucks Financial incident, Apocalyptics began protesting Starbucks Financial headquarters, and the company announced the complete suspension of its zombie retraining program, which got the hypo-ETE activists and support groups going again about the 60 percent zombie unemployment rate. Then, worst of all, some vigilantes came to Seattle from the country and killed a nineteen-year-old zombie girl with an antique hunting rifle, shot her outside a club and left her body outside a Starbucks Financial.

All because I'd wanted better service?

The dead zombie girl was all over the news-tweets. I couldn't stop staring at her photo. Her ashen-white skin glistened in the blue light. Of course, it wasn't Marci—it looked nothing like her—but I couldn't stop thinking about my old girlfriend. I sat that night in our apartment on Queen Anne Hill, staring at the results from my full-body scan, the doors and windows double-locked, music playing low, and I wondered if things might have been different.

3.

Marci had a cousin who went zombie a few years back, before it was called that. It was the usual thing: Stephanie came from a poor family, got low scores on her sixth-grade E-RADs — we're talking food-service low, manual-labor low. Imagine being a twelve-year-old girl and being told that all you can ever aspire to is greeter at a Walmart-Schwab. Stephanie had childhood diabetes, and since her parents' application for gene therapy had been rejected, her own chances of getting a childbirth license were nil. So she started snorting Replexen. This was right after kids in clubs discovered that grinding up the weight-loss/metabolism-boosting pill could give them an ungodly buzz, slow time, allow them to dance and screw all night; and although it was already connected to the symptoms of hypo-ETE — milky eyes, pale skin, increased hunger, slow-witted aggressiveness — it didn't stop them. For some, that only seemed to make the high better.

One day, Marci and I were watching sim-tweets of the Northeast Portland riots — during the debate over anti-harassment laws and the whole zombie rights campaign.

"Poor Stephanie," I said.

"I don't know," Marci said. "Maybe she knew what she was doing."

Afterwards, people at work would ask me, "Did you suspect?" Of course, after someone leaves, you find all sorts of clues, look back on conversations that suddenly have great significance, but honestly, that's the first thing I remember: Marci saying about her zombie cousin, *Maybe she knew what she was doing.*

Of course, I had known for some time that Marci wasn't happy. Our last couple of years had been tough on her, tough on both of us. Most of our friends had moved out of the city. Our apartment had lost most of its value. That fall, our procreation application had been red-flagged — Marci's gene scan uncovering some recessive issue. I told her I didn't care if we had a kid. But it became part of the class stuff between us: I was from money, Marci wasn't; I'd aced my E-RADs and Gen-Tests; she'd been borderline in both. None of that had mattered when we'd started seeing each other. And it still didn't for me. But when the procreation board said she couldn't have a kid? I guess it was too much for her.

But did I know Marci was using Replexen? I don't think so. It's hard to separate what you suspect from what you know later. Certainly, she seemed *off* that spring, disoriented, nervous, wearing more makeup, eating more yet somehow getting thinner. Then I got promoted at work, to the Asian desk, only days after Marci's job was eliminated. "We're fine," I kept telling her, and I meant financially. But it must have seemed insane to her, the way I just kept saying we were fine. That March there was a story on the sim-tweets about a couple in the Magnolia neighborhood that had chosen to go zombie. I turned away from the screen to Marci and I just . . . asked. *Would you ever?*

I think she'd been waiting for me to bring it up. "Yes," she said quietly.

"Yes what?" I asked.

Yes, she had used Replexen. A few times. Snorted it.

I asked, "Recently?" She slumped in her chair. "Yes," she said.

"How recently?"

"I'm using it now," she whispered.

We were in the living room. I stood. And for some reason, the question that popped into my mind was this one: "Where did you get it?"

She glanced up at me, and in that moment I suppose we were thinking the same thing: why, when Marci tells me she's taking the most dangerous club drug in the world, the first thing to pop into my mind would not be her health, but where she had gotten it.

A few months earlier, Marci and I had gone through an especially rocky time. Her company had just been bought up, and the inevitable squeeze had begun. Marci had wanted to leave Seattle, to move closer to her family, but my company was thriving, so I said no. She said I was imperious and blind to reality; I said she was defeatist. We split up for a few weeks before we realized we'd made a mistake and got back together. It was only after she came back that time that I began to suspect Marci had gone back to her previous boyfriend, Andrew. He was a club owner and a "nonbie," one of the lucky 15 percent who could use Replexen without any of the undesirable zombie side effects.

So I asked: "Did you get the drugs from Andrew?"

"No," she said, "I got them from a woman I used to work with."

"What woman?"

"You don't know her."

"Why would you do that, Marci?"

"Oh, Owen," she said, "this isn't about you. It's about me."

It was the cliché that got to me. ("Yeah, you're right, it's about you, Marci . . . *You're becoming a fucking zombie!*") I yanked her sleeve up and saw the red marks against her white skin, and Jesus, shooting it is twice as dangerous as snorting it. Once your skin starts to go, you've already done permanent damage. She shrank away from me, cried, apologized, promised to get treatment, and when we went to bed that night I honestly believed we could get through this, that we'd caught it in time. I spent the next day applying for loans from all the food-service/banks — Starbucks Financial, Walmart-Schwab, KFC/B-of-A. I would have debited my apartment, my car, my organs for her treatment, but I came home from work that night and she was gone. No sim, no note, no nothing.

I simmed our friends and her parents, her old coworkers, but no one had heard from Marci. I even went to see her old boyfriend, Andrew, at his club in what was still called the U District, even though the state university there had shut down years earlier. Andrew was bald and lean — a little taller than me, with a long neck and cavernous eyes, pockmarks on his sunken cheeks. Nonbies always have that feral look, as if they've just finished running a road race in their clothes, or they haven't slept in months. We had met once, in passing, but I would never have picked him out of a lineup, so many years had been put on his face. Andrew came from behind the bar and I could smell the nonbie on him — like a soup of sweat, smoke, and old bacon. He stared at my suit and tie, at my wool coat.

"Slumming, Owen?"

I looked around the seedy club but said nothing.

He crossed his arms. "What do you want?"

I explained that Marci had begun using Replexen and that she was missing. I watched his face to see if maybe he already knew what I was telling him. Andrew was wearing a black leather coat, too short on his arms. I saw one of his hands twitch. He stared at the door to his club. He let out a deep breath. "Was she snorting it?" he asked quietly.

"Needles," I said. His eyes closed, and I realized that he hadn't seen her after all. He asked about her skin. "Yes," I said, "milky."

"You didn't notice?" he asked. Then he looked down. "Sorry."

Even for nonbies, Replexen use shortens your lifespan. They are hard years spent on that shit. I followed Andrew's weary eyes as he looked around his own club . . . painted windows and scarred wood on the tables and floors. Did he wonder, *How did I get here?* This wasn't a full zombie club; it catered more to nonbies and first-timers; no, it wasn't hell, but it was the waiting room.

"I haven't seen her," Andrew said, and he turned and went back behind the bar. I could've just simmed him my number, but I wrote it on a piece of paper and slid it across the bar. He looked up. He was chewing on one of those pocked cheeks, and it looked as if he was trying to say something. I left before he could.

My guess was that Marci had disappeared into what was already starting to be called Z Town. And if that was the case, of course, I was too late. Seattle was one of the worst cities for derelict zombies—old Fremont had been turned over to the hardcore clubs, brothels, and shooting galleries, to bars that supposedly released rodents during happy hour—places that made Andrew's shitty club seem like a Four Seasons.

For two years after that, I waited for Marci to come back. But it wasn't until my last doctor's appointment and the bad news I got—it wasn't until after Brando snapped and the death of that poor zombie girl—that I finally felt compelled to go to Z Town and look for her, for the only woman I have ever loved.

4.

Wendy Gasson was the last of my neighbors to have a pet: Fidel. He was an indoor cat, and she was careful about making sure he didn't get out, but one day, as Fidel sat there by the window watching birds, Wendy came in with the groceries and the cat bolted out of the apartment, down the steps, through the door, and into the street.

After the initial sim-tweets about hypo-ETE, a new sector of the economy had appeared: private eyes who went into Z towns and looked for missing kids and spouses and took them to quack deprogrammers, or surgeons, a whole industry of people who promised—lied, really—that they could reverse the effects of long-term Replexen abuse. The sleaziest of these PIs would even take cat cases, usually for elderly people who just couldn't come to terms with the fact that Fluffy was *seriously* not coming back. Some of the private eyes just went to a pet store and got a tabby to match the pictures ("No, this is Fluffy; I'm sure of it"). Wendy told me she'd tried to hire one of these guys off the Craig-sim to find Fidel, but the guy only went after people. "Lady," he said, "your cat's gone."

I got the detective's name from Wendy, but I didn't contact him right away. I tried everything else I could think of first: simming Marci's friends and family, taking out Craig-sim ads. I even went back to Andrew's club in the U District, but it was closed; a Dumpster Divas secondhand food store was now in its place. Nobody knew anything. I had no choice.

So I simmed the detective and made plans to meet him outside my doctor's office. I stepped out into the cool air, chest still burning from the radiation, when a tall, gray guy in a long suede jacket stepped forward. "I'm Mick."

"Owen."

Mick was in his fifties, with a high forehead and severe blue eyes. I hadn't explained much in my tweet, but he didn't seem to want details. I followed him to an antique red hybrid and we climbed in. I asked where he found gas for this old car, and he just smiled at me, like it was proof of his investigative powers.

It was a flat rate, he explained as we drove, five thousand up front.

I pulled out my iVice to debit him the five grand, but he shook his head. "Cash," he said.

So we went to the nearest KFC/B-of-A, where I was preapproved for the highest food debits. I lied on the application and said it was for dinner at a nice restaurant. Mick counted the five grand, folded the bills, tucked them in his waistband, and started driving. He pulled a small bottle of homemade hooch from beneath his car seat and handed it to me. I took a drink. Vodka.

I pulled out my iVice to show him the pictures of Marci, to tell him about her, but he held up his hand. "Save it till we get there." We drove quietly along Westlake.

"Get where?" I asked.

He chuckled at something. "Hey, what'd one zombie say to another?"

I stared at him. "What did you say?"

"What . . . did one zombie say to the other?"

"Is . . . that a joke?"

"*Dystopia?* What dystopia? Dis da only 'topia dere is."

I stared at him.

"You *do* know what a dystopia is, right?"

I said I did.

It was dusk as we approached the Fremont Bridge. Even before Fremont became Z Town, the construction of the Aurora Tunnel had cut down on traffic crossing into Fremont. Now it was six o'clock and there were maybe a dozen cars on the road. The bridge's cross braces were covered with holo-boards warning about the dangers of Replexen abuse and reminding people it was illegal to transport "cats and other pets" into Fremont, and finally there was the big black-and-white sign: "WARNING: Entering Hypo-ETE Concentration District."

Mick held out the bottle again. "Couple looking for an affordable condo in Seattle calls a real estate agent," he said. "Agent says, 'I know a place, five rooms, city views. Bad news, it's in Zombie Town. Good news? It's very pet-friendly.' "

I took a drink of his vodka, my hands shaking. The streetlights in Fremont were tinted blue—it's calming for them—and this gave everything a strange underwater glow, like an aquarium. There were few people on the streets, zombie or otherwise, the buildings nondescript, simple brick storefronts. We turned and started back toward the water. We passed Gas Works Park, and I imagined I saw figures moving in the shadows of the hulking works, flashing matches, bits of skin.

"How many zombies does it take to screw in a lightbulb?" Mick asked.

I closed my eyes. "Please," I whispered.

"*UUUUNNNNGGG!*" he said.

We turned again, and again, and back again, down a street with no lights, and I had the sense Mick was driving serpentine to make me disoriented. Finally, we pulled up in front of a dark four-story building.

"This is it," Mick said.

I looked up at the building.

"You got those pictures of her?" he asked.

I held up my iVice.

Mick nodded and got out of the car. I followed him. We stood in front of the building. I could hear yowling in the distance. I shivered as I stared at the dark building in front of us. "You haven't asked me a single question about Marci," I said. "What makes you think she'll even be here?"

Mick shrugged. "What's the worst part about having sex with a zombie?"

I put my hands up. "Please. No more jokes."

"Burying your cat afterward."

We climbed the stairs and pushed open a heavy door. We came into a dimly lit foyer, closed heavy doors on either end. A wall-mounted eye cam pointed at us. Mick held up a pair of thousand-dollar bills. He crinkled them. Then he opened his coat for the camera, I guess to show that he had no weapons. Then he elbowed me. I did the same, opened my coat.

After a moment, an electronic lock clicked and one of the doors opened and a muscular young zombie kid in baggy shorts, a sweatshirt, sunglasses, and flip-flops came through. At first I thought it was Brando, but of course it wasn't.

"Follow me," the zombie kid rasped.

I looked at Mick. "Aren't you coming?"

"What's the difference between a zombie and a bagel?" Mick asked. I just stared at him. *"UUUUNNNNGGG!"* he said again.

The zombie kid grunted a kind of laugh. "Good one, Mick."

Mick shrugged. "It kinda works with anything. *UUNNGG!*" Then he turned and went back outside. I watched him go, wondering whether I should turn and follow him out. Instead I hurried after the zombie kid. It was cold in the long hallway, clammy. Closed doors lined the walls; strange sounds came from the rooms. At the end of the hall, we came to a set of doors that opened onto a huge ballroom, a lounge of some kind—heavy timbers and ornate molding, like an old social club, an Elks Lodge maybe, smoky, filled with the movements of people on overstuffed leather couches and chairs, and as my eyes focused I could see a bar at the front, and a couple of zombies serving drinks. Everywhere else, white-skinned women in scanty clothing lounged around, talking to men like me.

It was a brothel.

"This is a mistake," I said to the kid.

The zombie kid turned, and at first I thought he was staring at me, but he was looking at someone over my shoulder. "Dina," said the zombie kid.

"You have pictures?" a woman asked from behind me.

I turned. The woman, Dina, was in her thirties, with shimmery black hair and pale skin, her eyes that cloudy blue but somehow not entirely gone zombie yet, or just controlled in some way. Like the kid who had led me back here. In fact, there seemed to be a whole range here—not just zombies and nonbies but people who seemed to function under the effects of the drug.

"You have pictures of your wife?" Dina said again, her voice just betraying the slightest hint of hypo-ETE gravel.

"My girlfriend," I said.

She nodded and smiled warmly at me.

I pulled out my iVice and fumbled with it. "I don't know if she's . . . I mean . . . you don't think Marci is . . ." I glanced at the zombie prostitutes all around us. One of them took a man by the hand and led him away.

Dina, the zombie madam, reached out and steadied my hands. "It's okay. Relax."

Finally, I found a holo of Marci and me in our apartment—it was when she had short hair, but it was a great picture: her bemused chestnut eyes, long lashes, high cheekbones. The 3-D holo appeared blurry rising from my iVice, but then I realized it was my eyes. I wiped the tears. Dina smiled. "She's so pretty."

I nodded and pulled the image back into my iVice.

"How long ago?"

"Two years. She left . . . two years ago."

Dina nodded again. She took my hand. I looked down at our hands, her white skin against my sun-scarred hand. She led me across the darkened room. I felt the breath go out of me. I was terrified I might see Marci here—and terrified I might not.

We arrived at one of the couches, in the corner of the lounge, where a short-haired zombie girl was sitting, staring off blankly. On the table in front of her was a hypodermic syringe with a needle, and a bag of powder. "Is that—" I pointed at the drugs on the table.

Dina said, "It makes some men feel better to know what it's like."

"Oh, no," I said, "I don't want that." Then I looked closely at the girl on the couch, her brown hair and eyes, her high cheekbones. I reached out, tilted her chin up. "You know that's not Marci," I said.

"Of course it is."

"No, it's not even close. This girl's ten years younger than Marci . . . at least three inches shorter."

"Marci," Dina said, and the zombie on the couch looked up at me.

"See. It's her."

The zombie girl looked back down again.

"Joe," I said, and the girl on the couch looked up again.

Dina looked upset with me. She turned to face me, cocked her head, and took me in with those clear, translucent eyes. There was a hum to her, a vibration—like a dropped guitar. "What is it you want?"

"I told you. I want to find my girlfriend."

She smiled patiently. She reached out and took my hand again in hers. "No. What do you *want*?"

"What?" My throat felt raw from the radiation. "I just want to talk to her."

"About what?"

"I'm sick," I said, and at that moment, the burning in my chest was overwhelming. "Cancer. I just found out a few weeks ago. Ozone sickness—third stage. My application for gene therapy was turned down, so they don't know how much time . . . I wanted to see Marci and . . ." I couldn't continue.

Dina stroked my hand with her slick white hand. "Apologize," she said.

"What?" I felt the air go out of me.

"You wanted to apologize? It's been two years, and this is the first time you've come here," the black-haired woman said. And as she said it, I knew it was true, and I wasn't sure anymore that the burning in my chest was coming from the radiation.

"You didn't even look for her," Dina continued, her voice entirely without judgment. "In fact, when she left, you were sort of . . . relieved. Weren't you? Relieved that she left before it got bad."

I tried to say no, but I couldn't speak.

"You would never have said it out loud, but you knew where it was going and you didn't know if you could do it. Take care of someone so . . . sick."

The room swirled as the pale woman spoke.

"Your anger was useful. You told yourself that she *wanted* this; that she *chose* this; that she *chose* to throw her life away."

I nodded weakly.

"But now you know . . . don't you?"

I could barely see her through my teary eyes.

"Now . . . you know what we know." Her voice went even lower. "That nobody *chooses*. That we're all sick. We're all here."

"I . . . " I looked at the ground. "I just wanted to tell her . . ."

"Tell her what?" Dina asked patiently.

I wept into my hands.

"Tell her what?" Dina whispered as she rubbed my shoulder. Finally she turned to the other girl, sitting on the couch. "Marci?"

The zombie girl stood and grabbed the drugs off the table. "Tell her what?" Dina whispered.

"I'm here," I managed to say to the short-haired girl.

Dina nodded and smiled at me. Then she gently took my hand and pressed it into the other girl's pale hand. And Marci led me away.

WESLEY YANG

■

Paper Tigers

FROM *New York*

SOMETIMES I'LL GLIMPSE MY REFLECTION in a window and feel astonished by what I see. Jet-black hair. Slanted eyes. A pancake-flat surface of yellow-and-green-toned skin. An expression that is nearly reptilian in its impassivity. I've contrived to think of this face as the equal in beauty to any other. But what I feel in these moments is its strangeness to me. It's my face. I can't disclaim it. But what does it have to do with me?

Millions of Americans must feel estranged from their own faces. But every self-estranged individual is estranged in his own way. I, for instance, am the child of Korean immigrants, but I do not speak my parents' native tongue. I have never called my elders by the proper honorific, "big brother" or "big sister." I have never dated a Korean woman. I don't have a Korean friend. Though I am an immigrant, I have never wanted to strive like one.

You could say that I am, in the gently derisive parlance of Asian-Americans, a banana or a Twinkie (yellow on the outside, white on the inside). But while I don't believe our roots necessarily define us, I do believe there are racially inflected assumptions wired into our neural circuitry that we use to sort through the sea of faces we confront. And although I am in most respects devoid of Asian characteristics, I do have an Asian face.

Here is what I sometimes suspect my face signifies to other Americans: an invisible person, barely distinguishable from a mass of faces that resemble it. A conspicuous person standing apart from the crowd and yet devoid of any individuality. An icon of so much that the culture pretends to honor but that it in fact patronizes and exploits. Not just people "who are good at math" and play the violin, but a mass of stifled, repressed, abused, conformist quasi-robots who simply do not matter, socially or culturally.

I've always been of two minds about this sequence of stereotypes. On the one hand, it offends me greatly that anyone would think to apply them to me, or to anyone else, simply on the basis of facial characteristics. On the other hand, it also seems to me that there are a lot of Asian people to whom they apply.

Let me summarize my feelings toward Asian values: Fuck filial piety. Fuck grade-grubbing. Fuck Ivy League mania. Fuck deference to authority. Fuck humility and hard work. Fuck harmonious relations. Fuck sacrificing for the future. Fuck earnest, striving middle-class servility.

I understand the reasons Asian parents have raised a generation of children this way. Doctor, lawyer, accountant, engineer: These are good jobs open to whoever works hard enough. What could be wrong with that pursuit? Asians graduate from college at a rate higher than any other ethnic group in America, including whites. They earn a higher median family income than any other ethnic group in America, including whites. This is a stage in a triumphal narrative, and it is a narrative that is much shorter than many remember. Two-thirds of the roughly 14 million Asian-Americans are foreign-born. There were fewer than 39,000 people of Korean descent living in America in 1970, when my elder brother was born. There are around 1 million today.

Asian-American success is typically taken to ratify the American Dream and to prove that minorities can make it in this country without handouts. Still, an undercurrent of racial panic always accompanies the consideration of Asians, and all the more so as China becomes the destination for our industrial base and the banker controlling our burgeoning debt. But if the armies of Chinese factory workers who make our fast fashion and iPads terrify us, and if the collective mass of high-achieving Asian-American students arouse an anxiety about the laxity of American parenting, what of the Asian-American who obeyed everything his parents told him? Does this person really scare anyone?

Earlier this year, the publication of Amy Chua's *Battle Hymn of the Tiger Mother* incited a collective airing out of many varieties of race-based hysteria. But absent from the millions of words written in response to the book was any serious consideration of whether Asian-Americans were in fact taking over this country. If it is true that they are collectively dominating in elite high schools and universities, is it also true that Asian-Americans are dominating in the real world? My strong suspicion was that this was not so, and that the reasons would not be hard to find. If we are a collective juggernaut that inspires such awe and fear, why does it seem that so many Asians are so readily perceived to be, as I myself have felt most of my life, the products of a timid culture, easily pushed around by more assertive people, and thus basically invisible?

A few months ago, I received an email from a young man named Jefferson Mao, who after attending Stuyvesant High School had recently graduated from the University of Chicago. He wanted my advice about "being an Asian writer." This is how he described himself: "I got good grades and I love literature and I want to be a writer and an intellectual; at the same time, I'm the first person in my family to go to college, my parents don't speak English very well, and we don't own the apartment in Flushing that we live in. I mean, I'm proud of my parents and my neighborhood and what I perceive to be my artistic potential or whatever, but sometimes I feel like I'm jumping the gun a generation or two too early."

One bright, cold Sunday afternoon, I ride the 7 train to its last stop in Flushing, where the storefront signs are all written in Chinese and the sidewalks are a slow-moving river of impassive faces. Mao is waiting for me at the entrance of the Main Street subway station, and together we walk to a nearby Vietnamese restaurant.

Mao has a round face, with eyes behind rectangular wire-frame glasses. Since graduating, he has been living with his parents, who emigrated from China when Mao was eight years old. His mother is a manicurist; his father is a physical therapist's aide. Lately, Mao has been making the familiar hour-and-a-half ride from Flushing to downtown Manhattan to tutor a white Stuyvesant freshman who lives in Tribeca. And what he feels, sometimes, in the presence of that amiable young man is a pang of regret. Now he understands better what he ought to have done back when he was a Stuyvesant freshman: "Worked half as hard and been twenty times more successful."

Entrance to Stuyvesant, one of the most competitive public high schools in the country, is determined solely by performance on a test: The top 3.7 percent of all New York City students who take the Specialized High Schools Admissions Test hoping to go to Stuyvesant are accepted. There are no set-asides for the underprivileged or, conversely, for alumni or other privileged groups. There is no formula to encourage "diversity" or any nebulous concept of "well-roundedness" or "character." Here we have something like pure meritocracy. This is what it looks like: Asian-Americans, who make up 12.6 percent of New York City, make up 72 percent of the high school.

This year, 569 Asian-Americans scored high enough to earn a slot at Stuyvesant, along with 179 whites, 13 Hispanics, and 12 blacks. Such dramatic overrepresentation, and what it may be read to imply about the intelligence of different groups of New Yorkers, has a way of making people uneasy. But intrinsic intelligence, of course, is precisely what Asians don't believe in. They believe—and have proved—that the constant practice of test-taking will improve the scores of whoever commits to it. All throughout Flushing, as well as in Bayside, one can find "cram schools," or storefront academies, that drill students in test preparation after school, on weekends, and during summer break. "Learning math is not about learning math," an instructor at one called Ivy Prep was quoted in *The New York Times* as saying. "It's about weightlifting. You are pumping the iron of math." Mao puts it more specifically: "You learn quite simply to nail any standardized test you take."

And so there is an additional concern accompanying the rise of the Tiger Children, one focused more on the narrowness of the educational experience a non-Asian child might receive in the company of fanatically preprofessional Asian students. Jenny Tsai, a student who was elected president of her class at the equally competitive New York public school Hunter College High School, remembers frequently hearing that "the school was becoming too Asian, that they would be the downfall of our school." A couple of years ago, she revisited this issue in her senior thesis at Harvard, where she interviewed graduates of elite public schools and found that the white students regarded the Asian students with wariness. (She quotes a music teacher at Stuyvesant describing the dominance of Asians: "They were mediocre kids, but they got in because they were coached.") In 2005, *The Wall Street Journal* reported on "white flight" from a high school in Cupertino, California, that began soon after the children of Asian software engineers had made the place so brutally competitive that a B average could place you in the bottom third of the class.

Colleges have a way of correcting for this imbalance: The Princeton sociologist Thomas Espenshade has calculated that an Asian applicant must, in practice, score 140 points higher on the SAT than a comparable white applicant to have the same chance of admission. This is obviously unfair to the many qualified Asian individuals who are punished for the success of others with similar faces. Upper-middle-class white kids, after all, have their own elite private schools, and their own private tutors, far more expensive than the cram schools, to help them game the education system.

You could frame it, as some aggrieved Asian-Americans do, as a simple issue of equality and press for race-blind quantitative admissions standards. In 2006, a decade after California passed a voter initiative outlawing any racial engineering at the public universities, Asians composed 46 percent of UC-Berkeley's entering class; one could imagine a similar demographic reshuffling in the Ivy League, where Asian-Americans currently make up about 17 percent of undergraduates. But the Ivies, as we all know, have their own private institutional interests at stake in their admissions choices, including some that are arguably defensible. Who can seriously claim that a Harvard University that was 72 percent Asian would deliver the same grooming for elite status its students had gone there to receive?

Somewhere near the middle of his time at Stuyvesant, a vague sense of discontent started to emerge within Mao. He had always felt himself a part of a mob of "nameless, faceless Asian kids," who were "like a part of the décor of the place." He had been content to keep his head down and work toward the goal shared by everyone at Stuyvesant: Harvard. But around the beginning of his senior year, he began to wonder whether this march toward academic success was the only, or best, path.

"You can't help but feel like there must be another way," he explains over a bowl of phô. "It's like, we're being pitted against each other while there are kids out there in the Midwest who can do way less work and be in a garage band or something—and if they're decently intelligent and work decently hard in school . . ."

Mao began to study the racially inflected social hierarchies at Stuyvesant, where, in a survey undertaken by the student newspaper this year, slightly more than half of the respondents reported that their friends came from within their own ethnic group. His attention focused on the mostly white (and Manhattan-dwelling) group whose members seemed able to manage the crushing workload while still remaining socially active. "The general gist of most high-school movies is that the pretty cheerleader gets with the big dumb jock, and the nerd is left to bide his time in loneliness. But at some point in the future," he says, "the nerd is going to rule the world, and the dumb jock is going to work in a car wash.

"At Stuy, it's completely different: If you looked at the pinnacle, the girls and the guys are not only good-looking and socially affable, they also get the best grades and star in the school plays and win election to student government. It all converges at the top. It's like training for high society. It was jarring for us Chinese kids. You got the sense that you had to study hard, but it wasn't enough."

Mao was becoming clued in to the fact that there was another hierarchy behind the official one that explained why others were getting what he never had—"a high-school sweetheart" figured prominently on this list—and that this mysterious hierarchy was going to determine what happened to him in life. "You realize there are things you really don't understand about courtship or just acting in a certain way. Things that somehow come naturally to people who go to school in the suburbs and have parents who are culturally assimilated." I pressed him for specifics, and he mentioned that he had visited his white girlfriend's parents' house the past Christmas, where the family had "sat around cooking together and playing Scrabble." This ordinary vision of suburban-American domesticity lingered with Mao: Here, at last, was the setting in which all that implicit knowledge "about social norms and propriety" had been transmitted. There was no cram school that taught these lessons.

Before having heard from Mao, I had considered myself at worst lightly singed by the last embers of Asian alienation. Indeed, given all the incredibly hip Asian artists and fashion designers and so forth you can find in New York, it seemed that this feeling was destined to die out altogether. And yet here it was in a New Yorker more than a dozen years my junior. While it may be true that sections of the Asian-American world are devoid of alienation, there are large swaths where it is as alive as it has ever been.

A few weeks after we meet, Mao puts me in touch with Daniel Chu, his close friend from Stuyvesant. Chu graduated from Williams College last year, having won a creative writing award for his poetry. He had spent a portion of the $18,000 prize on a trip to China, but now he is back living with his parents in Brooklyn Chinatown.

Chu remembers that during his first semester at Williams, his junior adviser would periodically take him aside. Was he feeling all right? Was something the matter? "I was acclimating myself to the place," he says. "I wasn't totally happy, but I wasn't depressed." But then his new white friends made similar remarks. "They would say, 'Dan, it's kind of hard, sometimes, to tell what you're thinking.'"

Chu has a pleasant face, but it would not be wrong to characterize his demeanor as reserved. He speaks in a quiet, unemphatic voice. He doesn't move his features much. He attributes these traits to the atmosphere in his household. "When you grow up in a Chinese home," he says, "you don't talk. You shut up and listen to what your parents tell you to do."

At Stuyvesant, he had hung out in an exclusively Asian world in which friends were determined by which subway lines you traveled. But when he arrived at Williams, Chu slowly became aware of something strange: The white people in the New England wilderness walked around smiling at each other. "When you're in a place like that, everyone is friendly."

He made a point to start smiling more. "It was something that I had to actively practice," he says. "Like, when you have a transaction at a business, you hand over the money—and then you smile." He says that he's made some progress but that there's still plenty of work that remains. "I'm trying to undo eighteen years of a Chinese upbringing. Four years at Williams helps, but only so much." He is conscious of how his father, an IT manager, is treated at work. "He's the best programmer at his office," he says, "but because he doesn't speak English well, he is always passed over."

Though Chu is not merely fluent in English but is officially the most distinguished poet of his class at Williams, he still worries that other aspects of his demeanor might attract the same kind of treatment his father received. "I'm really glad we're having this conversation," he says at one point—it is helpful to be remembering these lessons in self-presentation just as he prepares for job interviews.

"I guess what I would like is to become so good at something that my social deficiencies no longer matter," he tells me. Chu is a bright, diligent, impeccably credentialed young man born in the United States. He is optimistic about his ability to earn respect in the world. But he doubts he will ever feel the same comfort in his skin that he glimpsed in the people he met at Williams. That kind of comfort, he says—"I think it's generations away."

While he was still an electrical engineering student at Berkeley in the nineties, James Hong visited the IBM campus for a series of interviews. An older Asian researcher looked over Hong's résumé and asked him some standard questions. Then he got up without saying a word and closed the door to his office.

"Listen," he told Hong, "I'm going to be honest with you. My generation came to this country because we wanted better for you kids. We did the best we could, leaving our homes and going to graduate school not speaking much English. If you take this job, you are just going to hit the same ceiling we did. They just see me as an Asian Ph.D., never management potential. You are going to get a job offer, but don't take it. Your generation has to go farther than we did, otherwise we did everything for nothing."

The researcher was talking about what some refer to as the "Bamboo Ceiling"—an invisible barrier that maintains a pyramidal racial structure throughout corporate America, with lots of Asians at junior levels, quite a few in middle management, and virtually none in the higher reaches of leadership.

The failure of Asian-Americans to become leaders in the white-collar workplace does not qualify as one of the burning social issues of our time. But it is a part of the bitter undercurrent of Asian-American life that so many Asian graduates of elite universities find that meritocracy as they have understood it comes to an abrupt end after graduation. If between 15 and 20 percent of every Ivy League class is Asian, and if the Ivy Leagues are incubators for the country's leaders, it would stand to reason that Asians would make up some corresponding portion of the leadership class.

And yet the numbers tell a different story. According to a recent study, Asian-Americans represent roughly 5 percent of the population but only 0.3 percent of corporate officers, less than 1 percent of corporate board members, and around 2 percent of college presidents. There are nine Asian-American CEOs in the Fortune 500. In specific fields where Asian-Americans are heavily represented, there is a similar asymmetry. A third of all software engineers in Silicon Valley are Asian, and yet they make up only 6 percent of board members and about 10 percent of corporate officers of the Bay Area's twenty-five largest companies. At the National Institutes of Health, where 21.5 percent of tenure-track scientists are Asians, only 4.7 percent of the lab or branch directors are, according to a study conducted in 2005. One succinct evocation of the situation appeared in the comments section of a website called Yellowworld: "If you're East Asian, you need to attend a top-tier university to land a good high-paying gig. Even if you land that good high-paying gig, the white guy with the pedigree from a mediocre state university will somehow move ahead of you in the ranks simply because he's white."

Jennifer W. Allyn, a managing director for diversity at PricewaterhouseCoopers, works to ensure that "all of the groups feel welcomed and supported and able to thrive and to go as far as their talents will take them." I posed to her the following definition of parity in the corporate workforce: If the current crop of associates is 17 percent Asian, then in fourteen years, when they have all been up for partner review, 17 percent of those who are offered partner will be Asian. Allyn conceded that PricewaterhouseCoopers was not close to reaching that benchmark anytime soon—and that "nobody else is either."

Part of the insidious nature of the Bamboo Ceiling is that it does not seem to be caused by overt racism. A survey of Asian-Pacific-American employees of Fortune 500 companies found that 80 percent reported they were judged not as Asians but as individuals. But only 51 percent reported the existence of Asians in key positions, and only 55 percent agreed that their firms were fully capitalizing on the talents and perspectives of Asians.

More likely, the discrepancy in these numbers is a matter of unconscious bias. Nobody would affirm the proposition that tall men are intrinsically better leaders, for instance. And yet while only 15 percent of the male population is at least six feet tall, 58 percent of all corporate CEOs are. Similarly, nobody would say that Asian people are unfit to be leaders. But subjects in a recently published psychological experiment consistently rated hypothetical employees with Caucasian-sounding names higher in leadership potential than identical ones with Asian names.

Maybe it is simply the case that a traditionally Asian upbringing is the problem. As Allyn points out, in order to be a leader, you must have followers. Associates at PricewaterhouseCoopers are initially judged on how well they do the work they are assigned. "You have to be a doer," as she puts it. They are expected to distinguish themselves with their diligence, at which point they become "superdoers." But being a leader requires different skill sets. "The traits that got you to where you are won't necessarily take you to the next level," says the diversity consultant Jane Hyun, who wrote a book called *Breaking the Bamboo Ceiling*. To become a leader requires taking personal initiative and thinking about how an organization can work differently. It also requires networking, self-promotion, and self-assertion. It's racist to think that any given Asian individual is unlikely to be creative or risk-taking. It's simple cultural observation to say that a group whose education has historically focused on rote memorization and "pumping the iron of math" is, on aggregate, unlikely to yield many people inclined to challenge authority or break with inherited ways of doing things.

Sach Takayasu had been one of the fastest-rising members of her cohort in the marketing department at IBM in New York. But about seven years ago, she felt her progress begin to slow. "I had gotten to the point where I was over-delivering, working really long hours, and where doing more of the same wasn't getting me anywhere," she says. It was around this time that she attended a seminar being offered by an organization called Leadership Education for Asian Pacifics.

LEAP has parsed the complicated social dynamics responsible for the dearth of Asian-American leaders and has designed training programs that flatter Asian people even as it teaches them to change their behavior to suit white-American expectations. Asians who enter a LEAP program are constantly assured that they will be able to "keep your values, while acquiring new skills," along the way to becoming "culturally competent leaders."

In a presentation to 1,500 Asian-American employees of Microsoft, LEAP president and CEO J. D. Hokoyama laid out his grand synthesis of the Asian predicament in the workplace. "Sometimes people have perceptions about us and our communities which may or may not be true," Hokoyama told the audience. "But they put those perceptions onto us, and then they do something that can be very devastating: They make decisions about us not based on the truth but based on those perceptions." Hokoyama argued that it was not sufficient to rail at these unjust perceptions. In the end, Asian people themselves would have to assume responsibility for unmaking them. This was both a practical matter, he argued, and, in its own way, fair.

Aspiring Asian leaders had to become aware of "the relationship between values, behaviors, and perceptions." He offered the example of Asians who don't speak up at meetings. "So let's say I go to meetings with you and I notice you never say anything. And I ask myself, 'Hmm, I wonder why you're not saying anything. Maybe it's because you don't know what we're talking about. That would be a good reason for not saying anything. Or maybe it's because you're not even interested in the subject matter. Or maybe you think the conversation is beneath you.' So here I'm thinking, because you never say anything at meetings, that you're either dumb, you don't care, or you're arrogant. When maybe it's because you were taught when you were growing up that when the boss is talking, what are you supposed to be doing? Listening."

Takayasu took the week-long course in 2006. One of the first exercises she encountered involved the group instructor asking for a list of some qualities that they identify with Asians. The students responded: upholding family honor, filial piety, self-restraint. Then the instructor solicited a list of the qualities the members identify with leadership, and invited the students to notice how little overlap there is between the two lists.

At first, Takayasu didn't relate to the others in attendance, who were listing typical Asian values their parents had taught them. "They were all saying things like 'Study hard,' 'Become a doctor or lawyer,' blah, blah, blah. That's not how my parents were. They would worry if they saw me working too hard." Takayasu had spent her childhood shuttling between New York and Tokyo. Her father was an executive at Mitsubishi; her mother was a concert pianist. She was highly assimilated into American culture, fluent in English, poised, and confident. "But the more we got into it, as we moved away from the obvious things to the deeper, more fundamental values, I began to see that my upbringing had been very Asian after all. My parents would say, 'Don't create problems. Don't trouble other people.' How Asian is that? It helped to explain why I don't reach out to other people for help." It occurred to Takayasu that she was a little bit "heads down" after all. She was willing to take on difficult assignments without seeking credit for herself. She was reluctant to "toot her own horn."

Takayasu has put her new self-awareness to work at IBM, and she now exhibits a newfound ability for horn tooting. "The things I could write on my résumé as my team's accomplishments: They're really impressive," she says.

The law professor and writer Tim Wu grew up in Canada with a white mother and a Taiwanese father, which allows him an interesting perspective on how whites and Asians perceive each other. After graduating from law school, he took a series of clerkships, and he remembers the subtle ways in which hierarchies were developed among the other young lawyers. "There is this automatic assumption in any legal environment that Asians will have a particular talent for bitter labor," he says, and then goes on to define the word *coolie*, a Chinese term for "bitter labor." "There was this weird self-selection where the Asians would migrate toward the most brutal part of the labor."

By contrast, the white lawyers he encountered had a knack for portraying themselves as above all that. "White people have this instinct that is really important: to give off the impression that they're only going to do the really important work. You're a quarterback. It's a kind of arrogance that Asians are trained not to have. Someone told me not long after I moved to New York that in order to succeed, you have to understand which rules you're supposed to break. If you break the wrong rules, you're finished. And so the easiest thing to do is follow all the rules. But then you consign yourself to a lower status. The real trick is understanding what rules are not meant for you."

This idea of a kind of rule-governed rule-breaking—where the rule book was unwritten but passed along in an innate cultural sense—is perhaps the best explanation I have heard of how the Bamboo Ceiling functions in practice. LEAP appears to be very good at helping Asian workers who are already culturally competent become more self-aware of how their culture and appearance impose barriers to advancement. But I am not sure that a LEAP course is going to be enough to get Jefferson Mao or Daniel Chu the respect and success they crave. The issue is more fundamental, the social dynamics at work more deeply embedded, and the remedial work required may be at a more basic level of comportment.

What if you missed out on the lessons in masculinity taught in the gyms and locker rooms of America's high schools? What if life has failed to make you a socially dominant alpha male who runs the American boardroom and prevails in the American bedroom? What if no one ever taught you how to greet white people and make them comfortable? What if, despite these deficiencies, you no longer possess an immigrant's dutiful forbearance for a secondary position in the American narrative and want to be a player in the scrimmage of American appetite right now, in the present?

How do you undo eighteen years of a Chinese upbringing?

This is the implicit question that J. T. Tran has posed to a roomful of Yale undergraduates at a master's tea at Silliman College. His answer is typically Asian: practice. Tran is a pickup artist who goes by the handle Asian Playboy. He travels the globe running "boot camps," mostly for Asian male students, in the art of attraction. Today, he has been invited to Yale by the Asian-American Students Alliance.

"Creepy can be fixed," Tran explains to the standing-room-only crowd. "Many guys just don't realize how to project themselves." These are the people whom Tran spends his days with, a new batch in a new city every week: nice guys, intelligent guys, motivated guys, who never figured out how to be successful with women. Their mothers had kept them at home to study rather than let them date or socialize. Now Tran's company, ABCs of Attraction, offers a remedial education that consists of three four-hour seminars, followed by a supervised night out "in the field," in which J.T., his assistant Gareth Jones, and a tall blond wing-girl named Sarah force them to approach women. Tuition costs $1,450.

"One of the big things I see with Asian students is what I call the Asian poker face—the lack of range when it comes to facial expressions," Tran says. "How many times has this happened to you?" he asks the crowd. "You'll be out at a party with your white friends, and they will be like—'Dude, are you angry?'" Laughter fills the room. Part of it is psychological, he explains. He recalls one Korean-American student he was teaching. The student was a very dedicated schoolteacher who cared a lot about his students. But none of this was visible. "Sarah was trying to help him, and she was like, 'C'mon, smile, smile,' and he was like . . ." And here Tran mimes the unbearable tension of a face trying to contort itself into a simulacrum of mirth. "He was so completely unpracticed at smiling that he literally could not do it." Eventually, though, the student fought through it, "and when he finally got to smiling he was, like, really cool."

Tran continues to lay out a story of Asian-American male distress that must be relevant to the lives of at least some of those who have packed Master Krauss's living room. The story he tells is one of Asian-American disadvantage in the sexual marketplace, a disadvantage that he has devoted his life to overturning. Yes, it is about picking up women. Yes, it is about picking up white women. Yes, it is about attracting those women whose hair is the color of the midday sun and eyes are the color of the ocean, and it is about having sex with them. He is not going to apologize for the images of blond women plastered all over his website. This is what he prefers, what he stands for, and what he is selling: the courage to pursue anyone you want, and the skills to make the person you desire desire you back. White guys do what they want; he is going to do the same.

But it is about much more than this, too. It is about altering the perceptions of Asian men—perceptions that are rooted in the way they behave, which are in turn rooted in the way they were raised—through a course of behavior modification intended to teach them how to be the socially dominant figures that they are not perceived to be. It is a program of, as he puts it to me later, "social change through pickup."

Tran offers his own story as an exemplary Asian underdog. Short, not good-looking, socially inept, sexually null. "If I got a B, I would be whipped," he remembers of his childhood. After college, he worked as an aerospace engineer at Boeing and Raytheon, but internal politics disfavored him. Five years into his career, his entire white cohort had been promoted above him. "I knew I needed to learn about social dynamics, because just working hard wasn't cutting it."

His efforts at dating were likewise "a miserable failure." It was then that he turned to "the seduction community," a group of men on Internet message boards like alt.seduction.fast. It began as a "support group for losers" and later turned into a program of self-improvement. Was charisma something you could teach? Could confidence be reduced to a formula? Was it merely something that you either possessed or did not possess, as a function of the experiences you had been through in life, or did it emerge from specific forms of behavior? The members of the group turned their computer science and engineering brains to the question. They wrote long accounts of their dates and subjected them to collective scrutiny. They searched for patterns in the raw material and filtered these experiences through social-psychological research. They eventually built a model.

This past Valentine's Day, during a weekend boot camp in New York City sponsored by ABCs of Attraction, the model is being played out. Tran and Jones are teaching their students how an alpha male stands (shoulders thrown back, neck fully extended, legs planted slightly wider than the shoulders). "This is going to feel very strange to you if you're used to slouching, but this is actually right," Jones says. They explain how an alpha male walks (no shuffling; pick your feet up entirely off the ground; a slight sway in the shoulders). They identify the proper distance to stand from "targets" (a slightly bent arm's length). They explain the importance of "kino escalation." (You must touch her. You must not be afraid to do this.) They are teaching the importance of sub-communication: what you convey about yourself before a single word has been spoken. They explain the importance of intonation. They explain what intonation is. "Your voice moves up and down in pitch to convey a variety of different emotions."

All of this is taught through a series of exercises. "This is going to feel completely artificial," says Jones on the first day of training. "But I need you to do the biggest shit-eating grin you've ever made in your life." Sarah is standing in the corner with her back to the students — three Indian guys, including one in a turban, three Chinese guys, and one Cambodian. The students have to cross the room, walking as an alpha male walks, and then place their hands on her shoulder — firmly but gently — and turn her around. Big smile. Bigger than you've ever smiled before. Raise your glass in a toast. Make eye contact and hold it. Speak loudly and clearly. Take up space without apology. This is what an alpha male does.

Before each student crosses the floor of that bare white cubicle in midtown, Tran asks him a question. "What is good in life?" Tran shouts.

The student then replies, in the loudest, most emphatic voice he can muster: "To crush my enemies, see them driven before me, and to hear the lamentation of their women — in my bed!"

For the intonation exercise, students repeat the phrase "I do what I want" with a variety of different moods.

"Say it like you're happy!" Jones shouts. ("I do what I want.") Say it like you're sad! ("I do what I want." The intonation utterly unchanged.) Like you're sad! ("I . . . do what I want.") Say it like you've just won $5 million! ("I do what I want.")

Raj, a twenty-six-year-old Indian virgin, can barely get his voice to alter during intonation exercise. But on Sunday night, on the last evening of the boot camp, I watch him cold-approach a set of women at the Hotel Gansevoort and engage them in conversation for a half-hour. He does not manage to "number close" or "kiss close." But he had done something that not very many people can do.

Of the dozens of Asian-Americans I spoke with for this story, many were successful artists and scientists; or good-looking and socially integrated leaders; or tough, brassy, risk-taking, street-smart entrepreneurs. Of course, there are lots of such people around — do I even have to point that out? They are no more morally worthy than any other kind of Asian person. But they have figured out some useful things.

The lesson about the Bamboo Ceiling that James Hong learned from his interviewer at IBM stuck, and after working for a few years at Hewlett-Packard, he decided to strike off on his own. His first attempts at entrepreneurialism failed, but he finally struck pay dirt with a simple, not terribly refined idea that had a strong primal appeal: hotornot.com. Hong and his co-founder eventually sold the site for roughly $20 million.

Hong ran hotornot.com partly as a kind of incubator to seed in his employees the habits that had served him well. "We used to hire engineers from Berkeley—almost all Asian—who were on the cusp of being entrepreneurial but were instead headed toward jobs at big companies," he says. "We would train them in how to take risk, how to run things themselves. I remember encouraging one employee to read *The Game*"—the infamous pickup-artist textbook—"because I figured growing the cojones to take risk was applicable to being an entrepreneur."

If the Bamboo Ceiling is ever going to break, it's probably going to have less to do with any form of behavior assimilation than with the emergence of risk-takers whose success obviates the need for Asians to meet someone else's behavioral standard. People like Steve Chen, who was one of the creators of YouTube, or Kai and Charles Huang, who created Guitar Hero. Or Tony Hsieh, the founder of Zappos.com, the online shoe retailer that he sold to Amazon for about a billion dollars in 2009. Hsieh is a short Asian man who speaks tersely and is devoid of obvious charisma. One cannot imagine him being promoted in an American corporation. And yet he has proved that an awkward Asian guy can be a formidable CEO and the unlikeliest of management gurus.

Hsieh didn't have to conform to Western standards of comportment because he adopted early on the Western value of risk-taking. Growing up, he would play recordings of himself in the morning practicing the violin, in lieu of actually practicing. He credits the experience he had running a pizza business at Harvard as more important than anything he learned in class. He had an instinctive sense of what the real world would require of him, and he knew that nothing his parents were teaching him would get him there.

You don't, by the way, have to be a Silicon Valley hotshot to break through the Bamboo Ceiling. You can also be a chef like Eddie Huang, whose little restaurant on the Lower East Side, BauHaus, sells delicious pork buns. Huang grew up in Orlando with a hard-core Tiger Mom and a disciplinarian father. "As a kid, psychologically, my day was all about not getting my ass kicked," he says. He gravitated toward the black kids at school, who also knew something about corporal punishment. He was the smallest member of his football team, but his coach named him MVP in the seventh grade. "I was defensive tackle and right guard because I was just mean. I was nasty. I had this mentality where I was like, 'You're going to accept me or I'm going to fuck you up.'"

Huang had a rough twenties, bumping repeatedly against the Bamboo Ceiling. In college, editors at the *Orlando Sentinel* invited him to write about sports for the paper. But when he visited the offices, "the editor came in and goes, 'Oh, no.' And his exact words: 'You can't write with that face.'" Later, in film class at Columbia, he wrote a script about an Asian-American hot-dog vendor obsessed with his small penis. "The screenwriting teacher was like, 'I love this. You have a lot of Woody Allen in you. But do you think you could change it to Jewish characters?'" Still later, after graduating from Cardozo School of Law, he took a corporate job, where other associates would frequently say, "You have a lot of opinions for an Asian guy."

Finally, Huang decided to open a restaurant. Selling food was precisely the fate his parents wanted their son to avoid, and they didn't talk to him for months after he quit lawyering. But Huang understood instinctively that he couldn't make it work in the professional world his parents wanted him to join. "I've realized that food is one of the only places in America where we are the top dogs," he says. "Guys like David Chang or me—we can hang. There's a younger generation that grew up eating Chinese fast food. They respect our food. They may not respect anything else, but they respect our food."

Rather than strive to make himself acceptable to the world, Huang has chosen to buy his way back in, on his own terms. "What I've learned is that America is about money, and if you can make your culture commodifiable, then you're relevant," he says. "I don't believe anybody agrees with what I say or supports what I do because they truly want to love Asian people. They like my fucking pork buns, and I don't get it twisted."

Sometime during the hundreds of hours he spent among the mostly untouched English-language novels at the Flushing branch of the public library, Jefferson Mao discovered literature's special power of transcendence, a freedom of imagination that can send you beyond the world's hierarchies. He had written to me seeking permission to swerve off the traditional path of professional striving—to devote himself to becoming an artist—but he was unsure of what risks he was willing to take. My answer was highly ambivalent. I recognized in him something of my own youthful ambition. And I knew where that had taken me.

Unlike Mao, I was not a poor, first-generation immigrant. I finished school alienated from both Asian culture (which, in my hometown, was barely visible) and the manners and mores of my white peers. But like Mao, I wanted to be an individual. I had refused both cultures as an act of self-assertion. An education spent dutifully acquiring credentials through relentless drilling seemed to me an obscenity. So did adopting the manipulative cheeriness that seemed to secure the popularity of white Americans.

Instead, I set about contriving to live beyond both poles. I wanted what James Baldwin sought as a writer—"a power which outlasts kingdoms." Anything short of that seemed a humiliating compromise. I would become an aristocrat of the spirit, who prides himself on his incompetence in the middling tasks that are the world's business. Who does not seek after material gain. Who is his own law.

This, of course, was madness. A child of Asian immigrants born into the suburbs of New Jersey and educated at Rutgers cannot be a law unto himself. The only way to approximate this is to refuse employment, because you will not be bossed around by people beneath you, and shave your expenses to the bone, because you cannot afford more, and move into a decaying Victorian mansion in Jersey City, so that your sense of eccentric distinction can be preserved in the midst of poverty, and cut yourself free of every form of bourgeois discipline, because these are precisely the habits that will keep you chained to the mediocre fate you consider worse than death.

Throughout my twenties, I proudly turned away from one institution of American life after another (for instance, a steady job), though they had already long since turned away from me. Academe seemed another kind of death—but then again, I had a transcript marred by as many F's as A's. I had come from a culture that was the middle path incarnate. And yet for some people, there can be no middle path, only transcendence or descent into the abyss.

I was descending into the abyss.

All this was well deserved. No one had any reason to think I was anything or anyone. And yet I felt entitled to demand this recognition. I knew this was wrong and impermissible; therefore I had to double down on it. The world brings low such people. It brought me low. I haven't had health insurance in ten years. I didn't earn more than $12,000 for eight consecutive years. I went three years in the prime of my adulthood without touching a woman. I did not produce a masterpiece.

I recall one of the strangest conversations I had in the city. A woman came up to me at a party and said she had been moved by a piece of writing I had published. She confessed that prior to reading it, she had never wanted to talk to me, and had always been sure, on the basis of what she could see from across the room, that I was nobody worth talking to, that I was in fact someone to avoid.

But she had been wrong about this, she told me: It was now plain to her that I was a person with great reserves of feeling and insight. She did not ask my forgiveness for this brutal misjudgment. Instead, what she wanted to know was—why had I kept that person she had glimpsed in my essay so well hidden? She confessed something of her own hidden sorrow: She had never been beautiful and had decided, early on, that it therefore fell to her to "love the world twice as hard." Why hadn't I done that?

Here was a drunk white lady speaking what so many others over the years must have been insufficiently drunk to tell me. It was the key to many things that had, and had not, happened. I understood this encounter better after learning about LEAP, and visiting Asian Playboy's boot camp. If you are a woman who isn't beautiful, it is a social reality that you will have to work twice as hard to hold anyone's attention. You can either linger on the unfairness of this or you can get with the program. If you are an Asian person who holds himself proudly aloof, nobody will respect that, or find it intriguing, or wonder if that challenging façade hides someone worth getting to know. They will simply write you off as someone not worth the trouble of talking to.

Having glimpsed just how unacceptable the world judges my demeanor, could I too strive to make up for my shortcomings? Practice a shit-eating grin until it becomes natural? Love the world twice as hard?

I see the appeal of getting with the program. But this is not my choice. Striving to meet others' expectations may be a necessary cost of assimilation, but I am not going to do it.

Often I think my defiance is just delusional, self-glorifying bullshit that artists have always told themselves to compensate for their poverty and powerlessness. But sometimes I think it's the only thing that has preserved me intact, and that what has been preserved is not just haughty caprice but in fact the meaning of my life. So this is what I told Mao: In lieu of loving the world twice as hard, I care, in the end, about expressing my obdurate singularity at any cost. I love this hard and unyielding part of myself more than any other reward the world has to offer a newly brightened and ingratiating demeanor, and I will bear any costs associated with it.

The first step toward self-reform is to admit your deficiencies. Though my early adulthood has been a protracted education in them, I do not admit mine. I'm fine. It's the rest of you who have a problem. Fuck all y'all.

Amy Chua returned to Yale from a long, exhausting book tour in which one television interviewer had led off by noting that Internet commenters were calling her a monster. By that point, she had become practiced at the special kind of self-presentation required of a person under public siege. "I do not think that Chinese parents are superior," she declared at the annual gathering of the Asian-American Students Alliance. "I think there are many ways to be a good parent."

Much of her talk to the students, and indeed much of the conversation surrounding the book, was focused on her own parenting decisions. But just as interesting is how her parents parented her. Chua was plainly the product of a brute-force Chinese education. *Battle Hymn of the Tiger Mother* includes many lessons she was taught by her parents—lessons any LEAP student would recognize. "Be modest, be humble, be simple," her mother told her. "Never complain or make excuses," her father instructed. "If something seems unfair at school, just prove yourself by working twice as hard and being twice as good."

In the book, Chua portrays her distaste for corporate law, which she practiced before going into academe. "My entire three years at the firm, I always felt like I was playacting, ridiculous in my suit," she writes. This malaise extended even earlier, to her time as a student. "I didn't care about the rights of criminals the way others did, and I froze whenever a professor called on me. I also wasn't naturally skeptical and questioning; I just wanted to write down everything the professor said and memorize it."

At the AASA gathering at Yale, Chua made the connection between her upbringing and her adult dissatisfaction. "My parents didn't sit around talking about politics and philosophy at the dinner table," she told the students. Even after she had escaped from corporate law and made it onto a law faculty, "I was kind of lost. I just didn't feel the passion." Eventually, she made a name for herself as the author of popular books about foreign policy and became an award-winning teacher. But it's plain that she was no better prepared for legal scholarship than she had been for corporate law. "It took me a long, long time," she said. "And I went through lots and lots of rejection." She recalled her extended search for an academic post, in which she was "just not able to do a good interview, just not able to present myself well."

In other words, *Battle Hymn* provides all the material needed to refute the very cultural polemic for which it was made to stand. Chua's Chinese education had gotten her through an elite schooling, but it left her unprepared for the real world. She does not hide any of this. She had set out, she explained, to write a memoir that was "defiantly self-incriminating"—and the result was a messy jumble of conflicting impulses, part provocation, part self-critique. Western readers rode roughshod over this paradox and made of Chua a kind of Asian minstrel figure. But more than anything else, *Battle Hymn* is a very American project—one no traditional Chinese person would think to undertake. "Even if you hate the book," Chua pointed out, "the one thing it is not is meek."

"The loudest duck gets shot" is a Chinese proverb. "The nail that sticks out gets hammered down" is a Japanese one. Its Western correlative: "The squeaky wheel gets the grease." Chua had told her story and been hammered down. Yet here she was, fresh from her hammering, completely unbowed.

There is something salutary in that proud defiance. And though the debate she sparked about Asian-American life has been of questionable value, we will need more people with the same kind of defiance, willing to push themselves into the spotlight and to make some noise, to beat people up, to seduce women, to make mistakes, to become entrepreneurs, to stop doggedly pursuing official paper emblems attesting to their worthiness, to stop thinking those scraps of paper will secure anyone's happiness, and to dare to be interesting.

CONTRIBUTORS' NOTES

Sherman Alexie is the author of twenty-two books, including *The Absolutely True Diary of a Part-Time Indian*, winner of the 2007 National Book Award for Young People's Literature, *War Dances*, winner of the 2010 PEN Faulkner Award, and *The Lone Ranger and Tonto Fistfight in Heaven*, a PEN Hemingway Special Citation winner. He is also the winner of the 2001 PEN Malamud Award for Excellence in the Art of the Short Story. *Smoke Signals*, the film he wrote and co-produced, won the Audience Award and Filmmakers' Trophy at the 1998 Sundance Film Festival. He lives with his family in Seattle, Washington.

Kevin Brockmeier is the author of the novels *The Illumination, The Brief History of the Dead,* and *The Truth About Celia;* the children's novels *City of Names* and *Grooves: A Kind of Mystery;* and the story collections *Things That Fall from the Sky* and *The View from the Seventh Layer.* His work has been translated into seventeen languages, and he has published his stories in such venues as *The New Yorker,* the *Georgia Review, McSweeney's, Zoetrope, Tin House,* the *Oxford American, The Best American Short Stories, The Year's Best Fantasy and Horror,* and *New Stories from the South.* He has received the Borders Original Voices Award, three O. Henry Awards (one, a first prize), the PEN USA Award, a Guggenheim Fellowship, and an NEA grant. Recently he was named one of *Granta* magazine's Best Young American Novelists. He lives in Little Rock, Arkansas, where he was raised.

Judy Budnitz is the author of two story collections, *Flying Leap* and *Nice Big American Baby*, and a novel, *If I Told You Once*. Her stories have appeared in various publications including *The New Yorker*, *Harper's*, *McSweeney's*, *Granta*, the *Paris Review*, and others. She is currently living outside of San Francisco and working on another novel.

Junot Díaz was born in Santo Domingo, Dominican Republic, and is the author of *Drown*, *The Brief Wondrous Life of Oscar Wao*, which won the John Sargent Sr. First Novel Prize, the National Book Critics Circle Award, the Anisfield-Wolf Book Award, the Dayton Literary Peace Prize, and the 2008 Pulitzer Prize; and also the story collection *This Is How You Lose Her*. He is the fiction editor at the *Boston Review* and the Rudge and Nancy Allen professor at the Massachusetts Institute of Technology.

Barry Duncan is the subject of the upcoming documentary film *The Master Palindromist* (www.masterpalindromist.com). Since being profiled by Gregory Kornbluh in the September 2011 issue of the *Believer*, Duncan has appeared on the National Public Radio programs *Here & Now* and *All Things Considered*, received numerous palindrome commissions, and collaborated with the dance company Monkeyhouse on the dance piece "Back Going No Going Back." He lives in Massachusetts.

Stephen Elliott is the author of seven books, including the memoir *The Adderall Diaries* and the novel *Happy Baby*. He is the founding editor of *The Rumpus*. His feature-film debut, *About Cherry*, is being distributed by IFC and opens in theaters in the fall of 2012.

Louise Erdrich writes from her home in Minneapolis and owns Birchbark Books, a small independent bookstore focused on Native titles. She is the author of many novels, including *The Plague of Doves*, a finalist for the Pulitzer Prize, and *The Round House*, which will be published in fall 2012. Her books for middle readers include *The Birch-*

bark House, *The Game of Silence*, *The Porcupine Year*, and *Chickadee*. She is a member of the Turtle Mountain Band of Chippewa.

Robert Hass received the Pulitzer Prize in poetry in 2009 for *Time and Materials* (Ecco Press). His most recent book is *What Light Can Do: Essays 1985–2011* (Ecco Press). He teaches at the University of California at Berkeley.

The most recent of **Adam Hochschild**'s seven books is *To End All Wars: A Story of Loyalty and Rebellion, 1914–1918*. The story of the British anti-slavery movement he refers to in his piece in this volume can be found in *Bury the Chains: Prophets and Rebels in the Fight to Free an Empire's Slaves*.

Phil Klay is a Marine Corps veteran of Operation Iraqi Freedom and a graduate of the MFA program at Hunter College. He has been published by the *New York Times*, the *New York Daily News*, and *Granta*, and has an upcoming short story collection to be published by Penguin Press.

Nora Krug's illustrations have appeared in publications internationally, including the *New York Times*, *The Guardian*, *Playboy*, *Comedy Central*, *Vanity Fair*, and the *Wall Street Journal*. Nora illustrated the children's book *My Cold Went on Vacation* for Penguin Putnam.

Robin Levi is the human rights director of the Oakland-based nonprofit Justice Now, a California-based human rights organization dedicated to building a movement among people in women's prisons to challenge violence and imprisonment. She also coedited *Inside This Place, Not of It: Narratives from Women's Prisons*.

Jeff, One Lonely Guy is **Michael Logan**'s first book. Excerpts from his book-in-progress, a work of nonfiction, have appeared in *Conjunctions*.

Anthony Marra is a graduate of the Iowa Writers' Workshop and is currently a Stegner Fellow at Stanford University. His first novel, *A Constellation of Vital Phenomena*, will be published in 2013.

Rick Moody's newest novel is *The Four Fingers of Death*, from Little, Brown. He has a new solo album, called *The Darkness Is Good*, released on Dainty Rubbish Records. Moody also plays music with the Wingdale Community Singers, whose recently released album is called *Spirit Duplicator*. Both albums are available at Amazon, iTunes, and CDBaby.com.

Julie Otsuka is the author of two novels. *The Buddha in the Attic* won the PEN/Faulkner Award and was a finalist for the National Book Award and the *Los Angeles Times* Book Prize. *When the Emperor Was Divine* won the Asian American Literary Award, the American Library Association Alex Award, and was longlisted for the UK's Orange Prize. Her fiction has been published in *Granta* and *Harper's*. She is a recipient of a Guggenheim fellowship and an Arts and Letters Award in Literature from the American Academy of Arts and Letters. She lives in New York City.

Michael Poore is a Chicagoland writer whose fiction has appeared in *Glimmer Train, Fiction, Talebones*, the *Southern Review, Asimov's*, and other magazines. His novel *Up Jumps the Devil* (Ecco/HarperCollins), a biography of the devil, is available now. Poore has been nominated for the Pushcart Prize, the Fountain Award, and the Theodore Sturgeon Memorial Award. He lives with his wife, writer Janine Harrison, and daughter, Jianna. Visit him online at www.mikepoorehome.net.

Eric Puchner is the author of the story collection *Music Through the Floor* and the novel *Model Home*, which was a finalist for the PEN/Faulkner Award and won a California Book Award. His work has appeared in *GQ, Tin House, Zoetrope: All Story, Glimmer Train*, and the *Best American Short Stories*. He has received a Pushcart Prize and a National Endowment for the Arts fellowship. He lives in Los Angeles and teaches at Claremont McKenna College.

Jeff Ragsdale has worked as an actor, comedian, and home builder. Ragsdale has been featured on NBC's *Last Comic Standing*, CBS's *Sunday Morning* and *The Early Show*, Fox's *The Morning Show with*

Mike and Juliet, Good Day New York, Geraldo at Large, the Science Channel, WPIX, NY1, CTV, among others. In 2009 Ragsdale won Whoopi Goldberg's game show, *Head Games*. Ragsdale is currently at work on a memoir about his time in Latin America and his New York stand-up comedy days. His Tumblr is a continuation of *Jeff, One Lonely Guy*: jeffonelonelyguy.tumblr.com

Mark Robert Rapacz is the author of the dime-store novel *Buffalo Bill in the Gallery of the Machines*. His short stories have appeared in a number of publications, including *Water~Stone Review, Southern Humanities Review*, and *Martian Lit*. He is a graduate from Hamline University's MFA program in fiction. In 2010 he received the Pushcart Prize's special mention distinction. He and his wife currently live in Minneapolis, where he continues to write stories.

Chaz Reetz-Laiolo graduated from the School of the Art Institute of Chicago's MFA program in 2005. His work has been featured in *Fourteen Hills*, the *Harvard Review*, the *Paris Review, Raritan, StoryQuarterly*, and the Italian daily *Corriere della Sera*. He lives in California with his daughter Isa.

Ryan Rivas is editor and publisher of Burrow Press and *Burrow Press Review*. More of his writing can be found at ryanrivas.net.

Jon Ronson is a writer and documentary filmmaker. His books include *Them: Adventures with Extremists, The Men Who Stare at Goats*, and *The Psychopath Test*. He's a contributor to the PRI show *This American Life*. His new collection, *Lost at Sea: The Jon Ronson Mysteries*, will be published by Riverhead.

George Saunders was awarded a MacArthur "Genius" Grant in 2006 for "bring[ing] to contemporary American fiction a sense of humor, pathos, and literary style all his own." He is the author of three collections of short stories, *In Persuasion Nation, Pastoralia*, and *CivilWarLand in Bad Decline*, and the novella *The Brief and Frightening Reign of Phil*. He also wrote a children's book, *The Very Persistent Gappers of Frip*, which was a *New York Times* bestseller. In 2000, *The New Yorker* named him one of the "Best Writers Under 40." His work appears regularly in *The New Yorker, Harper's,* and *GQ.* Saunders teaches at Syracuse University. Random House will be publishing his short story collection *Tenth of December* in 2013.

Saïd Sayrafiezadeh is the recipient of a 2012–2013 fiction fellowship from the Cullman Center for Scholars and Writers. His short stories and essays have appeared in *The New Yorker,* the *Paris Review, Granta, McSweeney's,* and the *New York Times Magazine,* among other publications. He is the author of the acclaimed memoir *When Skateboards Will Be Free,* for which he received a Whiting Writers' Award. The Dial Press will be publishing his short story collection in 2013.

David Shields is the author of eleven previous books, including *Reality Hunger: A Manifesto,* named one of the best books of 2010 by more than thirty publications, and *The Thing About Life Is That One Day You'll Be Dead,* a *New York Times* bestseller. His work has been translated into fifteen languages.

Mona Simpson worked as a journalist before moving to New York to attend Columbia's MFA program. During graduate school, she published her first short stories in *Ploughshares,* the *Iowa Review,* and *Mademoiselle.* She stayed in New York and worked as an editor at the *Paris Review* for five years while finishing her first novel, *Anywhere But Here.* After that, she wrote *The Lost Father, A Regular Guy,* and *Off Keck Road.*

Claire Bidwell Smith is the author of the memoir *The Rules of Inheritance* (Penguin, 2012). She is a therapist specializing in grief and lives in Los Angeles. She can be found at www.clairebidwellsmith.com.

John Jeremiah Sullivan is a contributing writer for the *New York Times Magazine* and the southern editor of the *Paris Review.* He writes for *GQ, Harper's Magazine,* and *Oxford American,* and is the author of *Blood Horses.* Sullivan lives in Wilmington, North Carolina.

Adrian Tomine is the author of *New York Drawings, Scenes from an Impending Marriage, Shortcomings, Summer Blonde, Sleepwalk,* and *32 Sto-*

ries. He is the creator of the ongoing comic book series Optic Nerve, and is a regular contributor to *The New Yorker*. He lives in Brooklyn with his wife and daughter.

Jose Antonio Vargas is an award-winning multimedia journalist and the founder of Define American, a new campaign that seeks to elevate the conversation around immigration. Formerly, he was a senior contributing editor at the *Huffington Post*, where he launched the Technology and College sections. Prior to that, he covered tech and video game culture, HIV/AIDS in the nation's capital, and the 2008 presidential campaign for the *Washington Post*. He was also part of the team that won a Pulitzer Prize for covering the Virginia Tech massacre.

Padma Viswanathan is the author of the novel *The Toss of a Lemon*. She lives in Fayetteville, Arkansas.

Ayelet Waldman, an attorney and former public defender, is the author of *Red Hook Road* and *Bad Mother: A Chronicle of Maternal Crimes, Minor Calamities, and Occasional Moments of Grace*. She also co-edited *Inside This Place, Not of It: Narratives from Women's Prisons*.

Jess Walter is the author of six novels, most recently the *New York Times* bestseller *Beautiful Ruins*. He was a National Book Award Finalist for *The Zero* and won the Edgar Allan Poe Award for best novel for *Citizen Vince*. His book of stories, *We Live in Water*, will be published in March 2013.

Peter Yang is a New York City–based photographer specializing in portraits and entertainment. Recent clients include Chevrolet, *ESPN the Magazine*, *Esquire*, Mobil, Nike, Pfizer, *Rolling Stone*, Verizon, and *Wired*. On his days off, Peter enjoys reading and grooming his mustache.

Wesley Yang is a contributing editor at *New York*. His writing has also been published in the *New York Times*, *n+1*, *Bookforum*, and the *Tablet Magazine*, among others, and has won the National Magazine Award. He lives in New York and is working on his first book for W. W. Norton.

THE *BEST AMERICAN NONREQUIRED READING* COMMITTEE

FOR ANOTHER YEAR, the student committee at 826 Valencia in San Francisco was joined from afar by a group of talented Michigan high schoolers at 826 Michigan in Ann Arbor. Together, these two contingents comprised the *Best American Nonrequired Reading (BANR)* committee and spent a year unearthing articles and stories, reading them, sparring over their merits and flaws, and helping with the sprawling task of putting together this collection.

Hanel Baveja is a junior this fall at Huron High School in Ann Arbor, Michigan. She does marching band, plays tennis, and reads for *BANR*. She enjoys writing plays and listening to poetry.

 Ezra Brooks-Planck is a junior this fall at Chelsea High School in Michigan, where he can be found sporting a Venetian Carnivale mask and speaking in a French monster voice. He enjoys reading, writing, running, cooking, and parkour.

Claire Butz is a junior this fall at Pioneer High School in Ann Arbor. She loves any orange-flavored drink except Sunny D and misses her former *BANR* sister. She loves the sound of rain from the inside of a tent and she would rather be on the eastern end of Long Island. Claire enjoys Christmas cards, remembering what movie "that guy" is from, museum gift shops, and Blokus.

Gabrielle Cabarloc graduated from Oakland Unity High School in California while working on *BANR*. She is a freshman this fall at Humboldt State University. She loves to hang out with her dog, go to concerts, and make new friends. She says the greatest part about being a student editor for BANR is that she got to learn from other students her age.

It is impossible to feel cool around **Sophie Chabon**. This is immediately apparent in conversation with her. Just when you think you've found your groove, she out-cools you in an instant. "I just finished knitting a vest in the shape of Steven Moffat's head," she might say. And the feeling guts you,

causes you to fall asleep every night on a pillow saturated with tears and snot, lamenting the fact that you've led such an uncool life in comparison. A decade and a half of unrelenting lameness. The emotional toll is a small price to pay, however, for being her friend. She is seventeen, a senior at Lick-Wilmerding High School in San Francisco, and lives in Berkeley. (Written by Paolo Yumol.)

Aimee Chase-Echols is seventeen years old and a senior this fall at June Jordan School for Equity in San Francisco. She plays the bass way too much, is absurdly happy, and occasionally sings Whitney Houston songs while writing essays. All she ever thinks about is politics, which her father considers an unhealthy habit.

While working on *BANR*, **Gabe Connor** graduated from Gateway High School in San Francisco. He now attends City College of San Francisco, where he studies art history and film. With each new edition of *BANR* comes another opportunity for Gabe to demonstrate his ineptitude at telling the truth in his

bio. This year, he is keeping it short and simple, and mostly nonfiction. Gabe is an avid reader (he loves the *Paris Review* and *The New Yorker*), but joining Twitter has caused him to make immediate value judgments about any writing once it goes beyond 140 characters.

Claire Fishman is a sophomore at Huron High School in Ann Arbor. This was her first year on the *BANR* committee. She enjoys reading, listening to podcasts, and the design qualities of metronomes. She also loves Academic Games, though she doesn't really expect you to know what that is. If you do, then, hey, that's pretty cool. Her favorite story from this year's collection is Julie Ot-suka's "The Children," because it's so haunting.

While editing this book, **Kitania Folk** finished her secondary education at Lowell High School in San Francisco. Now she is nineteen and a freshman at New York University, where her sensitive skin is suffering from the harsh winter. She loves editing because she loves reading and giving advice. She wonders how the skills she learned while working on *BANR* will serve her outside the basement. Nevertheless, she is glad to have them.

Estephania Franco is eighteen years old and graduated from Oakland Unity High School while editing *BANR*. Besides working, studying, or being in her house all day, she likes to hang out with her friends and go to parties. This fall she is a freshman at UC-Berkeley. GO BEARS!

Sarah Gargaro is a junior at Greenhills High School in Ann Arbor. She wages a constant battle with her eyebrows and Latin grammar. She has particularly small ears and average-sized feet. She has an affinity for felt-tipped pens and Ticonderoga pencils. Her favorite books include *Shadow of the Wind*, *I Am the Messenger*, and *Franny and Zooey*. This is her second year on the *BANR* selection committee.

Christian Giovanni Hernandez graduated from Oakland Unity High and now attends Cogswell College in California. He has a love for music that's deep like an abyss. Nothing excites him more than good times with friends. He sometimes rhymes when he writes, listens to all kinds of music, and believes there's meaning behind everything. He'll be the cat who walks around the city playing guitar.

Alberto Herrera is an eighteen-year-old student whose goal in life is to try everything. While editing *BANR*, he graduated from Mission High School and now attends City College of San Francisco. His favorite quote is by Albert Einstein: "Insanity is doing the same thing over and over again expecting different results." Alberto feels that we all tend to follow the same norm, hoping to find success and prosperity, thereby proving Einstein's remark on repetition. So, the only way to break free of insanity is to go against it by breaking social borders and living to your own satisfaction, not someone else's.

Quinn Johns is a junior at Huron High School in Ann Arbor. If you can't find him rowing on the Huron River with his school's crew team, then he is probably enjoying a good fiction story or historical account. He greatly enjoys his time with the *BANR* committee and plans to continue working with 826 Michigan.

Char Koelsch graduated from high school in Michigan while working on *BANR* and is now a freshman at an undisclosed university in the Midwest. Her favorite authors are the equally clairvoyant Christopher Hitchens and Carlos Ruiz Zafón. She is a side-sleeper, has a soft spot for anime villains, and fanta-

sizes about traveling to London. Additionally, Char appreciates alliteration and prefers spelling the color grey with an "e."

Linda Liu is a senior at Huron High School in Ann Arbor. She is very glad that she joined *BANR*. She spends her (limited) free time watching Asian dramas that apparently always include car crashes and memory loss.

Juju Miao is a senior at Huron High School in Ann Arbor. Through her awesome persuasion skills, she managed to drag Linda Liu to join the *BANR* committee. This was her third year with *BANR* and she feels old. She has not changed much since she began editing the collection and still finds the meetings to be the highlight of her week.

Flavia Mora, sixteen, is a junior at the Ruth Asawa School of the Arts in San Francisco. She wishes to expand her writing and explore other arts. She hopes to publish or perform a piece of her work and later be involved in activism.

Naoki O'Bryan is a freshman at City College of San Francisco. He graduated from Balboa High School and the Bay School. He plans to study journalism.

Milton Pineda is a senior at the Academy of Arts and Sciences in San Francisco. He is seventeen years old and has a fondness for Batman, microwavable foods, and YouTube. His hobbies include video games, sports, and hanging out with his friends and family. He plans to go to college and major in business administration.

Alex Pollak graduated from the Ruth Asawa School of the Arts in San Francisco and is now a freshman at Lewis & Clark College. In addition to working on *BANR,* he writes poetry, plays guitar, doodles, and tries to explore nature as often as possible. He hopes you enjoy the collection.

 Hosanna Rubio is a junior at the Ruth Asawa School of the Arts in San Francisco. Her life is based on the late rapper, poet, and actor Tupac Shakur. She listens to his greatest hits CD once a month. She appreciates the Peace Corps, Richard Wright, rap, Fashawn, and love. One day she wants to be a stoker and best friends with a reincarnation of Tupac.

Isabel Sandweiss is a junior at Community High School in Ann Arbor. She loves crepes, especially with lemon and sugar. At one point in life she owned seventy-three sock monkeys. On humid summer nights, particularly at dusk, her hair becomes strikingly similar to the mane of a lion. In twenty years she will be living on a sloth farm with her loving husband, James Franco. She strongly believes that Thursday is the most blissful day of the week.

 Abigail Schott-Rosenfield, fifteen, is a junior at the Ruth Asawa School of the Arts in San Francisco. She loves Wallace Stevens's writing and tries to learn dead languages by herself. This is her first year on the *BANR* committee. The experience has made her infinitely wiser.

Hannah Shevrin is a junior at Community High School in Ann Arbor. This is her first year on the *BANR* committee and she has enjoyed all the funny, quirky Tuesday nights. She will always have a fondness for Jimmy Fallon and mangoes. She has a talent for whipping out odd facts about U.S. presidents in awkward situations. She hopes to some day live in a place where there is both natural water and nice people who can ride unicycles safely.

Kate Shrayber is a sixteen year-old junior at Gateway High School in San Francisco. Kate has immersed herself in contemporary teenage pop culture, which in turn has influenced her love of glitter, cats, trashy magazines, and Lana Del Rey. Kate has a penchant for intense eyeliner, loves dresses, and has developed an unhealthy addiction to chai.

Sarah Starman is a junior at Pioneer High School in Ann Arbor. She enjoys sunshine, oranges, running, and meeting new people. She's also an optimist. If you find her with free time (which is unlikely), she'll probably be reading, listening to music, or watching reruns of *Pretty Little Liars*.

Carlos Reyes Tambis is eighteen years old and graduated from the Academy of Arts and Sciences in San Francisco. He is now a freshman at City College of San Francisco and plans to transfer to the University of New Mexico.

Paolo Yumol, seventeen. Raised on a squid farm in the tundra of northern San Francisco, he wrote his first short story at the age of eight and three-thirteenths in the ink of his pet squid, Shirley. When Shirley died, it reaffirmed his belief that writing was the career he wanted to pursue. Although he is rarely

seen without headphones around his neck, it has been said that he has the most beautiful lymph nodes in all the world. Paolo is a freshman at Oberlin College, where he is hiding under a piano until he completes his guide to the care of bipolar squids. He requests that all fan mail be addressed to his mother, as letter openers make him uncomfortable. (He previously attended Lick-Wilmerding High School—what a blast!) (Written by Sophie Chabon.)

Very special thanks to Daniel Frazier, Kendra Langford Shaw, Nicole Angeloro, Mark Robinson, Sam Weller, Jesse Nathan, Jill Haberkern, and Whitney Clark. Thanks also to 826 National, 826 Valencia, 826 Michigan, Houghton Mifflin Harcourt, Laura Howard, Andi Mudd, Ethan Nosowsky, Adam Krefman, Jordan Bass, Brian McMullen, Alyson Sinclair, Russell Quinn, Walter Green, Sam Riley, Molly Bradley, McKenna Stayner, Rachel Khong,

Sunra Thompson, Chelsea Hogue, Mimi Lok, Juliet Litman, Juliana Sloane, Gerald Richards, Ryan Lewis, Yalie Kamara, Valrie Sanders, Tim Ratanapreukskul, Raúl J. Alcantar, Emilie Coulson, Jorge Eduardo Garcia, Lauren Hall, María Inés Montes, Miranda Tsang, Kent Green, David Aloi, Vickie Vértiz, Daniel Gumbiner, Megan Roberts, Belle Bueti, Sarah Marie Sheperd, Ryan Diaz, Matt Gillespie, Hannah Doyle, Seph Kramer, Nate Mayer, Aimee Burnett, Joseph Nargizian, Samantha Abrams, Keziah Weir, Hayden Bennett, Joseph Cotsirilos, Virgil Taylor, Oona Haas, Francesca McLaughlin, Sabrina Wise, Melissa MacEwen, Ava Kofman, and Evan Greenwald.

NOTABLE
NONREQUIRED READING
OF 2011

MATTHIEU AIKINS
   Our Man in Kandahar, *The Atlantic*
STEVE AMICK
   Not Even Lions and Tigers, *Cincinnati Review*
CAROL ANSHAW
   The Last Speaker of the Language, *New Ohio Review*
DANIEL ARNOLD
   Cass McCombs: Scorpio Rising, *The Fader*

RICK BASS
   The Blue Tree, *Ecotone*
BARRY BEARAK
   Watching the Murder of an Innocent Man, *The New York Times Magazine*
TOM BISSELL
   The Last Lion, *Outside*
ALEX BLUMBERG & LAURA SYDELL
   When Patents Attack! *This American Life*
MARK BOAL
   The Kill Team, *Rolling Stone*
KATE BOLICK
   All the Single Ladies, *The Atlantic*

NATHANIEL RICH
  The Luckiest Woman on Earth, *Harper's*
DAVID RIORDAN
  Mutts, *Boston Review*
JANE ROGERS
  Red Enters the Eye, *Epoch*
TIM ROGERS
  Barrett Brown Is Anonymous, *D Magazine*
SANTIAGO RONCAGLIOLO
  Deng's Dogs, *Granta*
JON RONSON
  Robots Say the Damnedest Things, *GQ*
HELEN RUBINSTEIN
  Essy, Stepping into the Water, *Ninth Letter*
KAREN RUSSELL
  The Hox River Window, *Zoetrope: All-Story*
BENJAMIN RYBECK
  Dad Stuff, *Ninth Letter*

ELI SANDERS
  The Bravest Woman in Seattle, *The Stranger*
JENN SCOTT
  Brethren, *Gulf Coast Review*
TAIYE SELASI
  The Sex Lives of African Girls, *Granta*
RICH SHAPIRO
  The Incredible True Story of the Collar Bomb Heist, *Wired*
JIM SHEPARD
  HMS *Terror, Zoetrope: All-Story*
KAREN SHEPARD
  Girls Only, *One Story*
RUSSELL SHORTO
  The Way the Greeks Live Now, *The New York Times Magazine*
JOE B. SILLS
  The Ascendants, *Ninth Letter*
MARK SLOUKA
  1963, *Agni*

ABOUT 826 NATIONAL

Proceeds from this book benefit youth literacy

A LARGE PERCENTAGE OF the cover price of this book goes to 826 National, a network of youth tutoring, writing, and publishing centers in eight cities around the country.

Since the birth of 826 National in 2002, our goal has been to assist students ages six through eighteen with their writing skills while helping teachers get their classes passionate about writing. We do this with a vast army of volunteers who donate their time so we can give as much one-on-one attention as possible to the students whose writing needs it. Our mission is based on the understanding that great leaps in learning can happen with one-on-one attention, and that strong writing skills are fundamental to future success.

Through volunteer support, each of the eight 826 chapters—in San Francisco, New York, Los Angeles, Ann Arbor, Chicago, Seattle, Boston, and Washington, DC—provides drop-in tutoring, class field trips, writing workshops, and in-school programs, all free of charge, for students, classes, and schools. 826 centers are especially committed to supporting teachers, offering services and resources for English language learners, and publishing student work. Each of the 826 chapters works to produce professional-quality publications written entirely by young people, to forge relationships with teachers in order to create innovative workshops and lesson plans, to inspire students to write and appreciate the written word, and to rally thousands of enthusiastic volunteers to make it all happen. By offering all of our programming for free, we aim to serve families who cannot afford to pay for the level of personalized instruction their children receive through 826 chapters.

The demand for 826 National's services is tremendous. Last year we worked with more than 6,000 volunteers and over 29,000 students nationally, hosted 646 field trips, completed 220 major in-school projects, offered 387 evening and weekend workshops, welcomed over 200 students per day for after-school tutoring, and produced over 900 student publications. At many of our centers, our field trips are fully booked almost a year in advance, teacher requests for in-school tutor support continue to rise, and the majority of our evening and weekend workshops have waitlists.

826 National volunteers are local community residents, professional writers, teachers, artists, college students, parents, bankers, lawyers, and retirees from a wide range of professions. These passionate individuals can be found at all of our centers after school, sitting side by side with our students, providing one-on-one attention. They can be found running our field trips, or helping an entire classroom of local students learn how to write a story, or assisting student writers during one of our Young Authors' Book Projects.

All day and in a variety of ways, our volunteers are actively connecting with youth from the communities we serve.

To learn more or get involved, please visit:

826 National: www.826national.org
826 San Francisco: www.826valencia.org
826 New York: www.826nyc.org
826 Los Angeles: www.826la.org
826 Chicago: www.826chi.org
826 Ann Arbor: www.826mi.org
826 Seattle: www.826seattle.org
826 Boston: www.826boston.org
826 Washington, DC: www.826dc.org

826 VALENCIA

Named for the street address of the
building it occupies in the heart of
San Francisco's Mission District,
826 Valencia opened on April 8,
2002, and consists of a writing lab,
a street-front, student-friendly retail pirate store that partially funds
its programs, and satellite classrooms in two local middle schools.
826 Valencia has developed programs that reach students at every
possible opportunity—in school, after school, in the evenings, or
on the weekends. Since its doors opened, over fifteen hundred volunteers—including published authors, magazine founders, SAT
course instructors, documentary filmmakers, and other profession-
als—have donated their time to work with thousands of students.
These volunteers allow the center to offer all of its services for free.

826 NYC

826NYC's writing center opened
its doors in September 2004. Since
then its programs have offered over
one thousand students opportunities to improve their writing and to
work side by side with hundreds of
community volunteers. 826NYC has
also built a satellite tutoring center,
created in partnership with the Brooklyn Public Library, which has introduced library programs to an entirely new community of students.
The center publishes a handful of books of student writing each year.

826 LA

826LA benefits greatly from the wealth of cultural and artistic resources in the Los Angeles area. The center regularly presents a free workshop at the Armand Hammer Museum in which esteemed artists, writers, and performers teach their craft. 826LA has collaborated with the J. Paul Getty Museum to create Community Photoworks, a months-long program that taught seventh-graders the basics of photographic composition and analysis, sent them into Los Angeles with cameras, and then helped them polish artist statements. Since opening in March 2005, 826LA has provided thousands of hours of free one-on-one writing instruction, held summer camps for English language learners, given students sportswriting training in the Lakers' press room, and published love poems written from the perspectives of leopards.

826 CHICAGO

826 Chicago opened its writing lab and after-school tutoring center in the West Town community of Chicago, in the Wicker Park neighborhood. The setting is both culturally lively and teeming with schools: within one mile, there are fifteen public schools serving more than sixteen thousand students. The center opened in October 2005 and now has over five hundred volunteers. Its programs, like at all the 826 chapters, are designed to be both challenging and enjoyable. Ultimately, the goal is to strengthen each student's power to express ideas effectively, creatively, confidently, and in his or her individual voice.

826 MICHIGAN

826 Michigan opened its doors on June 1, 2005, on South State Street in Ann Arbor. In October of 2007 the operation moved downtown, to a new and improved location on Liberty Street. This move enabled the opening of Liberty Street Robot Supply & Repair in May 2008. The shop carries everything the robot owner might need, from positronic brains to grasping appendages to solar cells. 826 Michigan is the only 826 not named after a city because it serves students all over southeastern Michigan, hosting in-school residencies in Ypsilanti schools, and providing workshops for students in Detroit, Lincoln, and Willow Run school districts. The center also has a packed workshop schedule on site every semester, with offerings on making pop-up books, writing sonnets, creating screenplays, producing infomercials, and more.

826 SEATTLE

826 Seattle began offering after-school tutoring in October 2005, followed shortly by evening and weekend writing workshops and, in December 2005, the first field trip to 826 Seattle by a public school class (Ms. Dunker's fifth-graders from Greenwood Elementary). The center is in Greenwood, one of the most diverse neighborhoods in the city. And, thankfully, enough space travelers stop by the Greenwood Space Travel Supply Company at 826 Seattle on their way back from the Space Needle. Revenue from the store, like from all 826 storefronts, helps to support the writing programs, along with the generous outpouring from community members.

826 BOSTON

826 Boston kicked off its programming in the spring of 2007 by inviting authors Junot Díaz, Steve Almond, Holly Black, and Kelly Link to lead writing workshops at the English High School. The visiting writers challenged students to modernize fairy tales, invent their ideal school, and tell their own stories. Afterward, a handful of dedicated volunteers followed up with weekly visits to help students develop their writing craft. These days, the center has thrown open its doors in Roxbury's Egleston Square—a culturally diverse community south of downtown that stretches into Jamaica Plain, Roxbury, and Dorchester. 826 Boston neighbors more than twenty Boston schools, a dance studio, and the Boston Neighborhood Network (a public-access television station).

826 DC

826DC, National's newest chapter, opened its doors to the city's Columbia Heights neighborhood in September 2010. Like all the 826s, 826DC provides after-school tutoring, field trips, after-school workshops, in-school tutoring, help for English language learners, and assistance with the publication of student work. It also offers free admission to the Museum of Unnatural History, the center's unique storefront. 826DC volunteers recently helped publish a student-authored poetry book project called *Dear Brain*. 826DC's students have also already read poetry for President and First Lady Obama, participating in the 2011 White House Poetry Student Workshop.

SCHOLARMATCH

ScholarMatch is a nonprofit organization that aims to make college possible by connecting under-resourced students with donors. Launched in 2010 as a project of 826 National, ScholarMatch uses crowd-funding to help high-achieving, San Francisco Bay Area students who have significant financial need. But it takes more than money to ensure that students successfully complete college. That's why ScholarMatch also offers student support services and partners with college access organizations, nonprofits, and high schools to ensure that students have the network and resources they need to succeed.

More than 80 percent of ScholarMatch students are the first in their families to go to college, and over 50 percent of them have annual family incomes of less than $25,000. ScholarMatch students are resilient young people who have overcome harrowing challenges, and maintain their determination to seek a better future through college.

With commitments from donors, we ensure that young people in our community receive the education they need to succeed in a challenging economic landscape. To support our students' college journeys or to learn more about our organization, visit scholarmatch.org.